PERFECT SINNER

MAFIA WARS - BOOK SEVEN

MAGGIE COLE

PULSE PRESS

This book is fiction. Any references to historical events, real people, or real places are used fictitiously. All names, characters, plots, and events are products of the author's imagination. Any resemblance to actual events or places or persons, living or dead, is entirely coincidental.

Copyright © 2021 by Maggie Cole

All rights reserved.

No part of this book may be reproduced in any form or by any electronic or mechanical means, including information storage and retrieval systems, without written permission from the author, except for the use of brief quotations in a book review.

PROLOGUE

Gemma O'Hare

THEY SAY EVERY PERSON HAS A BREAKING POINT. I NEVER GAVE it much thought. I assumed I was mentally tough and too strong and independent for anyone to mess with me. That was before my half-sister, Orla Bailey, stalked, harassed, threatened, and even physically hurt me.

Anything I cherished, and things I didn't even think about, she stole from me. My freedom to go wherever I wanted disappeared. I can't step outside without worrying about my safety. The ability to live on my own and get a good night's rest evaporated into thin air when I woke up with rodents and bugs crawling all over my body. When I do sleep, it's not uncommon for me to wake up screaming and crying with sweat coating my skin.

My entire life, I was carefree and confident. Those traits eroded until they were nothing but a mere memory of who I used to be. Orla's determination to ruin me affected everything, including my career, which I loved and was great at.

Now, I no longer know who I am. Most days, I believe I'm going crazy. There just isn't any way to escape the unhinged thoughts going through my mind.

Except when I'm with Nolan.

Everything about him makes me weak-kneed, even when we're fighting. When I'm with him, I feel like a piece of my old self has returned. The times he leaves and I can't go with him, everything inside me feels off. And the fact he hates the Baileys, my blood relatives, as much as I do, seems to make me crave him more.

I don't know how he does it, but all I've lost seems manageable when I'm with him. The crazy feelings I have go away, and life becomes hopeful again. The notion I could have a future and not stay stuck in this world of fear and spiraling thoughts ignites and grows.

Then Orla finds her way back to me.

No matter what Nolan does to keep her away, she always maneuvers back into my life. Each time, the desperation to end her life or mine grows. And now, I'm kicking myself.

I got comfortable. Too much time passed without hearing from her. Maybe my mind needed the break from the anxiety, but the longer she stayed away, the more relaxed I became. I hoped she was somehow in the shoot-out and the police just didn't report it. After all, they still haven't reported the death of my father. Nolan promises me he saw Liam shoot my father in the head. He insists my father bled to death on the street. And Liam claims that the police often keep mafia activity under wraps due to different dynamics.

So the possibility Orla was in one of the cars and got shot isn't out of reach. The fact my father wasn't reported dead gave me too much hope she died as well.

Yet, I should have known better than to let my guard down.

Now, her threats aren't about hurting my sisters or mom. She decided to redirect her wrath to someone else. And if I lose this person, I will go crazy. I'll end up in a straitjacket or give in to the temptation to end my life.

Last night, when I saw the text, I couldn't breathe. Anxiety rushed back in, squeezing my heart. But this time, Orla's pushed me too far. She's set her evil sights on killing Nolan. So when this is over, I'll be the one pulling the trigger.

It's ironic, really. My father wanted me to step into my role in the family. I claimed it wasn't who I was and never would be. But that was before I ever laid eyes on Nolan.

Orla may be a mafia princess, but the blood swirling in my veins makes me just as much of one as she is. The only solution is to dig down and pull out all the evil that's inherently in me, then finish her off. In the end, only she or I will be standing.

She succeeded and broke me. But I won't let her destroy the only good thing I have left in my life.

1

Nolan O'Malley

SEAN'S WARNING SENDS NEW CHILLS DOWN MY SPINE. *"The Baileys are coming for you. Watch your back."*

It's not the first time he's warned me about something. I react the same way I always do. I sit up in bed and scrub my hands over my face. Cold sweat coats my skin, and my racing pulse doesn't seem to slow. No matter how many slow breaths of oxygen I inhale, my dead brother's face and voice don't go away.

After several minutes, I go into the bathroom and take a shower. It's four in the morning, but anytime Sean visits me in my dreams, which is happening more frequently these days and always with the same warning, I never can fall back asleep.

The hot water turns cold. I step out then debate about going to the gym but turn my laptop on instead. After a few hours, I pump my fist in the air. "Fuck yeah!"

I finally figured out the algorithm I've spent the last several months trying to decipher. Declan hacked into the server, and all the pressure was on me to do my part. It's the last significant piece needed to take down Jack Christian's company. My cousins, brothers, and I have to wait until it goes public, but once the price gets high enough, we're going to short the stock. We'll make billions as it falls. Everything Jack and his slimeball business partner Judge Peterson have worked for will go down the drain. Mack Bailey, Jack's other buddy, will also lose millions.

However, my excitement is short-lived. The hatred I have for those three men runs so deep, even financially destroying them isn't enough. Until all three of them have suffered and die, nothing will make me rest. Not one of them deserves another moment on this earth. The amount of anguish they've brought upon my family is enough for several lifetimes. When the day comes, and they're nothing but ground flesh scattered in Lake Michigan, that's when I'll maybe be able to regain some sense of peace in my life.

It's something I've not felt since my father died. A Bailey killed him. To screw with my family more, the Baileys set my brother, Sean, up with the Rossis, an Italian crime family. They killed him, and since then, any remaining tidbit of calmness or happiness has died.

A war rages inside me. I do the only thing I know how to try and control it. I put my socks and sneakers on then step outside. The cool morning air smacks me in the face—not atypical for Chicago. It's still dark out as I run along the shoreline and get to my family's gym.

My three brothers and two cousins are there. It's a rare occurrence for all of us to work out together. Killian and Liam are in the boxing ring with my uncle Patrick. He's been their trainer for as long as I can remember.

Finn spots Declan while he does bench presses. Declan is struggling to finish his set. I approach them, and Finn taunts, "Stop being a sissy and finish it strong."

Declan lets out a final grunt, pushes the weight up, and Finn helps place it back on the rack. Declan sits up, wipes the sweat off his face, and pants hard.

"I cracked it," I reveal.

Declan and Finn turn their heads toward me.

I continue, "Before I rewrite their algorithm, I need you to be ready to hack in and erase the blueprint."

"Don't do it before we're ready," Finn warns.

"I'm aware," I snap, pissed he would even think he needs to remind me. I know the plan and my role in it. Everything has to stay as is and profitable. Until the company goes public and the stock price hits what we've assumed it will, we can't disrupt anything.

Finn crosses his arms. "What's got you all riled up this morning?"

I ignore his question and turn to my brother. The last thing I'm going to do is go into detail about how my dead brother is constantly in my dreams, warning me about the Baileys coming after me. Or maybe Sean means all of us. Either way, I don't want it to come to fruition. I'd love to take out every human being who has Bailey blood flowing through their veins before I learn what Sean's warning refers to.

Before my father's death, I never thought I would kill anyone. My nana made us promise to stay away from my uncle Darragh's mob business. When Sean died, everything spiraled. Now, every thought of stealing the last breath from a Bailey brings me joy.

Killian killed Lorenzo Rossi, the son of the head of the Italian mafia. In conjunction with the Ivanov brothers, he pinned it on the Petrovs, another heinous crime family who has a vendetta against them. A silent war began between the two families. From time to time, it requires us to step in and take men from both sides out to keep the power even. It's something I never thought I'd do.

When Killian told Declan and me what he did, Liam and Finn were still in prison. My brothers and I had a small construction firm. Since then, we've shut it down. That one night changed everything for us.

Before my nana died, Darragh had promised her he would keep us away from his business. Part of me believes he feels guilty and it's why he allowed us to stay out of the drug and gambling side of the family activities. Instead, he had my brothers and me focus on Liam and Finn's plan to take down Jack Christian's company. He knew Declan and I played around on our computers as a hobby. Little did we know how closely our uncle monitored our pastime.

Once this deal goes through, the future income stream for our family will come from legitimate sources. Well, minus the way we got our funds to start the new tech company we'll create.

We allied with the Ivanovs. They aren't a true crime family. Their businesses are all legit. However, their ruthlessness is nothing shy of ours. Overnight, it felt as if my entire world shifted. The rage I felt over my father and Sean's deaths momentarily lifted when my brothers and I hunted Crosby and Cullen Bailey down. They orchestrated Sean's death and were two high-up members of their clan. It was the first time I ever sliced a man to pieces. The first cut felt like a sweet release. Some men might black out their wrongdoings, but I remember every moment of those few days. At times, I hear their screams and see their faces. I smell the decay and bodily fluids. When the flashbacks occur, the faint shimmer of relief fills me before returning to feeling all the rage I keep inside me.

Declan wipes his face another time then rises. He squints. "It won't be a problem. What's going on?"

"Nothing."

He studies me. "It's not like you to snap. Did something happen? You should be ecstatic you got the algorithm."

"I'm fine. I just didn't sleep well," I admit.

"You need to get laid. It'll make you sleep like a baby," Killian booms from behind me.

I spin and ignore him. My little brother thinks most of his issues can be solved through his cock. It's nothing new. Usually I'd laugh, but I'm not in the mood. Everything feels off since I woke up. My run did nothing to release any of my anger or grief. I state, "Tell Darragh I cracked the algorithm."

Liam's eyes widen, and he sighs in relief. He pats me on the back. "Your next drink is on me."

"Don't get too excited. I need to figure out how to create a better one to replace it," I warn him.

He pins his fierce gaze on mine. He confidently states, "You will."

"They set the date yet?" Killian asks.

Declan grabs a bottle of water from the nearby fridge then tosses one to Finn. "No. All speculation. Eric said they're estimating three to six months." Eric's one of the hedge fund traders who set up dozens of offshore accounts and positioned us to profit from the fall of Jack's company.

The pressure to figure out an algorithm better than Jack's reignites. It may take months for me to figure it out. I don't have a minute to waste. If I don't create it before the company goes public, we're screwed. I ask Finn, "Did you get the dirt we need on them?"

His face hardens. "Not yet."

"We will," Liam assures us.

My chest tightens. If they don't get dirt on Jack and the judge, it creates a possible hiccup in our plan. I ignore the nerves rising in my chest and walk toward the punching bag. I need to pound something and ease some of the unsettled anxiety I can't seem to shake. I grumble, "I have shit to do today."

I grab a pair of fingerless gloves and hit the bag until my arms burn and sweat pours out of me. I add in sets of push-ups, sit-ups, and planks then go back to the bag. After several rounds, Killian comes over. "You gonna tell me what's eating you?"

"Nothing," I reply and punch the bag again.

"Liar."

"I didn't get laid last night, remember," I jab.

"Nolan," he firmly states.

I stop punching and sigh. I stare at the ceiling and try to add more oxygen to my lungs. I finally admit, "Sean's been in my dreams again."

Killian shifts on his feet. He clears his throat. "What's he saying?"

The tightness in my chest returns. I meet my brother's eyes. "The Baileys are coming for you. Watch your back."

The loathing in Killian's expression at the mention of the Bailey name is like a dragon breathing fire. He grinds his molars then says, "We're going after them this time. They aren't getting any more O'Malleys."

I hesitate then glance behind me to double-check no one is around us. I don't want everyone else to know. Killian has had dreams before, too. Declan hasn't, and I don't want Liam and Finn to know. I'm unsure why, but I don't. I confess, "It's not the first time. He's talking to me almost every night."

Killian steps closer. "Darragh increased our surveillance. They can't move without us knowing about it."

I snort. "You and I both know it's a false sense of security. It's like having a gated neighborhood without someone standing at the entrance with a machine gun. You think you're safe.

You don't lock your door at night. And then people end up dead, and everyone asks how it happened."

Killian's jaw tightens. "They aren't getting to us again."

As much as I want to believe my brother, I can't shake Sean's warning. "I have to go. Who knows how long this algorithm is going to take to create."

"You showering? I'll drop you off on my way home."

"No. I'm going to run back. I'll see you later." I step past him.

He calls out, "Nolan."

"Yeah?" I glance back.

He firmly states, "I promise you, we're the ones in control this time."

"Your arrogance has always been your downfall, little brother. None of us can afford to assume the Baileys can't get to us," I warn.

"It's not arrogance. We aren't naive anymore. If they did surprise us, we wouldn't hesitate to handle them accordingly," he boasts.

I consider his words and can't deny that if any Bailey dared step foot in front of us, we wouldn't hesitate to deal with them differently than before my father or Sean died.

"Don't get cocky," I order then leave. I run back to my house, take another shower, and turn my computer on. I make the same smoothie I drink every morning then get lost in my work. Every avenue I take leads to a dead end. By nighttime, my eyes are burning from staring at the computer screen too long, and my stomach is growling. My phone rings and I answer, "Killian. What's up?"

"You still staring at the computer screen?"

I chuckle. "Yep."

"Take a break and meet us at the pub. It'll still be there tomorrow."

My stomach growls again. "All right. I need to eat anyway. But I'm not staying all night. I need to get back to this."

He groans. "You've got time."

"You don't know that," I reply.

"Yeah, I do. Now get your ass to the pub."

I glance at the clock on the wall then outside. It's already turning dark. "I'll see you soon." I hang up, throw on a pair of jeans and a fresh T-shirt, and my doorbell rings.

I slide my feet in my shoes and look at the security screen on the wall. Surprised, I open the door. "Darragh. What are you doing here?"

He steps past me. "Your place was on the way. Killian said you're going to see Liam tonight?"

"Word gets around fast," I mutter. Somehow, Darragh always knows everything that is happening.

He ignores my statement and takes off his tweed cap. His steel gaze assesses me. "I heard you figured out the algorithm?"

"Yeah. But I don't know the new one yet," I admit.

"But you will?" he asks.

No pressure.

I straighten my shoulders. "I'm working on it."

Darragh nods. His voice turns colder. "When you see Liam tonight, tell him it's confirmed."

The hairs on my arms rise. "What is?"

"The Zielinski boys. Just as we planned."

I freeze. Darragh pinned a crime Boris Ivanov committed on Bruno Zielinski's sons. Bruno is the head of the Polish mob. He and the Rossis formed an alliance. Darragh also framed the Rossis for killing Bruno's sons to break up their agreement.

"I'll tell Liam."

He pats me on the back. "Good. Let me know when you figure out the algorithm." He leaves, and I follow him outside. I get in my car and drive to the pub since I'm not drinking. No matter how much Killian tries to get me to stay and drink, I have to figure out how to make this algorithm a priority. I'm eating dinner then going home.

The pub isn't far from my house. Within several minutes, I park the car and step inside the pub. Liam and Hailee are at the bar, and he waves me over. The regulars attempt to talk to me, but I beeline toward him. "Liam. Your dad said to tell you it's confirmed."

His face darkens. "It went our way?"

I nod.

A woman next to him clears her throat, and I glance at her.

Jesus, help me.

There's a familiarity about her. She looks a bit like Hailee, but instead of appearing innocent, she has a confident, eat-me-up-and-spit-me-out aura about her. Hailee has cool blonde hair, but this woman's is strawberry-blonde. Against my will, my eyes drift down her body. I force myself to tear my gaze off her cleavage and perky breasts. I continue staring at her then finally find the power to stop ogling her. But it's too late. Her cheeks burn bright red, making her blue eyes pop even more, causing my dick to become hard as steel.

Play it cool.

She's trouble.

Unlike my brother, Killian, who always goes for the bad girl, I avoid them at all costs. They're drama, and I don't need it in my life.

I rip my eyes off her, turn and embrace Hailee, then kiss her on the cheek. "Hailee. How are you doing?"

She sweetly smiles. "Good. You?"

"I don't have any complaints."

The girl next to her sticks her hand out. "I'm Hailee's little sister, Gemma."

Gemma. I hold in my groan. Her name alone is a recipe for dirty thoughts, never mind her voice, which is the sexiest thing I've ever heard. It's like caramel dripping down your skin. Once you listen to it, you can't just wipe it away. It sticks with you.

"By a year," Hailee mutters.

Against all my restraint, I eye Gemma's body again. I take her hand. "Nice to meet you. I'm Nolan." The intensity from touching her is too much. She has an energy field around her, zapping me straight to my core. I drop her hand and spin toward the manager. "Hey, Darcey. Can I get a bottle of water?"

"Sure. You aren't drinking tonight?"

"No. I'm only staying for a bit. I have work to finish."

"Well, that doesn't sound like fun," Gemma taunts.

No. Fun would be putting you over my knee and slapping your naked ass.

I take a sip of my water, trying to cool off. I shrug without glancing at her.

Molly comes up behind the bar. She beams at me. "Hi, Nolan!"

"Hey, Molly."

"Thanks for fixing my mom's laptop," she says.

"No problem. Glad it's working again."

She turns to the women and smiles. "Hailee, is this your sister? You look a lot alike."

Hailee confirms, "Yes. This is Gemma."

Gemma steps closer to me, and my veins begin to hum. She gives Molly a dismissive smile and focuses on me. "So you're a computer guru? I thought you'd be the boxer, at first glance." She squeezes my biceps.

I dismiss the zings running down my arm. Gemma may be the hottest woman who's ever walked into this pub, but I don't like how she dismissed Molly. She's my best friend Colin's little sister, and my friend, too. Also, I'm not into snobs. It confirms Gemma's nothing but trouble, and I don't need any more of that than I already have. "Yeah? Well, I'm not. Nice meeting you." I turn to Molly. "Are my brothers in the game room?"

"Yes." Molly attempts not to look hurt, but I see it in her expression.

I smile at Molly, trying to make her feel better. I go to the game room, and Killian sinks the eight ball in the corner pocket of the pool table. He cockily looks up. "Hey..." He glances past me and raises his eyebrows. "Who's that with Hailee?"

I act like I don't care. "Her sister, Gemma." I grab the cue stick and twist the chalk on it.

He softly whistles. "I take it she's not a kindergarten teacher?"

I shrug. "Don't know, don't care. Rack 'em up." I motion to Declan.

He finishes his beer then grabs the triangle, placing every ball inside it. When he lifts the rack, I put the chalk down, line up my cue, and break the balls. Two solids roll into the pockets.

"Bravo!" Gemma's voice hits my ear, and I once again think

about sticky caramel. Only this time, I wonder how long I'd get to lick her and what she'd sound like moaning if I put it all over her body. Then I reprimand myself because everything about her is a road I don't travel down. She's Killian's type to a T. High drama, wild, reckless, and guaranteed to take all my concentration away from the only important thing right now—figuring out the next algorithm. It's too important for our family. If I don't get it right, the O'Malleys are never getting out of the drug and gambling business. And the money involved makes everything Darragh built look like chump change.

"Hailee, is this your sister?" Killian asks.

"Yeah. This is Gemma," Hailee replies.

Killian hugs her and kisses her on the cheek. I almost jab him in the stomach with my cue. It's an innocent gesture, but nothing ever is with Killian and a girl like Gemma.

What am I thinking? A woman like Gemma has never walked into this pub before. She makes all of Killian's women look like overpriced hussies.

Declan eyes her up and replicates Killian's moves. I grip the cue tighter. Finn is the only one I can stomach watching kiss Gemma's cheek, and that's only because I know he's obsessed with finding Brenna.

When everyone has their O'Malley hands off Gemma, I casually ask, "Can we continue our game now?"

"Gemma, do you play pool?" Killian inquires.

She laughs and flips her hair, then saunters up next to me. Her energetic buzz glides across my skin, and she isn't even touching me. "Sure. But I think I'd rather watch." She tilts her head and smirks at me.

"Suit yourself," I say and move to the other side of the table.

I line up my cue and lose my concentration when Killian steps next to Gemma. She takes a sip of her drink, and he leans down near her ear. "Want another drink?"

She puts her hand on his biceps. "Sure. You're the boxer, right?"

I screw up so badly, I scratch, and the cue ball flies into the middle pocket.

"Might want to sharpen your skills," Killian taunts.

I grunt and grab my water.

Killian holds his cue and assesses the table. Declan takes his place next to Gemma. He ogles her, and I hold myself back from smacking him. He licks his lips and questions, "What do you do for fun, Gemma?"

She bats her eyes. "I'm kind of a spur-of-the-moment gal, if you know what I mean."

Declan softly chuckles, and I swallow the bile climbing up my throat. I know his expression too well. She's a piece of candy he's ready to eat.

Caramel once again fills my mind, and I chastise myself.

"Ugh." Hailee groans at the table behind me.

"Chill. She's just having fun," Liam mutters.

"Yeah, right. Cut her off now."

Molly comes into the room. "Anyone want another drink? Nolan, are you sticking with water?"

"Yeah. I've got a lot—"

"Bring us another round, lass," Killian declares.

"I'm okay right now," Hailee chirps.

Declan taps Gemma's near-empty glass. "The rest of us need refills."

Another groan comes from Hailee. Liam and Finn both chuckle, and Molly glances behind her at Gemma, then looks back at me. "Do you want another water?"

"No, thanks, I'm good."

She smiles. "Okay. Let me know if you need anything."

"I will. Thanks."

Molly walks out, and Gemma crosses the room. She places her hand above mine and holds on to the cue. She grabs the chalk, grinds it on the tip, and blows. "There. You're all ready now."

I don't react. I'm not my brothers and not going to drool all over her. And she doesn't seem to have any issues flirting with them, so I'm staying as far away from her as possible. The last thing I need is someone in my life who flirts with other men. Liam's ex-fiancée Megan was a flirt. She had no problem getting with our cousin, Danny, the minute Liam got arrested. The judge hadn't even sentenced him yet when she dropped him for Danny. I tell her, "You're in my way."

She tilts her head and drags her finger down my chest. Her pouty lips curve, and she makes doe eyes at me. "Am I?"

Fuuuuck.

"Yeah." I step away from her and take my shot.

Molly brings more rounds, and Gemma tries harder and harder to get my attention, but I continue to ignore her. The more she drinks, the more it bothers her. Deep down, it's turning me on how much it's annoying her. My brothers continue to give her attention, and Finn talks to her, but she seems focused on getting me to acknowledge her.

The more she tries, the less I react, and the tighter my pants become. She jumps up on the corner of the pool table, crosses her legs, and leans over, revealing her perfect everything. She's drunk way too much, but everyone kept giving her more.

I've stayed longer than I should have, but I can't seem to make myself leave the room. I typically loathe drunk women unless I'm inebriated alongside them. Still, even in her annoying state, she's so damn beautiful and full of personality, I want to take her home and make up for not giving her any recognition all night.

"Time to get off the table, lass," Killian orders.

"But Nolan hasn't said please yet." She shoots darts at me with her eyes, and I finally have had it.

My balls are aching, and she's the reason. I'm starting to wonder why I'm avoiding her. I lean down to her ear. In a low voice, so no one else can hear, I say, "Get off the table, or I'm going to throw you out of here." Before I can finish telling her I'm going to take her to my house, put her over my knee, and slap the shit out of her ass, she reaches for my shirt.

She fists a handful of material and, in a loud voice, slurs, "You don't know who you're messing with."

Maybe I should just tell everyone to leave the room and fuck her right on this pool table. I growl, "Yeah? Who's that?"

She lowers her voice but not so much that Declan and Killian, who are behind me, can't hear. She huffs, defiantly glares at me, and claims, "I'm Rory Bailey's mafia princess. You can't handle what I'll do to you."

2

Gemma

I'VE SAID A LOT OF THINGS IN MY LIFE. NOT A LOT BOTHERS me. I don't consider myself a super-reserved person. Things some people take offense to, I roll my eyes at. My motto has always been, life is too short to worry about being uptight about what you say.

Well, at least before Orla, my half-sister I never knew about, I used to believe that. Since she came into my life, all I do is worry about what I say. Talking can now get people killed. But nothing has ever come out of my mouth that I regret as much as what I just said to Nolan.

His eyes turn to slits. He barks, "What did you just say?"

I hold my breath. All I want is for someone to protect me. Orla doesn't let a day go by without harassing me. My entire life is in shambles, and I never thought I needed anyone to protect me before she hunted me down. Since Liam met Hailee, I haven't worried about the Baileys getting to her. It only took one look to see how he'd kill anyone who attempts to harm her. I just wanted to come here tonight and leave with the same thing.

God, I'm stupid. But desperation makes people do crazy things, as I'm quickly learning.

I'm drunk and don't even know why I would say what I did. I hate that my blood makes me a mafia princess. Every time Orla tells me what I am, or when she made me visit my father in prison, and he called me it, I cringe inside. So why I chose to reveal it to Nolan doesn't make any sense.

Before Orla, I dated my fair share of bad boys. They were all sexy with a flair of danger. My dating life ceased after her arrival. Yet, none of them compares to Nolan O'Malley.

When Liam told me Nolan was into algorithms and the most intelligent guy he knew, I assumed he would be a boring nerd. He walked into the bar, and I thought he was Killian, the boxer. Everything about him screams bad boy athlete and not a tech geek. His neck, right arm, and hand have tattoos all over them. An open-mouthed, fierce snake is inked on the front of his neck. Celtic symbols and swords intricately weave together in the design. A few strands of silver run throughout his reddish-brown hair, matching his perfectly groomed short-cut beard and mustache.

Underneath his gray, form-fitted T-shirt is chiseled perfection. All that is mesmerizing enough until you see his eyes. They're green globes of smoldering intensity you could get sucked into and stare at for hours. My first look into them sent heat straight to my core, and it's something I've never experienced before.

He's everything Irish, bad boy, and dangerous. Like the other O'Malleys, you immediately feel his ferocity and virility. Every one of them is good looking, sexy as sin, and not to be messed with. I'm sure any of them could protect me against Orla and my father, yet, Nolan is the one I can't drag my eyes away from.

And now, he's stolen my breath with the hatred, rage, and betrayal in his eyes he's pinned on me.

I barely hear Hailee's voice when she says, "Gemma. What did you say?"

Nolan doesn't flinch. In a low, menacing tone, he repeats, "Say it again."

The room becomes silent. My chest tightens, and blood pounds so hard between my ears, I get dizzy. I attempt to slide off the table, but Nolan grabs me by the throat and makes me look at him.

My flutters go crazy in both fear and lust-filled desire. My head spins from too much alcohol.

"Nolan! Let her go!" Hailee yells.

"Nolan!" Liam growls and pulls at his arm. "What the fuck is wrong with you two standing there?"

Nolan's flaming green eyes never leave mine.

"Let her go," Declan barks.

Nolan releases me, steps back, and seethes, "Get out."

The next few minutes are scary. Liam attempts to go after Nolan, the O'Malley brothers step in, and Finn pulls Liam back. Words fly fast and ugly, and Nolan points to Hailee and me. "Ask the Bailey sisters."

My insides quiver harder. This isn't the way for Hailee to find out we're Baileys. Plus, Orla threatened to kill my mother if I told anyone. For months, during every difficult moment, I've not said anything. And now, I've put the people I love the most in danger.

Hailee firmly says, "My sister is obviously drunk. Our last name is O'Hare."

"How long have you been spying on us?" Nolan fumes. The loathing in his eyes is so deep and painful, it makes me hate myself. I don't know why he thinks I would spy on him, but it's clear he believes I would.

"I swear to God, Nolan, if you don't stop these accusations, you're going to leave in a body bag," Liam warns.

"It's true," I whisper, not able to lie with Nolan glaring at me. Plus, I've never been a liar before Orla showed up in my life.

Hailee spins on me. Her eyebrows pinch together. "What are you talking about?"

My stomach churns, and bile starts rising from my gut. "I'm going—" I put my hand over my mouth and run out of the room.

"Gemma!" Hailee yells, following me.

As soon as I get into the bathroom, I get sick. My sister holds my hair and rubs my back.

When I finish, I sit against the stall. Sweat and tears coat my cheeks. Hailee hands me wet towels, and I wipe my mouth, then start crying. "I'm sorry."

Hailee sits next to me and pushes my hair off my face. "Gemma, I'm so lost right now."

There's so much to tell her, and I don't even know where to start. Now that I let the cat out of the bag, I can't go backward. My sister isn't going to pretend I didn't say it. Through endless tears and all the fear I've felt over the last few months, I tell her things our mother should have told us.

I explain that our father is Rory Bailey. We have a half-sister named Orla, and she made me visit our father in prison. I watch the horror in my sister's eyes grow as I disclose our father's threat that we take our roles in the family and marry the men he chose. If we don't, he'll throw us in his whorehouse. The faces and voices of men breaking women in when Orla made me go and watch still haunt me. I tell her how Orla has been following me for months. Everywhere I go, she shows up or has one of her men there to scare me. They are mob, and Orla threatened to kill my mother if I told anyone what I knew.

Hailee tries to comfort me the entire time, but I've lost all ability to control my emotions.

I wipe my face. "Liam will protect you. I-I need to find someone to protect me, too. Please. I don't want to ever see them again."

"Shhh. We need to get out of here, Gemma. Let's go home."

More truths I've been hiding come out. I don't know where to go. Orla infested my apartment with rodents and bugs. I lied and said it was another tenant in my building. And I can't stay at my mom's anymore. I'm too afraid I'll tell her. Hailee keeps insisting we need to talk to her, but I'm scared she'll die. I beg her not to tell anyone.

She puts her shaking hand on her cheek. "Okay. I won't. Let's go home. We can't stay here all night."

I allow her to help me up. She goes to open the door, but I put my hand on it and stop her. "He wants to see you, Hailee."

Hailee's eyes widen. "I'm not—"

"Do you think Liam can kill them? Especially her. She's... Hailee, she's so horrible." I fall apart again.

Hailee freezes.

My Pandora's box is open, and I can't seem to keep anything in anymore. "She's everywhere. On my phone. In my building. At my work. Anywhere I go, she shows up. I'm going to go crazy."

Hailee tugs me into her again, and I sob. As much as I want to stop crying, I can't seem to. I wish I were strong how I used to be, but all I feel now is weak. Hailee instructs, "Let's go. We'll talk to Liam about how to protect you." She leads me out of the restroom. We take one step out and stop.

The O'Malleys are all lined up against the wall, scowling at us. A new fear fills me. I can't tear my eyes off of Nolan's.

"Is she lying?" Liam growls.

Hailee defiantly sticks her chin in the air. "My sister isn't a liar."

More guilt pierces my heart. I've been lying to my sisters and mom about things. My job, home infestation, and hundreds of other white lies I've told over the last few months trying to protect them.

"But you are?" he hurls back.

"We didn't know!" I cry out, not wanting Liam to hate Hailee. I've never seen my sister so happy with anyone, and Liam protects her. I don't want my inability to keep my mouth shut to hurt them or put my sister in more danger.

Hailee tugs me closer. "Why are you so angry about this? We're the ones who should be upset. We're the ones who just learned we're part of some family we've never heard of."

"Are you kidding me?" Nolan growls, and I jump. He's so mad. I don't know the history of the Baileys and O'Malleys, but Orla wasn't happy when Hailee started seeing Liam. Since then, Orla has stayed away but still calls and texts me daily.

"Nolan," Declan warns under his breath.

Hailee quietly asks, "Liam?"

"Your family helped murder our brother. It was after they killed our father. Let's start with that," Nolan barks then returns to shooting me a look so hateful, I want to die on the spot. It's not just his wrath. It's the pain and suffering swirling around it.

I tear my eyes away and turn to Hailee. "We need to go."

Hailee furrows her brows and quietly replies, "Let's go." We take two steps, and Liam steps in front of us. "The door is that way." He points to the back exit, and a new fear ignites that I didn't consider.

Is he going to kill us?

Hailee continues to be the strong one. She confidently states, "We aren't going in the alley. We're going out the front door. Now move, Liam."

His face darkens, creating a new chill in my bones. He declares, "No. My car is parked out back. You're coming with me."

My voice shakes. "You're going to hurt us now? Because we're part of a family that we don't want anything to do with?"

"Don't fall for it," Nolan warns.

"Watch your mouth," Liam barks.

Nolan steps toward him, but Killian grabs the back of his shirt. He yanks him backward.

"Get off me!" Nolan shouts.

"I said to calm down," Declan orders. He and Finn exchange a glance. They form a wall around Nolan.

Finn motions toward the door. "Go."

Liam puts his arms around Hailee and me and swiftly guides us past the O'Malleys and into the alley. His driver, Knox, opens the back door of the vehicle. He repeats, "Get in."

I look at Hailee for permission. I'm not sure what to do. Is it safe to go with him or not?

Neither of us moves. Liam quietly says, "I'm not going to hurt you, Hales. We can't stay here right now. Let's go."

She grasps my waist, as if to steady herself. "How do I know you won't hurt us?"

He glances at the sky then her. "I'm not the one who's changed, little lamb."

Hurt fills her eyes. "You think I have?"

"Didn't say that," he replies.

Her eyes turn to slits. "Didn't you?"

He avoids answering her. "Get in."

"Where are you taking us?" I demand.

He doesn't take his gaze off my sister. "My place. We need to talk."

"What if we don't want to go?" I ask. I wanted the O'Malleys to protect me, too, but now it seems like I might have invited more danger into our lives.

Liam glances over his shoulder at the door then at me. "Would it be better to go to your mother's? After all, I do have questions for her."

"No!" I blurt out then begin sobbing again.

Hailee firmly commands, "Get in the car, Gemma."

"But—"

"Please. Do what I ask." Her blue orbs beg me to obey her.

I climb in, not sure what else to do but trusting Hailee to make the right decision for us. The door shuts then the front door closes. I sit in the car, staring out the window into the blackness, wondering how I could have screwed up so badly.

Several minutes pass, and Hailee rips the door open. "Gemma, get out."

Liam says, "Hales—"

She spins. "They've threatened my sister. They want to kill my mother. My father, who I didn't even know the name of until tonight, has plans for Gemma and me. They scare the shit out of me. And if you aren't going to help us, then I don't have anything else to say. I don't answer to you, Liam."

He slams the door shut and steps forward so she's against the car. I debate about getting out of the other side, but Knox rolls the divider window down. He turns and attempts to joke, "Rough night?"

I don't answer. I put my hand over my face, wishing I could control my emotions. For so long, I covered it all up. The only time I cried was in bed when I was alone. Now, I can't seem to stop it. And I'm embarrassed I flirted with Knox earlier when Liam picked us up.

"Oh shit. Sorry, Gemma. Here." Knox hands me a box of tissues.

"Thanks," I manage to get out.

More time passes. My heart never stops racing, and I think I might get sick again. The door finally opens, and Liam and Hailee get in.

He protectively wraps his arm around Hailee, and she closes her eyes briefly, then refocuses on me. Concern and confusion lace her expression.

The ride to Liam's is quiet. I don't dare speak, afraid of what else I might say. When we pull into his driveway, another car parks behind us. Lights fill the backseat, and a door slams. New anxiety floods me. *Is this a trick and Liam is going to hurt us?*

He glances out the window then quietly speaks in Hailee's ear. "I'll handle this. Take your sister inside."

She asks, "Who—"

There's a knock on the windshield, and I jump.

"Let's go, Gemma." Hailee opens the door and gets out. She reaches in to help me out.

I take her hand, step out, then say, "Thanks. I—"

"We need to talk, Liam," Nolan's voice rings in the air.

I freeze, not expecting to see him again. I gather the courage to turn.

Liam gets out. "Not tonight. We'll talk tomorrow."

"No. I want to know why she said what she did," he seethes, scowling at me.

"We already know why," Liam claims.

"No. We don't know why. We know what she said, and that's it. I want to know why she said what she did to me," Nolan demands.

"I'm sorry! I shouldn't have," I admit, ashamed about what I said, what it represents, and how this entire night is my fault.

"Gemma," Hailee warns.

"Hales, take your sister inside!" Liam explodes.

"Come on." She attempts to guide me away, but I can't tear my eyes off Nolan's. Every part of me wants to make it right. I didn't know the Baileys killed his father or brother. I understand why he's so upset.

"Tell me," Nolan says to me.

Liam tries again. "Nolan—"

"Were you targeting me?" he asks.

"What? Nolan, go home. Don't you dare harass my sister," Hailee barks.

"Stay out of this," Nolan bites back.

"Don't talk to my woman like that," Liam warns.

"Your woman is a Bailey," Nolan growls.

"You have a five-second warning, and then I'm going to—"

"I'll tell him why!" I cry out.

The air turns silent. Nolan's green eyes seem to glow hotter next to Liam's. Nolan growls, "Tell me."

Nerves jump around my belly. "Can I tell you without Hailee and Liam?" What I said is embarrassing. I don't want my sister to hear it. Nolan deserves an explanation, so I'll deal with his anger.

"What? Gemma, no!" Hailee insists.

Liam starts to agree, "Yeah. I don't think—"

"Fine. Get in my car," Nolan thunders.

Hailee tugs me into her. "No. She's not—"

"Stop!" I shrug out of her grasp. "He has a right to know. I shouldn't have said it."

"What exactly did you say?" she asks.

"Nothing you need to know." I walk toward Nolan's car.

Hailee threatens, "If you hurt her—"

I spin.

Nolan declares, "I don't hurt women. I'm an O'Malley, not a Bailey. You should learn the difference."

"You grabbed my sister's neck," Hailee points out.

Nolan shakes his head. He keeps his eyes on Hailee and calls out, "Gemma, did I hurt you?"

My lower body pulses at the memory. I shove my ego to the side, clear my throat, and admit, "No."

"Did you like it?" More arrogance fills his voice.

Hailee glares at him. "You're an—"

"Yes," I hurriedly insist.

Hailee gapes at me. "What is wrong with you?"

I'm tired, over the entire evening, and not into being judged for what turns me on, especially after months of feeling nothing but fear. My sister never dated any bad boy before Liam, but I know what they're like. "Don't be a hypocrite, Hailee. I'm sure Liam is no saint around you." I open the door and slide into the car. I twist my fingers in my lap, watching Nolan swiftly approach the vehicle.

He gets in, and the air fills with a mix of sandalwood and coffee beans. I breathe deeply, trying to calm down, but it just sends my stomach in more flutters. Nolan's hardened expression turns on me. He demands, "Start talking, Gemma."

I open my mouth but shut it, not sure what I'm going to say.

"You wanted my attention. Now you've got it. Speak," he roars.

I understand he's mad, but now I am, too. My delivery is a mix of apprehension and attempted confidence, "Just give me a minute. You don't have to be so nasty."

"Says the Bailey mafia princess herself," he spits.

I close my eyes and turn away, ashamed of what I said. I whisper, "I'm sorry. I hate who I am."

He leans over the console and turns my chin. I gasp, and he enunciates, "Why did you say it?"

"I-I..." Tears fly fast down my cheeks and over his fingers. "You don't understand what she's done to me."

"Who is she?"

"Orla."

His eyes turn to slits. "What about her?"

"She's...she's our half-sister. We don't have the same mother, and I didn't know about her until she tracked me down. She's stalked me for months. Every day, she texts or calls me. There are always new threats and—"

"Give me your phone, now!" Nolan's expression morphs. I don't know what to think of it.

"Why?"

"Don't ask questions and stop talking. Now, give it to me."

I dig into my cross-body bag and hand my phone to Nolan.

"Security code."

Maybe it's dumb of me to give it to him, but I don't think. "Eight-two-five-five-five-five."

He shakes his head in annoyance and taps the screen, mumbling, "Any dickhead can hack that code." Several minutes pass, and his jaw twitches.

"What are you—"

"Quiet!" he commands.

I continue watching him, and he mutters, "Gotcha!" He looks up. "She's tracking you, but your microphone wasn't on."

"I turned that off. She seemed to know everything I said, so I got paranoid," I admit.

He raises his eyes in surprise. "That was smart."

"See, there's more to me than just good looks," I tease, but it falls flat.

The amusement in his expression disappears almost as quickly as it appears. "She had access to all your emails, texts, and social media."

My skin crawls. "I only thought she was tracking my location. I turned it off on my phone, but she still knew where I was."

He puts my cell in front of me then pulls up the screen. "She put a virus on your phone that overrode the settings. It didn't have the capacity to override your microphone."

I turn away, shameful that she can infiltrate my life in so many ways, and I'm clueless and unable to stop her.

For the first time in hours, Nolan's voice turns calm. "Why is she tracking you?"

I wipe my face and keep focusing on the darkness. "She made me visit my father in prison. I didn't even know who he was until she told me. I was a toddler when my mom fled with us in the middle of the night. They said my sisters and I have to take our place in the family and marry the men my father chose for us, or he'll throw us in his whorehouses."

Silence fills the air. I finally turn. His eyes surprise me. There's compassion in them. "Why did you say what you did, Gemma?"

I shake my head. "I don't know. I was drunk, and you were ignoring me. I-I kept all this to myself for months. Orla said she'll kill my mom if I tell anyone. And now...oh God! If my mom dies..." I cover my face.

He sighs then firmly asks, "Are you going to sit here and tell me you don't know who the O'Malleys are?"

I remove my hand. "No. I know who you are. I didn't know about your father or brother. I see how Liam protects Hailee, and I-I just wanted someone to protect me from her. I..." I put the heels of my palms over my eyes to stop the tears. I quietly admit, "I think about killing myself every day. I don't know how much more of her I can take."

The silence is deafening as shame, guilt, and disgust fill me. I don't believe in suicide. I think it's the coward's way out, but having to live like this isn't sustainable. I'm going to go crazy with paranoia and fear.

The door opens and shuts. I look up. Nolan comes around the car and opens my door. He holds out his hand. "Get out."

I gape at him, wondering how he can be so heartless and cruel when I just admitted what I did. He's going to drop me off at Liam's door. I'm not sure what I expected from him, but it feels so raw.

"Now."

I straighten up, trying to muster any self-respect I have left. He leads me up the sidewalk to Liam's house and opens the door. He holds out his hand. "Give me your phone, Hailee."

"What? No!" she says.

"Hailee, give it to him," I blurt out, fearful Orla might be tracking her.

"Why?" she asks.

I'm emotionally drained. I can only whisper, "Please. And stop talking."

Liam doesn't hesitate. He reaches into her purse and hands the phone to Nolan.

He gets the code from her, spends five minutes going through it, and finally hands it back to her. "It's clean."

Relief fills me.

Hailee and Liam want to know when I saw Orla last and what she calls me about. I answer their questions, regurgitating what I told Nolan, and Liam swears he'll keep us safe from the Baileys.

Then Hailee asks me about my job, and I shamefully tell her how I quit. I had to. Everywhere I went, Orla had her men threatening me. I couldn't even get a coffee or take an Uber.

Hailee blurts out, "I'm sorry I told you no. You can move in with me."

"No," Liam states.

She spins to him. "I'm not—"

"Neither of you are living on your own. You'll both move in here. I'll watch over you," Liam claims, and relief floods me.

She points to the mattress in the corner of the open space. Liam is remodeling and it's a construction zone. "There isn't even one bedroom right now."

"Gemma's coming with me," Nolan states.

I turn to him in shock.

"What are you talking about?" Hailee asks, as surprised as I am.

He crosses his arms. "She knows a lot more than what she's disclosing right now. She's going to tell me everything she knows about anyone associated with the Baileys."

"You aren't kidnapping my sister," Hailee claims.

Nolan's eyes turn to slits. "The attitude toward me is getting old."

"Don't talk to my woman like that," Liam barks.

Nolan focuses on him. "Don't let your dick cloud your judgment. They're Baileys. We're at more risk because of your relationship. Whatever she knows, she needs to disclose."

Liam steps toward him. "I said—"

"I'll go with him," I blurt out. Whatever he wants to know, I'll tell him if it means he'll keep me safe.

"What? No!" Hailee exclaims.

"He's right." I turn to Nolan. "If I go with you, nothing will happen to me? You'll protect me from them?"

"As long as you don't lie to me. If you utter one untruth and I find out, I'll throw you to the wolves like a piece of raw meat," Nolan threatens.

My insides shake at the thought of him handing me over to the Baileys.

"Jesus. You are not going with him. Liam," Hailee states, looking at him for help.

"I don't lie. It won't be a problem. Let's go. I'm tired," I proclaim.

Hailee tries again. "Liam—"

"Let her go. Nolan, if she lies, you bring her to me, not the Baileys," Liam orders.

"I don't lie!" I insist. Before Orla, I never did. Now that everyone knows, there is no point covering anything up anymore.

"Good. We won't have any issues, then." Nolan opens the door and motions for me to go.

"Gemma!" Hailee tries one last time.

I spin. "What do you want me to do? Go back to Mom's? Go to your place? I'm not safe anywhere. At least if I go with Nolan, I'm protected."

"Liam already has O'Malleys watching you. You don't need to go with him," she blurts out.

I freeze, feeling betrayed. "You allowed him to have people watch me, and you didn't tell me? No wonder why I'm so paranoid. I've got Baileys and O'Malleys following me. You should have told me."

"I only told her before you walked in. Unlike the Baileys, you won't notice them. We aren't trying to scare you. It's only for your protection," Liam informs me.

I shut my eyes and shake my head. How much about the O'Malleys following me is influencing whatever Orla is planning to do to me? I open my eyes and reply, "I'll talk to you tomorrow, Hailee."

"Gemma!" She reaches for me, but I shrug out of her grasp.

"Don't! I'm tired. I'm sick of talking. I'll see you tomorrow." I leave with Nolan in tow.

Hailee warns, "Nolan, if you hurt my sister—"

He spins, scowling. Anger emanates off him. "I'm not repeating this again. I'm not who you have to worry about. Liam, set your woman straight." He leaves.

Nolan escorts me to his car and opens the door. I get in, and we don't say a word the entire way to his house. He parks in the garage, closes the door, and leads me inside, straight to the kitchen. He takes a carton of coconut water out of the fridge, opens it, then holds it in front of me. "Drink this."

"I'm okay."

"No, you've been drinking and were sick. You need electrolytes. Now drink." He shakes it in front of my mouth.

I decide not to fight. I take a few sips.

"More. At least half of the bottle," he demands.

I do as he says, and when half is gone, I hand it back to him. "Thank you."

He says nothing, puts it back into the fridge, then leads me to the guest-bedroom suite. "There are toothbrushes, paste, and other toiletries in the bathroom. It's late. Go to sleep. Tomorrow, we're talking some more."

I take a deep breath and meet his eyes. "Thank you."

He opens his mouth then shuts it. He studies me for several moments. His eyes turn sympathetic. He says, "Get some sleep. O'Malleys are watching the house, and I'm down the hall. You don't need to worry about any Baileys getting to you here."

"Thank you." I express my gratitude again, only to get no response.

He nods and turns to leave then freezes. He spins back. "Don't do anything stupid, princess. Not under my roof."

I gape at him, not sure how to take his comment. Part of me thinks he meant it as a term of endearment, but the rational side of me knows Nolan doesn't trust me as far as he can throw me.

3

Nolan

There's no way to quiet my mind. A Bailey is sleeping under my roof. If Gemma's telling the truth, they're coming after her. Our protection makes my family an even bigger target than before. And all I keep seeing is her face, covered in tears.

I've welcomed the devil to reposition his fork straight at me.

She could be lying.

She wants to commit suicide, it's so bad.

Lifeless images of Gemma don't leave me all night. It's a contrast from her outgoing, fun personality. It tugs at my heart. I rotate between worrying about her and reminding myself she has Bailey blood flowing through her veins.

The news of who she is should end the attraction I feel toward her, but everything feels amplified. Visions of her pink ass with my handprint on it don't ever leave me. Unless she's playing me, she wants me. It doesn't help me turn off my racing thoughts of things I want to do to her.

Jesus. She's Rory Bailey's daughter. Nothing can happen between us.

After several hours of failing to sleep, I kick myself for wasting more time. I throw on my pajama bottoms and head to my office. The clock reads three in the morning. I fire up the computer and try to concentrate on cracking the new algorithm.

I might as well be staring at a blank screen for over an hour. All I keep visualizing is Gemma alive and Gemma dead. I debate about checking on her. My conscience finally wins, and I creep down the hall. I quietly open her bedroom door.

It takes my eyes a few minutes to adjust to the darkness of the room. I step closer. Everything in my body comes to life. She's hands down the most beautiful woman I've ever seen. She must have washed her face before bed. The makeup that stained her face is gone. Her cheeks have a natural blush and a few freckles. She must have covered them up with her foundation. Her pouty lips are a soft pink. Most women would pay for her lashes, but they have to be natural since they match her strawberry-blonde hair. For the first time since meeting her, she has a peaceful expression on her face.

Relief floods me that she's okay and didn't do anything to herself. It hits me how worried I was, and it's another thing I'm unhappy for feeling. I shouldn't care. She's a Bailey. I've vowed never to hesitate when it comes to one of them. Yet, here I am, not only hard as a rock from staring at her but caring way too much about her well-being.

A Bailey princess.

I need to get out of here.

My resolve is weak. Instead of leaving, I take a seat in the chair but immediately rise. It's lumpy, so I grab the items and realize I'm holding her folded clothes. At the same time, she stirs. She turns toward me, stretches her arms above her head, and hugs the pillow. Her creamy, flawless skin makes me think of dripping caramel on her again. I've never thought twice about the sticky substance before, but it's quickly becoming an obsession.

I tear my eyes off her momentarily. Her bra is black see-through lace. Her panties match. I don't know what they call them, but it's one of those pairs that show off the bottom of her ass cheeks. Unable to resist, I torture myself further and sniff them. An earthy scent, mixed with lavender, which I assume is from her laundry soap, flares in my nostrils. I hold back a groan then ball them up in my fist. I neatly stack her clothes and bra on the table next to me and clutch the panties.

She takes a deep breath, and a soft moan fills the air. I lean closer, studying every part of her. The urge to pull the blanket off her so I can see what she looks like naked grows until I make myself leave.

When I get to my bedroom, I glance at my phone. It's nearing six. I sniff her panties one more time and let out the groan I've been holding in all night. I place them in the nightstand drawer next to my bed. Then, I run my hand over my stack of O'Malley pub T-shirts and find the softest one I can. I wish I could take a picture of her in it and send it to her father just to piss him off. I take it to her bedroom. I put it on the chair and creep out again.

Since I'm worthless unless it involves obsessing over Gemma, I go into the kitchen and find my shaker bottle and metal ball for my smoothie. I normally use a blender, but I don't want to wake her. If she's telling the truth and hasn't been sleeping, this might be the first time she's gotten rest in a while.

Sometimes I use fresh or frozen fruits and vegetables, but I also have flash-dried produce that got turned into a powder-like substance. I add that to my bottle, along with several supplements, put the cap on, and shake it for several minutes. I open the lid, grab an egg out of the fridge, and crack it open.

"Tell me you aren't drinking that with a raw egg." Gemma's slightly raspy voice cuts through the air.

My heart stammers. She's in nothing but my T-shirt. She can't be. I have her panties, and her nipples are poking straight at me. I lock eyes with her. I pour the egg into my smoothie, put the lid back on, then shake it again. Against my will, my eyes travel down the length of her body. Satisfaction grows seeing her in an O'Malley T-shirt. I don't think she catches me ogling her though. When I reach her face again, she's gaping at my torso.

"My eyes are up here, princess," I cockily state.

Her cheeks erupt into crimson flames. She recovers and straightens her shoulders. "You wouldn't happen to know where my panties are, would you?" She smirks.

Heat climbs up my neck and floods my face. I curse myself. What was I thinking? I open the lid, reply, "Nope," then take a long drink to try and cover up my reaction.

She steps so close, her aura pounds into my flesh just like the previous night. She tilts her head up and bats her eyelashes. In a sweet, innocent tone, she asks, "So if you're not the panty thief, who is?"

I finish the rest of my smoothie faster than usual in an attempt to calm my skyrocketing pulse. I get done, step to the side, and wash out my cup. "Not my fault if you can't keep your clothes together. Maybe you didn't wear them and forgot?"

She huffs. "Hmm. I've never forgotten something like that before. But that means I leave the house without wearing panties. Is that your assumption of me?"

Amused, I can't help it and grin. I look down and meet her blue eyes. "Are you saying you've never gone out of the house without underwear on?"

"Is that what you do?" she fires back.

"Depends on if the boys need to breathe."

She lets out a small laugh, and her face lights up further. "So they get sweaty often? Is that what you're trying to tell me?"

I turn it on her again. "Is that how you decide to wear your panties in public or go bare?"

"And we're back to the mystery of who the panty thief is," Gemma chirps.

"Not sure what you're talking about," I lie.

"My clothes were on the chair when I went to sleep. I woke up, and they were on the table. The chair only had this T-shirt." She tugs at the chest and then releases it.

"Huh. You might want to get some things from your mom's place today."

Her face falls.

My initial thought is that she doesn't want to stay here longer. But then I remember her concerns about Orla killing her mother. I firmly declare, "I have questions. She's going to answer them."

She scrunches her forehead and blinks hard. "I don't want my mom to die."

"She won't. She's under O'Malley protection. And right now, you all increase the Bailey threats on my family. So I'm going to ask, and she's going to answer," I insist.

Gemma tugs on a lock of her hair. "Are you always so insensitive?"

My gut twists. Yesterday wasn't normal for me. Sean's warning to me in my dream set me off. Finding out Gemma and Hailee were Baileys intensified my already edgy state. I reply, "No. I'm a really nice guy, but I'll never have any love or trust for a Bailey as far as I can throw them."

Her body stiffens and she turns away.

I instantly regret being such a dick. But maybe it's better we keep the lines clear. She's a Bailey. I'm an O'Malley. If she doesn't want any part of them, I'll protect her, since it's in my family's best interest. Other than that, she shouldn't expect much. Her family hurt mine too many times to count. Even if she's telling the truth, her blood makes it impossible for me to ever fully trust or like her. Liam may not be able to cut off ties with Hailee, but once this is over and Rory, Orla, and whoever else is coming after Gemma are dead, we'll go our separate ways.

She clears her throat and moves away from me. "Is it okay if I make some coffee?"

"I don't drink coffee."

She spins. "Seriously?"

"Yeah. That shit is acidic, addicting, and overall bad for your body," I claim.

She looks at me as if I'm crazy. "You do realize eating raw eggs puts you at risk of salmonella, right?"

"My eggs are pasteurized. Do you eat sushi?"

"Yeah. I love it. Why?"

"It's raw. You have the same risks."

She rolls her eyes. "If you get sushi from a quality restaurant, your risk is extremely low."

"Yeah. Same with eggs."

She sighs. "Okay. You have fun when you get food poisoning. Where can I go to get a cup of coffee around here?"

"Get dressed. I'll take you to the cafe down the street."

"Can I take a quick shower?"

"Yeah."

"Thanks." She leaves the room, and I stare at the back of her, wishing I could watch her remove my T-shirt.

I scrub my face in frustration, reprimanding myself for my thoughts. I throw my cup in the dishwasher and go into my bedroom. I take a shower, throw on a pair of gray joggers and a faded green T-shirt with the O'Malley pub logo. It's different from the one I gave to Gemma. It's also soft, since Nora can't stand selling stiff T-shirts.

Gemma's waiting on the couch when I get out to the main room. Her hair is twisted and tied into a messy bun. She rises, and my dick twitches. She twisted the T-shirt I gave her into a knot on her stomach. If I look close enough, a hint of her abs is showing. Her skirt from last night hugs her hips perfectly, displaying her bare legs that I want to lick caramel off of.

She catches me ogling her again and says, "Did you forget your underwear in those pants?"

Shit. I tear my gaze from her thighs, realizing I've got a semi, and she's watched it develop. I grab my keys and arrogantly reply, "Nope. Full coverage, princess, unlike you. Let's go."

Her face turns maroon.

I spin away from her while texting my cousin so I can attempt to get control of my cock. He's in charge of adding extra security to us wherever we go, so I tell him we're going to the cafe. I lead her to the garage and open her door. She slides in the car, keeping her legs pressed firmly together.

I take a few deep breaths before I get in the driver's seat, reminding myself she's a Bailey, and not just any Bailey. She's

Rory's daughter. Besides his brother, Mack, there might not be a more disgusting human being on this planet.

We get to the cafe, and I put my hand on her back and lead her inside. Three of my cousins are already inside. Another three are behind us. No one would know they are watching us.

It's a typical weekday morning. The line is long but moves quickly. We get to the front of the counter. The male barista eyes Gemma over. My guess is he's in his late twenties. He says in a chipper voice, "Welcome to Morning Bean. What will you be drinking today, doll?"

I scowl at him. Before I can stop myself, I blurt out, "Do you call all your customers doll?"

He cocks an eyebrow at me. "Just being friendly."

"Keep your side comments to yourself," I warn him.

I ignore Gemma's questioning, or maybe it's an amused stare. I keep my eyes on the punk in front of me and ask, "Gemma, what do you want?"

She clears her throat, and that goddamn raspy voice of hers tortures me further. "I'll take a double espresso long, please."

I have no idea what that drink is, but the fuck-me eyes the barista is continuing to give her pisses me off further. He has the balls to ask, "Got a hard day in front of you?"

Gemma sweetly replies, "No. Just a—"

"How much is it?" I interject.

He gives Gemma a frustrated look then punches the order into the computer. "Five eighty-two."

Gemma digs into her purse, but I toss six bucks at him.

He picks up the money then hands me the change. "What's your name, doll?"

"Are you looking for issues?" I growl.

"Nolan," Gemma mutters and pulls on my arm.

"I need it for the drink," he states.

"Nolan. That's all you need to know." I lead Gemma to the other end of the counter and cross my arms.

She doesn't say anything until we get her drink and sit down. "Are you always so rude to restaurant workers?"

I snort. "Says the woman who was super disrespectful to Molly last night."

She gapes at me. "I was not rude to her."

I accuse, "You were a total snob. You dismissed her like she wasn't good enough for you. Do you have something against waitresses?"

"I was not a snob. And she was fawning all over you with her lovesick puppy dog eyes."

"That's not true," I claim.

"Yeah, it is. Do you two have a thing or something?"

"You're kidding me, right?"

She shakes her head then takes a sip of her espresso. "No? If you don't have a thing, then does she know it?"

"You're out of line," I reply.

"Oh? How so?"

"Molly's brother is my best friend. I've known her forever. He's in Europe, and I promised him I'd watch out for her. We're friends. That's it," I insist, and it's the truth.

"Well, you should tell her that."

I fire back, "You should be nice to her."

"You should be nice to innocent baristas doing their jobs."

I groan. "Doll? You think that was an appropriate comment to make to you?"

She laughs. "You don't have any idea what random men say to me. That was tame. And especially when I used to waitress. So no, I'm not a snob against servers."

My chest tightens. The feeling I want to kill someone pops up. "What do they say?"

"Nothing. Let's drop it."

"No. I want to know," I insist.

She avoids answering me. "Can you take me to my mom's after this? I'll pack and tell her I'm staying with Hailee."

My focus snaps back to our reality. "We already discussed this. I have questions I need answers to."

Worry floods her expression. She lowers her voice. "Nolan, my mom doesn't even know about Orla contacting me or that I know who my father is."

"You need to tell her."

Gemma pins her big blue eyes on mine. "I told you why I can't."

I lean closer to her. "Listen to me. The time of hiding this is over. Your other sisters need to know what is going on, too. They need to be aware in case anything out of the ordinary happens to them."

She swallows hard. "Liam said the O'Malleys would protect them."

"We will. But everyone needs to be aware of things. And their phones need to be checked, too," I advise.

She closes her eyes and turns toward the window.

I shouldn't touch her, but watching her grapple with this is painful. I reach across the table and grab her hand. She looks at me.

I sternly say, "I'm not trying to be a dick. If you want my protection, you have to trust me. I know what needs to happen in this situation."

She studies me. Her lips curve into a frown. "Doesn't really seem fair I have to trust you, yet you'll never trust me."

The truth hangs in the air. I want to tell her I regret saying what I did this morning, and that it's not the case, but I can't. She's still a Bailey, with their DNA in every cell of her body.

My phone rings, and I answer, "Liam?"

"Hailee called her other sisters. I'm swinging by to pick you and Gemma up. Hailee wants to talk to her mother," Liam says.

I tighten my grip on Gemma's hand. "We're at Morning Bean."

"I'm two blocks away. Meet me outside," Liam instructs.

I hang up. "This issue is solved. Hailee called your sisters and mom. We're going over there now."

She purses her lips in anger and shakes her head.

I calm my tone. "Don't be upset, princess."

She glares at me. "Can you stop reminding me what I am? And Hailee should have talked to me first."

"I think that goes both ways."

"What does that mean?" she spouts.

I shrug. "Maybe Hailee thinks you should have told her."

"I told—"

"I know. You have your reasons. She has hers. It's all I'm saying. But I think you have more issues to deal with than adding holding a grudge against your sister to your plate." I release her hand and rise.

She stands, picks up her coffee, and looks up. "No matter what you think of me, my mother was severely beaten by my father. I still remember it even though I was a toddler. She fled North Carolina in the middle of the night with four daughters. My sisters weren't even one. I know you have your agenda, but I'd appreciate it if you and Liam let us talk to our mom without you verbally assaulting her. My father abused her enough."

My insides flip with rage. Any man who abuses a woman should be dead in my book. I can only imagine what Rory put her mother through. Imagining what Gemma described makes me feel bad for all of them. "I'm not out to hurt any of you."

Her face hardens, but her lips shake. "Good. If you meet my mom, please remember she's been through a lot. Don't talk to her how you talk to me."

Her words are a slap in my face. It stings. I've never had any woman claim I'm anything but nice to them. I usually get told how sweet I am. But ever since my father died, the mere mention of a Bailey sets me off. A lump forms in my throat. I swallow it and try to find the right words, but everything seems wrong. I hate that I've been a dick to Gemma. If she weren't a Bailey, I wouldn't think twice about watching everything I say and how I deliver it. But she is, and it makes me feel unbalanced. My immediate reaction is to apologize, yet I can't seem to find the words or swallow my ego. I finally settle on, "I'll be nice."

She nods and turns. I almost reach for her and pull her into my arms. I want to tell her I'm sorry and I'll stop being a dick. Something inside me won't allow me though.

She moves toward the door, and I follow. Liam's car pulls up, and we get inside.

"Gemma, you okay?" Hailee asks.

Gemma quietly replies, "You should have asked me about this."

Hailee sighs. "They all need to know."

Gemma twists her fingers in her lap and stares out the window. No one says anything the rest of the ride.

Liam and I stand in the hallway outside their mother's condo for over an hour. We barely speak, and we suddenly hear the women shouting.

Her mother opens the door, and Liam steps in front of her. I step to the side of him and let him talk, trying to remember my promise to Gemma that I will be nice to her mom.

At one point, her mother asks who I am, wants to know what I want with Gemma, then asks, "So my daughter is your prisoner?"

Gemma cries out, "Mom! Stop! That's not—"

Her mother spins fast and cuts her off. "You do not know what you are doing or what these men are capable of. This isn't a game or a wild night out, Gemma."

Gemma's eyes fill with tears, and I suddenly feel suffocated. "You don't think I know that? They've destroyed my life in the last nine months. I've lived in fear, quit my job I worked my ass off for and was good at—no, I was amazing at it—and now I've become a hermit to the point my friends won't even talk to me. My half-sister infested my home so badly, I can't ever walk in there again without the feeling of rats crawling on me because the one night I took a sleeping pill, I woke up with them all over me. Every night, I get in bed and can barely sleep. My stomach feels like an acid pit eating at me all day. So don't stand there and tell me what I know or don't know. I'm fully aware this isn't a game, Mother."

Her mother covers her mouth with her hand and whispers, "I'm so sorry. I didn't know. You should have told me."

"Like you should have told us who our father is?" Gemma fires back.

Her mother breaks down in sobs, and Gemma brushes past her. I'm about to go after her, but Hailee does. She eventually comes back into the room and avoids looking at me. It's then I realize so many things.

Unless Gemma is the biggest con artist in the world, there's no way she's lying about this. Orla has destroyed her life. She's living in a constant state of fear, but I see something else.

It's shame. The realization cuts me to the core. I finish going through her sisters' and mother's phone. I demonstrate how to turn off their microphones and do a search twice a day for trackers. Liam and I discuss security measures. I'm careful to keep my tone calm. The entire time, Gemma stands at the window, staring out at the Chicago skyline.

She packs a bag before we go. I say goodbye to her mother, but she says nothing to me and walks away. It shouldn't bug me her mother hates me. They are still Baileys, and my loathing for Baileys hasn't diminished. But Gemma no longer seems to fit the box I've thrown all Baileys in.

And I'm not sure what to do with it or her.

4

Gemma

Nolan won't let me carry my overnight bag. He also grabbed my suitcase. He wheels it into my bedroom and sets the bag on my bed.

My insides haven't stopped quivering since we left my mother's house. It's not any different since Orla came into my life. The time when I felt happy and energetic no longer exists. My old life is becoming a mere memory. The more I analyze it, the deeper I fall into a darker space.

Nolan doesn't move, studying me. I haven't said anything since we left. I'm not in the mood to fight or hear anything else today about how much he detests me.

"Thanks. I'm going to unpack." I open my suitcase, hoping he'll leave. His presence is just a reminder of who I am and what I now can't have.

"Are you okay? That got a bit intense at your mom's," he acknowledges. His voice is softer than I've heard before, and it throws me for a loop.

"Don't start being nice to me now," I attempt to joke, but my voice shakes. I pull a stack of shirts out of my suitcase and open the white dresser drawer.

"Gemma—"

"I'm fine. I'm sure you have lots to do today, so don't let me get in your way." I shut the drawer and return to my suitcase then pick up the pile of my underwear.

"You haven't eaten today," Nolan says.

I shrug. "So? It's not like I work out anymore." I used to make sure I ate throughout the day and fueled my body for my workouts. I've always been an athlete. The last few months, as more depression set in, I stopped doing at-home workouts. It's okay as a one-off but boring and another reminder I'm not free.

"Why aren't you working out?"

I continue to avoid looking at him. I open the second drawer and add my panties. "The last time I ran outside was months ago. One of Orla's guys ran next to me. He threatened me the entire way home. The same guy jumped on the treadmill at the gym a week later."

Nolan stays quiet for a few minutes. I grab some hangers out of the closet, blinking hard. Working out was something I did for fun and my sanity. It also allowed me to compete. All of that is gone now.

He finally says, "How far do you run?"

I sarcastically laugh. "I don't anymore."

"When you did. How far?"

I put a black dress on the hanger. I mumble, "What the hell was I thinking when I packed?" Like I'll be going anywhere that requires a dress, much less a cocktail one.

"Two miles? Five miles? How far?" he asks again.

"It depends. Normally at this time of the year, I would start training for the triathlons or races I do every spring, summer, and fall," I admit.

Nolan grabs my sneakers out of my suitcase. "Great. I haven't run today. Get ready. We'll run down to Nora's and have lunch after."

I finally look at him. "That's several miles away."

"Four."

"Did you hear me say I haven't run in months?"

His eyes drift over my body, and heat rises to my cheeks. He cockily raises his eyebrows. "You'll be fine. Unless you're scared you can't keep up with me?"

I tilt my head. "What do you run a mile in?"

"Eight and a half minutes if I'm not trying."

In my peak form, I run five to six-minute miles. Nerves jump around in my stomach, but I agree, "Okay. Fine."

He grins. "Good. Get ready. You can unpack later." He leaves the room.

I dig through my suitcase. I'm unsure why, but I packed running clothes for the cold. It's only March, and it's a warmer day than normal in Chicago but still chilly. When I'm ready, I lace up my shoes and go out to the family room.

Nolan hands me a tube-like packet of gel. "Take this before we go."

I glance at it. "I'm fine."

He shakes his head. "You haven't had anything but your carton of acid today. If you don't eat it, we aren't going."

"We're running to lunch."

"Gemma, when's the last time you ate?" He crosses his arms.

I rack my brain. "Yesterday at Hailee's school. I had a few chicken nuggets."

"And you were sick last night. I don't need you passing out on the way to the pub. Now, eat."

I sigh. I'm not hungry, but I really want to run, especially since it's a nicer day outside. I tear open the packet and swallow all the gel. "There, happy?"

"Yup." He grabs the empty wrapper and tosses it in the trash. We do some stretches and then he puts his hand on my back and steers me outside. "If I need to slow down, let me know."

I usually would laugh at that statement. I've always been a fast runner. But my butterflies fill my gut again. I don't know what to expect after being inactive for so long.

Nolan sets a leisurely pace. As we get farther into our run, I naturally start to speed up. We run on the scenic Lakefront Trail along Lake Michigan. Since it's nice out, many people are on it. Several men pass me. My chest tightens and paranoia begins. I glance around, wondering if Orla's men are following us.

Nolan glances at me, grabs my bicep, and stops. "Gemma, you okay?"

I try to catch my breath and look over my shoulder again.

"There are six O'Malleys circled around us. You don't need to worry," he gently states.

I blink hard, trying to stop the flood of panic from overtaking me.

"Why don't we grab a cab to Nora's?" Nolan suggests.

I wipe my face. "No. I want to finish." I don't wait for him to respond and return to running, ignoring the urge to look around me. We turn onto the street the pub is on. I focus on the O'Malley's sign a mile down the road. The closer I get, the faster I run.

Nolan's beside me the entire time, and when we get to O'Malley's, I stop. We both continue walking past it.

"I'd hate to run with you when you're in shape," Nolan mutters, breathing hard.

I laugh and glance up. Sweat drips down his face and his cheeks are red. "You didn't ask me what my timed mile is."

He arches an eyebrow. "What is it?"

"Five-twenty-two is my record."

He whistles. "Seven-fifteen is the best I've ever done."

"That's legit," I say.

He snorts. "Don't patronize me."

We walk a few more minutes, turn around, then go into the pub. Instead of taking a seat, he leads me to the kitchen.

A very pregnant, gorgeous, redheaded woman is sitting at a table. There's a large machine, and she pushes potatoes through it, and they come out as fries. She looks up and smiles. "Hi!"

Nolan grabs a chair and pulls it out. I sit, and he takes the seat next to mine. "Nora, this is Hailee's sister, Gemma."

Her face lights up even more. "Nice to meet you! I love Hailee!"

"Thanks. Nice to meet you, too."

Nora glances between us. "So, how did you two meet?"

I'm sure my cheeks are still red, but they grow hotter thinking about the previous night.

Nolan quickly says, "Last night. Gemma made a bet I couldn't keep up with her running." He rises. "Did the avocados and goat cheese come in?"

"Yep."

He opens the fridge, removes a loaf of sprouted bread and other ingredients. "I hope you aren't picky, Gemma. Once you eat this, you're going to want it all the time."

I assess the food he placed on the counter. "What is it?"

"It's an avocado grilled cheese. Nora, you want one?"

She shakes her head. "Boris will be here to pick me up soon. I've got a doctor's appointment. Molly needed some overtime, so she's coming in to finish these potatoes up."

I make a mental note to be overly friendly to Molly so Nolan doesn't continue to believe I'm a snob. I ask, "When are you due?"

"In a few weeks."

"Do you know what you're having?"

She shakes her head. "We decided to let it be a surprise. Liam's parents insist I'm having a girl."

"Aww."

"Guess I'm missing the party," a dark-haired man with a slight Russian accent says and comes into the kitchen. He dips down and kisses her cheek.

"This is my husband, Boris. This is Hailee's sister, Gemma," Nora says, making the introductions.

Something passes in his expression, but it fades quickly. It makes me wonder if he knows who I am. He nods. "Nice to meet you, Gemma. You ready, Nora?"

"Yep." She rises, and we all say goodbye.

Nolan washes his hands and puts a skillet on the stove. He turns it on and starts buttering the bread.

"Can I help?" I ask.

"Nope. I've got this down to a science," he claims.

"Oh, I forgot. You're a genius, right?"

Amusement crosses his expression. "I wouldn't claim that."

"Liam pretty much did."

He shrugs. "I'm good at what I'm good at, that's all."

I get up and wash my hands. Then I jump on the counter next to where he's cooking. "I assume you're good at math and science?"

"Yeah. It's easy for me." He stops slicing the avocado and pins his green orbs on me. "What do you do?"

"Nothing. I quit, remember?" I say it as if it doesn't bother me, but the sting ignites in my belly.

He studies me, and my flutters take off. "What did you do?"

"I was a Director of Marketing at Sustainable. It's a smaller turnkey firm. There were under one hundred of us. I oversaw ad and branding campaigns, everything from the pitch, to creative, to the final placement." A happy and sad nostalgia ignites within me.

Nolan chops up basil and remarks, "So you have a creative brain?"

"Yeah."

"You loved it?"

"Mmhmm." I take a deep breath and focus on the avocado. "I've never heard of this sandwich before."

"It'll be your new addiction," he boasts.

I laugh. "You're pretty sure about this sandwich."

He wiggles his eyebrows. "You'll see." He layers the bread, cheese, and other ingredients in the skillet. "What was it about your job you loved?"

I think for a few moments. "Everything. The people I worked with were fun. Being able to create a concept out of nothing and see it come to life... I don't know. There's something magical about it."

His lips twitch.

"Sorry. That sounded stupid," I state.

His face falls. He gazes at me intensely and lowers his voice. "No, it didn't. You have passion for it. Passion's a good thing, don't you think?"

My butterflies take off. I quietly agree, "Yeah."

He tears his eyes away, and I breathe deeply. He flips the sandwich.

I grab his hand and trace the green ring on his middle finger. "Is this a real emerald?"

He glances at it, and his face hardens. He seems to grapple with what to say.

Moments pass, and I assure him, "You don't have to tell me. Sorry."

His grief-stricken expression meets mine. "My daideó gave it to my father. When he died, the Baileys sent his hand to my nana. She gave it to my brother, Sean. When the Rossis killed him, they sent it in a box with his heart."

My pulse increases and jaw drops to the floor. I freeze in horror, but then ask, "I thought the Baileys killed your brother?"

More hatred pops on his face. "They are just as responsible. They set him up with the Rossis."

I grip his hand tighter. "I'm so sorry."

He sniffs hard and focuses on the ceiling. "Sean's wife Bridget moved to New York. She's an O'Connor."

Confusion fills me again. "Sorry. Should I know who they are?"

He tilts his head. In a soft tone, he asks, "You really are naive, princess, aren't you?"

I'm not sure how to answer or if he even expects me to.

Pain laces his expression. In a dry voice, he continues, "They're another crime family on the East Coast. Our family has strong ties with theirs."

"Did they have kids?" I ask.

He shifts on his feet. "Yeah. Bridget doesn't want her children to have any part of our family. She thinks only her family can keep them safe. Before they left, she gave me the ring and said Sean would want me to have it. I told her it should go to one of my nephews, but she didn't even let them keep the O'Malley name, claiming it was too dangerous."

I reach up and stroke his cheek. His painful gaze reaches mine. My voice shakes, and my eyes water. "I'm so sorry. For all of it. Your losses. What I did and said last night. All of it."

He says nothing, nods, then removes the sandwiches off the skillet. He puts them on a plate, cuts each into two triangles, then picks a piece up. He blows on it then holds it in front of my mouth. "Try this."

I take a bite and softly moan. It's the most delicious thing I've tasted in months. The herbs mix into the goat cheese and avocado perfectly.

His eyes light up. "Good, right?"

I nod then lick my lips.

He steps closer, reaches for my face, and brushes his thumb over the corner of my mouth, then slowly over my lips. My heart races faster. The scent of sandalwood and coffee beans, along with raw, male sweat, flares in my nostrils. I nervously hold my breath.

He removes his thumb and slides the tip in his mouth, sucking on it while staring at me so intensely my insides pulse. He picks up the sandwich. His deep, calm voice is like lava rolling down my spine. Cocky arrogance fills his expression. "Ready for another bite?"

"Nolan. I didn't know you were here," Molly's annoying voice rings in my ears.

Shit, shit, shit! Of course she would show up right now.

Be nice, so he doesn't think you're a snob.

Nolan assesses me one more second then steps back. "Hey, Molly. Do you want a sandwich?"

She pins her eyebrows together. In a low, hurt voice, she replies, "You made avocado grilled cheese?"

My chest tightens. Is this something he's done with her? Has he wiped cheese off her lips and sucked it off his thumb, too? Is it his signature move with women or something?

Nolan tilts his head. It's slight, but I notice it. He firmly replies, "Yes. Do you want one?"

She glances at me then him. "No." She grabs an apron and puts it on then washes her hands. She sits where Nora did, picks up a potato, and forces a smile. In a borderline snotty voice, she asks, "Are you feeling better?"

In an attempt to hide my embarrassment, I slide off the counter and match her smile. "I am. Thank you."

"Good. You left your bracelet on the floor. It's behind the cash register. At least I think it was yours. The stall smelled like vomit." She smirks.

Heat flies to my cheeks. I glance at my wrist and realize for the first time my bracelet is missing.

"Molly," Nolan reprimands.

She innocently claims, "What? It's safe and sound. She should thank me for finding it."

I stand straighter. "Thank you." I step toward the door, but Nolan stops me. "Where are you going? You didn't finish your sandwich."

"Going to get my bracelet. And I'm not hungry anymore," I say and shrug out of his grasp. If he thinks I'm going to eat his grilled cheese sandwich he uses to win women over with, he's wrong. And I'm not staying in the same room to have Molly rub it in my face that I was a drunk idiot last night.

I leave the room and go to the bar. "Hey, Darcey. I don't know if you remember me from last night—"

"Sure, I do. Are you feeling better?" Unlike Molly, her concern is genuine.

My face heats further. "Yes. I'm sorry—"

"Girl, don't apologize. No one stands a chance when the O'Malley boys are ordering drinks. They gave me the hangover from Hell last weekend. And I've worked here for years and know better."

I gratefully smile. "Thanks. Molly said my bracelet is behind the cash register?"

She turns and pulls it out of a small box. "Here you go!"

"Thanks." I slide the rose gold cuff over my wrist.

"Sure."

I walk toward the kitchen, and Nolan steps out with a to-go bag. "Ready to go home?"

"Yep," I curtly respond.

"Did you get your bracelet?" he asks.

Molly steps out and puts her hand on Nolan's biceps. In a sticky-sweet voice, she says, "Nolan, I forgot to tell you something."

I can't help it and roll my eyes. Of course she did.

He spins. "What's that?"

She beams at Nolan, and my stomach flips. "Colin's coming home soon. His assignment is over."

Nolan's face lights up, and excitement fills his voice. "When?"

"He thinks within the next month. As soon as his current project finishes, he said he's back here for good," she informs us.

"That's great, Molly."

"My mom will want to have a party for him."

"Just let me know when."

She squeezes his biceps and releases him. "I will." She turns to me. Her voice sounds as if she's my best friend. "Bye, Gemma."

Not falling for your fake niceties. I return her goodbye and leave. I step out of the pub, and Nolan grabs my arm and spins me into him.

"What are you doing?" I accuse.

His green eyes flare with flames. He growls, "You never go outside without me or one of the guys saying it's okay."

"Sorry. You don't have to be nasty about it."

He takes a deep breath and slowly lets it out. He lowers his voice. "The car's here."

I gaze behind me, and a black car pulls up to the curb. "Who's that?"

"One of my cousins. Let's go." He steps to the car and opens the door.

I get in, and he follows.

He opens the bag and pulls out a box. He lifts the lid, picks up the grilled cheese, and holds it to my lips. "Finish your lunch."

"Not hungry."

"Do you have something against my sandwich all of a sudden?" he attempts to tease, but I'm not budging.

I roll my head toward him. "Maybe you should have fed it to Molly."

"And we're back to this crazy notion you have that I mess around with my friend's sister," he fumes.

"Claim whatever you want. I'm not blind. And she's not innocent."

He groans. "This is getting old, princess."

"Tell me about it, prince charming," I bark back.

"You know what? Starve." He takes a bite of the grilled cheese.

I don't say anything. As soon as the car pulls in to his driveway, the garage door goes up. I go into the house and peel off my sweaty clothes. I get in the shower and stand under the hot water, wondering if I'm overreacting. It felt good to get out and run. Up until Molly showed up, things were nice between Nolan and me. But then I remember how hurt she looked, and I can't help but wonder what their history is and if he's lying.

Nolan's a bad boy. I know his type all too well. It's who I always date and why I'm still alone. In the end, you can't trust them. And one thing about a bad boy is they always have a plethora of women they want to hide.

I get out of the shower. A plate is on my bed with the grilled cheese sandwich, reheated. It smells good, and my stomach growls. I cave and eat it, but all I keep torturing myself with is the same question.

What has gone on between Molly and Nolan?

5

Nolan

Gemma goes straight to her room. I start to follow her but change my mind. What exactly am I going to say? I don't even know why she's so pissed. Molly wasn't nice. I reprimanded her when Gemma went to get her bracelet. Molly said she was rude to her the previous night, which I couldn't deny, but I still told her to let it go and be nice. I'm not sure why Gemma's upset with me for it.

After more debate, I reheat her sandwich and knock. She doesn't answer. I can hear the shower. I inch the door open, verify she's in the bathroom, and put it on her bed. I leave, take a shower in my bathroom, and almost knock on her door again.

Almost.

I stop myself mid-knock. I still don't know what I'm trying to achieve. Hating her was so much easier, but at some point, it changed. Last night, I could only see her as a Bailey. Now, I'm not sure what I feel toward her or what bucket to place her in.

She's still a Bailey.

An unwilling one.

Her blood is still theirs. She'll always be part of them.

My phone rings, and I glance at the screen. I answer, "Darcey, everything okay?" Since Nora is about to have the baby, my brothers and I told Darcey to call us and not her if something is wrong at the pub.

"Nolan, are you free?"

The hairs on my arms rise. "Yeah, why?"

"Molly sliced her hand on the potato machine. Killian wrapped it, but he said he's doing something for Darragh tonight. She's kind of hysterical and thinks she needs stitches."

"And do you?"

"Umm...not sure."

"How the heck did she do that?" The potato machine is pretty self-contained. I wouldn't think anyone could hurt themselves on it unless they're trying to.

Darcey sighs. "You know Molly. She's accident prone."

I glance toward Gemma's bedroom door. "Okay. I'll be there in a minute. Keep it wrapped." I hang up, and my gut flips.

I knock on Gemma's door. She opens it and pushes her wet hair behind her ear. "Hi. Thanks for the sandwich."

I smile, happy she ate, especially after our run and not eating for days. "You're welcome."

She waits for me to speak.

I open my mouth then shut it. Mentioning Molly is only going to piss her off again. "I have to go out. Something came up."

"Oh." Worry and a bit of fear cross Gemma's face.

My heart stammers. It shouldn't bother me so much, but I hate seeing her expression. "You don't have to worry. My cousins all have the house surrounded. If you want, I can have one of them come inside?"

She shakes her head. "No. That's okay. I'll be fine if you're sure no one can get in?"

"They can't," I assure her.

"Okay. Umm...will you be gone long?"

"Hopefully not."

She takes a deep breath and smiles. "Okay."

An awkward silence follows. I start to reach for her then stop. "I'll see you later tonight."

"Sure. Have a good night."

I slowly step back and leave. I talk to the guys guarding the house and tell them to send another one over so he can be right on the doorstep. A strange feeling fills me as I drive away, but I'm not sure what to make of it.

"*The Baileys are coming.*" Sean's voice comes flying at me from nowhere.

I grip the steering wheel tighter. The first thought is Gemma's in my house and she could be playing me. Everything could be an act. It isn't the first time a mafia family would have planted someone in another family's life.

Gemma holding her palms over her eyes pops into my mind. All I hear is her saying, "*I think about killing myself every day. I don't know how much more of her I can take.*"

I don't have long to analyze why Sean's voice came into my head at this particular moment. I pull up to the back alley of the pub, and Killian is waiting with Molly. Her hand is wrapped in white gauze. He opens the door, and she gets in.

"You all right?" I ask.

Her brown eyes fill with tears, and she starts to weep. "It hurts so bad." She leans toward me, and I pull her into me for a hug.

"All right, lass. You probably only need one or two stitches. They might even use glue." Killian rolls his eyes and mouths, drama queen. He always called Molly that. I usually get angry with him for being disrespectful, but tonight it's not bothering me.

I pat Molly's back. "Let's get your belt on."

Killian stretches the belt toward me, and I clasp it in the buckle. He puts her purse on her lap. "Darcey called St. Joseph's. They said it isn't a long wait right now."

"Got it."

Killian shuts the door, taps the hood, and I take off.

"How did you manage this one?" I ask.

Molly sniffles. "One of the potatoes got stuck under the grate. I tried to get it out."

"Did you push another potato through?" Nora gave a strict training about the new machine. Everyone had to be there. She was very clear. All you have to do is push another one through and not touch the grate.

Molly sobs. "No. I wasn't thinking straight."

I turn my blinker on and glance at her. "At least you didn't cut your finger off. Next time, don't touch the grate."

"Sorry. Did I ruin your date with Gemma?"

I freeze. "I wasn't on a date with Gemma."

"No? She sure seemed awfully possessive of you," Molly states.

My chest tightens. "I think you misread things."

"Why was she with you after all the craziness that happened last night?"

Rain hits the windshield, and I turn on the wipers. Lightning flashes across the sky. "We went for a run."

"But you're not dating her?"

"No." I turn to Molly. "Why are you asking me this?"

She pushes her brown hair behind her ear. "Aren't we friends? Isn't this what friends talk about?"

I've dated plenty of women. Not once have I discussed them with Molly. She once dated a Rossi thug without knowing who he was. He came into the pub, started a fight, then came back and torched the place. It's the only time I interrogated her about who she sees. Something about talking about Gemma with Molly makes me uncomfortable, even though nothing is going on between us. "Well, I'm not dating Gemma, so let's change the subject." I pull up to the emergency room entrance. "Go inside, and I'll meet you."

Molly gets out, and once she's safely inside, I park the car. I jog through the rain and enter the hospital. We go through all the procedural stuff and take a seat and wait.

"You should call your mom and tell her we're here," I advise.

"She isn't home. She went on a girls' trip for the weekend," Molly says.

"Oh. Where to?"

"Vegas. She won't be home until Monday."

I cross my arms and stretch my legs.

"I like your joggers," Molly says.

"Thanks." I bite on my smile, thinking about Gemma and my conversation before we went for coffee.

"What's so funny?" Molly asks.

"Hmm?" I raise my eyebrows at her.

"You look like you want to laugh."

"Nothing."

"Oh, come on. You can tell me," she insists. She leans closer to me. "It'll be our secret."

"Nothing's funny. How's your hand?"

She glances at it and scrunches her face. "It really hurts, Nolan."

Maybe Killian is right and she is a drama queen.

"On a scale of one to ten, ten being the most amount of pain, what is it?" I ask.

She sniffles several times. "At least a seven."

"A seven! Wow! Killian has to beat me in the face in the boxing ring several times for a seven. You gotta toughen up, girl," I declare and elbow her in the arm.

She puts her good hand over her face and groans. "Nolan! You know I can't handle pain well."

I'm about to agree with her when a nurse yells her name.

She gets up then turns. "Aren't you coming with me?"

"Do you want me to?"

"Please!"

"Okay." I rise and go with her. The nurse unwraps the gauze and smiles. "It's not bad. You'll be fine. We'll wash it out to make sure it isn't infected, and my guess is the doctor will tell me to use skin glue on it."

I glance at the gash. It's barely an inch long and not deep at all.

"What about stitches?" Molly questions.

"I don't see any reason you'll need those," the nurse says.

We spend another hour and a half waiting for the doctor, who ends up telling the nurse to add some skin glue to her finger. After another half hour, the nurse brings her discharge papers.

Molly and I get in the car. It's dark, and the thunderstorm is loud and bright. When we get to her house, I walk her to the door to make sure she gets inside okay.

"Will you come inside? It freaks me out to be here by myself," she says.

"Molly, you know the O'Malleys watch your house. No one is inside." Since her brother, Colin, did many things for Darragh before he went overseas for work, the O'Malleys have always protected them.

She grips my biceps. "Please, Nolan!"

"Fine. I'll sweep the house. Then you can turn your security system on. But then I need to go, Molly."

"Okay. Thank you."

We step inside. I go through each room, and when I get done, Molly asks, "Do you want a drink?"

"No. Molly, I have to go. Turn on your alarm. Get some rest." I nod and turn to leave.

"Nolan!"

I spin. "Yeah?"

She throws her arms around me. "Thank you for taking me. I'm sorry I'm such a cry baby."

I pat her back. "You're fine. Now get some rest."

She looks up but doesn't let go of me. "Okay. Thank you."

I step back, feeling slightly uncomfortable. I curse Gemma for getting in my head about my relationship with Molly. But then I think of Gemma alone in the house, and all I want to do is go home and make sure she's okay. I sternly say, "Good night, Molly. Lock up."

She reluctantly releases me. I leave, drive home, and go into the house.

Everything is dark. I glance at my watch. It's after ten. The lightning bursts through the sky, and the house rattles as the thunder follows. I'm not sure if Gemma will be awake or sleeping, so I slowly open her door.

I'm unprepared for what I see. At first, I think my eyes are playing tricks on me. But they aren't.

"What are you doing?" I growl.

Gemma jumps, and a handful of pills scatter all over the floor. The cup of water tumbles to the ground. She turns her tear-stained cheeks toward me. Her entire body is trembling.

I rush over to her and kneel in front of her. I put both hands on her cheeks. My heart races so fast it hurts. I repeat, but gentler than before, "What are you doing, princess?"

She shuts her eyes, and tears stream over my hands.

"Gemma."

She begins to sob, and my heart breaks.

I pull her into my chest and stroke her head. "Shh. Everything is going to be okay," I tell her, but I wonder if it is.

Her skin is clammy, and she only cries harder. I'm trying to figure out what could have led to this when her phone lights up on the bed.

I grab it and punch in her code while holding her tightly to me. My stomach drops.

An onslaught of text messages from Orla is on the screen. Hundreds of messages, videos of what I can only assume are women being raped in the Bailey whorehouses, along with two different messages.

Orla: *In case you forgot what she sounded or looked like.*

I gape at the screen, realizing Orla must have taken Gemma to one of their whorehouses to watch this.

The other message is also consistent.

Orla: *You're next if you don't agree to marry who Dad wants you to.*

Mixed in with all these horrors are pictures of Gemma's sisters and mother with captions about what men will do to them or how Orla may kill them.

There's a video of her father, in his orange jumpsuit, demanding she take her place in the family and marry his thug. Then there's another video of the man they want her to marry, telling her all the ways he's going to defile her.

My head gets dizzy as I keep scrolling what seems to be a never-ending list of threats. And they all arrived while I was gone.

Every five messages, the same text occurs.

Orla: *You should kill yourself since you aren't good enough to be a Bailey.*

My mouth is dry. I swallow the lump in my throat and continue trying to calm Gemma, but I don't know what to do. I turn off her phone and toss it on the bed. A rage I've never felt builds in my gut. It takes everything in me to stay calm on the outside.

A long time passes before her sobs turn into whimpers. I mumble into her hair, "I'm taking you to my room."

She says nothing. I rise, pick her up, and carry her to my bedroom. I get a T-shirt, remove her pants and top, and put it on her. I tuck her in bed, strip down to my underwear, then slide next to her.

I tug her into my arms and stroke her back. She's still shaking, and I pretzel all my limbs around her.

She finally looks up. Her blue eyes fill with more tears, and her face crumbles all over again.

"Shhh. Everything is all right," I whisper, holding her as tightly as I can.

For the first time in my life, I'm willing to break the one moral code I have left.

I'm willing to kill a woman. And God help Orla if she gets near Gemma or me. I won't show her any mercy.

6

Gemma

WHEN I WAKE UP, IT'S BLACK. NOLAN HAS HIS LIMBS WRAPPED around me, and I'm confused. I don't move while trying to remember how I got in his bed, lying on his warm, hard flesh.

I was contemplating killing myself.

She wouldn't stop.

Jesus, he saw.

Shame fills me as the memories of last night flood me. I slowly lift my head. Nolan's eyes are closed, and he's breathing softly. I attempt to move, and he tightens his arm around me.

I have to get out of here.

I wait several more moments then carefully untangle my body from his. I manage to slip away to creep out of his bedroom and down the hall to mine. When I step inside, I freeze.

Sunlight shines through the window. I never pulled the shades down and realize Nolan must have his blackout curtains pulled down in his room. It's later than I assumed. Pills cover the floor next to my bed. My phone is off, and I panic. I quickly turn it on. It's one of Orla's rules. My phone is to stay on at all times. While it's firing up, I kneel and pick up the pills.

"What are you doing?" Nolan's voice growls.

I inhale sharply and freeze. I close my eyes, embarrassed. I avoid looking at him and clear my throat. "Cleaning up my mess."

The screen of my phone illuminates, and he races over and snatches it off the bed. "You're getting a new phone number."

"No. I can't. It's her rule. She's going to come after me for turning it off last night," I fret. I finally look at him, and my pulse picks up. As embarrassed as I am, Nolan, in nothing but boxers, is a hard man to tear your eyes away from. His torso of ripped perfection has Celtic knots with a large cross tattooed down the side. The same side has Celtic arrows pointed down and outlining his V.

Jesus.

"She's not coming near you. And that includes communicating with you," he claims.

My insides quiver, and I refocus my attention off his body. I blurt out, "You don't understand. The last time I turned my phone off, I woke up with rodents and bugs on top of me."

His face hardens, and I assume he's mad at me again. "She's not getting to you here. The O'Malleys are protecting you."

I pick up more pills, but my hand is shaking from the feeling of mice and spiders crawling on me. Several pills miss the container and fall back on the floor.

Nolan kneels next to me and takes the bottle. He softly says, "Let me do this."

"No. It's my mess." I hold my trembling hand out. "Give me my phone so I can see if she sent me something I have to respond to her about."

His eyes turn to slits. "Absolutely not. You're never talking to her again."

I close my eyes in frustration and exhale through my nose. "It's not—"

"You were going to kill yourself. This isn't up for debate," Nolan barks.

So much humiliation fills me, I cover my face. I manage to get out, "Can you let me clean this up and leave, please?"

He doesn't reply. I don't move, trying to figure out how to get past the embarrassment. He gently says, "We need to talk."

I remove my hands from my face. The pills are in the bottle, and he's still gripping my phone, except it's turned off. I shake my head. "I'm sorry she got to me last night. It won't happen again. Let's drop it."

He studies me and firmly says, "No. We're talking about this."

My shame turns into anger. I rise off the floor. "No, we aren't. You aren't my therapist."

"Who is?" he asks, rising off the floor.

I spin to leave, but he reaches for my upper arm. I angrily spout, "Nolan—"

"Who's your therapist, Gemma?"

"I don't have one. What would I say? My psychotic half-sister is threatening to kill me and is part of the mob?" I blurt out.

He clenches his jaw.

I lower my voice. "Thank you for taking care of me. I'm fine. Next topic."

"You can't let her get to you."

"Jesus, Nolan. Do you think this is a choice for me? You think I like being this weak woman I never was before she came into my life?"

"You aren't weak."

A sarcastic laugh bursts out of me as I wipe the tear falling off my cheek. "I know me before this, and I know me now. I'm just trying to hold on. And until you know what that's like, don't tell me what's weak or not." I point to myself. "This isn't the person I was or want to be. So, if you can drop this conversation and let me be humiliated in peace, I'd appreciate it."

Sympathy fills his expression.

"I don't need your pity, either, Nolan."

He keeps his intense gaze on me. "What do you want me to do, Gemma? Act like this never happened?"

"Yeah."

"Not possible. You scared the shit out of me."

"Sorry. It won't happen again." I attempt to grab my phone, but he holds it in the air. I jump up, but he's too tall. "Nolan!"

"You'll get your phone back when I remove all this crap she's sent you. Until then, you aren't looking at it. And I'm blocking her," he demands.

Pains shoot through my heart. "Do you not listen?"

"I think you're the one not hearing me. I said she can't get to you here," he claims.

I put my hand on my hip. "You're arrogant. She can get to me anywhere. She's proven it dozens of times."

"The O'Malleys weren't watching you. She hasn't come near you since Liam added protection to you. Now, get dressed," he rants.

"Don't boss me around."

He raises his eyebrows. "You want your morning acid?"

I roll my eyes. "Coffee is not—"

"You've got ten minutes." He walks out of the room, taking my phone and the pill bottle. The door shuts.

I close my eyes and take a few deep breaths.

The door reopens, and I glance at him. He grabs my purse and dumps the contents on the bed.

"What are you doing?" I cry out.

He ignores me, unzips the inside pockets, then tosses the bag on the bed. He goes into the closet and opens the suitcase.

"Nolan!"

"These are your pills, not mine. You got any more?" he asks. He pulls my duffle bag off the shelf and rummages through it.

"Please, stop!" Tears fall down my cheeks. This is beyond embarrassing. I had one bottle of headache tablets. It was the only thing I could think of that was in my room. I was too scared to leave it last night with him gone.

He ignores my plea and checks my shoes, further humiliating me. I finally think he's going to leave, but he doesn't. He pulls all my clothes out of the dresser.

"Stop!" I beg again, but he doesn't.

He puts the clothes back in the drawers and the items in my purse. I think he's finished, but he's not. He checks my pillows then lifts the mattress.

"Why are you doing this?" I sob.

He puts the mattress back on the box spring then spins. His green flames flare into mine. "You're under my roof. Under my protection. I'll be damned if you're going to do something stupid under my watch."

I fire back, "You're released of your duties. I'll go back to my mom's."

"No. You won't. And you have two choices. Get dressed, and you get coffee. Otherwise, attempt to have a temper tantrum and pack. I'll tie your ass up and force-feed you if I have to, so help me God, Gemma. Make your choice. You have ten minutes." He spins and storms out of the room.

I sit on the bed, with my hand covering my face, wondering how I got here. How is this my life when I had everything going for me?

"Three minutes," Nolan yells through the door.

I finally succumb and put on yoga pants, a T-shirt, and a sweatshirt. I throw my hair in a bun and stare at my tear-stained cheeks in the mirror. My eyes are bloodshot. I splash cold water on my face.

Nolan comes barging into the room. "Time's up."

"Can I put my socks and shoes on?"

He motions for me to leave the bathroom, and I glare at him when I pass by. I finish getting ready and take a pair of over-sized sunglasses out of my bag. I go into the kitchen. He picks up two smoothie cups off the counter then guides me out to the car.

I get in and buckle my seat belt.

Nolan slides into the driver's seat, puts one drink in the cup holder, then hands me the other smoothie. "Drink this."

"I'm not eating raw eggs."

"I didn't put it in yours. Now, drink."

"Stop bossing me around."

He sighs, runs his hand through his hair, and turns toward me. "There are going to be some new rules in this house."

"I'm not your child."

He snorts. "Then stop acting like one."

"Can you stop this? I'm already embarrassed enough." I swipe my finger under my glasses.

He lowers his voice. "You aren't talking to her again. I don't care what she threatened you with. She's not getting to you. And you're going back to eating and working out. Until we track her down and I kill her, there's plenty of opportunities for marketing and branding work from home. I'll help you find them. You aren't going to sit around and waste away."

I gape at him.

"Got any questions?"

"You're-you're going to kill her?" I stutter. It's what I wanted Liam to do, but hearing him say it sends a shock through my system.

"Yeah. Next topic."

My stomach flips. "How?"

"I said, next topic. Are we clear on what you'll be doing?" he asks.

It's not a secret the O'Malleys are dangerous, but Nolan's so confident in his statement, I blurt out, "You've killed people before?"

His face hardens. He holds the smoothie in front of me again. "Half of this needs to be drunk before we go into the cafe. I suggest you start now."

"Can we go back to you not talking to me like I'm a child?"

His lips twitch. "I'll think about it. Now, drink."

"You're such a dick."

He turns the car off, crosses his arms, and leans his head against the headrest.

"What are you doing?" I ask.

He rolls his head toward me. "Now you're going to drink all of it before we leave."

I reach for my seat belt, and he grabs my hand. "If you attempt to get out of this car, my threat to tie you to a chair and force-feed you will come to fruition. I'm not joking, Gemma. I don't make threats I don't follow through on. Now, drink your smoothie, or you're not getting coffee today."

As much as I want to fight him, I don't want to test him and see if he's bluffing. I mutter, "So my mom was right. I am your prisoner."

Hurt crosses his face, but he quickly recovers. "Five minutes to finish it, or we're getting out of the car and you'll receive the consequences."

I let out a frustrated breath and drink the smoothie. It's a perfect combination of sweet and savory, but I don't tell Nolan. When I finish, I glare at him. "Happy now?"

"Yep." He sets his empty cup in the holder and gives me a satisfied smile. "It's good, isn't it?"

I grip the cup tighter so I don't slap him. "No. It was gross. Can we get my coffee now?"

"Acid, coming right up," he mutters and starts the car. We ride in silence. When he parks, I reach for the door handle.

"Don't open it!" he exclaims.

"Why?"

"I told you. You don't go outside without being given the all clear," he reminds me.

I release the handle and sit back. He gets out, comes around, then opens the door. He reaches in to help me out and tugs me into him. As much as I want to push him away, I don't. I sink into him and let him lead me inside with his arm wrapped around me as if I'm his.

The line is like the other morning. He keeps his arm protectively around me. I recognize a man's face from the previous day, and my body stiffens.

Nolan leans down to my ear. "Relax, princess. It's my cousin."

I tilt my head, and his mouth is only inches from mine. "Is it that obvious I'm paranoid?"

He shakes his head. "No. Now, what are you ordering today?"

"Same as yesterday."

"Large acid long?" He cocks an amused eyebrow.

I bite my smile. "Have you never had coffee?"

"Nope. It's bad for you."

"There are plenty of studies to show it's good for you," I claim.

His eyes dart to my lips. "Is that how you convince yourself? You read some study published by some kook on the internet?"

I groan. "You're very annoying."

"I'm—"

"Look who's back. Good morning. What can I get you, doll?" the barista chirps.

Nolan's arm tightens around me. He growls, "Did we not have this conversation yesterday?"

"Nolan," I reprimand, but deep down, I kind of like his super possessive, jealous side. It's one of the reasons I've always fallen for the bad boys.

The barista ignores Nolan. "What can I get you?"

"Double espresso long, please," I reply.

"Same as yesterday. Got it." He punches the order into the system. He gives me a big grin. "Those glasses are hot on you, doll. And sorry, I didn't catch your name yesterday."

"Nolan. And you're really asking for it," Nolan growls.

The barista smirks at Nolan then returns to the screen.

Nolan shoves six dollars at him and doesn't wait for his change. He guides me to the end of the counter, seething.

I tell him, "You need to chill."

"That guy is a douchebag."

Just to get under Nolan's skin, I study the barista. I tilt my head. "Hmm."

"What does that mean?" Nolan asks.

"I don't know. He's kind of cute," I say.

Nolan's eyes widen. "You have to be kidding me."

I shrug. "He has the I'm-almost-thirty-and-cocky thing down."

"Bet he doesn't even know what to do with his cock," Nolan mutters.

I hold in a laugh.

A female barista yells out, "Double espresso long for Doll."

Nolan's eyes turn to flames. The male barista glances at him and throws him an arrogant smile.

"That's it." Nolan picks up my drink, escorts me to the car, and opens my door.

"Is there a fire somewhere?" I ask.

He grunts.

I get in the car then he shuts the door and walks around to the other side. He gets in, starts the car, and drives the opposite way we came.

"Where are we going?"

"To the store."

"For what?" I ask.

"An espresso machine. I'm not having that dickhead check you out every morning," he states.

I take a sip of my coffee and try to ignore my flutters. I turn toward Nolan. "Why do you care?"

He glances at me but only momentarily then refocuses on the road. He doesn't answer my question.

I decide it's time to turn the tables on Nolan. I've been embarrassed all morning. It's his turn. "Does this have to do with you stealing my panties?"

A faint blush creeps up his neck. "Told you I don't know anything about that."

"Are you saying someone else was in your house while I was sleeping? Should I be worried, or is one of your cousins a panty thief?" I innocently ask.

"Maybe they're under the bed," he offers.

"Hmm. Since you ransacked my room today, I think we would have found them," I add.

He veers into the other lane then turns in to a parking lot.

I ask again, "So why do you care so much about the barista checking me out?"

"It's rude." He pulls into a parking spot.

"It's not if it doesn't offend me," I reply.

He shuts the car off and turns toward me. "Are you into him?"

I snort. "Not at all."

Relief fills his face.

Once again, I ask, "Why do you care?"

He opens his mouth then shuts it. He licks his lips, stares at mine, then gets out of the car. He opens my door, leads me into the store and down the coffee maker aisle.

I reach for a cheap one, and he puts his hand on the box. "This isn't an espresso machine."

I shrug. "It'll work."

He shakes his head, looks around, then guides me into the next row. He points to a huge box. "This work?"

I stare at the price tag. "That's over a thousand dollars!"

"Will it make what you drink?" he asks.

"I guess, but a normal coffee machine is fine," I reiterate.

He grunts. "If you want espresso, you're getting espresso, princess."

7

Nolan

Several Weeks Later

"Oh! Wow!" Gemma exclaims.

I glance up. I'm working on creating the new algorithm...or at least trying to. She's on the couch with her laptop, in the shortest pair of shorts I've ever seen. My thoughts about caramel have now switched to honey, since it occurred to me liquid caramel would burn her skin. I've gotten a total of fifteen minutes in without staring at her thighs, wondering for the millionth time what she tastes like. I ask, "What's going on?"

She furrows her eyebrows, reads something else on the screen, then excitement erupts in her voice. "I got a job."

I jump up and sit next to her. "Where?"

She points to the screen. "It's a start-up. They only need a basic branding package, but they want to know when I can start. They said they liked my portfolio." She spent several days creating sample graphics and slogans for fake companies to showcase her skills. We came up with all sorts of crazy names at the pub one night. When she created the designs and slogans, they all blew me away.

I slide my arm around her shoulders and tug her into me. Without thinking, I kiss the top of her head. "That's my girl."

She tilts her head, and my heart races faster. The last few days have gotten harder for me not to touch her. Once we got past the new house rules, we fell into a routine. We wake up, drink our smoothie, then go for a run. After, we do different isometric exercises. She then makes her espresso, and I harass her about putting acid in her body. The rest of the day, we spend on our laptops. I make sure she eats three meals and two snacks a day. At night, we watch movies, play cards, or go to the pub. But every moment spent with her is more torturous than the last. The constant flirting comes from both our sides, but neither of us has gone past that. Each night, we go into our separate rooms. I toss and turn, wishing she were with me. I always end up sneaking into her room and watching her sleep. And it's the first time I've kissed her on the head since the night she slept in my room.

Her blue eyes meet mine, and she sweetly smiles.

Time seems to stand still. She looks so happy. Over the last few days, she doesn't seem as stressed. I know she can't see it, but I catch glimpses of who she is and not who she thinks she's become. The more I see, the more I'm attracted to her. It's creating real issues for me when I analyze our situation.

She finally says, "Thanks for making me do this."

"You did it. I just threatened you," I tease.

She laughs, and my cock twitches. Something about her laugh lights something inside me I haven't felt before. It's getting harder to resist making a move on her. Part of me no longer remembers why I'm not. After everything Orla has put her through, I wonder if it's fair to still assume we can't be together since she's a Bailey. Liam seems to have gotten over it within minutes of learning the truth about Hailee. I wonder why I'm still holding on to it or if Liam is crazy.

Gemma glances at my lips. "Well, thanks."

Before I can analyze it, I say, "Let's go celebrate tonight."

She slowly licks her lips. "How?"

I internally groan. That tongue of hers is driving me insane. "Let's go out."

"To the pub?" she asks.

I shake my head. "No. Somewhere nice. Wear your blue dress."

She cocks an eyebrow. "My blue dress?"

"Yeah. The one in your closet." Ever since I saw her blue minidress hanging in the closet, I've imagined her in it.

Her lips twitch. "Okay. Do I get to pick your outfit?"

If I get to see you in your blue dress, you can pick my clothes for life. I casually reply, "Sure."

She shuts her laptop, rises, and I get a view of her perfect ass. She glances behind her. "Are you coming?"

I rise and we go into my closet.

She flicks through my clothes and every now and then holds a shirt or sport coat up to me. She finally settles on a pair of jeans, a form-fitted white T-shirt, and a navy fitted sport coat. She asks, "What time are we going out?"

I remove my phone from my pocket and pull up the app to see what's open. The high-end sushi restaurant I want to take her to doesn't have any openings, so I text my friend who owns it. He replies, and I say to Gemma, "We'll leave in two hours."

"Guess I better get in the shower, then," she chirps. She pats me on the shoulder and passes me.

I reach for her. "Hey."

"Yeah?"

"Congratulations."

Her face lights up, and my balls ache some more. "Thanks."

I wink, and she leaves.

I shower, get ready, then pace my bedroom. I'm suddenly nervous.

Is this a date or no?

Do I want to cross the line with her, or am I just asking for more trouble?

No. I shouldn't cross the line. We're living together. I don't need things to get uncomfortable or to cause any drama.

When it gets closer to the time we need to leave, I've convinced myself we're two friends going to dinner to celebrate her success. That's it. We'll go to dinner, have a night out, then come home.

Keeping it in the friend zone.

I go into the family room. Gemma comes out. My heart almost beats out of my chest. Her blue dress matches her eyes. It showcases her legs and cleavage. She's wearing four-inch silver stilettos. I love her without makeup, but I decide I love her just as much with it. And her long hair hangs in waves. She freezes and scans my body. She softly says, "You look nice."

I check her out again. "You look gorgeous."

Neither of us moves for a moment. She spins and says, "Can you zip me up?"

The dress is backless. She's not wearing a bra, and it takes everything I have not to push her dress off her. I step forward and drag my finger down her back. A small gasp slips from her lips. A muted floral scent makes my blood hotter. I take my other hand and move her hair over her shoulder then refrain from unzipping the part she was able to, in order to see if she's wearing panties. I slowly zip her dress up.

She spins into me. In her stilettos, the top of her head is just under my nose. She glances up, I look down, and our breaths merge. I hold myself back from kissing her. "Are you hungry?"

She blushes, and her eyes roam to my lips. "Yeah."

"Good. I won't have to tie you up and force-feed you, then," I tease.

She tilts her head and smirks. "Ha ha. You're suddenly Mr. Funny, I see."

"I'm always funny."

She squints. "Mmmm...are you?"

I chuckle. "Yep. Let's go." I help her into her coat then lead her out of the house and to the car waiting in the driveway. I open the door to the back seat.

"Fancy." She smirks.

I pat her ass. "Get in, princess."

Her face flushes as she obeys.

I take a deep breath of fresh air before joining her in the car. It does nothing to calm my nerves. She crosses her legs, and I roll my head toward her. "Are you wearing panties tonight?"

She smirks. "Do you always ask women you take to dinner if they're wearing panties?"

"Nope. Just you. And you aren't wearing a bra." I glance at her cleavage, unable to stop myself from being a total pervert.

She peeks down at my pants, walks her fingers over my leg, and stops next to my dick. Her index finger strokes my inner thigh, sending zings through my groin. She moves her head closer to mine. "Are these your boxers, or did you leave them at home?"

"Maybe if you're a good girl at dinner, you'll find out when we get home," I blurt out before I can stop myself.

Her hand freezes, her breath hitches, and she swallows hard.

I curse myself for going where I shouldn't. At the same time, I lean an inch from her lips and dig myself deeper in the hole. I murmur, "I think my bed misses you."

She takes a deep breath. "Is that why you watch me while I sleep? Because your bed misses me?"

I freeze. Blood pounds between my ears. "You know I watch you?"

She bites her lip and slowly nods.

My stomach flips. "Does it bother you?"

She shakes her head.

I trace her jawbone. "Why is that?"

She opens her mouth to speak, and the door opens.

I jerk my head and bark, "Ever heard of knocking, Korrigan?"

My cousin grunts. "Easy. We're here." He steps aside.

I glance out the door to the line snaking around the building. "Next time, knock," I reprimand and slide out of the car. I reach in and take Gemma's hand. When she's out of the car, I tug her close to me and go to the front of the line.

"Nolan. I haven't seen you in a while," the bouncer says and holds out his fist.

I bump it. "Good to see you, Kai. This is Gemma."

He eyes her over, and for the first time ever, I want to punch Kai.

"Nice to meet you, Gemma."

"You, too," she replies with a kind smile.

He nods for us to go inside. I quickly guide her past him to the hostess station. We immediately get escorted to a private area. Black curtains hang on both sides of the two-top table. Small candles give Gemma's face a soft glow, making my head spin faster.

The hostess hands me a wine menu. "Your server, Akari, will be with you shortly." She leaves.

I open the wine menu. I scan it, and my nerves vibrate. I'm not a huge wine fan and never know what to order. It's one of those things I should probably figure out but haven't yet. I ask, "Do you drink red or white?"

Gemma winces. "I don't like wine."

"Thank God," I say and shut the menu.

She laughs. "You don't, either?"

"Not really. I'd rather have real alcohol."

She beams. "And we finally agree on something."

"I guess so. You always drink a martini at the pub. Is that what you want?"

"Mmm...nope. I think tonight I'll have a Sidecar."

Her answer surprises me. I grew up in a pub but never heard of it. "What's in it?"

"Cognac, orange liqueur, and lemon juice," she reels off.

"Is it sweet?"

She shrugs. "A bit."

"I'll take a Macallan, then."

Her lips twitch. "You're so Irish."

"And you aren't?"

"How am I Irish?"

The server pulls the curtain back. "Good evening, I'm Akari. Did the hostess tell you the specials tonight?"

"No," I respond.

Akari smiles. "For starters, I highly recommend the Tuna Tartare Tower. It's enough for two. The chef also has a twelve-piece sashimi sampler, and there are three new signature rolls. Would you like to know what's in them?"

"No. I eat anything and like to be surprised," Gemma claims. She smirks at me. "But I'm sure Nolan would want to know."

"Oh? Why is that?"

She turns to Akari. "He's very particular about what goes into his body. He's never even drunk coffee."

Shock fills Akari's face. She turns to me. "Never?"

"It's super acidic and full of toxins," I claim.

She raises her eyebrows at Gemma. "Guess I'll go through it all."

"Nope. Just bring us one of everything," I say.

Gemma tilts her head. "It's okay. You can know the ingredients."

I shake my head. "Nope. I bet there isn't anything here I don't like."

Akari grins. "Okay. Anything else?"

"Gemma?" I ask.

"No. I'm good."

Akari takes our drink orders, steps back, and pulls the curtain for privacy.

Gemma leans closer. "You were saying I'm super Irish?"

I trace the bones on her hand. "Yep. Hot tempered. Stubborn. Sexy as hell." I pin my gaze on her, and my stomach somersaults. I can't seem to keep my mouth shut tonight. I'm still not sure it's a good idea. I rethink if I should even drink the alcohol I ordered.

Her cheeks turn red. "Is that your way of nicely saying I'm a hot mess?"

"Your words, not mine."

She shifts in her seat. She nervously darts her eyes to her water then back to me. "So I haven't overstayed my welcome yet?"

"No. I kind of like having you around," I admit.

She takes a sip of water then asks about the elephant standing in front of our relationship. "Even though I have Bailey blood swirling in my veins?"

I skirt around the question. Maybe it's my stubbornness, but I can't seem to say it's okay. It's not fair to her, but something about admitting it's okay she has Bailey DNA seems like a betrayal to my father and Sean. But the urge for me to make her mine is only intensifying, and I don't know how to stop it. I respond, "If you didn't have their blood, I guess we wouldn't be in this position, would we?"

She furrows her eyebrows and sits back in her seat. She moves her hand on her lap. "What if I didn't? What if you met me on the street or in the pub? Say the night we met, I wasn't as crazy as I was, and what happened didn't happen. Imagine I was my normal self that night. Would we be sitting here?"

The server opens the curtain and sets down our drinks. Gemma's gaze never leaves mine.

"Need anything else right now?" Akari asks.

"No. We're good," I reply and watch her leave, to try and gather my thoughts.

"We wouldn't, would we?" Gemma asks.

I tap my glass of Macallan. I quietly admit, "No. I would have stayed away from you."

She looks away. "Why?"

"You're more Killian's type," I say without thinking.

She snaps her head toward me. "What does that mean?"

The feeling I just majorly slipped up annihilates me. "Nothing bad. He just always dates wild women."

Her voice turns cold. "Wild women?"

"I didn't mean to offend you. I'm just telling the truth," I reply, but my chest tightens.

She takes a sip of her drink, licks her lips, and sets her glass down. "So Killian dates wild women. Who do you date?"

"The non-wild women," I attempt to tease, but it falls flat.

Her knee begins to bounce next to mine. "I see. So why is that? What about them do you like? Is it the fact they do whatever you say? Or that they never embarrass you? What is it about them?"

"Easy. I think you're taking this the wrong way."

"I'm fine. I'd just like to know what you find so attractive about them."

"Let's talk about something else," I suggest.

"No. You said it. I'd like an explanation, please," she pushes.

I take a long drink.

"Nolan!"

"Fine. I'll tell you. There isn't any drama. It's easy. They aren't reckless. I can trust them."

She nods and rises. "I need to use the restroom."

I get out of my seat. "Gemma—"

"I'll be back in a minute."

"Don't be upset—"

"I'm not. I need the ladies' room. Do you know where it is?"

I sigh. "Yeah. Come on." I escort her through the restaurant and wait outside, kicking myself for not shutting my mouth. Quite a while passes, and she finally comes out.

"Gemma—"

"Everything's fine. Let's change the subject." She smiles and walks past me.

I follow her back to our table, and a server has the Tuna Tower and sashimi platter. He sets it down. We get in our seats, and she avoids me, filling her appetizer plate with tuna, mango, and avocado. She focuses on eating.

Several minutes pass. I attempt to rectify things again. I calmly state, "I didn't mean to sound like I was calling you those things."

She sets her chopsticks down and finally acknowledges me. "But I am, aren't I?"

"Only sometimes," I tease, trying to lighten the mood. It only digs the hole deeper.

She doesn't say anything, but hurt fills her face.

"I'm not saying things right tonight," I claim.

"Sure you are. You're just speaking your truth." She takes a long sip of her drink then says, "Let's change the subject."

I feel guilty changing the subject. It's as if I'm taking the coward's way out. "Okay. But first, tell me this. If you met me outside of the family issues and you hadn't been looking for someone to protect you, would you have even given me a second glance?"

She sits up straighter and looks me straight in the eye. "Yeah. I would have. You're exactly the type of guy I'd be into. And then I'd realize what a mistake you were after a few months in and kick myself for dating another guy like you."

My gut feels like she punched me. "What does that mean?"

"What do you think it means?"

"I don't know. Why don't you fill me in?"

She sticks a piece of salmon in her mouth, chews it, then washes it down with her Sidecar. She wipes her mouth with the black napkin. "Let's see. After you swept me off my feet and got in my pants, you'd start standing me up. I'd find out you were cheating on me, and then you'd deny it and try to convince me I'm the crazy one but you still love me."

"That's not me at all," I claim.

She huffs. "Yeah. Sure. That's what all guys like you say."

My pulse beats harder. "Guys like me?"

"Yeah."

My anger builds, and the curtain opens. The same male server places a tray of rolls down and tells us each of the names. I barely hear him, staring at Gemma, who's focusing on the server.

"Need anything else?" he asks.

"We're good. Thank you," she sweetly replies.

He leaves and shuts the curtain.

"So what kind of guy am I, Gemma? Because I'm not a cheater. I don't use women. And I've never stood a woman up," I tell her.

She stares at the rolls then picks one up with her chopsticks. She puts it on her plate then selects a few more. "You're a typical bad boy. Dangerous. Totally alpha. Super into your body and looking good."

I sit back in my chair and grip the edge of the table. "So I'm a cheater who stands women up because I work out and eat right?"

She shrugs. "Just calling it what it is. No shame in your game. It's who you are." She pops a piece of sushi in her mouth and continues to not look at me.

"And this is coming from a girl who competes in all sorts of athletic competitions? The same girl who has a six-pack?"

"I'm not a cheater."

"Neither am I," I insist, insulted she would even assume I am after living with me for several weeks.

She puts her chopsticks down and takes another drink. "Can we change the subject?"

I don't answer her. I swallow half my glass of Macallan. It burns my throat as it slides into my stomach.

"You should eat." She points to the sushi.

"I've lost my appetite," I state.

"Oh? Want me to tie you to the chair and force-feed you?" She shoots me a wide-eyed innocent expression.

The curtain opens. In a chipper voice, Akari asks, "How are we doing?"

"Fine. Can we get our check, please?" I ask.

She looks at the table. "Is something wrong with your food?"

"No."

"Do you want a box?"

"No."

"Yes, please. I can have it at home during one of my feeding times," Gemma digs.

Akari glances at us, confused, but recovers. "Sure. I'll be right back with boxes and your check."

"Great. Thank you," Gemma replies.

I tap the table, finish my drink, and scowl at her. "Glad to know what you think of me."

"Ditto." She finishes her drink then chases it with water.

Uncomfortable silence fills the air. I wonder how I got it so wrong. Or how I screwed up so bad. Part of me is too pissed about what she thinks of me to attempt to make things right. The other half of me only sees the hurt in her expression and body language. Either way, I'm at a loss for how to move back to where we were.

Akari comes back with the check. I pay while Gemma boxes up the food. We leave. The car ride home is quiet. We're a few blocks from my house when I mutter, "This isn't how I wanted tonight to go."

She sighs. In a hurt voice, she says, "No. You wanted to get in my pants even though you still hate me because of who my father is and you despise everything about me."

I turn toward her. "That's not true."

"Isn't it? Can you sit here and say you're perfectly accepting of who I am and the blood that flows through my veins?"

My heart beats faster. I want to tell her she's wrong, and I do accept everything about her. That no matter who her family is, I don't care. But my father's and Sean's faces pop into my mind, and it takes me a while to find my words.

The car pulls into the driveway, and we get out. I pull her into me and slide my hands on her cheeks. "Listen. I'm like you in this. I don't—"

"Nolan!" Molly's voice calls out, and my gut drops.

I close my eyes then spin toward my front porch. "What are you doing here?"

She rises off the step. "I lost my keys. My mom isn't home. You're the only person who has an emergency set."

Shit.

"How did you get here?"

"I took an Uber. But I can see I'm interrupting. I'll go home and wait for my mom." She begins to walk away.

"Molly, stop. Just give me a minute."

She sniffles. "Okay."

I turn back to Gemma.

She shakes her head. Her sad expression makes my heart sink. She steps away from me. "I'm going to bed."

"Gemma, wait." I reach for her arm.

She shrugs out of it and mutters, "I hope you're happy with your non-wild, drama-free girl."

"Gemma!"

She walks past Molly and into the garage. The door slams and I cringe.

I lead Molly inside the house and get my keys. Gemma is nowhere around. I hand Molly the spare and say, "I'll have Korrigan take you home."

Her face falls. "Okay. Umm, can I have a glass of water first?"

I groan inside. Molly is quickly becoming a pain in my ass. "Sure." I go to the fridge and get her a bottle of water. I expect her to take it with her, but she sits on the barstool.

"Nolan, I need some advice," she states.

"Can we talk some other time?" I ask.

She looks away, and her voice shakes. "Ummm...sure." She rises.

Guilt fills me. She's always been a troubled girl. I promised Colin I'd look out for her. "Molly, sit back down. What do you need to talk about?"

8

Gemma

I open my door to get a bottle of water and hear Molly talking. It's past midnight. Hurt and anger intensifies. Nolan prefers to spend his night with a train wreck like her but claims I'm drama. Not sure why he can't see how big of a mess she is but has no problem pointing out mine.

Okay, maybe that isn't fair. He didn't exactly point out my shortcomings. But he did make it clear I wasn't a choice he'd ever make. And I'm not willing to be his spur-of-the-moment, wild-girl guinea pig for him to test out, only to say he tried it out once and proved his theory right.

I shut my door and crawl back into bed. I toss and turn but freeze when the door opens. I close my eyes.

Like every night, Nolan stares down at me. I can feel him. My heart beats harder. Several minutes pass and then he sits on the chair.

I always keep my eyes shut. I usually fall asleep, feeling safe when he watches me. Tonight, there's no way it's happening. Instead of pretending, I slowly open my eyes.

It takes a moment for them to adjust. Nolan's in his boxers, displaying every inch of his muscular flesh. A crystal whiskey glass is in his hand, and he's tapping the side of it with his index finger.

His green eyes glow in the dark. They fixate on mine, and I don't blink. I don't know if time stands still or moves forward. It feels like forever and nothing at all before he sets the glass on the table, drops to his knees, and is in front of me.

I hold my breath when his hand strokes my cheek. Flutters ignite in my belly. The intoxicating scent of sandalwood and coffee beans swirls in the air. He opens his mouth then shuts it.

Against my will, his face becomes a blur as tears fill my eyes. I don't want to fight with Nolan. I don't want to be the girl he doesn't want or would never choose. And I don't want him to be another guy I regret.

He takes both hands, slides them in my hair, and dips his face in front of mine. The blazing green fire in his eyes burns brighter. The pulsing in my veins quickens. His hot breath, sweet from whiskey, merges with mine.

I open my mouth, and before I can say anything, his lips are on mine. His delicious tongue slides so quickly into my mouth, I gasp. My body trembles as he flicks it in and out, exploring every part and rolling it against my tongue.

I kiss him back with a fury, unable to stop myself from responding or ending what both of us know we shouldn't do.

His strong hand slides down my back, and his other hand throws the covers off me. He palms my ass and pulls me into a sitting position so I'm facing him. Before I know what's happening, he wraps my legs around his waist, lifts me up, and carries me down the hall. He never takes his mouth off mine or reduces the intensity of our kisses. It grows hotter and hotter until I feel like I'm about to combust.

He sets me on the bed, removing his lips from mine, only to pull his T-shirt I'm wearing, over my head and tossing it on the floor. His mouth consumes me again, and when our warm skin makes contact, a deep groan rumbles in his chest.

I hold on to him as if he's mine, pushing the thoughts about why I should stop this to the back of my head. He's a perfect concoction of hard flesh, pulsing skin, and aggressive confidence you don't ever want to let go of. It's in his eyes and hands and lips. Every move he makes, he takes possession of me further until I'm so engrossed in his body, I forget I'm not part of him.

His mouth inches down my torso, controlling my every whimper, creating an inferno so fiery, pellets of sweat burst out on my skin.

When he reaches my pussy, his eyes lock on mine. I come almost as soon as his tongue and lips ravage me. It feels like forever since a man last touched me, but everything about Nolan is different.

I cry out, dizzy from the adrenaline. It only encourages him more. He reaches up, pushes my head back, then sticks his hand over my face. His fingers slide down until two are in my mouth, muffling my moans as another wave of endorphins ricochets through my body.

He drags his tongue up my torso, sucks on each breast, then returns to kissing me.

The sound of the drawer opening hits my ears. Somehow, he puts a condom on without ever taking his mouth or body away from mine. Tingles ignite on the back of my thigh when he pushes it up. He presses his forehead against mine and sinks into me.

I gasp. He closes his eyes then his green orbs drill back into mine. "Shhh," he murmurs, caressing my head.

I lift my hips then realize he's not entirely in me.

"Go slow, princess." He continues kissing me, thrusting deeper inch by inch, then glides his arms under my back and rolls over, taking me with him.

My knees sink into the mattress. He sits up and wraps his arms around me, fisting my hair and tugging it. His lips assault my neck, and I take more and more of him in until there's no more to take.

His erection expands my walls to the point I wonder if he's going to break me in two. I grind my hips on top of him, closing my eyes, feeling the intensity of all that is Nolan.

Every touch is possessive. Each kiss feeds a craving. All the parts of him swallow me whole until only life surges through me.

"You're mine, princess," he murmurs then licks the back of my ear.

I want it to be true. I don't know if it is, except for in this moment. So I push any questions or worries away and fall deeper under his spell.

He kisses me again, gently biting my lip, then holds my face in front of his. He commands, "Tell me you're mine."

I nod, attempt to kiss him again, but he holds my hair tighter so I can't.

"Say it," he demands. His eyes glow like a wild animal that just woke up and needs to be fed.

My voice comes out in a quiet rasp. "Yes."

"Yes, what?"

"I'm yours."

His smoldering expression burns hotter. He flips me on my back and pins my wrists above my head.

"Oh God!" I cry out as he thrusts harder.

"Jesus, Gemma," he mumbles then buries his face into the curve of my neck, biting on my collarbone.

Tremors ignite in my toes. My body spasms against his, and I clutch him wherever I can as my eyes roll.

"That's it, princess," he growls then his erection violently pumps inside me, stretching me to another breaking point.

We lay there, sweaty, breathing hard, flesh throbbing against flesh. He finally picks his head up and stares at me.

I open my mouth, not even sure what I'm going to say, but he puts his finger over it.

"Don't talk. Let's not ruin this," he says then consumes my mouth, as if it's a drug he can't get enough of. Or maybe I'm the one taking hit after hit of him. I match every ounce of affection he gives me with a hunger and greed I don't ever recall feeling.

We come up for air. He rolls off me, tugs me into his arms, and pretzels his limbs around mine, just like the only other time I slept with him. He kisses my head, strokes my back, and I fall asleep on his chest.

When I open my eyes the next morning, he's breathing softly and evenly.

Shit. What did we do?

The covers are over me but not the one side of his body. I stare at his chest, covered in ink, attempting not to freak out. But I'm unable to hold back and trace the Celtic arrows on his V.

"You can go lower," his deep voice teases.

I freeze then glance up. His eyes are still closed, but his lips twitch. I walk my fingers farther down the V and discover the biggest erection I've ever felt.

He opens one eye. "How much energy do you have?"

I nervously laugh, still not sure if we should be doing this. "That's an odd question."

He reaches in the drawer then flips me on my back. I sharply inhale, and an arrogant expression fills his face. "I wonder if I wear you out first, if you'll still beat me today."

"Beat you?"

He kisses me then lowers his head to my neck. "Mmhmm. I have a surprise for you."

Flutters fill my belly. He licks my nipple, and I squeak out, "Oh?"

His soft chuckle fills the air. His hand slides over the curve of my waist until it's between my legs. He pinches my clit, and I gasp.

The alarm on his phone blares through the air. He groans then reaches for it. He mutters, "We might have to run there," then slides off me and stands up.

I sit up to get out of bed, but he yanks me toward him. I yelp, and he smirks. His hands grab my hips, and he flips me on my knees. His hot breath hits my ear. "This is for categorizing me with those dickheads." His palm hits my ass cheek.

A loud crack rings through the air, and I jump. He tightens his arm around my waist.

"Nolan!" I scream. No one's ever slapped my ass before.

He rubs it out and tingles spread under his hand. "Naughty girls get spanked." He hits me again, and the sting intensifies before he rubs it out.

I think he's going to repeat it when his cock slides inside me.

"Oh God!" I yell.

He doesn't inch in me like the previous night. His pelvis is soon against my ass cheeks, and I'm whimpering and shaking on all fours. Zings fly up my spine as his tongue slides up it.

"Holy...oh..."

His fingers circle my clit, and his lips hit my ear. "If you beat me today, I'm licking your pussy at the pub tonight."

"What?" I still don't understand what he's talking about by me beating him.

"Mmhmm. And if I win, you're going to drop to your knees and suck my dick like it's a Tootsie Pop you can't get to the center of."

I burst out laughing, but it's short-lived. He starts to thrust and circle faster, and I break out in a sweat. Endorphins fill all my cells, and I scream, "Nolan! Oh God!"

He splays his hand on my back, pushes me down on the mattress, and grasps my hip with his other hand. Each thrust creates new tremors in my body until I'm so dizzy, I see stars.

He grunts loudly, his body becomes a piston detonating in mine, and I think I might blackout from the rush of adrenaline.

I try to catch my breath, but he pulls me on my feet and spins me into him. Cockiness floods his expression. "Get dressed, princess."

"For what?"

He tsks me. "And you call yourself Irish?"

I stare at him in confusion.

"It's St. Paddy's Day. We have a race to get to."

It takes me a minute to process. I didn't even realize it was March. St. Paddy's Day is my favorite holiday. "5K or 8K?"

"What do you think?"

"Eight?" I ask, hopefully.

"Of course."

"On the Riverwalk?"

"Is there any other one?"

"Really?"

"Yep. We're all signed up under fake names. We even have ID cards," he says.

I clap then throw my arms around him. "Thank you!"

He pats my sore ass cheek. "Get your clothes on. We're going to be late."

We slide into our running gear, leave the house, and jog down to the Riverwalk. "It's so pretty!" I exclaim, staring at the green water. Every year, Chicago dyes the water in the lochs for the holiday.

Nolan grabs my hand and maneuvers me through the large crowd. For the first time in a long time, I don't feel scared or paranoid. I'm just excited about taking part in one of my favorite races. He leads me to the registration table, and we stand in line. He leans down to my ear. "Your name is Crystal Waters."

I raise my eyebrows. "Seriously? What's yours?"

"You don't want to know."

"Oh, please tell."

"Dick Wood."

I laugh so hard, tears come to my eyes. "Who came up with these names?"

"One of my brothers. Who do you think?"

"Killian?"

"Yep."

The person in front of us leaves, and Nolan slaps down two fake IDs. The woman reads our cards, smiles, and studies us. Nolan puts his arm around my shoulder, and I attempt not to laugh. We get our packets and pin the race bibs on our shirts. The announcer says it's time to line up. Nolan grabs my hand and leads me to our designated starting area.

The nervous flutters I always have whenever I start a race ignite in my belly. Nolan leans down and says, "Don't forget our bet."

My butterflies intensify. I tilt my head up. "Umm, did we make a bet?"

His eyes sparkle. "Yeah. You subconsciously agreed."

"Hmm. I guess I'll have to remember we have this cosmic ability to consent."

He wiggles his eyebrows. "You know, if—"

The starting pistol blasts and we start to move with the crowd. The first quarter-mile it's jam-packed, but the runners begin to spread out. I hit a comfortable speed but don't go as fast as I usually would. There's no way I'm breaking away from Nolan until the end.

We weave around the other runners who started in the zone before us, making our way down the green river. A few miles in, we get to the ship canal and turn to run alongside Lake Michigan.

It's sunny, but the wind picks up, smacking me in the face. I push harder to keep my pace. About a mile until the finish line, Nolan pants, "You're killing me, princess."

I glance over. "Do you need me to slow down?"

"No." He scrunches his sweaty face in determination.

I wait until we're a quarter-mile to the finish line and decide it's safe for me to go all out, since Nolan will be right behind me. There's no way I'm losing this bet he created.

Nolan surprises me and continues running side by side with me until the final turn. I find my second wind and run faster, breaking away from him and shooting through the finish line. I cross, continue running, then morph into a jog before transitioning to a walk. My blood is pounding in every cell of my body, and I feel like my old self. I turn to see Nolan sprinting past the marker. He replicates my actions and puts his hands above his head.

"Speedy Gonzalez!" he puffs.

I grin, unable to stop the happiness I feel. I boast, "I won!"

He smirks. "Did you win, or did I?"

I bite on my smile, feeling the happiest I've felt in a long time. We walk toward his neighborhood, and he tugs me into him.

I glance up. "Thanks for arranging this. It makes me feel like me again."

"I know, princess. Let's get your acid and you can drink it on the way home." He opens the door to a cafe. It's the same chain as the one near his house. We get in line and I ask, "So we're going to the pub later today?"

"Yeah. You didn't think I'd let you miss St. Paddy's Day, did you? That would be blasphemy," he teases.

"Very true."

His stomach growls. "I think we should eat sushi for breakfast when we get home."

Guilt about last night fills me. "Hey, I'm sorry about—"

"We're both at fault. Let's forget about it." His green eyes fill with remorse.

I nod. "Okay."

He smiles. "Since this is your first O'Malley St.—"

"Well, if it isn't my missing sunshine. Did you take part in the run, Doll?" the same barista from the cafe near Nolan's house asks. His eyes scan my body, and he licks his lips. "Sweat looks good on you."

Nolan's body stiffens. He growls, "If you hit on my woman one more time, I'm going to reach over this counter and drag you outside."

I bite on my smile and tug on his arm. "Nolan."

The barista's smug expression gets cockier. He addresses me. "Same order as always, Doll?"

"Yeah."

"Stop calling her Doll," Nolan barks and throws six bucks on the counter.

"But she is. Look at her," he gloats and checks me out again.

Nolan's face turns red, and he starts to reach over the counter.

I jump in front of him. "Easy. Let's go wait for my espresso."

He snarls and points at the barista. "You better watch it."

I tug him toward the end of the counter, and he mumbles, "That guy is going to see an early grave."

"I think he's doing it to get under your skin. You shouldn't let him bother you."

"No. He's eyeing you up like a piece of fresh meat," Nolan insists.

I attempt not to smile.

"You find this funny?" Nolan asks.

"Double espresso long for Doll," the other barista yells and sets my drink down.

Nolan growls and exchanges a look with the barista who hit on me.

I lead Nolan outside, and we walk home. We take showers, and I put on jeans and the green, long-sleeve O'Malley T-shirt he had hidden in his closet for me. It's soft like the ones of his I wear to bed. I pull out the sushi from last night, and we only take a few bites before the doorbell rings.

"Expecting company?" I ask.

"Nope." He goes to the door and opens it. "Molly. What are you doing here?"

My gut drops.

Her annoying voice fills the room. "I wanted to say thank you for helping me last night. Sorry to be such a pain, but you're the only one I can talk to about these things. Anyway, I know you love my fish stew, so I made you a pot."

Nolan clears his voice. "Thanks. That was nice of you."

"Are you going to the pub today?"

"Yes. Of course."

Her voice gets chipper. "Great. I'm heading there now for my shift. I'll make sure I save one of the chilled mugs for you before we run out."

"Thanks. I'll see you later," Nolan says.

"Okay. Bye, Nolan," she almost sings, and I want to throw up in my mouth.

Nolan shuts the door and brings a large plastic container into the kitchen.

I put my chopsticks down and glare at the container.

"She's just trying to be nice," Nolan offers.

"Sure. Ms. I-Want-to-Suck-Your-Dick-All-Night can't stay away for more than twelve hours, can she?" I sneer.

Nolan puts the stew in the fridge. He spins me on the barstool and tilts my chin up. "Nothing is going on between

Molly and me. Are you going to let this ruin the St. Paddy's Day I planned for you?" He arches an eyebrow.

I take a deep breath. Until Molly showed up, things were perfect. Everything he did today has been for me. I sigh. "No."

He slides his hands to my cheeks and brings his face to mine. His lips twitch. "Good. Let's finish our sushi. You're going to need lots of food in your stomach to handle an O'Malley St. Paddy's Day."

9

Nolan

It has barely hit noon when we get to the pub, and it's already at max capacity. There's a line around the corner of the building. My cousins are on the front doors. Leo, the Ivanov bouncer who usually is outside their gym, is in the alley.

O'Malleys usually take care of all the security, so I ask, "Leo, what are you doing here?"

Leo's thick Russian accent fills the air. He crosses his arms. His natural scowl is on his face. "Boris didn't like the situation that occurred last year. He decided it's best to let the Irish party and have a Russian on this one."

I can't argue with Boris's reasoning. Nora brings in a heated tent and creates more seating on St. Paddy's Day. You can't enter, only exit. Last year, my cousin was in charge of alley duty. He decided to drink the whiskey shots his girlfriend kept bringing him. He let people in, and we were over capacity. A fight broke out in the alley. Boris, Sergey, my brothers, and I, had to break it up.

"Should I make you go to the front?" Leo seriously asks.

I reply, "When did you become the comedian?"

He grunts, lifts the rope, and motions for Gemma and me to go through.

I lead her through the tent and into the hallway. A wave of heat and loud noise hits me. There's a crowd waiting for the restrooms.

"This is insane," Gemma shouts.

I grin. "Yep."

Killian steps out of the stairwell with a keg. Declan is behind him, carrying two cases of alcohol.

"About time you showed up. Next keg, you're getting," Killian states.

"How long have you been here?" Gemma asks.

"Six."

"Wow."

"I told you we were running the race this morning," I remind him. I've always been at the pub at six on St. Paddy's Day. It's the busiest day of the year. We open early, and none of us go home until closing time. But things are different this year. Nora is due to have the baby any day. Boris insisted she stays out of the pub, worried about the large crowd. Nora tripled her staff, Boris took over the security, and her manager, Darcey, has things under control.

Before I signed up for the 8K, I spoke with Nora. Gemma's always run that race. She told me it was one of her favorites. I wanted to do something to make her feel like her old self. And I always wanted to run it but never could because of the pub. Nora assured me she had everything sorted and to sign up.

Killian shakes his head and passes us. "Excuses me, lasses. Green beer coming through."

"Why's he so pissy?" I ask Declan and grab the top case he's holding.

"No idea." He leans over and kisses Gemma on the cheek. "How was your race?"

She beams. "Awesome. I beat your brother."

Declan chuckles. "That isn't hard. He's slow."

"Shut up. You run like a turtle," I claim.

"I'm a gazelle and you know it. And I always let you win so I don't make you look bad."

I snort. "Is that what you tell yourself?"

"Yep." He pushes through the crowd.

I nod for Gemma to go and follow them. We get to the bar and set the cases down. Killian is switching out the keg. Declan removes his pocket knife and rips open the boxes.

Gemma reaches in and pulls fifths of green apple schnapps out.

"I'd say take a seat, but there aren't any," I tease.

"It's okay. I'd rather help."

"Those go at the shot station in the game room." Molly comes up behind us. She has her hand on her hip and an annoyed expression.

Gemma takes a deep breath then smiles. "Okay. I'll take them over." She puts the bottles back inside.

"I'll do it." Molly tries to pick up the box but barely lifts it. She turns to me. "It's kind of heavy. Can you carry it for me, Nolan?"

Before I can pick it up, Gemma grabs the box and steps away from the bar. She grumbles, "It's not that heavy."

Molly rolls her eyes. When Gemma is several feet away, she asks, "Why is she here?"

"Molly, we're too busy for you to be chatting. Table sixty-six wants to cash out, and they've been waiting," Darcey reprimands.

Molly leaves, and I spin. "Hey, Darcey."

She pats me on the shoulder. "Any chance you can cover the shot station for about an hour? Nicky and Tyler need a break."

"Yep. On it." I go into the game room. Gemma is helping Nicky open fifths. I can't help but smile. I didn't bring her to work all day, but I like how she just jumped in. Plus, she looks hotter than I imagined in her O'Malley fitted T-shirt and skinny jeans.

I sneak up behind her and slide my palm on her ass. I lean into her ear and whisper, "Did you get a shot yet?"

She tilts her head and smiles. "Nope. These are cute though. I've never seen Lucky Leprechauns."

I reach around her and grab a green shot glass with gold sparkles on the rim. I hold it in front of her and tease, "And you call yourself Irish?"

She laughs. "You seem to enjoy accusing me of not being Irish today." She picks up another shot and clinks the one I'm holding. "Sláinte is táinte."

I chuckle, impressed she knows the Irish verbiage toast meaning health and wealth. "Sláinte is táinte."

We take the shots. I tell her, "They need a break. I'm going to cover them for a bit."

"I'll help."

"You want to be my shot girl?" I wiggle my eyebrows.

"I told you I used to work in a bar, right?"

"You did mention it." I turn away from her. "Nicky, Tyler, go take a break."

They smile gratefully and leave.

Gemma starts dipping the shot glasses in the gold sparkles, and I pour the whiskey and schnapps into the shaker. As soon as I pour the alcohol, it seems like they are gone. The waitstaff keep filling their trays, and the line in the game room gets longer.

Killian joins us and shouts, "Cash only! Use your server if you have a tab."

There's a groan, and half the people get out of line.

"Glad to see you have sprinkle skills, Gemma." He picks up a shot. "Here. Have some fun while you're doing this."

She takes it, Killian and I take another one, we clink glasses and all say, "Sláinte is táinte."

He roars, "All right. Lasses first. If you have a dick, step to the back of the line."

The men start grumbling. Gemma gapes at Killian.

I yell, "If you're an O'Malley and don't move your ass to the back, Declan's going to kick it all the way outside for not having manners."

There's more shouting and men shuffling to the back.

Gemma picks up a tray of shots and yells, "If you're an O'Malley and think you're better looking than Killian or Nolan, form a line here!"

Hoorays and cheers fill the air. My extended family is huge. There are relatives I barely recognize that only come here once a year or for family events.

"Oh, you're out of line now, lass," Killian states.

Gemma smirks. "Looks like everyone thinks they're better looking than you."

"They're blind when they look in the mirror," he replies.

"All tips go to Killian's erectile dysfunction fund," Gemma shouts.

The game room explodes in laughter.

"No blue pill needed here, lass. We're not sure about Declan though," Killian barks back.

My third cousin, Lorcan, says something in Gemma's ear. Her cheeks turn to fire, and my chest tightens. I don't trust him or any of my single cousins not hitting on her. The same goes for the men in line I haven't seen before. I move to the other side of Killian. I growl at the line of men, "Pay, take your shot, and move along. And I better not find out you said something indecent." I scowl at Lorcan until he leaves, knowing full well he said something that will piss me off.

Over the next hour, the three of us make and sell hundreds of Lucky Leprechauns. For every comment Killian or I make, Gemma fires back with something to top it. I don't remember laughing so much. Four staff members come over and relieve us of our duties.

I steer Gemma behind the bar. "What do you want to drink?" I point to the chalkboard with the green drinks.

"Ooh. I'll have a Green Whiskey Smash."

"Good choice." I create two then steer her to the back of the room. Nora keeps a large table reserved for our family and the Ivanovs. Sergey and Kora, Maksim and Aspen, and Declan are seated at the table. I pull a chair out for Gemma, and she sits.

"Is Hailee coming?" she asks.

"She texted they were on their way," Aspen says.

"Darragh insisted they have brunch together," Declan adds then takes a sip of his green beer.

I sit next to Gemma, and Killian slides onto the seat next to me. A server brings over a tray of appetizers. He sits down avocado pesto with a bread and cracker tray, tiny green goddess grilled cheese sandwiches, Irish potato bites sprinkled with chives, and spinach balls with a dill-lemon dip.

"Looks like we're just in time for more food," Hailee chirps and leans over Gemma's back to hug her.

Gemma's face lights up. "Hi! How was brunch with Liam's parents?"

"Good."

Liam kisses Gemma's cheek, slides out a chair for Hailee, and sits in the one next to hers. "What did I miss?"

"Gemma collected tips for your erectile dysfunction." Killian snatches a potato bite off the plate and stuffs it in his mouth.

The table erupts in laughter, and Kora asks, "Have some issues, Liam?"

"Actually, it was for Killian's," Gemma smirks.

"Still think you're confusing Liam with me," Killian replies.

Liam huffs. "Definitely not. I can assure you, I have no issues." He puts his arm around Hailee.

Declan pours a beer. "Hailee, you want this or something else?"

"That works."

Declan hands one to her and one to Liam. I make a plate that has everything on it and put it between Gemma and me.

Hailee turns to Gemma. "When did you get here?"

"Around noon. Nolan and I ran the 8K today."

"You did? That's great!"

"Finn coming?" I ask Liam.

Liam's face hardens. "No. He said he's not into the crowd. Can't say I blame him." Liam glances around the packed pub.

Molly brings a tray of Jell-O shots. The bottom layer is green, the middle is white, and the top is orange. "Darcey said to bring these to you."

"Thanks," everyone says.

She stands next to me and directs, "Try it and tell me if it's good. Darcey said she used the lime gelatin instead of the green apple. She wants your opinion."

Gemma stiffens next to me. I wish she'd stop feeling uncomfortable about Molly. I'm not sure what to do about it.

Everyone takes the shot. Declan proclaims, "Tell Darcey it's a keeper."

"Do you like it, too, Nolan?" Molly asks.

"Yep," I reply, wishing she'd leave. Lately, it feels like she's hanging on me, and I assume it's Gemma's accusations messing with my head. I'm usually not self-conscious about the attention Molly gives me. I'm sure I'm paranoid. Still, I wish she would go to the next table.

She looks at Aspen. "Your bracelet is beautiful."

Aspen smiles. "Thanks. Maksim got it for me in Vegas."

"Did you just go?"

Aspen's lips twitch. "No. It was where we met."

"Wow. You bought it for her right away? So was it love at first sight?"

Aspen and Maksim exchange an intimate look. Maksim speaks, and his Russian accent is thicker than normal. "I answer yes to that."

"But you didn't exactly feel it the first time you saw him?" Molly asks Aspen.

Killian clears his throat. "Molly, your table over there is waving at you."

"Oh! Sorry." She squeezes the top of my shoulder and leaves.

I hand Gemma a fork.

"Is it feeding time?" she mumbles in a bitchy tone, but it's enough for Hailee to hear.

"What does that mean?" Hailee glares at me.

"Nothing." Gemma drinks half her Green Whiskey Smash.

"Might want to slow down, princess," I snap, annoyed at her nasty comment after all the fun we've had today.

"And prince charming is back," she seethes.

"Are you not treating my sister right?" Hailee fires at me.

I scowl at her. "Stay out of our business."

"Watch your tone," Liam warns.

I lean closer to him. "Your woman needs to focus on something else."

"Jesus. Knock it the fuck off. It's St. Paddy's Day," Declan bellows.

I rise and fume, "I need some air. Watch the princess for me."

"You're such an asshole," Hailee mutters.

Gemma mutters, "Hailee—"

"Go ahead and tell your sister what an ass I am to you while I'm gone," I tell Gemma.

Guilt crosses her face.

I shake my head at her and leave. I go out into the alley and behind the outdoor bar. I pour a glass of whiskey and drink it while trying to calm my rage.

Everything was going well. Why she can't just let Molly be Molly and ignore her, I don't know.

Killian joins me, tops off my drink, and fills one for himself. "What's going on with you two?"

"Nothing." I let another mouthful of whiskey burn my throat on the way down. The last thing I want is to admit anything to Killian when I don't even know what Gemma and I are.

He grunts. "It's obvious you two are screwing."

"No, we aren't," I lie, not looking for his unsolicited opinion.

He takes a long sip and gives me his, *I don't believe a word you're saying*, look. "If you're going to mess around with a girl like that, you better set some ground rules."

"A girl like that? What the fuck does that mean?" I ask, my rage transferring from Gemma to him.

"You know what I mean."

I step closer to him. "No. I don't. Why don't you tell me?"

He shrugs, and arrogance fills his face. "Fun. Outgoing. Sexy as hell and knows it. Also, not someone who likes rules."

I scrub my face. "You just told me I needed to set rules, proving you don't even know what you're talking about."

"Sure, I do. You have to set them and hold her to them. If you don't, she's going to get attached."

"Jesus. You're a dick. You know that?"

I add more whiskey into my cup, feeling slightly buzzed from the quick alcohol intake.

"If you can't handle a girl like her, you shouldn't play around with her. All you're going to do—"

"I said no entry," Leo's Russian accent barks.

Killian and I glance over at him. He's standing up, and four men are surrounding him. Everything about their appearance screams they aren't here to have a good time. They have on matching black hoodies and wool hats. They don't seem fazed by Leo, who's one of the strongest, most intimidating men I've ever come across.

"Who's that?" I ask.

"No idea," Killian says as we both make our way toward Leo.

"This is a free country. Or don't you know this isn't Russia?" one thug with a deep Polish accent states.

Killian and I exchange a glance. Since Darragh set up Bruno Zielinski's sons for Boris's crimes and then arranged to have them killed in prison, retaliation isn't out of the question.

"You aren't welcome here. I suggest you leave," I growl. Killian and I step next to Leo.

"You discriminate against Poles?" one man snarls.

From the corner of my eye, I see the man who insulted Leo stick his hand in his pocket, and the hairs on my arms rise. I didn't bring my gun or knife, since we would be drinking, security is covering the pub, and our drivers have weapons.

Killian steps past Leo. "If you don't turn around and leave in three seconds, you're going to wish for months you did."

None of them flinch. One steps right up to Killian's face. "If you don't let us in—"

Killian throws a right hook at him, landing on his cheek. The other man whips a knife out of his pocket, and I go after him. Two guys lunge at Leo.

Customers scream. I get a left hook into the man's stomach. He gasps but still manages to flick his knife open. He slashes it toward me and cuts through my T-shirt. There's no time to think. I barely feel the pain and grab his neck with one hand then reach for his other arm. I push his neck up and yank his arm until it snaps.

He screams and drops the knife. I punch him in the face, break his nose, and he falls to the ground.

Leo smashes the other two guys' heads together, and they go down.

Killian is on the ground. He has blood on his lips, and he pounds his fists into the guy's face.

A police siren blares into the air and a cruiser pulls into the back alley. Two officers jump out of the vehicle with their guns pointed at us.

There are more screams from the patrons.

"Get on the ground. All of you," the police officer commands.

Killian punches the guy again.

"Now, or we'll shoot!" the officer yells.

I rip Killian off the man and bark, "Killian, get down!"

The seven of us lay on the cold asphalt. I gaze into my brother's crazed eyes.

"You're bleeding," he mutters and glances at my bicep.

"Shut up," the officer growls.

"What the fuck is going on?" Declan demands.

"Everyone stay back," the officer orders.

The next few minutes are a blur. The police handcuff us, read us our rights, and more police cars pull into the alley, along with two ambulances.

"Don't say a word," Declan advises as we get shoved into the police car.

"That goes for you as well," Maksim instructs Leo.

The door slams shut, and I glance out the window. Gemma is standing with her hand over her mouth and tears flowing down her cheeks. Hailee has her arm protectively around her. Liam is on the phone, his jaw clenched, and I'm assuming he's calling Darragh.

I tear my eyes away from them and look straight ahead. The three of us don't say a word, but it's like sardines stuffed in a can. We're all tall and built. When we get to the police station, I walk off the cramps settling in my legs.

We go through the booking process. Mugshots, fingerprints, and a full body search are all conducted. They confiscate our personal property. We get thrown into a cell.

It's crowded. Most of the men are drunk. Some of them have swollen faces or hands. Killian, Leo, and I go to the corner of the cell. Killian peels back my bloody sleeve. He studies it for a brief minute then says, "You're fine. That goon barely scratched you."

"Next time, don't let him hit your face," I reply, staring at his swollen, bloody lip.

He grunts.

Leo steps closer. He glances behind him then leans into us. "Were they Bruno's guys?"

"I don't know. I haven't seen them before. Have you?" I ask.

Leo's face hardens. "No. But his men have made themselves known outside the gym."

"Why would they surface around the Ivanovs?" I ask.

"They better not be coming after Nora or the baby," Killian fumes.

"Calm down." Leo glances behind him again. "Have you talked to Adrian or Obrecht about Dasha?"

Killian jerks his head back. "Adrian's ex-wife?"

"Yeah. She's back. And she got in bed with Kacper."

My gut drops. "Bruno's son?"

Leo nods.

"Jesus. That girl has always been nothing but trouble," Killian claims.

We spend several hours in the cell when a guard finally calls out, "Leo Ivanov. Killian O'Malley. Nolan O'Malley." He opens the cell and leads us down the hallway. When we step into the lobby, Darragh is waiting with his arms crossed. He says nothing, and we follow him to his SUV. We all get in the back seat.

"Were they Zielinskis?" Killian asks.

Darragh puts his tweed cap on his lap, takes his pipe out of his coat jacket, and lights it while deeply inhaling. He cracks the window, slowly releases it, then scowls. "You weren't sure if they were?"

My gut flips. "They had a knife, and who knows what else they were packing."

Darragh addresses each of us, "You broke the guy's arm, the two thugs you hurt have concussions, and the police said you were on the verge of killing the goon."

Leo crosses his arms and grunts. "Good. Next time, I'll do it harder so they don't wake up."

Darragh's eyes turn to slits. "Yeah? What if they weren't Zielinskis?"

"What are you saying, Uncle Darragh? You want us just to sit back next time and let a bunch of thugs enter Nora's pub? And maybe they're an enemy, but we should ID them to find out?" Killian barks.

Leo chuckles, and Darragh snaps, "This isn't funny, Leo."

Leo leans forward. His face turns dark. He licks his lips. "You're not my boss, Darragh. Don't lecture me about how to control thugs."

Darragh's face reddens with rage. "No, I'm not. But you were working for my niece, protecting the pub my mother built. Next time, restrain, but don't put men in the hospital. We have enough problems without creating more. As public as that was, now I owe the police chief. And I don't like owing anyone."

"No. I was working for the Ivanovs. Don't you forget it." The car stops, and Leo reaches for the door. "Thanks for the ride."

Darragh's anger continues to fester. Killian and I say nothing. Darragh is both right and wrong. There was nothing I would do differently if the situation happened again.

Darragh smokes the rest of the way to my place. When the car pulls into my driveway, he says, "You're Liam's advisors. I expect both of you to be smarter."

"Did you want us to be the ones who ended up in the ambulance?" Killian asks.

Darragh sighs. He takes another hit off his pipe, releases it, then says, "I was your age once. Both of you need to find more wisdom, and fast. You're trained fighters. You know how to defend without going overboard. Liam is going to need you. The O'Malleys need you. Remember that at all times."

I shake my head. I'm over Darragh's lecture. "Happy St. Paddy's Day, Uncle Darragh." I get out of the car, slam the door, then make my way past Liam's private black vehicle.

When I get inside, Gemma runs up to me. "Are you okay? You're bleeding."

I don't answer, brush past her, then pull Liam into my office. As soon as I close the door, I blurt out, "Your dad is pissed."

"About what?"

"How bad we beat up those Zielinskis."

Liam raises his eyebrows. "Why?"

"Says we shouldn't have been so rough on them."

Liam's face darkens. He stays quiet.

"Since your dad reminded me I'm your advisor, I thought I'd give you some advice."

Liam closes his eyes and crosses his arms. He sighs and meets my gaze.

"The O'Malleys don't let anyone, whether they're a crime family or not, threaten our family. If they don't listen to our warning, then they don't get our mercy. Your dad seems to have a different opinion. At some point, you're going to have to remind him of that. And let me be clear, as the leader of our clan, you better never hesitate," I warn.

Liam glances at the ceiling, sniffs hard, then nods and pats my back. "Clean up your arm. I'm glad you broke that fucker's bone." He leaves the room.

I stare out the window, watching him and Hailee leave, wondering how we're going to continue protecting the O'Malleys from all the different never-ending threats.

10

Gemma

LIAM AND HAILEE LEAVE. THE PIT IN MY STOMACH EXPANDS. I wait for Nolan to come out, but he doesn't. I finally go to his office and knock on the door.

He opens it and crosses his arms. A hardened look fills his face. He says, "I'm not in the mood, Gemma."

My insides quiver. I softly ask, "The mood for what?"

"To fight. To be accused of whatever you're going to accuse me of," he states.

"I'm not here for that."

The green flames in his eyes grow hotter. "Then what are you here for, Gemma?"

I take a deep breath. "To see if you're okay." I reach for his bloody bicep, but he shrugs away from me.

"I'm going to take a shower." He pushes past me and goes down the hall to his room.

I debate about what to do. I'm mad that I got bent out of shape over Molly, but that girl is pushing my every button. Nolan seems oblivious to it all. I can't stop wondering if anything has ever happened between them even though he claims it hasn't.

I sit on the couch, twisting my fingers. It grows dark outside. I rise to go into his bedroom and see if he's going to ignore me all night or come out, when he steps into the room.

He's wearing all black. He grabs his keys and says, "I have to go out. I might be gone for a few days. Tiernan and Fergal will escort you wherever you need to go."

My chest tightens. "What?"

His hardened expression never changes. "Don't go anywhere without them. One of them will stay in the house so you aren't alone."

"Nolan! Where are you going?" I demand.

His eyes lock on mine. "I have O'Malley business to deal with. Stay inside the rest of the night. Tiernan and Fergal can run with you in the morning if you want." He walks past me and opens the door.

"Nolan! Stop!"

He spins. "I'm late, Gemma. Stay inside." He shuts the door, and I stare at it for several moments.

The door opens, and Tiernan steps inside. "Hey, Gemma. You need anything?"

I clear my throat. "No."

He smiles then locks the door. He turns back to me. "Did you have a good St. Paddy's Day?"

"Yeah." I almost add, until Molly had to continue hanging on Nolan, but don't.

Tiernan runs his hand through his red hair. "Nolan said you haven't eaten. Do you want me to order something?"

Seriously? He says he's disappearing for possibly days and sends his cousin in to make sure I eat?

"I'm not hungry. It's been a long day. I think I'm going to bed," I state.

"Are you sure? It's only seven. I can have something delivered in case you get hungry later?" he suggests.

I shake my head. "No. I'm fine. Thank you." I leave the room and go into my bedroom. I shut the door then turn on my phone and text Nolan.

Me: *Did you leave because you're upset with me?*

Minutes pass, and I realize he's probably driving. I call him.

"Gemma, what's wrong?" he curtly answers.

I blurt out, "I'm sorry about what happened at the pub. If you left so you don't have to see me, I'll move back to my mom's."

"So you think I'm immature, too?" he questions.

My pulse beats so hard, I sit down. I soften my voice. "I didn't say that."

"I don't have time to talk about this, Gemma."

My voice shakes. I admit, "This is freaking me out."

He sighs and lowers his voice. "I don't have a choice right now. Please stay inside tonight. Eat some dinner. Tomorrow, if you want to go out, Tiernan and Fergal will take you."

I stare at the ceiling. "When will you be back?"

"I don't know. I have to go. Goodnight, Gemma." The line turns silent.

I stare at the phone, and a message pops up.

Nolan: *I instructed Tiernan to check on you every few hours. If you're sleeping and wake up, don't freak out.*

Me: *That isn't necessary.*

Nolan: *It's not open for debate.*

Me: *So he's going to watch me while I sleep, the way you do?*

Nolan: *No. I'd kill him if he did that.*

Even though I'm worried and upset, I smile, happy he's giving me some indication he's still into me.

Nolan: *I'm not going to have phone access anymore. Please do as I ask.*

Me: *Okay. Please be safe.*

Nolan: *I'll be fine.*

Me: *It would help if you told me what you're doing.*

He doesn't respond.

I pace my bedroom for hours, wondering what he's taking care of for the O'Malleys. My stomach growls, and I realize I haven't eaten since we ate sushi after our run. The plate filled with appetizers pops into my mind, and I decide it's best to follow Nolan's orders. I go out to the kitchen. Tiernan is watching TV. He sees me and rises.

I motion to the couch. "You can sit. I'm just going to make some dinner."

"I just had some of the fish stew I found in the fridge. Did you make it? It's delicious," he raves.

My stomach flips, and I take a few breaths. I reply, "No."

"You want me to heat a bowl for you?"

"Nope." I open the fridge and see the container Molly brought over. I'm tempted to pour it down the sink then light the plastic on fire. But I restrain myself.

I pull spinach, strawberries, and some leftover chicken out. I make a salad, add walnuts, then take half a lemon and squirt it over it.

Tiernan comes and sits on the barstool next to me. He glances at my salad. "That looks healthy."

"It's good."

He gives me a boyish grin. "Is Nolan a health freak?"

I laugh. "Why do you say that?"

He shrugs. "Everything in here is super clean. I've seen him eat at the pub, and he doesn't seem super picky. He makes his own food a lot, but I never really paid attention to why. Does he buy anything not organic?"

I bite on my smile. "Not a lot."

Tiernan leans closer. His face turns serious. "Are you jonesing for a piece of bread or something?"

I set my fork down. "He has bread."

"It's sprouted."

"Have you tried it?" I question.

He furrows his eyebrows. "No. But I'm Irish. It's blasphemy not to eat real bread, don't you think?"

Amused, I spin in my chair toward him. "Are you hungry?"

"I'm always hungry."

"How old are you?"

He wiggles his eyebrows. "How old do you think I am?"

"Mmm...twenty-five?" I guess.

"Nah. I'm almost thirty. I should probably grow a beard so I look older." He rubs his chin.

I peer at him closer. "Nolan said I could go out tomorrow with you and Fergal."

He nods. His face turns serious. "That's right."

"How old is Fergal?"

"Twenty-eight."

I tap the counter. "No offense, but have either of you been bodyguards before?"

"Sure."

"Have you killed anyone?"

He shifts in his seat. He clenches his jaw.

I quickly add, "Sorry, you're just young."

"How old are you?" he asks.

"Thirty-six."

He snorts. "You aren't that much older than me."

My pulse increases. "But if someone came after me—"

"I would shoot them and not think twice. So would Fergal," he assures.

I release a nervous breath. "Okay. Sorry to interrogate you."

He smiles, and I once again think about how young he looks. "It's all right. I understand your concern. But you don't need to worry."

"Great. Do you want something to eat?" I ask.

He glances at my salad. "I'm not really a rabbit food kind of guy."

I laugh. "I can make you a sandwich."

"On sprouted bread?"

"Yep."

"No, thanks. I already ordered a cheeseburger and fries. It should be here any minute."

"I thought you ate fish stew?"

He nods. "Yep. But you can only eat so much of that without proper bread. Plus, it was a few hours ago."

"Alrighty then." I return to eating my salad, and the doorbell rings. Tiernan answers it. He comes back to the kitchen with a bag of food. He holds a burger out to me. "I got two. You want one?"

The smell goes right to my stomach. I reach for it. "Sure."

We eat then I say goodnight and start walking toward my bedroom but spin around before I get there. "I know Nolan said you have to check on me, but I'm fine. It won't be necessary."

He crosses his arms. "Sorry, but I'm under strict instructions."

Shame floods me. "What was the reasoning Nolan gave you to check on me?"

He shakes his head. "No reason. He never gives a lot of reasons for anything. Nolan says jump, and I ask how high. It's easier than asking questions."

Relief replaces my shame. I'm grateful Nolan didn't tell Tiernan about what I almost did. "Okay. Goodnight." I go into the bedroom, shut my door, and put on one of Nolan's T-shirts. I pick up my phone to see what time it is, and a text message pops up.

Nolan: *Sleep in my bed.*

I freeze and stare at the message for several minutes.

Me: *Why?*

Nolan: *Because it's where you belong.*

My flutters go crazy, and I debate about what to send back.

Me: *Are you going to surprise me in the middle of the night?*

Nolan: *No, princess. Get some rest. I won't be texting you again.*

My heart sinks, and worry starts all over. I stare at the wall then finally take my phone and go into Nolan's room. His bedsheets smell like him. I sink into the pillow, deeply inhaling his scent and eventually drifting off to sleep.

I don't wake up until the sun has risen. It's peeking through the blinds I forgot to shut. I look over where Nolan would be, but he's not here. My phone doesn't have any new messages. I send him a text.

Me: *Are you coming home soon?*

My message never shows it's delivered, which makes me think his phone is off. Anxiety creeps into my chest, so I do some deep-breathing exercises.

He said he'd be fine.

Where is he?

I get out of bed and go into the bathroom, do my business, then look at his personal items on the counter. I pick up a bottle of cologne and spray it on my wrist then inhale it.

So that's why he smells like sandalwood and coffee even though he doesn't drink it.

My insides quiver hard. I spray another pump on my neck, close my eyes, and keep breathing.

He'll be home today.

He said it could be a few days.

Is that two? Three? What does that mean?

I stare at myself in the mirror, telling myself to pull it together. The last thing I need is to go into a panic attack just because Nolan isn't here.

But what if something happens to him?

What if it already did?

This isn't helping.

I need to stay busy today.

I throw a sweatshirt of Nolan's over his T-shirt then go down to my room. I put on a pair of yoga pants, go into the kitchen, and make a smoothie and espresso. Tiernan is asleep on the couch. He's snoring and didn't even wake up when I blended my smoothie. His hand is in his pants, grabbing his junk.

So much for watching over me.

I take my smoothie and espresso. I go into the office and put everything on the table then open my laptop. For the next five hours, I become engrossed in my new job. Everything they need for their branding, I create. The owner and I email back and forth, and he says he loves it all, then gives his final approval on everything.

The rush I used to get at work surges, and I happily glance over at Nolan's desk, but reality hits. He's not here. The nervousness about where he's at and if he's safe builds again.

Tiernan knocks on the door. "Are you doing okay?"

"Yeah."

He steps inside and reveals a plate he hid behind his back. "I have something for you."

"What is it?" I ask, and my stomach growls.

"Darcey sent leftovers from the pub." He sets down a plate full of St. Paddy's Day appetizers.

I meet his gaze. "Thank you. I didn't eat yesterday before the fight broke out."

He plops in the chair across from me, grabs a piece of bread, and slathers it with the avocado pesto spread. "This stuff is amazing." He shoves it in his mouth.

I put some on a cracker and pop it in my mouth. The herbs mix with the smooth avocado texture flawlessly. "Mmm."

He points to the spinach ball and says, "You can have all those."

"Not a fan?"

"Spinach is for rabbits."

I raise my eyebrows. "For someone as fit as you appear to be, you sure don't seem to eat like it."

He pats his stomach. "My mama raised me on meat and potatoes. I'm a real man."

"And right now, you're in your twenties with a fast metabolism," I warn.

He snorts.

There's a loud clap of thunder. I jump then turn to look out the window. Rain pours down so thick, I can hardly see out. I mutter, "Crap. Now I can't go for a run."

"Not outside. We can take you to the gym if you want." He grabs another piece of bread.

My chest tightens. I haven't been to the gym in months, since Orla's thug threatened me.

"You have a gym membership, right?" he asks.

"Yeah."

"Okay. So Fergal and I will check things out, give you the go-ahead, then you can get your workout in," he says, as if it's no big deal, then shoves more bread in his mouth.

"You sure it's okay?" I nervously ask. I shouldn't think twice about this. There were thousands of runners in the race I ran with Nolan the previous day. Then, I was in a packed bar. But something feels a bit off.

"If it isn't safe, we won't let you go inside. And we'll be there the entire time," he confidently states.

I consider what to do and decide I probably am anxious over not knowing where Nolan is and when he'll return. Working out will help ease my worries and take my mind off things. "Okay. Let me eat and then I'll change."

We finish everything on the plate, I put my workout clothes on, and we leave. When we get to the gym, Tiernan and Fergal go inside. I stay in the car with the driver and another bodyguard I haven't met before. After ten minutes, Tiernan and Fergal come outside.

"It's all clear," Tiernan informs us.

I ignore the flutters in my belly and step out of the car. I go into the gym, put my bag in the locker room, then find an empty treadmill. Everyone around me is engrossed in their workout, and I put my earbuds in.

For forty-five minutes, I run. I get lost in the music and adrenaline then spend another hour lifting weights and stretching. As much as I love to run outside with Nolan, it feels nice to return to the gym I've been a member of for years.

When I finish, I glance at Tiernan and Fergal stationed near the door. I run over to them. "I'm going to go into the sauna for ten minutes then shower quickly. If I'm not out in twenty minutes, storm the locker room," I tease.

Tiernan gazes behind me then wiggles his eyebrows. "I'll volunteer for that. Especially if you can get her to go in there."

I glance behind me at the woman doing squat presses then back at him. "Yeah. I'll work on that for you." I grin and stroll into the locker room.

I strip out of my sweaty clothes, put a towel around me, then go into the dry sauna. No one else is in it. I set the timer on the wall for ten minutes and lie down on the wood, deeply inhaling the dry, warm air. It's so comfortable, I close my eyes and almost fall asleep.

When the timer dings, I get up and rinse off in the shower. I wrap a fresh towel around my body then make my way to my locker. No one is in sight, which I find odd but don't dwell on.

As soon as I turn the corner, a hand covers my mouth, and I get yanked into a woman's body. My pulse darts to the sky. I attempt to scream, but a knife goes to my throat.

"Shut up." Orla's cold voice sends chills down my spine. "You think you can hide from me?"

My mind is a whirlwind of how not to get my throat sliced, stop the growing tremors taking over my body, and not allow my tears to escape.

She presses the flat part of the blade against my throat. "I'm going to destroy all of you. Your sisters won't know what hit them. And that mother of yours, the one who killed my mother, she's going to watch you all suffer before I take her out."

My heart almost stops. I'm unsure what she's talking about. My mother isn't a killer.

She laughs. "Oh, you didn't know, did you? Is it not something your mother talks about?" She grips my mouth so tight, it may bruise.

A tear slips down my cheek and over her hand. Chest pains stab me. There's no way my mother could be a murderer. Did Orla decide to come after me from this notion she has in her head?

"I'm through with your—"

"Let her go, or I shoot!" Tiernan growls, pointing his gun at our heads. Fergal rounds the corner, steps next to him, and positions his weapon in the same manner.

My insides shake harder.

Orla tightens her grip on my body and doesn't release me. She laughs. "You don't have the balls."

"I said, let her go!" Tiernan demands.

"Don't test us," Fergal barks.

Orla moves her head behind mine and backs us away. She sneers, "How good is your aim? Will your bullet hit her or me? Or will I slice her neck before you dare to pull the trigger?"

I stare at both Tiernan and Fergal, but they keep their attention on Orla.

"Neither of us miss. You have three seconds to release her," Tiernan threatens.

Fergal counts, "One. Two."

Orla kicks my heel, so my leg moves outward, quickly lowers the knife, and slices through the towel. The blade tears the inner skin on my thigh, and I scream as her hand leaves my body. She pushes me forward and lunges behind the locker.

Fergal takes off after her, and Tiernan rushes toward me. Fergal yells, "Door's secured."

"Gemma, let me see your leg!" Tiernan reaches for me, but I step back.

"No."

"You're bleeding all over the place."

I glance down at the bloodstain expanding on the towel and the tiny pool forming on the floor.

"We need to get you to a hospital," Fergal states.

I shake my head. "I'm going in the shower." My hands shake as I unlock my locker. I take out the pouch of ace bandages I keep in it for the days my knee is bothering me.

Tiernan argues, "Gemma—"

"Give me some privacy!" I yell, on the verge of losing it from the pain and humiliation of Orla getting to me again. And I still don't know why she said my mother killed hers.

"You need medical attention," Fergal claims.

I spin on him, angry I assumed I could be normal and come to the gym. My past experience with Orla proves she will always get to me. And my gut told me Fergal and Tiernan wouldn't protect me. "Why don't you do me a favor and make sure no one else gets to me while I clean up." I grab my clothes, ignore their guilty expressions, and return to the shower.

Once the water is on, I peel the towel away and stare at the bloody gash. It's horizontal, from the inside of my thigh to the front, a few inches below my female parts.

Jesus. She could have cut me there.

I resist the urge to break down. I take a handful of the antibacterial soap and wash it off. The sting is deeper than the cut. It's already starting to clot. I cringe but get through it. I dry it off. It's still bleeding, but I don't want to go to the hospital and become a sitting duck for Orla to attempt to kill me again. I press a clean, dry washcloth on it, wrap the ace bandage as tight as possible around my wound, then slip into my yoga pants. I throw my bra and sweatshirt over my head then slide into the sandals I keep at the gym for showering.

"Let's go," I instruct Tiernan and Fergal.

"You need a doctor," Tiernan insists.

Tears fill my eyes. My lips shake. "Can you please get me out of here? I need to go home."

He sighs, nods, then protectively puts his arm around my shoulder.

Fergal goes first, gives the all clear, and Tiernan maneuvers me through the gym and into the car. They sit in the back with me. I ignore their concerned faces and stare out the window, telling myself to keep it together.

The car pulls into the garage, and I jump out. I go directly to Nolan's bedroom and into his bathroom. Blood spots darken my black pants. I open the cabinet, trying to find a first aid kit. Nothing appears, and the pain in my thigh gets worse. Yet, it's nothing compared to the shame and fear I feel.

The tears start to fall. I stop and put one hand on the counter to steady myself and the other over my face.

"Gemma!" Nolan's voice rings through my sobs. I attempt to shut down all the emotions assaulting me. He comes flying into the bathroom and wraps his arms around me.

It only makes me sob harder.

He holds my head to his chest and says into my hair, "Shh. Let me see your leg."

I can't seem to pull it together. For months, Orla warned me she won't hesitate to kill me. She could have today. The reality of what could have happened mixes with my relief Nolan is here. I glance up and cry out, "I'm sorry."

He tugs me into his chest again. "Shh. Don't apologize for her." He kisses my head. "I need you to calm down, princess, so I can see your wound."

I force myself to take deep breaths. I finally tilt my head and meet Nolan's worried gaze. "She got to me."

His expression turns to stone. He vows, "And we're going to hunt her down for doing so."

11

Nolan

An hour earlier

ALL NIGHT, MY BROTHERS AND I TAKE CARE OF THE POLISH thugs who attempted to enter Nora's pub. Declan called Killian and me. While we were in the slammer, he got with my cousins, who know how to keep their mouths shut. They rounded up the goons when they got out of the hospital. Since Darragh got involved, their side and ours both had all charges dropped.

Declan thought it was best if Darragh didn't know what he was doing, since he was so vocal about his distaste over the fight. He claimed it was better to ask for forgiveness later and talked to Maksim. Since Adrian's ex-wife Dasha put the Ivanovs on the Zielinski's radar, Maksim was more than happy to give us access to use their garage. Adrian and

Maksim showed up, eager to jump in and help torture the thugs to see what information we can get out of them.

My phone is off, but something is bugging me to turn it on. It's not something I ever do in the middle of an event like this, but I've never had Gemma to worry about before. No matter how many times I slice through one of these men's skin, or do some other vile deed, I can't shake her out of my mind. I toss my gloves on the plastic and step into the front room. All our phones and personal items are on the desk. I pick mine up, turn it on, and my gut drops.

Tiernan: *There's been an incident with Orla. Gemma's leg got sliced. She's refusing to go to the hospital. We're a few minutes from the house.*

Blood slams against my skull. I dial Tiernan, but he doesn't pick up.

Tiernan: *We're in the car. I don't want to upset her more.*

Me: *Answer the goddamn phone.*

Tiernan: *I'll call you in a few minutes in private.*

Me: *Now.*

Tiernan: *Just chill for a few minutes.*

Pissed by his lack of following my orders, I call his phone. He has the audacity to send me to voicemail. When it beeps, I shout, "I'm going to fucking kill you for so many different reasons!" I hang up and grab my keys.

"What's going on?" Declan says, stepping into the room.

"Tiernan isn't picking up. Orla sliced Gemma's leg," I inform him and swallow down the bile rising in my throat. The visual of Gemma's perfect leg bloody and Orla anywhere near her creates a mixture of rage and nausea that floods me.

Declan's eyes widen. "Is she okay?"

"I don't know. Did you hear me say that little punk isn't picking up the phone? I told Liam and Darragh they were too inexperienced, and he assured me they could handle it. The one time I step away, that bitch gets to Gemma." I move toward the door, and Declan positions himself between it and me.

"Move," I growl.

He crosses his arms. "You know the rules. Shower first."

"Did you hear what I said?"

He points to the bathroom. "Go. Now. You can't leave here with blood on you."

I pull my hair. He's right. I strip and throw my clothes in the burn barrel, go into the shower, and scrub every inch of my body. Declan comes in with fresh clothes when I get out. I quickly put them on, grab my wallet and keys, and trot out to my car. It's the middle of the afternoon but raining. I drive as fast as I can without getting into an accident and run into the house. As soon as I step inside, I shout, "Gemma!"

Tiernan and Fergal jump off the couch. Tiernan says, "She's in your room."

I point at both of them. "I don't have time to deal with you two right now. Get out of my sight before I slice your throats." I shove past them and run into the bedroom.

Gemma's hand shakes over her face. Her tears fall next to her other hand, which is gripping the counter so tight, her knuckles are white.

I pull her into my arms, feeling like my heart's going to explode in my chest. She sobs harder, and I spend several minutes trying to calm her down. I kiss her head and tell her, "I need you to calm down, princess, so I can see your wound."

Several minutes pass, and she finally looks at me. Her blue eyes meet mine and a part of me dies. There's so much humiliation and fear in them. My guys, my own cousins, didn't keep her safe. I don't know how I'll ever trust anyone with her again or forgive myself for not fighting Liam and Darragh about my gut feeling.

Gemma chokes out, "She got to me."

More rage annihilates me until it's oozing out of every cell in my body. I'm unsure what to do with it. If Gemma weren't in my arms right now, I'd run out of this house to personally go after Orla. I still should, but I'm a weak man around her. Not one part of me will move to part from Gemma right now. All I can do is tell her the truth of what's in store for Orla. If it's the last thing the O'Malleys do, I'll make sure of it. I vow, "And we're going to hunt her down for doing so."

She sniffles and takes a shaky breath.

I slide my hands over her cheeks, kiss her forehead, then give her a chaste one on the lips. "Let me see your leg."

She slowly removes her pants, and I try to remain calm. Blood covers the ace bandage. When it comes off, there's a bloody washcloth stuck to her skin.

I slide my hands under her armpits and prop her up on the

counter. There's no way to remove the washcloth without hurting her. When I pull it off, it reopens the scab that started to form. She winces, and I say, "I should take you to the hospital."

Gemma grabs my arm. "No! It looks worse than it is. Please! I don't want to go where she might be able to get to me."

I slowly inhale and stare at the mirror.

Her voice shakes. "I'm sorry. Please don't be mad at me."

I fist her hair and dip my face in front of hers. "Why would I ever be mad at you about this?"

So much pain swirls in her blue eyes, chipping further at my heart. She scrunches her face. "I should have known better than to go to the gym."

"That isn't your fault. It's Tiernan's and Fergal's. And they're going to receive the consequences for putting you in danger," I promise her.

Her eyes widen. "What? No! Don't hurt them!"

A low growl comes out of my chest. I swallow the growing lump of anger in my throat. "I'm not going to hurt them. But they aren't keeping their jobs. Darragh can move them somewhere else. They aren't ready for this responsibility."

"But—"

"We aren't discussing it any further." I'm not going to fight with her all night over those idiots not protecting her. And Liam is going to get a visit from me. I release her hair, open the drawer, then pull out the first aid kit.

She utters, "Oh. The drawer."

I open the box and glance at her in question.

"I looked in the cabinet," she admits.

"Maybe I should give you a tour so you know where everything is." It comes out before I can analyze it. My nerves flip in my stomach. I've never wanted any woman to have access to all the things in my life. I ignore the uncomfortable feeling in my gut, take out antiseptic cleaner and skin glue, then open the bottle of cleanser.

She sniffles. "How's your arm?"

"Better than your leg."

"Kind of insane we both got sliced by a knife," she adds.

"Yeah." I steal a quick kiss then move her leg over the sink. "This might sting. Grip my good arm if you want."

She clutches my forearm, and I pour the solution over her wound. Her nails dig into my skin, and she tries to be brave but grimaces.

"Sorry, princess." I look closer at the gash, which only angers me further. She's lucky Orla didn't slash her privates. "It isn't super deep. But I'd feel better if you let a medical professional look at it."

"No. I'm fine. The glue should work. Please," she begs.

I sigh, unwrap some sterile gauze, and dab the wound until it's dry. Blood is still seeping out of it, but it's not horrible. "I'm going to attempt to glue this, but if this doesn't stick or has any sign of infection, we're going to the hospital. Understand?"

She nods. "Okay."

I press the gauze on the wound and put my lips in front of hers. "While this is drying, give me a kiss and show me how much you missed me."

Her face falls. "I did. I was worried about you."

Hearing her admit this stirs the same unfamiliar feeling. "Did you sleep in my bed?"

"Yes."

I can't help but smile and ask, "Where's my kiss?"

She locks her fingers in my hair. In a quiet voice, she asks, "Did you miss me?" Her eyes fill with a vulnerability I haven't seen in her before.

My heart skips a beat. I start to analyze what to say then stop. I don't know what's happening between Gemma and me, but she's becoming an obsession I can't shake. I decide to once again tell her the truth. "You're all I thought about when I shouldn't have been thinking anything about you."

The corners of her mouth curve. She pulls me closer and presses her lips on mine. Our tongues connect instantly, and I momentarily forget about her leg. Kissing Gemma is like turning on the heater when the sun has been beating down in your car on a boiling summer day. It grows hotter and hotter until every ounce of my blood is pumping violently in my veins. I mumble in her mouth, "I need to glue your thigh."

"Mmhmm." She moves closer to me and massages my head.

I find the strength to pull away. "Let me do this before the gauze sticks to it." I remove the white cloth, press her skin together, then apply the glue. I dip down and blow on her skin to help dry it.

"Guess I should say a Hail Mary she didn't cut my important parts," Gemma jokes.

I take my finger and glide it over her panties. "Hail Mary."

She squirms on the counter.

I place my hand on her good knee and move it as far as it'll go. I kiss the skin above her wound, and she strokes the side of my head. I mumble, "Did you eat while I was gone?" I slide my hand down her unharmed inner thigh and slip it under her panties and through her slit. I blow on the glue some more.

"Yeah," she breathes.

I slowly circle my thumb on her clit. "All your meals?"

"Mmhmm."

I blow one last time and touch the skin adhesive to see if it's dry. It is, so I drop to my knees. I circle my arm around her ass and tug her to the edge of the counter. I glance up. "Good girl."

She gasps and swallows hard.

"You know what I kept thinking about?" I position her legs over my shoulders and deeply inhale her scent.

"What?" she whispers.

I move her panties to the side. She shudders as I slip two fingers in her then return to rolling her clit with my thumb, staring at her throbbing pink paradise. "I didn't get my meal at the pub."

She inhales deeply. "I'm sorry. I—"

"Yeah. Me, too. Did you wonder how I was going to make good on my bet with all those people there?" I curl my fingers inside her and circle my thumb faster.

She whimpers and slightly rocks on my hand.

"Has a guy ever done that to you in a pub before?" I lash my tongue on her clit a few times then return to rubbing it.

"No." She pants and grips my head tighter.

"No sex in any bars?" I flick my tongue against her more intensely.

"No. Oh God!"

I pull away, reposition my thumb on her, and inch my fingers in and out of her wet heat. She moans, and I lock eyes with hers. "That's the problem with bad boys, princess. It's the difference between them and me. They're boys. I'm a man. And no matter where we are, I'll find a way to eat this sweet pussy, or fuck you in public, or get you off when you least expect it. So, you should remember good girls get rewarded. Bad girls get nothing."

"I'm sorry," she repeats and closes her eyes. Her cheeks flush, and my dick throbs. She's frustratingly beautiful, a pain in my ass at times, and wrecking me in too many ways to count.

"Should I remind you what good girls get?" I kiss her pussy and pull my fingers out of her.

Her eyes open, heavy with need and greed. She nods, and I grunt.

My pulse quickens. I smirk. "I didn't hear an answer." I pinch her clit.

"Oh God! Please!"

Satisfied, I shove my hand up her body and put my two fingers that were inside her into her mouth. She sucks on them as I devour her like I'm on death row and she's my last meal. I rotate between licking, sucking, and biting her with precision.

She cries out like a caged animal. Her thighs sweat against my cheeks. She digs her claws deeper into my head while grinding her trembling body into my face.

"Holy...holy...oh Jesus!" she screams as her body erupts into violent tremors.

I tug her closer to me, latch on to her harder, and continue feasting on what I'm claiming as mine. Whatever beefs she has with me, she's going to have to get over. We've crossed this line and I'm not sure how to step backward.

Her raspy voice cries out, "Nolan!"

I drop my pants, shimmy up her, and fist her hair. Our lips connect the moment our hot breath merges. My aching erection slides into her, and I groan. Her body around mine is sheer perfection. Every thrust I make, she matches. Each slide of her tongue keeps the buzz in my veins electric. The way she wraps her limbs around me makes me feel like I'm the only one she could ever want.

"Isn't the good girl option better?" I murmur in her ear then lick the back of it.

"Yes," she breathes. Her walls spasm around my cock so intensely, my balls tighten.

"Christ, Gemma."

"I...oh...oh..." she moans, and it ricochets off the bathroom tile like a song I want to hit the replay button on to drown out the rest of the world.

Her body convulses harder, taking me over the edge. I pump my seed hard into her, mumbling her name into her neck.

She clings to me, and neither of us moves. I finally lift my head and pull out then realize what I did. My stomach drops. "Shit, Gemma. I'm sorry. I wasn't thinking."

She glances down. The color drains from her cheeks. She quickly looks away. Her chest rises and falls faster again.

How could I not have put on a condom?

I stare in the mirror for a minute, cursing myself.

Don't be a coward and freak her out more.

I pull her chin toward me. "This is my fault. I'm sorry."

She doesn't say anything, just swallows hard.

"I'm clean. I just had my physical right before I met you."

She nods and nervously licks her lips then blinks hard.

"Are you on anything?"

Her eyes fill with tears, and she shakes her head.

My stomach flips. "Okay. Let's not get ahead of ourselves."

Her lips tremble. She blurts out, "I missed my gyno appointment. I was too scared to go out, and I didn't get my birth control refilled. I haven't been on it for months."

My heart races. I attempt to stay calm and keep my eyes locked on hers. "Tomorrow, we'll make you a doctor's appointment."

"But what if—"

"Then we'll deal with it. Just don't get worked up about something that isn't a reality yet."

She sniffles. "All right. I don't have anything. Just so you know," she adds quickly.

I stroke her cheek. "Thanks for telling me." I kiss her then say, "I have to sort out your security. We should get dressed and go."

She takes a deep breath. Guilt fills her expression. "All right. I-I'm sorry I didn't go to my appointment."

I stroke my thumbs under her eyes. "Stop with the sorries. Now go get ready."

12

Gemma

LIAM ISN'T ANSWERING HIS PHONE AND NOLAN SAYS WE'LL GO to Darragh and Ruth's house if Liam isn't home when we drive by. I clean myself up the best I can. The entire time, I keep thinking about how our little mistake could end up with significant consequences. I've always had safe sex and taken the pill. Nolan said it was his fault, but I can't only blame him. I curse myself over and over for letting Orla scare me so much, I made bad decisions. I've always wanted children but with the right guy. I barely know Nolan. The last thing I need is to bring a baby into this screwed-up situation I'm in due to my bloodline.

I'm adding my last layer of mascara when Nolan comes into my bathroom. He stands behind me, leans over, and I look up. "You almost ready, gorgeous?"

My flutters erupt. "Yep."

He gives me a peck on the lips then steps back. We leave the house and get in his vehicle. Once he backs out of the driveway, he puts it in drive, then clasps his hand in mine. In a low voice, he asks, "How's your leg feel?"

"It's throbbing a bit, but I can deal."

Guilt fills his expression. He glances quickly at me. "I'm sorry those idiots didn't do their job."

I sigh. "Nolan, I don't want to get them in trouble."

He refocuses on the road and clenches his jaw. "They had one job. It was to protect you. They didn't. They aren't a server at a restaurant and gave you the wrong dinner by accident. This is your life."

"Well, they did come in before she sliced my neck," I offer, trying not to wince at the thought.

"There aren't any excuses," he firmly states. "Liam's house is dark. Let's go to Darragh's." He veers into the left lane. "What did Orla say before they came in?"

My chest tightens. A pain shoots through my heart. Everything about what Orla said doesn't make sense. How could my mom kill anyone? She doesn't have it in her.

Or does she?

"Are you going to tell me?" Nolan gently asks.

"Oh, sorry. Umm..." I twist my fingers in my lap. Nolan already doesn't have a good impression of my mom. He didn't say it, but I could see it on his face. If he wasn't an O'Malley and my mother didn't have her preconceived notions, I'm sure they'd like each other. And what if Orla is right? Surely, I shouldn't tell anyone my mother killed someone?

"Gemma?"

Once again, Orla makes me into a liar. I blurt out, "She said she was going to kill me since I turned off my location services on my phone." Guilt eats me. I hate that I've become so used to fibbing, I can do it on a whim without thinking. Nolan's warning the first night we met flies into my mind, and I cringe inside.

"She hasn't reached out since I changed your phone number, has she?" Nolan asks.

"No."

"But she didn't say anything about that?"

"No."

Nolan pinches his eyebrows together. "So she hasn't tried to contact you in a few weeks after harassing you daily?"

My face grows hotter from continuing not to tell the truth. "She didn't say. Can we not talk about it anymore? I want to forget about it."

Nolan studies me briefly before turning in to a driveway. He parks and turns to me. "Was there anything else she said?"

I dig myself deeper. "No. The guys came in."

"At least they did one good thing," he grumbles then opens his door. I get out and meet him at the front of the car. He puts his hand on the small of my back and guides me to the front door.

He rings the bell and tugs me closer. "I'll need to talk to Darragh in private."

"I understand."

He kisses the top of my head.

Ruth opens the door. Her eyes are red, and she looks like she's been crying.

"Auntie Ruth. Are you okay?" Nolan questions.

She sniffles and nods. "Come in. Sorry, Darragh didn't tell me you were coming over."

"Sorry to pop in. Is he here?" Nolan steps forward and kisses her on the cheek.

Darragh's loud hack fills the air. Ruth closes her eyes, and Darragh steps into the room. His face is beet red and his eyes bloodshot. His handkerchief has blood spots on it. He catches his breath. "Nolan, what are you doing here?"

"We need to talk."

Ruth takes my hand. "Why don't I make us some tea, Gemma?"

"Okay."

"Ruthie, are you okay now?" Darragh asks.

She lifts her chin and smiles at him. "Yeah."

He pats her on the back. "I'm going to talk to Liam about this."

"No. You don't have to."

"What happened?" Nolan asks.

Ruth attempts to dismiss it. "Nothing—"

"Liam and Hailee kicked Ruth out of the house," Darragh angrily states.

"What? That's not like my sister," I claim.

Ruth firmly states, "Hailee didn't do anything." She turns to Darragh. "I told you, it was all Liam."

"Details," he mutters.

"Important ones," she insists.

He kisses me on the cheek then gives Ruth one. "Nolan and I will be in my office."

Ruth motions for me to follow her. We go into the kitchen, and she pulls out a chair. "Please, sit."

I obey. Garlic, onion, and other aromas fill the air. My stomach growls.

"Do you want tea or something else?"

"Tea would be nice," I reply.

She sets a wooden box in front of me then adds water to the kettle. It's green and gold, with Celtic hearts on it.

"That's beautiful," I say.

She sets it on the stove then sits across from me. "Thanks. Darragh gave it to me on our first anniversary. He had it shipped over here from Ireland."

"Wow. It looks new."

She smiles. "I try to take good care of it."

Hunger gnaws at my stomach. "What are you making? It smells great."

She glances at the slow cooker. "Corned beef and cabbage. It should be ready soon. It's Darragh's favorite. We had brunch for St. Paddy's Day with Liam and Hailee. Nora always has a platter of food sent over from the pub, so I don't ever make it until a few days after."

"Yum. I love corned beef and cabbage. My mom used to make it all the time when we were little. It smells delicious." My stomach growls.

She laughs. Her face lights up, and she reminds me of Liam. "Do you and Nolan have plans tonight? We'd love to have you stay."

The tea kettle whistles and the steam flies out of it.

Ruth gets up and removes it from the stove.

"I don't know what Nolan has planned. I'm free," I state.

She hands me a mug of hot water. "It would be nice if you can join us. I don't get to spend a lot of time with any of my nephews. They are all so busy."

I open the tea box and sort through it. "Wow! You have a good selection!"

She beams. "Thanks. Darragh only drinks Irish Breakfast Tea, but I like to switch it up."

"Me, too." I pick up an exotic fruit blend and smell it. "This is yummy." I stick it in my cup.

She opens the slow cooker and fills a small bowl. She sets it in front of me with silverware. "Why don't you test it out for me?"

I put my arm in the air for a victory pose. "Thank you. I'm starving."

"Oh! Hold on!" She opens the bread bin and pulls out a crusty loaf. She tears a piece off and sets it on the plate. "Do you want butter?"

"No, thanks. This smells so good." I pick up my fork and separate the meat. Then I dip the bread in the bowl, add the beef and other ingredients to it. I take a bite of my concoction then moan.

Her eyes twinkle. "Is it done?"

"Mmhmm." I finish chewing and swallow. "This is delicious. Honestly, the best I've ever tasted."

"Really?"

"Yes." I stick more bread in the bowl and add a layer of pure Irish deliciousness to it.

"I'll teach you how to make it if you want. It's really easy," she offers.

"Really? I'd appreciate that." I shove another bite in my mouth.

Nolan and Darragh enter the room.

"Ooh! You made corned beef and cabbage?" Nolan licks his lips.

"It's soooo good! Try this." I offer a piece to him.

He leans down and bites it then groans.

"Can you stay for dinner, Nolan?" Ruth asks.

He looks at me for permission, and I nod. He quickly takes the seat next to me, and a boyish grin I've never seen fills his face. "Feed me, Auntie Ruth."

Joy explodes across her face. Her green eyes glow. "Great. Sit down, Darragh." She motions to the seat next to Nolan and turns to the counter.

Darragh sits, and she serves us dinner. We spend several more hours at their house, talking and laughing. It's been so long since I did anything family oriented, and it feels nice. When we leave, I give Ruth a big hug. "Thanks again."

She embraces me back. "You're welcome any time. Let me know when you want to learn how to make my recipe."

"I will. Thank you," I gratefully reply.

We leave and get in the car. I turn to Nolan. "That was fun."

His mouth turns up in a nostalgic smile. "Yeah. I don't get to do that very often. When my mom died, Auntie Ruth and my nana did everything they could to help us. She used to have my brothers and sisters over several times a week for dinner."

My heart almost stops. I knew about Nolan's father's death but not his mother's. "Your mom passed?"

His face falls. He mumbles, "Yeah. A year after my father got murdered, my mother drowned in a lake. It was on the Fourth of July."

A chill runs down my spine. I reach for his hand. "I'm so sorry for your loss."

He clears his throat. "It happened a long time ago."

I squeeze his hand and keep it secure in mine. "You said, sisters. Do you have another one besides Nora?"

He takes a deep breath. "Erin and Nessa. They're twins and older than all of us. The four of us don't talk to them a lot."

"Why?"

He glances at me. "They're nasty, greedy, and jealous. My nana gave the pub to Nora when she died. Erin and Nessa thought they should have gotten it even though they barely stepped foot in it the past decade besides to party. Nora worked her butt off. She's spent her entire life in the pub. No one deserves any part of ownership, except Nora."

I hesitate to dig deeper but decide if he doesn't want to tell me, he'll say something. "Is the pub the only thing that drove a wedge between all of you?"

He sarcastically laughs. "Nope. They've always been like that. When my mother died, they took all her jewelry and cleaned out the safe. They claimed nothing was in it, but we all know my father kept a large sum of cash in it. My mother never touched it. Killian was at the house the week before she died. He sold some of my dad's tools, and she put the money in the safe. He saw it was still full."

"Wow. That's..."

"As I said, nasty, greedy, and jealous." He pulls into the garage and shuts the car off. We get out and go inside.

"Hey, what did Darragh say? Are Tiernan and Fergal in big trouble?" I ask, feeling bad if they are.

His eyes turn to slits. "Don't worry about them. And Darragh is sending for two of our top guys. They're out of state right now. It'll take a bit for them to wrap up what they are doing and get here."

My pulse increases. "Who will protect me when you aren't here?"

His eyes scan my body. He pins his green gaze on me. His lips twitch. "No one. Until they arrive, you and I might as well be attached at the hip."

13

Nolan

Lightning streaks through the sky. The boom is so loud, Gemma jumps. I put my arm around her tighter. "Everything is fine. It's just storming."

She tilts her head up, and her sleepy, blue eyes make the unfamiliar feeling that's attacking me too often wake up. I twist her strawberry-blonde hair around my finger. She rolls her warm body on top of me. "What time is it?"

"Who cares." I palm her ass and tug on the lock of hair.

She arches an eyebrow. "Do you have plans to keep me in bed all day?"

"Depends on how much of a dirty girl you'll be."

Her lips twitch. "Meaning?"

"We're out of condoms," I state.

"Okay," she enunciates. Her forehead wrinkles, and she stares at me in question.

I lean into her ear. "Do you trust me to pull out?"

She freezes then brings her face in front of mine. I'm playing with fire, fully aware of it, but unable to stop myself from wanting more. All night, we went at it. I didn't know I was low on condoms and am shooting myself, but it is what it is. And I've been watching her sleep for the last hour, debating how I want to take her again.

The more she stares at me, the more the thumping in my chest grows. I add, "No pressure."

She traces my lips. "And how does this make me the dirty girl?"

"You'll see." I tighten her hair around my finger and fist the rest of it. "By the way, your first orgasm won't be on my cock."

She furrows her eyebrows. "Does that mean I'm going to be left to get myself off when you do?"

"No, princess. You're going to ride my face when you come," I cockily reveal.

She puts both elbows on my chest. "After you pull out?"

"Yep."

She smirks, pushes her knees into the mattress, and sinks on my erection. Her wet heat encases me like a glove, and she leans into my ear. She flicks her tongue on my lobe, and tingles shoot down my spine. "Are you sure you can handle pulling out?"

I tug her head back, stick my tongue in her mouth, and pinch her nipple. She whimpers and begins lazily rolling her hips.

"Wrong way, princess," I mutter, steal a few more kisses, then sit up. I grab her hips, lift her off me, and instruct, "Turn."

She bites a smile, changes positions, and sinks back on me. She turns her head and asks, "This is what you think is dirty?"

I move her hair over her shoulder and kiss the back of her neck. "Stop asking questions and work that perfect pussy of yours on me."

Her eyes widen, and she bats her lashes. "You want me to go faster?" She rocks quicker.

I grab her hips, slow her down, and set the pace so my cells light with fire but it doesn't take me over the edge. I instruct, "Just like this. Bad girls get punished, so be a good girl."

Pink begins to crawl up her cheeks. She taunts, "Are you going to spank me?"

I grin. "Not right now. You like it too much." I slide my hand over her breast and play with her nipple.

She moans.

I kiss her neck. "You like riding me this way?"

In a raspy voice, she whispers, "So much."

"Good. You feel good, princess. Now keep this pace if you want your reward." I fist her hair and tug it so she's looking at the ceiling. I put my cheek next to hers. "Just a warning, if you want me to stop, you're going to have to tell me."

She freezes. "You aren't going to pull out?"

"No. I wouldn't lie to you about that. Relax."

She closes her eyes, returns to the rhythm I set, and whimpers. "Okay. Do you like that?"

I turn her head so I'm looking into her eyes. "I love everything about your tight little cunt." I steal another kiss. "Now be a good girl and let me watch you ride me."

She does what I want. I drag my fingers down her spine, and she shudders. Then I grab her wrists and hold them behind her back. I lay back on the mattress. If I didn't know better, I'd swear on the Holy Bible she's a mystical goddess. Her skin is smooth as silk. Her hair hangs in long, natural waves. And her ass that I can't stop thinking about is rounded magnificence. She's as Irish as any woman can get, and I never found one I was attracted to before. So everything about her fascinates me.

"Oh God," she whispers, and her insides grip me tighter.

I take a deep breath to control myself then reach into my drawer and pull out lube. Her skin turns dewy. The scent of her arousal gets more robust. I'd spray it on me and sniff it all day if I could. Her walls clench my shaft more intensely. It's bliss and torture, and I growl, "Don't you dare come."

"Please! I...holy...oh...No!—"

I grab her hips with two hands, lift her off me, and pull her lower body to my face. She yelps, and I tug her hot sex on my mouth.

"Oh fuck!" she yells.

I splay my hand on her spine, push her down, then reach for the back of her head. I position her face over my dick.

She deep throats me in one motion, and I groan. Her mouth is a naughty fantasy I could only dream about. She works my cock as hard as I work her, and I remind myself not to blow my wad.

I put lube on my finger then spread her ass cheeks and circle her forbidden zone.

She freezes.

I suck on her clit, and she moans like a wild animal, trembling in my mouth. She sucks harder, and I push past the hard ridge.

My cock falls out of her mouth, and she arches her back.

"Don't stop riding me, princess. I'm not done with you yet." I flick my tongue and smack her ass cheek.

"Nolan!" she screams.

I rub it out, inch my finger in her farther, keep flicking, then smack her again. Every time my hand makes contact with her ass cheek, she cries out and grinds her pussy in my face.

Her body becomes an earthquake of violent tremors. I smack her again and shove my tongue inside her. My fingers pump into her, and her body spasms on every piece of me that's inside her.

She rides my face harder, making incoherent noises that I would bottle up and listen to every night if I could. When I'm getting too close to coming, I push her forward on all fours. I cage my body over hers and slide my cock in her ass.

"Oh fuck!" she cries out.

I kiss her cheek. "Shh. Take a deep breath, princess."

Her eyes flutter open and shut. Her mouth hangs open as she tries to find air. Sweat pellets on her skin. She collapses on her forearms.

My body stays with hers, skin to skin, sweat mingling. I grip her waist, holding her steady. She obeys and takes deep breaths, allowing me to inch in and out until my pelvis hits her cheeks. "Good girl."

She tries to focus, but her eyelids keep opening and closing. And I thought I knew what she sounded like moaning, but when I move my hand and begin working her clit, the wild sounds coming out of her are an all new obsession for me.

"Jesus. You're driving me crazy, Gemma," I mutter in her ear.

She loses all control over her body. She's a rag doll in my arms, and with every thrust I make, she spasms harder.

I murmur in her ear, "You're ruining me. Every minute of every day. I can't think when you're around. How you feel right now, with your head spinning, is how you're tormenting me." I glide my finger in her sex and keep my thumb on her clit.

Barely audible, fragile breaths of air escape her lips. The scent of our fornication thickens around us. I suck on her shoulder and thrust harder, unable to hold myself back any longer.

Our cries of ecstasy twist together, competing with the violent storm outside. Wind slams against the house at the same time I pound into her. An explosion of adrenaline makes me dizzy. I collapse over her, my chest on her back and forearms holding me above her. We inhale and exhale air like one person instead of two people. Minutes pass. I pull out of her, and she flips underneath me.

Her face can only be that of an angel. Pink cheeks and blue eyes stare at me. I swipe her sweaty lock of hair off her forehead, saying nothing, mesmerized by the beautiful creature in front of me.

She reaches for me and locks her fingers behind my head. She tugs my lips to hers, stealing all the oxygen in my lungs.

The spark in my chest that I can't seem to shake reignites. Instead of trying to decipher it, I lean into it, kissing her back with every ounce of passion I possess.

Her stomach growls, and I laugh. "Did I work you into starvation mode?"

"I think it's all the food you've been making me eat. I'm constantly hungry."

I peck her on the lips. "What do you think about omelets?"

Amusement enters her expression. "No smoothie?"

"Nope. I think we should indulge today."

She beams. "I love omelets. With espresso, of course."

I groan. "Don't worry. I'll make you your acid."

She leans into my neck and inhales deeply. "Kind of ironic you buy cologne with coffee beans in it, don't you think?"

"What are you talking about?"

"Have you not looked at the scents in your bottle?"

"No."

She strokes my jaw. "You must want to be a coffee drinker deep down."

"Nope. That stuff is horrible for you." I lean down and give her another chaste kiss. "What do you think about a hot shower? Then you come back to bed, and I'll make breakfast."

She hesitates then nods.

My chest tightens. I roll onto my elbow and drag my finger over her collarbone. "What's wrong, princess?"

She shakes her head. "Nothing." Her cheeks grow hotter.

I put the back of my hand over them. "Why are you blushing?"

She bites her lip and nervously meets my gaze. "I um..."

I slide my arm under her neck. "What is it?"

There's more hesitation. She takes a deep breath and admits, "I hadn't done that before."

Shit. I assumed she had done everything. She claimed to have dated bad boys. I swallow the lump in my throat. "Did you not like it?"

Her face turns maroon. "No. I liked it."

"You did? Because if you didn't—"

She reaches out, grabs my head, and pulls it to her. She kisses me so deeply, I lose my breath.

"You shouldn't question a woman when she tells you she likes something," she murmurs.

"Does that include me?" I blurt out. My pulse beats in my neck, and I'm suddenly worried about what she might say.

Her face softens. "Yeah."

Relief fills me. "Good. I like you, Gemma. More than anyone I've met in a long time," I admit.

Her eyes turn glassy. She blinks hard. "Really? Even though I'm a mess?"

I caress the side of her head. "You aren't a mess. And I see you. Every part of you. This person you think you are now versus before, it's all in your mind. Both those people are you. They're both kind and funny and super sexy. Orla didn't steal any part of you. It's not hers to take. All she did was get you to peel a few layers back. You're multidimensional. That's a good thing in my book. It makes you real and special."

A tear drips down her cheek, and I kiss it. "Let's go shower." I pull her off the bed, lead her into the bathroom, and we take a hot shower. After we dry off, I tuck her back in bed. I lean down and direct, "Stay here and rest."

"Yes, sir." She salutes me.

"Don't get smart with me. I'll put you over my knee and slap your ass," I warn.

She bats her eyes. "Didn't we establish I like it when you do that?"

I groan. "Don't tempt me. You want toast?"

Her face lights up. "I forgot to tell you about what Tiernan thinks about your eating habits."

The sound of his name makes my blood boil, and I struggle to let it go. I'm still pissed he made such a bad call. I take a deep breath. "Why was he talking about that?"

Her stomach growls again. "Go make my food. I'll tell you over our omelets, sprouted bread, and espresso."

"Yes, ma'am." I kiss her forehead, throw on a pair of pajama bottoms, and go into the kitchen. I start the espresso machine then remove eggs, kale, mushrooms, garlic, goat cheese, and chopped onions.

Gemma comes out in one of my O'Malley T-shirts.

"What are you doing up?" I ask.

"Feel guilty. Want any help?"

I kiss her forehead. "No. Don't feel guilty. Your espresso is almost ready."

She reaches up and puts her arms around my neck. "Can I make dinner tonight?"

I grin. "Sure. What are you making?"

"It's a surprise. I'll order the ingredients to be delivered."

"Deal." I peck her on the lips then pat her ass. "Go get your mug of acid."

"Ha!" She steps back, takes her cup, and sits on the counter. "Do you have a thing about goat cheese?"

I add a drop of coconut oil in the skillet and turn the burner on. "What's not to love about goat cheese?"

She takes a sip of her espresso. "Nothing. It's yummy. But you rarely have other cheese in your house."

I claim, "It's good on everything. Plus, it's healthier than other cheeses."

"How?"

"It's packed with vitamins, minerals, and healthy fats. Plus, it helps reduce inflammation." I open the container of onions and put two spoonfuls in the pan.

She laughs. "Tiernan would love this conversation."

My pulse increases. "He's lucky he's family, or he wouldn't have his limbs right now." I flip the onions.

Gemma's voice softens. "I like Tiernan. He's just young."

I snort. "Yeah. Him and Fergal both have a lot to learn," I grumble then toss the mushrooms in the pan and put the lid on.

"Well, he's funny and was really nice. He helped take my mind off worrying about you," she adds.

The strange feeling creeps into my throat again. I step in front of her and put my hands on both sides of the counter. "You don't need to worry about me if I say I'll be fine."

She cups my cheek. "Where were you?"

Knots form in my stomach. "I told you I had O'Malley business to deal with."

She swallows hard. "What does that mean?"

I close my eyes briefly. I wish I could tell her everything, but I can't. "It means I'm doing things that I'll never discuss. Not with you, not with anyone."

Hurt appears on her face.

"It's for your protection. If I could tell you, I would," I try to assure her.

Silence fills the air. Blood slams against my skull. I worry I insulted her in some way.

She finally asks, "Do you always go away for days?"

"Sometimes. I try to stay out of those issues."

"What do you mean?"

I glance over her head, trying to figure out what to disclose. I lock eyes with her again. "You know I work on algorithms, right?"

"Yeah."

I choose my words carefully. "This isn't public knowledge, so keep it between us. We're forming a new tech company soon. It'll shift the way the O'Malleys earn their money. But I have to create the algorithm for it."

Her eyes widen. "Wow. That's impressive."

"It won't be if I don't figure it out soon." I straighten up and step back. The anxiety in my chest returns. I've been so obsessed over Gemma the last few weeks, I've not gotten very far. I lift the lid on the skillet, stir the onions and mushrooms, then add the kale.

Gemma says, "You will."

I shrug as if it isn't a big deal, but it is. "But once this happens, I shouldn't have to deal with certain things anymore."

She stays quiet a minute then smiles. "Okay. Thanks for telling me."

I change the subject. "What did you do while I was gone?"

Her face lights up. "I spent yesterday creating the branding for that company. They loved it."

I crack an egg into a glass bowl. "Of course they did. You're super talented. Do I get to see what you did?"

"Sure. Let me grab my laptop. It's in your office." She gets down from the counter and slaps my ass as she passes me.

"Hey! I'm the one who does the slapping," I tease.

"Bring it on," she smirks.

"Go get your laptop. Better yet, print it out," I suggest then return to making the omelets.

When she returns, she has a handful of papers. The omelets are ready, and we sit on the barstools. I turn and hold a forkful up to her. "Try this."

She opens her mouth, and I put the omelet in it. She chews and moans.

"Good, right?"

She swallows and nods. "So good. I think I'm getting a new obsession with goat cheese."

I wiggle my eyebrows. "Maybe you're just getting an obsession with me."

She traces a Celtic knot on my bicep. "Maybe you're the one with the obsession and it's over me?"

Zings race up my arm. I lean closer to her mouth. "Maybe I am."

Her pouty lips curve up, and she opens her mouth.

The doorbell rings, and she raises her eyebrow. "Expecting company?"

"Nope. Let me send whoever it is away." I rise, kiss the top of her head, and go to the door. Since the guys won't allow anyone near my front door who I don't know, I don't look out the peephole. I open the door, and my gut drops.

Not what I need right now.

"Molly, what are you doing here?"

She stares at my chest a moment then holds a laptop bag in front of her. "Did you not get my mom's message? She said she left you one that I would stop by this morning."

"Message?"

"Yesterday. She left you a voice message asking if you could fix my computer. She was on it and clicked something. I think she got a virus or something," Molly states, and a bolt of lightning streaks through the sky, followed by a crash of thunder. She jumps.

I force myself not to groan out loud. I open the door wider. "Come inside before you get electrocuted."

She steps in and pushes the hood of her green raincoat off. "Did you not get her message?"

"No. Sorry. I was dealing with something and haven't checked them," I say.

She winces. "Sorry to bother you. My mom's trying to get all her doctor appointments scheduled and they went to an online system. She lent her laptop to her friend who's going through cancer treatment, so she didn't want to ask for it back."

Crap. Now I need to fix it today. "Okay. Let me look at it quickly."

She reaches for my bicep and traces the skin glue over my cut. "Thanks, Nolan. Umm, I'm glad you're okay. I was really worried about you. Those guys had a lot of nerve coming to the pub."

I step out of the way so she isn't touching me. "I'm fine. Let me see what's going on." I spin and Gemma's eyes meet mine. I roll mine to show her I'm annoyed, but hers turn into flaming blue slits.

"Gemma. What are you doing here?" Molly asks.

Gemma crosses her arms. "About to eat breakfast. Why are you here?"

Molly looks Gemma up and down. "Trying to get my computer fixed. My mom needs to schedule her doctor appointments."

Gemma clenches her jaw and shakes her head at me. She leaves the room, and my heart squeezes.

Shit. Now she's pissed again.

I sit on the barstool, staring at the omelet, wondering how things always seem to be complicated between us. When I turn on the computer, my frustration grows. There are so many viruses on the laptop, I'm going to have to clean everything, then reupload everything so Molly's mom can use it. It's going to take hours. "How did this happen? I installed software to defend against this crap."

"Oh, you know my mom," Molly states.

"Did she turn the software off?" I ask.

Molly sits next to me. "Not sure."

"This is going to take hours. Why don't I drop it off?" I wishfully suggest, hoping she'll take the hint and leave.

"I'll wait if you don't mind. The storm seems to have gotten worse, and I hate driving in it."

Of course you do. I grumble, "Fine."

She picks up the stack of papers of Gemma's work. "What's this?"

I snatch it out of her hand. "Nothing." I turn them upside down and set the stack on the other side of me.

Molly chirps, "That omelet looks and smells great. Did you make it?"

I move Gemma's plate in front of me and hand mine to Molly. My appetite is suddenly gone. "Here. Have mine."

14

Gemma

AFTER TWENTY MINUTES PASS, I PUT CLOTHES ON AND GO INTO the kitchen. Molly has an empty plate in front of her and a cup of espresso. My anger grows deeper.

Nolan has an uneaten omelet in front of him that may or may not have been mine. A bit is missing. My espresso is on the other side of Molly. Frankly, it's exactly how she's making me feel—shoved aside. She's blabbing about something I don't even comprehend. I can't. My blood is boiling so much, I have to remind myself not to pick up a knife from the butcher block and start stabbing her.

All I see is her leaning close to Nolan. His hardened expression focuses solely on the computer screen, and his fingers are typing quickly.

He always looks like that when he's working.

How many times does her computer need fixing? Didn't he fix it the first night we met?

The more time Nolan spends trying to fix Molly's computer, the more pissed I become. I pick up my mug of cold espresso and go to the other side of the counter. I rinse out my cup and put it under the machine to make a fresh drink.

Nolan stops typing. His voice is softer than usual. "Your omelet's here. Want me to heat it up for you?" His green eyes meet mine.

"You should. It's delicious. Of course, Nolan's always been a great chef." Molly smiles at me, as if we're best friends. Then she turns toward him. "Do you remember the baked eggs with swiss chard and green olives you made a few months ago? Omgeee! It was soooo good!"

I glare at Nolan. "No, thanks. I seemed to have lost my appetite." I hit the button for my espresso. It's bad enough he made her the same goat cheese sandwich he grilled for me, but he made her breakfast, too?

He tilts his head, licks his lips, and stares at me.

"You were so kind to take care of me the night before." Molly puts her hand on his bicep and gives him puppy dog eyes.

I swallow the bile coming up my throat. I fixate on the black liquid coming out of the machine and curse myself. Bad boys are all the same—liars, cheaters, and total players. Nolan is no different.

He didn't cheat on me.

Not yet.

He lied about their relationship. Something has gone on.

How exactly did he take care of her?

Nolan's jaw clenches. He mutters, "You shouldn't have drunk so much." He rises, picks up the laptop, and sits in the oversized armchair.

Molly smirks at me.

A debate rages in my head about throwing hot espresso on her and if I could go to jail for it. Is it a type of assault and battery if I burn her? I fixate on the black liquid coming out of the machine. As soon as it's filled, I pick it up, along with my laptop. I leave and go into the office. I've already finished everything for the one job I had, so there's nothing to do. Instead, I go down a path I shouldn't.

I pull up my social media accounts. I type in Nolan O'Malley, but his account is on lockdown. Since we aren't following each other, I can't look at anything. Even his profile picture is blank.

I type in Declan next, but it's the same. Killian's, however, is full-blown public. He has hundreds of thousands of followers. Instead of getting drawn into all of Killian's selfies, shots of him boxing, and the girls hanging on him, I scroll his connections.

There you are, you little brat.

I click on Molly's. It's just as public as Killian's. Once again, I might get sick. Her profile only has photos of a few girlfriends, her mom, and her brother, which looks like it's only from video conferencing calls. There are a few random photos of the staff at O'Malley's, Nolan's brothers, and Nora. But there are tons of her and Nolan. She's usually hanging on him. Most of their pictures are at the pub, except a few that catch my eyes.

One is of her in Nolan's T-shirt. My stomach flips. It's the one I was wearing this morning. She's holding the phone in front of her and Nolan is in the background. His back is in the photo and he's facing his stove. She looks rather rough. Her makeup from the night before is still on her face and her hair is down but not brushed. The captions reads, *He saves me and cooks! Glad nothing bad happened to me last night! I hope I can stomach this since he's going to so much trouble to take care of me this morning.* The post after is a picture of food with the caption, *Baked Eggs with Swiss Chard and Green Olives. Soooooo yum!* It's dated several months ago.

Then there's the night Nolan left me alone and found me with a bottle of pills. She posted a photo of him talking to a medical professional. She tagged the location as St. Joseph's hospital. Her caption reads, *Soooooo grateful I have this guy in my life to make sure I'm okay!*

It was less than an hour after he left the house. So why didn't he come home for hours? My heartbeat picks up. I take several deep breaths and torture myself further by continuing to study it.

He never told me he was with her.

He lied to me.

Did he?

No. He just avoided the truth.

I was about to kill myself, and he was taking care of her.

I have no right to be angry. We weren't together. But something about him getting a phone call and leaving me to take care of her stings. And not like a mosquito bite. It's like a thousand bees attacking my body and all feasting on my skin at different times.

The picture and caption on my screen mock me. I don't know how long I stare at them until I shut my laptop. Nothing calms me. I stay in the office, too afraid of what I might say or do. The wound on my thigh itches. And my reality comes flying back to me.

Why did Orla say that about my mother?

I pace the office for hours. Another war rages in my mind about whether Orla could be telling the truth or not. I want to convince myself my mother can't be a murderer, but I never thought she was involved with the Irish mob until a few months ago.

Nolan comes into the room, and I freeze. He softly says, "Sorry that took so long."

I jerk my head back. "That's all you have to say?"

He scrubs his face. "What do you want me to say, Gemma?"

Millions of comebacks come into my brain, but nothing seems like it's ever going to make Nolan see Molly as the woman she is instead of his best friend's little sister. She's a conniving, manipulative woman who calculates her moves. I don't trust her around Nolan. She's trying to do everything to make him hers. Plus, he couldn't tell me about the night he was at the hospital with her. I don't even want to know what he did to take care of her months previously that required him to make her breakfast the next morning.

"I don't want you to say anything. You're pretty good at that anyway," I fire back and brush past him.

"What does that mean?" he asks, following me.

"Figure it out. I'm over this entire thing, whatever this is." I go into my bedroom and lock the door.

He attempts to open the door. "Gemma!"

"Go away. In fact, why don't you run down the street to Molly."

"That's not fair. I didn't know she was coming over," he claims.

"So what? You didn't have any problem inviting her in."

"Her mom needed to make her doctor's appointments. What did you want me to do? Her mother has severe diabetes and other health issues," he states.

I turn my phone on and blast the music. I flop down on the bed and bury my face in the pillow.

"You're acting like a child," he shouts then bangs on the door.

"Go away!" I yell.

He bangs on the door again, but I don't respond. "Fine. Be immature."

I assume he walked away. Song after song plays. I try to quiet my mind about all the questions I have regarding my mother, along with those about Nolan and Molly. But it's an atomic bomb going off, and I'm underneath it.

Nolan bangs on the door. "You have five minutes to get out of this room with your workout clothes on. And pack a bag if you want fresh clothes when we're finished. We aren't coming directly home."

"It's raining!" I yell.

"We're going to the gym."

I jump off the bed and yank the door open. "Are you trying to remind me that Orla assaulted me yesterday?"

He scowls. "Not your gym. My gym. Get ready, or I'm carrying you out of the house in your current clothes."

"Wow! I see you're back to prince charming."

He ignores me and leaves while warning, "Five minutes."

Irritated, I slam the door, throw on my workout clothes, and pack a bag. I meet him in the family room, and we say nothing. He leads me to the car, we get in, and drive to the gym in silence.

He protectively puts his arm around me when we get out of the car. I should shirk out of it, but I don't. As soon as we get inside, he releases me.

I freeze. A boxing ring is in the middle of the room. Imprinted on the floor is a Celtic cross. The Celtic letter O in the middle of it, and a ring of Celtic knots is behind the cross. Written under it is O'Malley.

Speed bags and heavy bags used for kicking or punching hang from the ceiling. One corner has exercise equipment. Several younger guys are working out with trainers, but the gym is pretty empty.

"This way," Nolan mutters.

I follow him, and he leads me down a hallway. He points. "Lockers are in there. And you don't have to worry in this gym about Baileys being here."

"Heard that before," I mumble and go inside. I choose a locker, throw my bag in it, and change my shoes. After I go to the bathroom, I wash my hands, but the water is only cold.

I meet Nolan near the punching bags. "There's no hot water in there."

"Yeah. It's been like that for a while."

"Why don't you fix it?"

He shrugs. "Women don't come in here. The men's works fine."

I huff.

He ignores me and hands me a pair of fingerless gloves. He instructs, "Put these on."

"I'll just go run on the treadmill."

He arches his eyebrows. "Too scared to try something new?"

I grab the gloves from him and shove my fingers in them. "Fine." I take a swing, and the bag flies forward, then back at me.

Nolan catches it a moment before it hits my face. "You have to stand in the correct position. Like this." He demonstrates.

I sigh and stand how he is.

He takes a few minutes to instruct me how to punch then steps back once I get into a rhythm. "Good. Let me know when you get tired."

"I'm not going to get tired," I claim, but my arms are already burning.

He snorts. "Sure." He picks up a rope and begins jumping.

Several minutes pass, and I think my arms might fall off. Something beeps. Nolan tosses the rope on the ground. "Switch."

I do what he says, relieved to stop punching. I pick up the rope and jump, watching him hit the bag like a pro, wishing he didn't look so damn sexy.

There's another beep. He stops and says, "Plank time," then drops to the ground.

I move into the plank position, concentrating on squeezing my core. It burns when the beep fills the air.

"Back to the bag," Nolan orders.

I return to punching it, imagining Orla's and Molly's faces. The beep fills the air, and we do several more rounds.

"Gemma. What are you doing here?" Liam's voice fills the air.

I stop punching the bag and spin. I tug my shirt to wipe my face. Something about seeing Liam sets me off again. "Can't exactly work out at the gym I go to when Orla got herself a membership there, now can I?"

His face hardens. "When did this happen?"

I angrily shake my head. "Last night. Nolan said it was all clear, but apparently, your guys aren't well versed in checking out women's locker rooms. I thought I was going to get my neck sliced off."

Liam turns to Nolan. "Who was guarding her? Why didn't you tell me?"

Nolan stops jumping and drops the rope on the floor. "Tiernan and Fergal. I told you they were too inexperienced for this."

Liam defensively says, "They've done security for my dad for over ten years."

"They aren't the smartest representation of the O'Malleys now, are they?" Nolan grabs a bottle of water and downs a quarter of it.

More anger erupts. "Gee, thanks for telling me I was in good hands and safe when you had concerns, Nolan."

Guilt crosses his face, but it disappears quickly. "Go back to punching your bag. Get it out before we get home."

"I know what I'd be happy to punch. If you'll excuse me, I think I'll go work out in peace instead of near the man who would be happy if I got slaughtered in public." I glare at Nolan and move to the other side of the gym.

I work out for a few minutes when Nolan calls out, "Gemma, we're leaving in fifteen minutes. Be ready to go."

I do a few more exercises then decide I need to shower. Nothing is calming me down anyway. I walk toward the locker room, and Liam says, "What did Orla say to her?"

I step next to him and quickly spout my lie, "I violated a rule when Nolan turned off my location tracker on my cell phone. I got this lovely new scar when your cousins realized they hadn't checked that area of the gym out and held a gun pointed to both our heads. I guess I should be grateful it was my leg instead of my neck, which is where she held the blade on me originally." I shoot Nolan another dirty look.

"Not sure why you're looking at me. Liam decided who was watching you when I can't," Nolan fires back.

Liam scans my body. "Where on your leg?"

"My upper thigh. Near all my reproductive organs," I state.

"Stop being dramatic. Your inner thigh isn't where your reproductive organs are," Nolan chastises me.

Liam glances at my leg. "Are you okay? Did you go to the hospital?"

My cheeks turn crimson, thinking about how Nolan glued my thigh then ate me out. "No. Nolan said it wasn't deep and cleaned it up. I'm going to get changed." I brush past them and go into the locker room. I remove my bag and turn on the shower, but the water is cold.

"Shit." I turn it off and close my eyes. "Screw this." I pick up my bag and go into the men's room.

Two men in their twenties are sitting on the bench. One is wrapping the other guy's hand with tape. He looks up and says, "Can I help you, sweetheart?"

I smile. "Point me to the showers?"

The other man turns and eyes me over. "Need some assistance?"

"Nope. Think I can handle it, but thanks."

The first guy points. "Around that corner."

"Thanks!" I wave and make my way to the showers. I freeze when I get to them. There are twelve showerheads, all in an open area.

"She came in with Nolan. He'll kill you," one of the men says.

I take a deep breath, turn on the water, and drown out their voices. When the water turns hot, I peel off my clothes and step under it and close my eyes.

"What do you think you're doing in here?" Nolan booms, and it echoes off the tiles.

I jump. "Taking a hot shower. There's a cold one in the women's room waiting for you."

Loud snickers fill the air, and Nolan spins and disappears. He shouts, "Get the fuck out!"

"Chill out. We can't see her."

"Now!" Nolan bellows.

I pump a handful of shampoo into my hand from the wall container and rub it in my hair. I'm rinsing it out when Nolan steps into the shower naked and turns on the other faucet. He scowls and steps in front of me. Sweat coats his body, and I force myself to stare at his eyes and not his ripped, inked flesh. He comments, "Not sure what you're trying to accomplish, princess."

"Stop being such a hypocrite," I accuse then return to rinsing my hair.

"Hypocrite?" he foams.

"Yeah. You want to get all bent out of shape due to a few guys being in here where they can't even see me. Yet, you spend all morning with your... what should I call her? Your ex? Your fuck buddy? What exactly is she?"

Red bursts into his cheeks. He steps closer until I'm pinned against the wall. "How many times do I have to tell you she's my best friend's sister? I've never been into her and never will be."

"Yeah, well, maybe if you were Mr. Full Transparency, I'd be able to believe what comes out of your mouth," I accuse.

He grabs my chin and brings his face in front of mine. "What are you talking about?"

"Next time you say, 'I have to go out. Something came up,' I'll remember it means your dick misses her and not to wait up," I roar.

His eyes turn to green fire. "I'm getting sick of being accused of shit I haven't done."

I laugh sarcastically then point in his face. "Next time you want to hide something, make sure your girlfriend doesn't take pictures and post it all over the place."

He steps so close to me, his skin touches mine. He lowers his voice. "What in God's name are you talking about?"

My insides quiver. Emotions hit me like a brick to the face, and it's too many things packed into the stone. There's the shame of what I did that night. All the years of dating men who cheated, and I took them back only for them to do it again, just because I wanted to be loved so badly. And then there's the worst reality of all. It's the fact that Nolan seems like he's a thousand times the man any of them ever were, yet it feels like the same thing. I blink hard and look away, not wanting to show him anything I feel. I've given too many men my tears, and I'm not giving them to him.

He slowly but firmly states, "Gemma, I need to know what you meant by that statement."

I find the courage to lock eyes with him. "Where were you the night you left me home, and Orla wouldn't stop messaging me?"

The color drains from his face. He swallows hard. "It's not what you think."

I shove him, but he's too strong and doesn't budge. "Jesus. Do you know how many times I've heard that?"

"Darcey called from the pub. She cut her hand. I had to take her to the hospital—"

"Why? Because no one else could? Because you had to be the one to rescue her? And what did you do after for all those hours? What did she do for you since she was 'soooooo grateful you were making sure she was okay?'" I put my fingers in quotes.

He runs his hands through his hair and closes his eyes. "Gemma, I need you to listen to me."

I shake my head. "No. I'm finished listening, Nolan. The time for me to listen was weeks ago. You chose not to talk. And for someone who's a computer guru, it sure is amazing how you don't cover your tracks."

Confusion fills his face. "What does that mean?"

"Move!" I push him again.

"Gemma—"

"I need you to move, Nolan. I mean it!" I push him again, and this time he takes a step back. I get out of the shower, grab the towel, and wrap it around my body.

He turns the water off and follows me. He grabs my shoulder. "Gemma—"

I spin on him. "How do you not see what everyone else does? Have you never looked at her social media account?"

He shakes his head. "Why would I look at her account? I barely go on mine."

I stare at the ceiling, a million different ways about how to end this conversation spin through my mind. I finally pin my gaze on his. "I'm done playing second fiddle to other women. And I'll be damned if I play it to Molly."

15

Nolan

"I would never ask you to play second fiddle," I try to assure Gemma, but it sounds weak coming out. I don't care about social media. Killian loves it, but I have better things to do with my time. I'm not sure what Molly put on her page, but I'm going to find out.

Gemma steps into her panties and doesn't reply. She clasps her bra and tugs a T-shirt over her head.

"Gemma—"

The door opens, and Killian walks in.

"Get out!" I bark.

His eyes widen, and he spins toward the door. "Good to see you, too, Nolan. Gemma, how are you doing, lass?"

"Fine," she mutters and pulls her jeans up. "I'm dressed. You can turn now. I'll be waiting by the door." She leaves.

Killian spins, smirking. "You gonna put some clothes on?"

"Shut up," I explode.

"Hey, I'm not the one playing locker room games."

"You're two seconds away from getting your face smashed in," I warn.

He opens his locker. "Easy, killer. What the hell did you do to piss Gemma off?"

I almost tell him to keep his nose out of it, but I'm so far in with Gemma, I don't know how to get myself out. "Molly stopped by the house this morning."

Killian groans. "Let me guess. She wanted you to drop your pants so she could lick your balls for breakfast?"

"Jesus! Why do I even talk to you," I grumble and open my locker.

Killian cockily licks his lips. "Because I'm the good-looking, fun one?"

"Keep telling yourself that," I mutter and put my shirt on.

Killian shuts his locker. He backs against it then crosses his arms. "So why was Molly at your house?"

"Her mom caught a virus on their laptop again. She needed to schedule her doctor's appointments. I didn't listen to my messages when I got home last night, so I didn't know she was sending Molly by with it," I admit.

Killian asks, "And Gemma didn't like Molly fawning all over you?"

I groan. "Not you, too."

Killian tilts his head. His face drops. "Molly's had a thing for you for a while. I tell you this all the time."

My stomach flips. "You make asshole comments. I thought you were just being your normal prick self."

"Nope. She wants your cock." He puts his shoe on the bench and ties the laces. "I always wondered if you ever did anything with her."

"Are you kidding me? One, I'm not the slightest bit attracted to her. She's a total train wreck. Two, she's Colin's little sister," I remind him.

He raises his eyebrows. "Wouldn't be the first time someone violated bro code. It didn't stop Boris from seeing Nora behind my back."

"Yeah, well, I'm not Boris and not interested in her." I scrub my forehead with the butt of my palm. "Look, I don't want to hurt Molly, but it's never happening."

"Tell her," Killian says.

My stomach twists. I don't want to believe Molly thinks of me as anything but a big brother. The thought of doing anything sexual with her makes me ill.

Killian takes his phone out of his pocket and takes a selfie. He types something.

I shake my head in annoyance. "Don't you get sick of posting photos of yourself all day long?"

"The lasses would be disappointed if I didn't."

I stuff my gym shoes in my locker. Then realize there's no time like the present. I order, "Pull up Molly's account."

"Why?" Killian questions.

"Gemma said I needed to open my eyes and look at it. Pull it up," I repeat.

Killian obeys and flicks his finger across the screen. He pins his brows together and mutters, "Yeah. Girl has it bad for you. If I didn't believe you, I'd think you were her boyfriend."

My pulse shoots through the roof. I grab the phone, and my gut sinks. "Shit."

"Yep."

"Why didn't you tell me I was all over her page?"

He snorts. "You think I go on social media and look at Molly's page?"

"You're connected to her."

"So? I'm connected with hundreds of thousands of people. I have plenty of smoking-hot lasses to look at and interact with instead of trolling Molly's page," he boasts.

I ignore pointing out how half of his followers are dudes who want to suck him off and tell him so on a daily basis. "Great. So what the hell am I supposed to do?"

"Sit her down and tell her it's never happening. Good luck with that." He pats me on the back then leaves.

I slam my locker shut. I slide my feet into my shoes and sling my bag over my shoulder. When I step outside the locker room, Gemma is standing next to the door. She's looking at her phone. Her face is white as a ghost, and her hand trembles.

"Gemma, what's going on?"

She shakes her head, avoids looking at me, then slips her phone into her pocket. "Nothing. Let's go."

I study her. It isn't just her hand trembling. Her lips are, too. I slip my arm around her, lead her out to the car, and once we're inside it, I hold my hand out. "What did Orla send you?"

She scrunches her face and looks out the window.

"Gemma, be pissed all you want but don't hide this from me. Did she figure out your new number?"

Her glistening blue eyes meet mine. She nods.

I stroke her cheek and soften my voice even though my insides are back in vengeful chaos. Orla should never have gotten her new number. No one knows it except her sisters, mom, Liam, and me. I ask, "What did she say?"

She closes her eyes. "Nothing new."

I pull the phone out of Gemma's pocket and punch in the code. My stomach flips. It's similar footage of the night I found Gemma with the pills. It's from the Bailey whorehouse. This time, it also shows every painful expression in Gemma's face while Orla made her watch the vile rapes. There's one message.

Unknown number: *I wouldn't have killed you yesterday. This is your fate, and I'm going to watch when they break you in.*

Abhorrence gnaws at my stomach. I set the cell in the cupholder. "I'm getting you a burner phone."

Gemma takes a deep breath and stares out the windshield. She quietly says, "Nothing is ever going to be normal again."

I lean toward her and slide my arm around her. "It will. We'll find her, and all this will stop. I promise."

She turns her face. Her eyes fill with tears. "Even if she's dead, my father will come after me."

My heart races. "We're going after your father, too. Make no mistake."

Her phone vibrates, and she grabs it before I can. "What the..."

I take it from her, and my stomach pitches. Bile sprints up my throat. A picture of Gemma, naked and with blood all over her pops up.

"How did she get a photo of me without clothes on?" Gemma asks.

I stare closer. It looks so real, but it isn't. I turn to Gemma. "It's edited. This isn't your body. It's not your abs or breasts."

"Let me see." She reaches for the phone, but I hold it away from her and turn it off.

"No. You aren't looking at these vile threats anymore." I slide the phone in my pocket near the door.

"Nolan—"

"I said no. There isn't any point in torturing yourself any further."

She leans back into the headrest and closes her eyes. "It's only a matter of time before she gets to me."

"No. It's a matter of time before I get to her," I vow.

She sighs. "Can we not talk about it anymore? Where are we going?"

"I wanted to check on Nora. I haven't talked to her in a few days. Do you mind if we stop by their place?" I ask.

She rolls her head toward me. "Why are you asking me?"

The feeling I can't shake, the one I don't understand, swirls in my chest. I tease, "You make it sound like you don't have any choices with me."

She stares at me.

My gut drops. In a low voice, I ask, "Is that what you think?"

"I didn't have a choice earlier about coming here, did I?"

Guilt is like a woodpecker, hammering into my heart. "We were both angry."

Her eyes turn to blue ice. "Yeah. And you got to order me around how you always do."

The hammer pounds harder. I quietly ask, "Am I that bad?"

She takes a deep breath. "No."

Uncomfortable silence fills the air. I debate about digging deeper into how much of an asshole she thinks I am or talking to her about the Molly situation.

I open my mouth, but Gemma asks, "Can we go? Hanging out in vehicles like this freaks me out. I feel like a sitting duck."

"Sure." I start the car, and we ride in more silence. My phone rings, and I glance at it, then answer, "Boris. Is Nora okay?"

Boris replies, "She's in labor. We're heading to the hospital now."

"Gemma and I were just on the way over to visit. Should we meet you there?" I ask.

"No. Nora said to hold off so you're not waiting around. I'll let you know what they say when we get there. Can you let your brothers and mine know? I tried calling Killian, but it just rang."

"Sure. Let me know if you need anything."

"Thanks." He hangs up.

I put my phone down.

"Is Nora okay?" Gemma asks, her voice full of concern.

I smile. "Yeah. She's in labor. They're on their way to the hospital. Can you text my brothers and Maksim? Tell them Boris said he'll let us know when to come, but Nora doesn't want anyone waiting around the hospital." I hand her my phone.

"Sure." She texts them and puts my cell in the cupholder. "Are you excited?"

"Yeah. I'm undecided whether it'll be cooler for her to have a girl or boy." I veer into the other lane and head toward the house. I cautiously ask, "Are you hungry?"

She glances at me. "I'm starving."

The vision of her uneaten omelet makes me cringe inside. "If you could have any type of food right now, what would it be?"

She doesn't hesitate. "Mexican."

"What's your favorite restaurant?" I ask.

"It's a hole in the wall in Lawndale."

"Miguel's?"

Surprise fills her face. "You've been there?"

"Yeah. It's my favorite, too. Want to go?"

She tilts her head. Her lips twitch. "Are margaritas on the lunch menu?"

"Sure. Should I drop the car off, and I'll have a driver take us?" My stomach somersaults, waiting for her to answer.

"Probably safer," she finally replies.

I don't ask anything else. I call my cousin to meet me at the house. He's waiting when we arrive. We get in the car, and as soon as the door shuts, I tug Gemma onto my lap.

"What are you doing?" she asks.

"Trying to make things right between us," I admit.

She sighs and turns away from me.

My nerves eat at my stomach. I pull her chin so she can't hide from me. "I understand why you're upset."

She doesn't say anything.

"Killian pulled up Molly's profile. I don't go on social media a lot. I haven't seen her page in years. What she posted isn't how it appears," I insist.

Gemma swallows hard. "And what do you think it looks like?"

The air in my lungs becomes stale. "That we're together."

She arches an eyebrow.

My gut dives. I hate how I feel guilty about something I've never done, but I do. I reiterate, "We aren't now, nor have we ever been."

"Why did you cook her breakfast? Her post made it appear as if she slept over," Gemma asks.

My heart races. "She did. She got super drunk at the pub and was throwing up. Her mom was out of town, and I didn't want to leave her on her own. I didn't think it was a big deal. She stayed in the guest bedroom."

The color drains in Gemma's face. "In my room?"

My chest tightens. "Yeah."

Gemma blinks hard. "Did you stare at her while she slept?"

I tighten my arm around her. "No. I've only ever watched you."

"I don't want to be lied to, Nolan."

"I'm not. I wouldn't do that to you," I insist.

Hurt fills her voice. "Then why didn't you tell me about the hospital?"

"You were already upset about what happened at the pub when she commented on your bracelet. I didn't want to piss you off again," I admit, then add, "But I didn't lie."

"No. You just omitted the truth," Gemma fires.

I nod. "Yeah. I did. I'm sorry. I won't do it again."

She looks at the ceiling and bites her lip.

"Gemma, look at me."

Her eyes slowly drift to mine.

I firmly state, "I won't lie to you or cheat on you. I'm not one of those dickheads you dated."

She stays silent.

"What do you need me to do so you believe me?" I ask.

"Make it clear to Molly you aren't interested."

"Have I done something to make her think I am?" I blurt out, still shocked Molly even thinks it's possible we could be together.

Gemma's eyes turn to slits. "You drop whatever you're doing and take care of her. She thinks she can just come over whenever—"

"She's never done that until recently. Not this frequently, at least. And I only take care of her because I promised Colin I'd watch out for his mother and her. He's coming home soon. I won't have to deal with her. But I'll sit Molly down and make it very clear it's never happening between us," I state.

"You will?" Gemma asks, as if she doesn't believe me.

"Yes. I promise you. I didn't know she had feelings for me. Honest. If I did, I would have set her straight immediately. And I'll tell her no more popping over. I don't want to hurt her, but she's obviously confused."

Gemma bites on her lip and twists her hands in her lap. Time seems to stand still.

I finally blurt out, "Gemma, I really like you. I'm not a saint. There's plenty of sins I'll pay for someday, but doing anything other than treating Molly like a little sister isn't one of them. And I'd never sleep with you and someone else at the same time. Are we going to get past this?"

Her lips twitch. She slides her hand up my chest and around my neck. "Sounds like you're a perfect sinner, then."

I cock an eyebrow. "Does this mean you forgive me, and we can pick up where things were before our breakfast got interrupted?"

She brings her lips an inch from mine. "Okay. You're forgiven. How dirty do you want to get?"

My dick perks up. "I'm always down to get filthy with you, princess."

She laughs. Her eyes sparkle. "Good. I have a craving for dirty nachos. I'll let you decide what comes after."

16

Gemma

MIGUEL'S IS A DIVE BAR. IT'S DARK, HAS LOUD LATIN MUSIC AT all times of the day, and you can smell the chefs smoking weed in the kitchen. Their margaritas are two for one at lunchtime, and Nolan and I have had several. Most of the crowd has died down, except for the regulars.

We're sitting in the back booth. I sink farther into his chest. We've laughed since we got here, lost in our own world, without anyone interrupting us but the server from time to time.

"I think it's time for me to clean you up," he murmurs in my ear then takes his finger and smears nacho cheese on my lips. He slowly licks the width of my lips until it's gone. Then he glides his tongue in my mouth and possessively takes control of our kiss, fisting my hair, and sliding his other hand in my pants and palming my ass. His tongue is an intoxicating mix of tequila and jalapenos. He could assault me every day with it and I'd be in happy paradise.

"Did you enjoy your cheese?" I mumble.

"Mmhmm." He kisses me deeper then moves his lips to my neck. "One of these days, I'm pouring honey all over you."

I softly laugh. "Why honey?"

"Caramel will burn." He pushes my shirt to the side and sucks on my collarbone.

"Why caramel?" I breathe.

He moves his face in front of mine. His green eyes brighten. "It's sticky. I might have to lick you for hours to get you clean."

I bite on my lip. "Well, I wouldn't want to deny you that."

He grins. "I think we need a restroom break, don't you?"

I smirk. "Is this your way of asking me if I want to screw you in the bathroom?"

"No. They don't clean very well here. The men's room is a mess," he states.

"Okay, then why—"

"Stop asking questions. Get your sexy little ass up, or I'm going to bend you over this table and smack you in front of the regulars."

"You wouldn't." I laugh.

His arrogance comes out as a hard sniff. In a solemn voice, he warns, "Want to bet?"

I'm unsure if he's joking or not, but I decide not to call his bluff. I rise, and he quickly escorts me down the hallway, which is even darker than the restaurant. He pulls me into the men's room.

"I thought—"

"Shh." He pulls a quarter out of his wallet and shoves it into a machine.

"They have a condom machine here?"

A packet falls. He wiggles his eyebrows then grabs the foil square. He guides me back into the hallway, toward the exit sign.

"Are we going outside?" I ask.

"Shh," he reprimands again. Right when we get to the exit, he opens a side door and pushes me inside. It's pitch black, and the walls shake as if they're going to break apart from the music.

My skin crackles with anticipation. "Where—"

His spicy-sweet tongue slides against mine, and he backs me into the wall. My nerves become electrified with the vibrations coming off the cold drywall and Nolan's body taking possession of mine.

In under a minute, my jeans are at my ankles, and his hands grip the back of my thighs, holding me up. He sinks his cock in me in one thrust, and I cry out, "Holy!"

"I'm not holy, princess. I'm a sinner," he growls. His green eyes glow like an unfed animal, and he reunites his mouth with mine.

The life I always feel when I'm around him intensifies. I grasp him, closing my eyes, buzzed from alcohol and him. All my worries fade. I forget all my fears and realities.

Men's voices speaking in Spanish ring through the air. The smell of weed mixes with the scent of our arousal. Nolan leans into my ear. "I'd say let's go take a hit, but you already make me high." He flicks his tongue on my lobe.

I inhale his scent, breathing in the essence of him, wanting nothing more than to get any part of him in me I can. His erection glides against my walls, creating currents of endorphins ready to explode in all my cells. My whimpers turn into loud cries, competing with the festive music.

"Jesus. You always feel so good, Gemma," he mutters then thrusts faster.

"Oh...oh!" Adrenaline batters my being and completely unravels me. It's a mayhem of explosions in every atom of my body. I tug his hair, trembling in his arms.

"Fuuuuuck," Nolan groans, stretching my body farther as he erupts deep within me.

A minute passes as he catches his breath. He returns to my mouth and kisses me with the same intensity as when we first got into this room. When he pulls back, I'm still breathless.

"Are you ready for me to pay the bill?" he asks, his green eyes full of cocky amusement.

I laugh. "Maybe you should release my legs and let me put my pants back on first."

He chuckles, pecks me on the lips, then puts me back on the ground. He bends over and pulls my jeans up. It's still dark, and I can't see anything except his green eyes.

"Where are we?" I ask.

"No idea."

"You don't know what room this is?"

"Nope. But I always wondered."

I burst out laughing, and he opens the door. My eyes take a minute to adjust to the light even though it's not much brighter.

Nolan quickly guides me through the restaurant, throws cash on the table, and leads me to the car. Day is turning into night. We get in the back seat. He puts his arm around my shoulders.

I sink into his warm chest and tilt my head up. "Thanks for a fun lunch."

He grins. It's an expression I love on him, but I don't get to see it very often. "It was. I like us this way."

My flutters erupt. I admit, "I do, too."

His eyes study mine. "Have you ever been to Ireland?"

I shake my head. "No."

"Me, either. We should go. See if it's all it's cracked up to be."

I laugh. "Should I pack my bag? Can we leave tonight?"

His eyes twinkle. "Do you have a passport?"

"It expired."

"You should renew it."

My pulse increases. "You're serious about going?"

His face falls. "With you? Yeah. I think we'd have fun, don't you?"

I smile. "Yeah. We'd have a lot of fun."

He gives me a chaste kiss on the lips. "Let's fill out your passport paperwork when we get home. We can get your picture taken tomorrow."

My butterflies intensify. "Okay."

Satisfaction crosses his expression. "So, what countries have you been to?"

I turn toward him more. "I went to Cancun for spring break in college."

"So cliché," he teases.

I laugh. "Yep."

He strokes my shoulder. "Where else?"

"Canada for work. Aruba and St. Martin for vacation. That's the extent of my international travels. What about you?"

He groans. "I don't even want to admit this."

"What?"

Pink creeps into his face. "My passport is stampless."

I gape at him. "You're forty-one."

He covers his face. "Ugh. I know."

"Why haven't you gone anywhere?"

He shrugs. "There's always so much going on with my family. All my trips have been short getaways to Florida or Vegas. My brothers and I didn't like leaving my nana on her own to deal with the pub. Since Sean died and Nora owns it, we're even more vigilant. We don't ever all go away at the same time. Two of us are always here."

"Always?"

"Yeah. When Dmitri had his bachelor party in Vegas, Declan and I stayed back," he admits.

I reach up and caress his head. "You're a good brother. Nora's lucky to have you." The car stops, and I look out the window. "Wow. That was quick. Home sweet home."

There's a loud knock and Nolan turns toward his window.

"Nolan. We've got a problem," Tiernan barks.

Nolan closes his eyes, sighs, then kisses my head. "Stay in the car for a minute."

My flutters turn to nervous ones. "Okay."

He steps out, shuts the door, and talks to Tiernan. Nolan's body stiffens. The garage door opens. A black sedan with tinted windows is parked next to Nolan's SUV. They walk over to it, open the trunk, then talk for several more minutes.

Something is wrong. I can feel it. I can't see what's in the trunk, but it can't be good.

Nolan shuts the trunk then makes a phone call. He runs his hand through his reddish-brown locks. After several minutes, he hangs up and gets back into the car.

"What's wrong?" I fret.

The previously relaxed atmosphere disappears. Nolan's hardened expression is back. He replies, "A man was lurking around the neighborhood. Tiernan recognized him from the gym. He's in the trunk."

My stomach flips. "He's a Bailey?"

"Yes."

My lip quivers, and I sober up. "He was watching us?"

Nolan tugs me into him. "Listen to me, Gemma. I'm dropping you off at Maksim's. You stay with Aspen. I trust his security. We're going to find out what his orders were and hopefully find out where Orla is."

Confused, I ask, "Maksim is going?"

Nolan nods. "Yes. I can't get ahold of my brothers. Let's go pack a bag."

Panic fills me. "How long will you be gone?"

He cups my face with both hands. In a firm voice, he states, "Gemma, you'll be safe at Maksim's."

"What about you?"

He leans closer. "You don't have to worry about me. We're the ones in control. Now, I need you not to freak out, pack a bag, and try to relax. I don't want to be worried about you while I'm gone."

I take a deep breath. "Okay."

He quickly kisses me. "Good girl."

We get out of the car and go into the house. I pack an outfit, one of his T-shirts to sleep in, and my toiletries.

He brings my laptop bag into the bedroom. "I thought you might want this?"

"Thanks." I reach up and lock my fingers around his head. "Do you think you'll be gone for a long time?"

"I'm not sure. I'll get you as soon as it's over."

I want to ask him what he's going to do to Orla's thug, but I know he won't tell me. Instead, I say, "I want to see him."

His eyes widen. "Why?"

"I-I just do. Please. Can I see him?"

He studies me for several moments, uncertainty in his eyes.

"Nolan. Please."

He exhales loudly. "All right." He slings my overnight bag over the same shoulder that my laptop bag is on then leads me to the garage. We stand in front of the trunk, and he nervously glances at me. "You sure you want to see this?"

"Yes," I adamantly state.

He takes the key and opens the trunk.

My heart races, and pains shoot through it. I grip Nolan's forearm so tight, I'm sure it'll leave nail marks. The goon has duct tape over his mouth and his face is bloody. He scowls, and even though his face is swelling, I'd know those eyes anywhere.

"Gemma?"

I tear my eyes off the man who haunts my dreams. I pin my gaze on Nolan. My voice shakes. "That's the man who stalked me at my work and gym."

17

Nolan

Neither of my brothers, Liam or Finn, answered their phones. Maksim is the first person I turned to when none of them responded to my calls. Normally, I'd go to Darragh with this, but after he disapproved of how Killian and I handled the pub incident, I'm not taking any chances.

Before I called Maksim, I didn't even know the thug my cousins caught was the guy who'd been stalking and harassing Gemma. Now that I know this, I'm even more grateful Maksim is here. I initially called him to help me keep the guy alive long enough to find out information on Orla's whereabouts. I didn't trust myself not to kill him within the first five minutes. He was only in my neighborhood to watch Gemma and do God knows what to her. Now that I'm aware he's the guy who spent months threatening her, the war raging in my belly is tenfold.

"I need you to make sure I don't kill him too soon," I admit, taking deep breaths.

Maksim flings his blade across the rectangle stone, sharpening it. His Russian accent fills the car. "I will. He was by himself?"

"Tiernan swears no one else was around."

Maksim sets his knife down and holds out his hand. "Give me your knife."

I take it out of my pocket and pass it to him. He repeats the same movements. "You've been drinking a lot today?"

Memories of laughing and feeling stress-free with Gemma seem like longer than only a few hours ago. "Gemma and I were in Longdale at Miguel's."

Maksim stops sharpening my blade. His icy-blue eyes meet mine. "Lunchtime margaritas?"

"Yep. You're familiar?"

He chuckles. "Aspen's a big fan. How many did you have?"

I shrug. "Not sure. Three? Maybe four? Possibly five. But I'm sober enough to kill this motherfucker now."

Maksim arches an eyebrow. "You smell like you took a shower in tequila. No matter how sober you think you are, you aren't."

"I'm fine," I assure him.

"You said you're ready to kill."

"I am."

Maksim sniffs hard. "Thought the goal was to torture him and get information? Make him suffer as long as possible and once he has nothing left to tell us, then kill him?"

"It is," I claim.

Maksim returns to sharpening the knife. "Then make sure you keep that in mind at all times. If you don't, you'll cut too deep, and he'll bleed to death too fast."

"I have done this before," I remind him.

Maksim snorts. "How many times have you done this after lunchtime margaritas?"

I scrub my face. "None."

Maksim hands me the knife back. "All right. If I say stop, you freeze. If I tell you to back off and let me take over, you don't question it. Understand?"

"Fine. You're in charge," I grumble.

He smiles. "Let's get this done quickly. Hopefully, we'll get the call soon about the baby."

I glance at my phone to double-check Boris hasn't texted, but there's no message. I say, "Darragh thinks it's a girl. Let's hope if it is, she looks like Nora."

"An O'Malley-Ivanov. What has the world come to," he mutters.

I grunt. "No shit. I can't wait to see her though."

His eyes light up. "Agreed. It'll be nice to have something good happen with all this going on."

Maybe it's the alcohol, or the fact I've always been able to say whatever to Maksim, but I admit, "I was having such a good time with Gemma before we pulled into the driveway."

His face hardens. "These interruptions to everyday life seem to be getting more frequent. Before Aspen, it was never this intense. Now that I have her, it seems there are so many more threats."

"Yeah. It's getting worse."

He studies me then asks, "Is Gemma your light?"

A lump grows in my throat. The feeling in my chest I keep getting that I can't explain pops up. I swallow hard.

"What do you mean?"

Maksim's steel gaze drills into mine. "Lately, I always wonder how I would get through it all if I didn't have Aspen. She makes the darkness disappear for me. At least until the next thing arises. It seems like something is going on between you and Gemma, so I'm wondering if she's your light."

I glance out the window at the passing Chicago skyline. "I don't know what's going on between Gemma and me. It's complicated."

Maksim huffs. "If it were simple, you should run."

I turn to him. "Why is that?"

He arches an eyebrow. "If it were too easy, she wouldn't be challenging you. You can't be a better man if your woman doesn't put you in your place every now and then."

I groan. "Don't worry. Gemma knows exactly how to push my buttons."

The car stops, and Maksim shuts his knife. "Sounds like a keeper to me." His face turns solemn. "Remember, I say stop, you don't move. I say back off, you let me take over."

I sigh. "You're taking all the fun out of this."

"You'll thank me later." He opens the door and gets out. I follow, and the driver leaves. We step into the garage and go to the back room.

Tiernan and Bodgen, Maksim's younger cousin, are both in the back. The moment Maksim agreed to let me use the garage and come with me, he had Tiernan pick Bogden up before bringing Orla's thug to the garage.

"What's his name?" I ask, assessing the naked man. His arms and ankles are tied with ropes and stretched as far as possible.

Tiernan's voice turns cold. "Rafferty Bailey. Third cousin to Orla. He came to the United States a few years ago."

Bogden steps in front of him and tilts his head. His Russian accent fills the room. "I've seen you before, haven't I?"

Rafferty scowls and says nothing.

I ask, "Where have you seen him?"

Bogden takes his knife out. "Let's be clear on how this is going to go. We ask questions, and you answer." He holds the blade at Rafferty's neck with the point on his Adam's apple. "Tell them where I've seen you."

"Go fuck yourself," Rafferty replies in a thick Irish accent.

Bogden tsks and slowly slices a line under his eye to his jaw.

Rafferty attempts not to scream, but his breathing picks up. Sweat pops out on his skin.

Bogden makes a cross on his chest at the same slow speed as the last cut. "I was coming out of Boris and Nora's building. You were in the lobby cafe, acting like you were reading a paper and lived there. But you don't belong in that building, do you?"

Short whimpers come out of Rafferty's mouth. He closes his eyes.

Maksim steps behind him and growls in his ear, "Why were you in my brother's building?"

Rafferty continues his silence, and piss drips down his leg. His body trembles.

Maksim places his knife on his spine. "Three...two...one—"

Rafferty cries out, "The baby! She wanted me to get the baby."

Chills fill my body. I lunge in front of him, pushing Bogden aside. I squeeze his throat and bark, "What did you say?"

He coughs, and his face turns red. I relax my hand slightly, and he scrunches his face. "Orla wants the baby."

Maksim leans into his ear. His voice turns colder. "And you were going to kidnap her?"

Rafferty closes his eyes and swallows hard.

"Where is Orla?" I demand.

"I don't know," he claims.

"Liar!" I yell, squeezing his throat tighter.

"Nolan, take a step back," Maksim commands.

But I don't. I can't. Something in me snaps. He stalked and threatened Gemma. He plotted to kidnap Nora's baby.

I scream in his face, "Where is Orla?"

His face turns purple as he gasps for air.

"Nolan!" Maksim shouts then pushes me.

I release Rafferty, breathing hard, and pull out my knife. I open it and hold it against his balls. "You're going to tell me right now where she is. If you don't, I'm going to—"

His eyes roll, and foam runs out of his mouth. His entire body violently convulses.

"Fuck!" Maksim mutters.

"What's happening?" Tiernan asks.

"He's having a heart attack or seizure, maybe both," Maksim replies.

I grab his neck again, completely out of control with rage leading my actions. I roar, "Where is Orla?"

Maksim claims, "You're wasting your energy. He's probably got less than a minute left."

Darragh's voice pops into my mind. *If he only has a minute left, make it painful.*

I stab my knife all over his body, as if it could somehow give me the information I need or make all the bad shit disappear. Blood flies all over the place. I get lost in a violent trance.

Maksim pushes me away, bellowing, "That's enough!"

I struggle to find oxygen and wipe my forearm over my blood-spattered face. Maksim's eyes are two slits. He calmly says, "He's dead."

I glance over his shoulder at Rafferty's corpse. His eyes are frozen open. Foam and blood cover his body, pooling at his feet, mixing with his piss. "Fuck!" I drop my knife on the ground, angry we didn't get any information about where Orla is hiding.

Maksim picks up my knife. He addresses Bogden and Tiernan. "Clean it up." He turns back to me. "Shower. Now."

I glance down at my clothes, frozen, wondering what Orla will do next to come after Gemma or Nora's baby.

"Nolan," Maksim snaps.

I look at him.

"Shower. Now," he repeats.

I close my eyes then open them and strip. I go into the bathroom and stand under the hot shower. Blood swirls down the drain. When the water runs clear, I finally pick up the soap and begin to scrub my body. After I shampoo twice, I put my forearm on the cold tile and rest my forehead against it.

Sean's voice fills my ears. *"The Baileys are coming for you. Watch your back."*

I gaze around the small space. Sean is nowhere, of course, but I hear it again.

"The Baileys are coming for you. Watch your back."

I swallow down the emotions crawling up my throat and turn off the water. I dry off and step out of the bathroom.

Maksim studies me a moment then nods to the shelf. "Get some clothes on. Have a seat. I'll be out soon."

I follow his instructions, getting changed and sitting at the desk. My knife is so clean, it looks brand new. I shut the blade and put it in my pocket. Then I pick up my phone and check to see if Boris called, but there's nothing. Gemma's cell is in my house, so I can't even call her. Not that I know what I would say. My heart races. I cover my face and breathe into my hands.

Maksim comes into the room, grabs clothes, and puts them on. He picks up his personal items. "Let's go."

I follow him outside. His driver is waiting, and we get in the car. My head is spinning with worry and fear. I'm unsure how I lost so much control, and I'm also embarrassed. Maksim told me to obey his orders, and I didn't. It's his garage. He did me a favor letting me bring Rafferty on his turf.

Maksim rolls down the divider window. "St. Joseph's then Club Seventy-Six."

I turn. "Why are we going to Club Seventy-Six?"

He raises his eyebrows. "Boris needs to know. Then, you need a drink."

"Pretty sure I've had enough today," I mutter.

Maksim grunts. "You can't go home to Gemma like this. Tonight, we drink vodka."

18

Gemma

"Gemma, stop pacing," Aspen orders.

I stop in front of the window. All of Chicago blinks against the dark night sky. My insides haven't stopped quivering since Nolan left. The sound of that man's Irish voice, along with his piercing eyes, brought up all the flashbacks of him threatening me. I remind myself he was tied up, and Nolan is the one in control, but I can't seem to shake the feeling something bad is going to happen.

Music blares through the room, and Aspen picks her phone up. She answers, "Maksim."

I race over to her.

She smiles at me. "You are?"

My heart beats faster. What if Nolan's hurt? Or he found out where Orla is and he's going after her now?

"Okay. See you in a few hours. Love you." Aspen hangs up and says, "Everything is fine. They handled the situation and are going for a drink."

"A drink?"

She nods. "That's what Maksim said."

"Is that normal after these types of situations?" I ask.

She bites on her lip and shakes her head. "No. But they're fine, not anywhere near the environment they were in, and will be home in a few hours." She slides her arm around my shoulder. "You can relax now. Why don't we have a drink, too?"

"No. You go ahead. I've had too many margaritas to count," I admit.

Aspen's eyes light up. "Ohh. Where from?"

"Miguel's."

She groans. "I'm so jelly. Those are the best. Did you get the dirty nachos?"

Thoughts of Nolan licking nacho sauce off my lips make me smile. "Yeah."

Aspen takes my hand and pulls me to the couch. "Sit." She grabs a blanket. As soon as I obey, she joins me and puts the throw over our legs. She leans in. "Okay. Now that we know they're okay, tell me what's going on between you and Nolan."

"Nothing," I lie. Aspen and Hailee have been best friends for as long as I can remember. Nolan and I don't even know what's going on between us. Talking about it with my sister's bestie doesn't seem like a good idea.

"Oh, come on," Aspen whines. "You looked like you were having a blast on St. Paddy's Day, and everything was great until Molly showed up."

"Ugh! Don't mention that little brat!"

Aspen holds her hands in the air. "Sorry." She wiggles her eyebrows. "Let's just talk about Nolan, then."

My pulse pounds in my neck. I turn to her. "Do you tell my sister everything?"

Aspen's lips twitch. "I don't have to."

I tilt my head. "Seriously. I don't want Hailee to know anything. I don't want to hear her lecture me about him or any other part of my severely screwed-up life."

Sympathy fills Aspen's expression. She softly says, "Your life isn't screwed up."

I blink hard. "Really? Has Hailee told you everything about who we are?"

Aspen nods. "Yes. She told me how it all came out and that your mom didn't ever tell you who your dad was. And she's really worried about you."

Tears fill my eyes. "She doesn't know the half of it."

Aspen's voice fills with concern. "What do you mean?"

Shame consumes me. "Nothing."

"Gemma—"

I rise. "Can I take a shower? I still smell like Miguel's."

Aspen gives me a small smile. "Sure."

"Thanks." I go down the hall and into the bedroom Aspen had me put my bag in when I arrived. There's an attached bathroom, and I turn on the water. I strip then study myself in the mirror.

My face looks like it's aged ten years. Little worry lines are now etched in the corner of my blue orbs. They weren't there nine months ago. My bloodshot eyes are probably from the alcohol. But before Nolan, they looked like this a lot from not sleeping. My body isn't in nearly as good of shape as it used to be. I've lost a lot of the muscle I worked hard to develop. Many people would look at me and not understand why it bugs me. I can put on any undergarments and nothing looks terrible to the ordinary person. But I know what I've lost. And I don't feel like me inside this body anymore.

I step into the shower, letting the hot water soak my hair. The stench of tequila and weed mix with the steam. I didn't smoke any, but it's one of the parting gifts you get when you leave Miguel's.

There are several bottles of shampoo. I smell them all and choose one with lavender in it, hoping it'll calm my nerves. I rinse, condition, then continue to let the hot water beat down on me.

When I finally get out, I brush my teeth and comb my hair. I debate about wearing the outfit I brought for tomorrow or Nolan's T-shirt, which is screaming for me to put it on. But since Nolan is coming back in a few hours, I opt for my yoga pants and an oversized sweatshirt.

Aspen's always been in my life, and I love her, but I don't want to answer her questions about Nolan right now. So I sit on the bed and open my laptop, wondering if anyone is looking to hire me.

I open my email, and my gut drops. There's only one new message besides all the junk emails. It's from Orla. There are only two sentences.

She killed her. You will all pay.

I swallow the bile rising in my throat and stare at the screen. Then it hits me that I don't even know if Orla is telling the truth. Was her mother even murdered?

I pull up my search bar and type in, Riona Ryan of North Carolina.

My stomach pitches so fast, I have to put my hand over my mouth. A picture of a woman resembling Orla fills the screen. Article after article discusses how authorities discovered her dead body from a drug bust gone wrong.

The date of her death might as well be a flashing neon sign. I know that date. My mother had a wall calendar to keep all our activities straight. Each year, she marked January fifth with a number. It increased each new calendar. One year, it said ten. I realized it was the anniversary of when she left my father. And each time it rolled around, my mother would buy herself a bottle of wine and drink the entire thing. Besides January fifth, my mother usually didn't consume alcohol.

I get so engrossed in reading article after article, I don't realize how much time has passed. The door opens, and Nolan stumbles in.

I close the laptop and jump up. "Hey! Are you okay?"

His green eyes drill into mine. In a low voice, he says, "I fucked up, Gemma."

I reach for his cheeks. "What do you mean?"

He shakes his head. Guilt fills his expression. "I don't know where she's at."

My gut sinks. "It's okay."

"No. It's not." He slides a lock off my forehead then tugs my hair. His finger traces my lips. "Do you know how pretty you are?"

My flutters kick off. I bite on my smile. "What have you been drinking?"

He rolls his eyes. "Vodka. I was with the Russian."

I laugh. "Are we staying here or going home?"

He palms my ass and tugs me into him. Then he dips his face over mine. "I like that you call my house home."

My butterflies go crazy, and I reprimand myself. He's drunk. I shouldn't think twice about anything he says. I repeat, "Are we going there or staying here?"

He scans the room then leans into my ear. His tongue flicks my lobe, and when he talks, his lips graze it. "I prefer you in my bed, princess. Don't you prefer to be in it?"

"Yeah," I say truthfully.

"When I'm there or on your own?" He arches an eyebrow.

I caress the sides of his head. "With you."

"Good. Let's go home, then." He brings his lips to mine, slides his tongue in my mouth, and massages his fingers on my scalp. "You're my light, princess," he mumbles then fucks me with his tongue.

"Mmm." I'm jelly in his arms, his to claim and possess all he wants. Drunk, sober, it doesn't matter. Any part of him he'll give me, I want. And whenever I'm with him, all the realities of my life— like what DNA is swirling in my body and Orla's latest threat—all seem to disappear.

"You taste like toothpaste," he claims.

"You taste like vodka," I reply then return to kissing him.

He retreats, studies me, and strokes the side of my head. "I mean it, Gemma. You're the most beautiful woman I've ever seen."

I can't help but smile. "You're drunk."

"No, I'm not."

I raise my eyebrows.

He grins. "Drunk over you, princess."

I laugh. "Now you're getting corny."

"I'm Irish. I'm supposed to be drunk and corny in love." He slides his hand in my pants, palming my ass, and tugs me against his erection.

My pulse skyrockets as he assesses me more. He's drunk, and he didn't say he loves me. He just said supposed to be, I tell myself.

He lightly kisses my forehead, under my eyes, nose, and lips. Then he steps away, picks up my bag, and puts my laptop in the case. He slings both over his shoulder then puts his arm around my lower back. His hot breath hits my neck, and his lips brush against my ear. "Let's go home and stay in bed all day tomorrow."

I tilt my head. "We don't have condoms."

He wiggles his eyebrows, removes his phone out of his pocket, and starts texting someone.

"What are you doing?" I ask.

He grunts, finishes, then announces, "Making Fergal go get extra-large condoms."

I bite on my smile. "Seriously?"

"Yep." He proudly grins. "Now, let's go." He guides me through Maksim's, we say goodnight, and go down to the car. As soon as the door shuts, he tugs me onto his lap, and his stomach growls.

I question, "Did you eat dinner?"

"No. Did you?"

"No."

He tilts his head and drags his finger over my breast. "You were supposed to make me dinner."

"I forgot all about that. This morning seems like forever ago," I admit.

His face darkens. "Yeah. So many good parts today. And so many bad ones."

I slide my hand through his hair. "Nolan, are you okay?"

He turns toward the window. "So close."

"What do you mean?"

"Rafferty. He knew where Orla is. But he died too soon." He turns back to me and sniffs hard. "At least I made his last minute more painful for ever hurting you and coming after the baby."

The hairs on my arms stand up. "Baby? Nolan, what are you talking about?"

He shakes his head. "Nothing. I'm drunk. Ignore me."

I firmly hold his cheeks. "Nolan, tell me right now what you meant."

He closes his eyes. When he opens them, the emotion swirling in them steals my breath. There's hatred, pain, and fear.

"Tell me," I insist.

He swallows hard. "He was stalking Nora, too. Orla wanted him to kidnap the baby."

A chill zaps me. It courses through every atom I have. I gape at him, my breath coming out in short bursts.

"Don't worry. Boris has iron-clad security on Nora. The baby won't be in any situation for Orla to take her."

"She can get to anyone," I state, convinced she's a ghost who can magically appear and disappear at her convenience.

Nolan's eyes turn to slits. "She will not get anywhere within a mile of my sister or her baby. Ivanovs and O'Malleys will make sure of it."

The car stops at a light. I glance out the window at the pedestrians walking around late at night. I used to do that. I never felt fear. Now, I wouldn't do it unless Nolan protectively had his arm around me and several of his men were following us. It's all because of Orla. If I don't stand a chance against her, how can a helpless baby? I quietly say, "You don't understand how she is. Once she sets her sights on something, she'll stop at nothing to destroy it. Do not let anyone in the hospital touch the baby unless Boris and Nora are there. Make sure the baby doesn't get put in the nursery."

Nolan sits up straighter. "Maksim and I already stopped at the hospital. Boris is aware."

A tiny bit of relief comes out in my shaky breath.

Nolan's face hardens further. His voice gives me more chills and also some comfort. He adamantly states, "I promise you, princess, if it's the last thing I do, I will have my day with Orla. And it will be her last one on earth."

19

Gemma

NOLAN'S WARM BODY IS PRETZELED AROUND MINE. HE'S A cocoon of safety I could get lost in, but I woke up over an hour ago, unable to stop thinking about my mom.

Could she have killed Riona?

No. It's not possible. My mother doesn't have it in her.

But I never thought I would kill anyone, and there are times I think I could kill Orla.

I attempt to move Nolan's arm, but he tightens it. He sleepily asks, "Where are you going, princess?"

I reach up and stroke the side of his head. "I was going to make breakfast. I think you need some sustenance after last night."

He pulls me on top of him. His eyes open. He winces then shuts them. "Might be a good idea based on the hammer in my head."

"Aww." I press my lips to his for a quick kiss. "I have the solution for that. Let me work my magic."

He slides his palms on the back of my thighs then tugs them so my knees are next to his hips. The tip of his erection touches my wet heat. He mumbles, "Maybe we should work it out a different way."

I softly laugh and inch my body higher on him, away from the temptation. I tease, "Eat first. Then you won't have a headache and can concentrate on me."

He opens his eyes. "Concentration on you won't ever be an issue."

I peck him quickly then push on his chest. "Let me take care of you for once."

His lips twitch. "Last night's a little fuzzy, but from what I recall, I think you're taking care of me all right."

My smile widens. "Be a good boy and release me. I'll show you how I reward you when you obey me."

He cocks an eyebrow. "Deal." He pats me on the ass cheek then lets go of me.

I roll off him, rise, and throw on his T-shirt he wore the previous night. I wag my finger. "Don't get out of bed. If you do, I'm not going to give you good boy status."

He salutes me. "Yes, ma'am."

I leave the room, fill a glass with coconut water, then take it to him. "Drink this while I'm making breakfast."

He sits up and takes it. "I think I could get used to you serving me."

"I'm usually the giver in my relationships," I state then heat creeps up my cheeks. Are Nolan and I in a relationship? Again, I'm not sure what we're doing.

He wraps his arm around my ass so I can't turn and run. "You don't think I'm a giver?"

I ruffle his hair. "Never said that. Now get the coconut water down you."

He smirks. "What do I get after I drink it, Ms. Giver?"

I smirk back. "Breakfast."

He playfully slaps my ass. "Good thing I'm starving."

I go back to the kitchen and pull out bacon, eggs, and bread. I set a skillet on the stove and ignite the burner. While it's heating up, I turn my laptop on.

My search from last night continues. I click on images. A few dozen of Riona Ryan appear. She's rarely smiling unless she's next to my father. I choose one, and it fills my entire screen.

Something feels off, and I can't put my finger on it. It's as if I know her. Surely, I wouldn't remember her if I was only a toddler? There are few things I recall about North Carolina. One was hiding in the closet with Hailee and my infant sisters. The second is my father's violence, which led to my mom's bloody body at times. The final thing is the night my mom fled with us.

I glance closer at the picture of the woman with red hair. It's remarkable how much she resembles Orla. I figure that must be why I feel like I've seen Riona before.

Nolan comes out of the bedroom in pajama bottoms. "What are you looking at?"

I slam the laptop shut. "Nothing."

He sets his glass in the sink and crosses his arms. "Had to be something."

My mouth turns dry. I blurt out, "I have a confession."

He waits for me to speak.

"I'm addicted to those pimple popper videos." It's actually the truth. I find them fascinating. I can get sucked into them for hours.

He scrunches his face. "Before breakfast?"

I shrug. "Any time of the day. The bigger, the better. I should concentrate on breakfast. Sorry, I shouldn't have pulled it up. I get nothing done when they're on." I put my laptop back in my bag.

Nolan cocks an eyebrow. My insides quiver, wondering if he's going to call my bluff. He finally admits, "I might have gotten sucked into a few videos on organ removal."

"Ewe. That's disgusting," I claim.

He picks up the pack of bacon. "More than your obsession?"

"Yeah. A lot more." I bump my hip into him. "Get out of the kitchen. You're supposed to be in bed."

Arrogance fills his face. "I'm feeling so much better. In fact, I think this should come off." He fists the T-shirt I'm wearing.

I huff. "And replace it with what?"

His face lights up. He opens the drawer and pulls out an apron with the O'Malley logo on it. "This."

Heat creeps into my cheeks. "And then what?"

A dirty grin appears. He points to the barstool. "I'm going to sit there and watch you cook for me. And my present for being a good boy is you get to sit on my cock while feeding me."

I laugh. "Is that so?"

"Yep." He tugs the T-shirt over my head so I'm naked then puts the apron on me and ties the strings. He spins me and leans into my ear. "Remember I said I'm a giver?"

I glance at him in question.

He splays his hand on my spine and pushes me over the counter. His foot moves my ankle toward the wall. He directs, "Stretch your arms and grip the edge of the counter. Keep your eyes on your hands."

There's no thought. My body is his to do with as he pleases, and I'll enjoy every minute of whatever it is he wants me to do. I reach forward and wrap my digits around the sides of the quartz.

His hand slips between my body and the apron. He glides two fingers in me and rubs my clit with his thumb.

I whimper.

A loud crack fills the air, and a delicious sting erupts on my ass cheek. I clench his fingers and cry out, "Oh God!"

He skims his nose up my spine, breathing deeply. He licks behind my ear. "I love how you smell, princess."

My toes curl as he circles his thumb faster. I blink to focus and whisper, "I'm gonna...oh..."

More zings fly from my ass cheek to my pussy as he smacks me again, rubs it out, then repeats it. His fingers and thumb manipulate me more intensely. Incoherent sounds fly out of my mouth as I orgasm so many times, my knuckles turn white. My legs turn to Jell-O, and my knees buckle.

"That's my girl," he growls in my ear and slides his hands up the sides of my body. The scent of my arousal fills the air. He shoves his fingers in my mouth, and I suck them. His hard erection presses into my tingling ass cheek. He murmurs, "Now I get to stare at my handprint on your ass and your flushed face while you cook for me. Perfect way to start the day."

I turn my head as more heat burns my cheeks. He pulls his fingers out of my mouth and pins his arrogant green eyes on mine. I say, "Glad you're feeling better."

His lips twitch. He gives me a chaste kiss and steps back. I slowly straighten up and spin into his chest. I drag my fingers down the side of his torso. "Why did you get a Celtic cross?"

Laced in his smile is sadness. "My mother said that unless Jesus was a tattoo artist, we weren't marking our bodies up. Sean and I got drunk one night and found a tattoo artist named Jesus. We even took his card to show my mother."

I gape at him then say, "You're lucky. He did an excellent job."

"Not exactly. The guy I use now had to do a lot to make it look like this. It was pretty bad."

"Really?"

"Yeah. Sean's was worse. His wasn't black. It was Kelly green and red."

"No!" I cover my mouth.

He nods, and his smile leaves his face. He hesitates then says, "My brother always did crazy things. He would have liked you."

Something about that statement chokes me up. I blink hard and take a deep breath. "I wish I could have met him."

Uncomfortable silence fills the air. I want to ask Nolan how Sean got involved with the Rossis or on the Bailey's radar, but I don't. He dips down, pecks me on the lips, and squeezes my ass. "Go make my bacon."

I laugh. "Are you a bacon lover?"

He steps back and looks at me like I'm crazy. "Is that a real question?"

"Guess not." I pick up the bacon package, open it, then lay the strips on the skillet. "Do you want scrambled or fried eggs?"

"Fried, but the yolks need to be runny."

I glance behind me. "Is there any other way to eat fried eggs?"

He grins. "Nope. Want me to put the toast on?"

"No. I got it. Sit down."

He plants himself on the barstool and picks his phone off the counter then sticks the charger cord in it. "Great. I hope I didn't miss a message about Nora and the baby."

"She can't still be in labor, can she?" I ask.

He snorts. "O'Malley women all have long labors. It's like a curse."

I put the bread in the toaster and push it down. "I guess it was nice of Nora not to want everyone waiting around the hospital."

"Yeah. Hospitals are the worst. Boris said she was only dilated to a four when we saw him last night."

I flip the bacon. "That sounds horrible. Crispy or floppy?"

"Crispy," Nolan replies, like it's a sin not to eat only crispy bacon.

"Another thing we agree on," I add. "So what are we doing today?"

He groans. "I hate to say this, but I should do some work while we're waiting for the baby. If I don't get this algorithm figured out, I'm going to be in trouble."

"It's okay. I have stuff to do on my computer anyway."

"Did anyone else get back with you about hiring you?" he asks.

My gut drops. It's disappointing not hearing back from anyone else. "No. But I thought I'd apply for some more."

Nolan states, "They're idiots not to hire you."

The toast pops up. I put a paper towel on a platter, add the bacon, and then crack the eggs into the skillet. I put the toast on a plate and butter it.

Nolan comes behind me and puts his arms around me. He softly says, "Hey."

I tilt my head up. "Yeah?"

He pins his green orbs on mine. "You're super talented. I'm proud of you for going after it. I know it sucks to not hear back or get what you want."

My heart skips a beat. "Thanks." Guilt eats at me for lying to Nolan. As soon as I can get on my laptop, I'm doing more research about Riona's death. I want to prove Orla wrong. Maybe if I can, she'll leave my mom, sisters, and me alone.

I finish making breakfast, Nolan pulls me on his lap, and we eat. After, he throws me over his shoulder and carries me kicking and screaming into the bathroom. We have some intense shower games then dress and go into his office.

For hours, I get lost reading everything I can about Riona's death. I go down the trail I've also gone down too many times since Orla appeared in my life. I research my father and anything I can find on the Baileys.

"Earth to Gemma," Nolan calls out, waving his hands in the air.

"Oh. Sorry!"

He chuckles. "Are you finding lots of new things to apply for?"

More guilt annihilates me. "Yeah. So what's up?"

"Want to go for a quick run then have sushi delivered for lunch?" he asks.

I smile. "Sure."

He studies me. "You okay?"

I shut my laptop. "All good. That sounds perfect."

We run and then shower. Once we get dressed, the sushi arrives, and we eat again before heading back into Nolan's office. Like before, I get engrossed in my search. It turns dark outside. An email pops up, and my chest tightens.

Dozens of pictures of my mother, sisters, and me are attached. We were in North Carolina. My twin sisters must have just been born. My father is in them, and I shudder. He's younger than when I visited him in prison, but his cruel eyes are the same. In almost all of them, my mother is scowling at Riona. I read Orla's message.

THINK YOUR MOTHER ISN'T CAPABLE? I DON'T SEE MY MOTHER *glaring, only yours. Time is running out for all of you.*

THE LONGER I STARE AT THE PHOTOS, THE SICKER I FEEL. I can't deny my mother's stare. She looks like she wants to kill Riona. I've never seen her have so much hatred on her face.

Another email arrives.

. . .

PERFECT SINNER

STILL DON'T BELIEVE ME? INTERESTING HOW THE SCARF YOUR mother wore in several of these pictures ended up at the crime scene, isn't it?

I click on the attached photo and study the scarf the police officer is holding. Then I look at the other images, already knowing it's the same one.

My stomach pitches. I leave the office, grab my phone from the counter, and go into the bathroom attached to my room. I stare in the mirror, hyperventilating and attempting to pull it together.

Nolan knocks on the door. "Gemma, you okay?"

"Yeah. I'll be out in a minute."

"Okay. Nora had the baby!"

I splash water on my face, dry it, then force myself to smile. I'm excited about the baby, but the thought that my mother could be a murderer haunts me. And it's not about her killing Riona. If she was anything like Orla, I can't say I blame my mother. But do I know anything about my mother if she could hide this from us after everything we've been through lately?

I open the door. "Is it a girl or boy?"

Nolan has never looked so excited. "It's a girl. They named her Shannon, after my nana. Boris said she has red hair, too!"

I reach up and hug him. "That's awesome. Congratulations, Uncle Nolan!"

He lifts me off my feet and kisses the top of my head. "They said we could come visit."

"Perfect. Let me throw on some makeup and I'll meet you in the family room," I say.

He nods and leaves. I grab the phone and call Hailee.

She answers after a few rings and chirps, "Hey, Gemma."

I clear my throat. "Are you going to the hospital to see the baby?"

Hailee's voice drops. "Yes, why?"

I close my eyes. "Okay. I need to talk to you when we get there."

"Are you all right?"

"Yes. I'll talk to you soon. Bye." I hang up before she can ask any questions or Nolan catches me on my phone. I hide it in the drawer next to the bed then put on some makeup.

Nolan and I go to the hospital. As soon as I see Hailee, I drag her to the corner of the room.

She hugs me tight. All the emotions I've been trying to choke down and hide from Nolan all day threaten to explode out of me. Hailee asks in a worried voice, "Are you okay? Liam just told me Orla cut you?"

It seems like so long ago. I haven't even thought about my thigh, consumed with whether my mother killed Riona or not. I nervously glance around to make sure no one can hear us. I reply, "I'm fine. But I need to know something."

Hailee furrows her eyebrows. "Okay. What is it?"

I lower my voice. "Did Mom say anything to you about Orla's mother, Riona?"

She shakes her head. "No. She's not said anything else besides what she revealed when we all met with her. I've not exactly been taking her calls, either. I blew her off again last night with an *I'm busy* text. Why do you ask?"

My heart races. I bite on my cheek, glance behind me, then tell Hailee, "Orla said something to me before the O'Malleys got to the locker room."

"About disabling the location services on your phone?"

I double-check no one is near us. "No."

In a firm voice, Hailee questions, "Gemma, what did she say?"

"I-I didn't tell Nolan or Liam."

"You didn't tell them what?"

The air in my lungs becomes stale. It's hard to breathe. I admit, "What she really said."

Hailee's eyes widen. "You lied to them?"

My eyes fill with tears. Guilt annihilates me. I've lied to Nolan after all he has done to protect me. The last day, we've come so far after everything that's happened between us, and it's tearing at my heart I can't tell him what's going on. If he finds out I lied, he's never going to forgive me. I stare at the wall and blink hard then put my hand over my mouth, trying to gain control of my unstable emotions.

Hailee wraps her arms around me. She whispers in my ear, "Just tell me. We'll figure out what to do with the information together."

I whisper back, "I-I-I researched it. I think Orla is telling the truth."

She tightens her hold on me. "About what?"

I swallow hard. "She told me she's going to destroy all of us. You, Ciara, Ella, and me. Only after the four of us suffer is she going to take Mom out."

Hailee freezes. "Why?"

My body begins trembling. "Everything matches, Hailee. The dates we left North Carolina line up perfectly."

Confusion fills Hailee's voice. "What matches?"

"The date her mother died. Orla..." I grip my big sister's hand. "Sh-she said our mother killed hers."

Hailee stares at me like I have two heads.

Nolan walks up to us. "We can go in and see the baby now." He assesses us. "What's wrong?"

I release Hailee's hand and wipe my eyes. "Nothing important."

"What did you say to Gemma?" Nolan asks Hailee.

Hailee gapes at him.

I state, "Nolan, she didn't—"

"My sister and I are allowed to talk. Mind your own business." Hailee hugs me and whispers, "We'll talk tomorrow."

I squeeze my arms around her then take a step back. I turn to Nolan and force a smile. "Ready to see the baby?"

His eyes dart between my sister and me. He reluctantly puts his arm around my back and says, "See you later, Hailee."

We go to Nora's room. Declan is talking to Boris in the hallway. We exchange congratulations with Boris and step inside. Killian is holding the baby. He kisses Shannon's head and says, "You did good, Nora."

"Time to hand her over," Nolan demands.

Nora turns to us, and her face lights up. "Hi!"

Nolan bends down and hugs her. "How are you doing?"

She smiles. "Tired, but good."

"O'Malley curse," Nolan comments.

She snorts. "You have no idea."

I hug her. "Congrats."

She holds my hand. "Thanks. Is my brother being nice to you?"

"Hey, I'm always nice," Nolan claims.

I smile. "Yeah."

Nolan holds out his hands, and Killian grumbles but passes Shannon to him. She curls into Nolan's chest, and it warms my heart. He's a natural with her. It hits me what a good father he'd make.

When it's my turn to hold the baby, I get teary-eyed again. "She's gorgeous. I can't believe all the red hair she has."

"Thank God she looks like her mother," Boris says, coming into the room.

We stay for an hour then leave. When we get in the car, Nolan asks, "What was going on between you and Hailee."

My stomach flips. "Nothing. Just sister stuff."

He slides his arm around my shoulders. "Are you okay?"

I straddle him and cup his cheeks. "I'm fine. Now tell me the dirtiest thing you've ever done in a car."

20

Nolan

A Few Days Later

A PHONE RINGS, WAKING ME UP.

Gemma stirs on top of me. Her groggy voice answers, "Hello."

I open my eyes, and she lays her head on my chest with the phone against her ear.

"Who is it?" I mumble, still getting used to the morning light.

Gemma replies, "Yeah. Where else would I be? It's super early in the morning." She yawns.

"I agree. Too early for talking." I yawn, too.

She traces my Celtic cross and says, "Nolan." She moves the phone away from her mouth and pecks me on the lips before asking, "What's going on that you had to interrupt my beauty sleep?"

I palm her ass and grunt. "As if you need beauty sleep."

Gemma furrows her eyebrows. She frantically questions, "Now?"

I refrain from cursing, knowing we're about to have our morning ruined.

She groans and sarcastically remarks, "I almost forgot all the realities of our awesome family dynamics."

The hairs on my neck rise. Anything to do with the O'Hare women never seems straightforward.

"See you soon. Bye," she chirps and hangs up.

I ask, "Who was that?"

"Hailee. She's coming over."

"What's going on?" I demand.

The same look Gemma gave me in the hospital appears. She claimed it was sister crap, but she didn't convince me it's not more. I asked her several times last night. She kept avoiding talking about it. Her eyes are focused on my tattoo as she traces it. I get the same response from her. "Just sister drama. Nothing for you to worry about."

I tilt her head so she can't ignore me. "Gemma, if something is going on—"

"It's nothing you need to worry about. I've told you this." Her voice is firm, but something in her eyes tells me there is more to whatever is going on between her and Hailee. She closes her eyes. "Please. You have O'Malley issues I'm not privy to. This is an O'Hare matter. Just let me deal with it on my own."

My pulse beats hard in my neck. I take a deep breath. She's right. I don't allow her access to every O'Malley issue. It's only fair I give her the same courtesy. Against my gut, I agree, "Okay."

She opens her eyes and exhales hard. "Thank you. I should get something to wear besides your T-shirt before Hailee comes."

The doorbell rings.

I give her a chaste kiss. "Stay here. I'll grab something from your room and answer the door."

She smiles, lighting up the world. The strange feeling in my chest rises. Every day, it's getting stronger, and I'm still not sure what to do with it. She chirps, "You're spoiling me now."

I pat her ass and rise. Without thinking, I blurt out, "Maybe you should get used to it."

She bites on her lip, and her cheeks flush. My heart pounds against my chest. She softly replies, "Maybe I should."

I wink. "I'll go grab your clothes." I throw on my pajama bottoms then go into her room. I select a black satin pajama set and take it to her. "This is nicer than my T-shirts you always wear."

"I like your T-shirts. They smell like you."

The flutters in my chest intensify. "I better get the door." I leave the room and answer the door. Gavin is standing next to Hailee. She gapes at my torso.

I tease, "My eyes are up here."

"Shut up." She shoves past me. Heat crawls up her cheeks. "Where's Gemma?"

I motion for Gavin to come inside. "Good morning to you, too, Hailee. Gavin, you want some espresso?"

"Nah. I'm good. Thought you didn't drink coffee?" Gavin asks.

"The princess requires it. She isn't a fan of my morning drink," I report, even though I make Gemma a smoothie without the raw egg.

"Smart girl. That shit is gross," Gavin replies.

"See, I'm not the only one who doesn't agree with raw egg smoothies." Gemma smirks, stepping through a doorway and into the room. She's wearing her black silk pajama shorts and a matching button-up top. My morning wood gets stiffer, and I make a mental note to see what other outfits she has in her room.

Hailee suspiciously glances between Gemma and me. "You two do know it's past eight, right?"

"Your point?" Gemma asks.

Hailee rolls her eyes. "The rest of the world is awake and has clothes on."

"Clothes are overrated," Gemma chirps. She takes a mug and fills it with espresso. "Want one?"

Hailee replies, "No, thanks. Can we talk in your bedroom?"

Gemma's face falls. "Sure." She motions for Hailee to follow her.

My radar that something isn't right and it's more than just O'Hare drama goes off. I tell myself to stop thinking the worst all the time and give Gemma the benefit of the doubt.

Gavin clears his throat. "You got a minute? I wanted to ask you something."

"Sure. What's up?"

Gavin shifts on his feet. He nervously runs his hand through his chestnut hair. "Luke saw Bridget and the kids."

The blood drains from my face. It's been so long since we heard anything from Sean's wife. And we all miss her and my nieces and nephews more than anyone could ever imagine. "In New York?"

"Yeah. You know my brother. Can't stay away for more than a month from that city."

Worry fills me. I hate not being able to see or watch out for them. "Are they okay?"

He nods. "Yeah. They were finishing their dinner. Bridget's father, Tully, was there. Luke talked to them for a few minutes then went to leave. He got in his car, and he said something told him to wait. Tully escorted Bridget and the kids to his car. But he didn't go with them."

Blood pounds between my ears. "Where did he go?"

Gavin pins his brows together. "He got in a car with Angelo Marino."

Goose bumps break out on my skin. Angelo is the head of the Italian mob in New York. He hates the Rossis, but I still don't know what business Tully would have with him. "Did you talk to Liam or Darragh about this?"

Guilt crosses Gavin's face. "No. Out of courtesy, I thought it was best to talk to you or your brothers first, since it regards Sean's wife and kids."

I pat his back. "Thank you. I appreciate you telling me. For now, can we keep this between us?"

"Of course." He opens the door and steps out.

I go into the bedroom and pick up my phone. I text my brothers.

Me: *We need to talk at some point today.*

Declan: *Is shit hitting the fan?*

Me: *No. But I just learned something, and I'm not sure what to make of it.*

Killian: *Your dick got hard, and you wonder why you want to stroke it?*

Me: *Did you set up that porn site yet so all your gay followers can watch you wank yourself off?*

Declan: *It's a shame to have all those videos you take of yourself go to waste, Killian.*

Killian: *Did you get your prescription for the blue pill yet, Declan?*

Declan: *Told you, little bro. My dick is stronger than steel. But I worry about yours with some of those lasses you've shagged.*

There's a knock on the door.

Me: *I'll text you later to meet up.*

I open the door, and my gut sinks. In an unfriendly tone, I ask, "Molly. What are you doing here?"

Hurt appears on her face, and I instantly feel guilty. She holds out a plate with foil over it. "I'm sorry. Is this a bad time? My mom and I were making cookies and made extra to say thanks for fixing our laptop again. And I have news about Colin."

I sigh and open the door.

There's no time like the present. I might as well get this over with.

"Come in." I sit on the couch and motion for her to sit in the chair across from me.

She puts the cookies down, takes a seat, and beams. "My brother arrives Saturday. My mom wants to have a surprise party for him. Can you come?"

I can't help but smile. I haven't seen Colin in years and miss him. Plus, it'll be great to hand him the reins back and not have to watch over his mom or Molly, especially since it bugs Gemma so much. "Sure. I talked to Colin last week, but he said he didn't know when he was flying out."

Molly's smile grows. She excitedly reveals, "He called this morning. Well, I should go. I know Gavin is waiting for you outside."

Hailee steps into the room. "Hi, Molly! He's with my driver."

Molly's face falls, and she scrunches her forehead. "Oh. Hi, Hailee. I didn't know anyone else was here."

"Gemma's showering then we'll be leaving," Hailee informs her.

Molly's face turns red. She looks at me in question. "Oh. Sorry. I didn't know she was still here."

I shift in my seat, not happy I have to tell Molly my business, with Hailee breathing down her neck. It may be inconvenient Molly likes me, but I still don't want to hurt her. I admit, "Yeah. She lives here right now."

Molly looks at the floor. Her hand slightly shakes and she rises. "Right. Okay. I'll see you later." She starts moving toward the door.

Crap.

I follow her. "Molly. Hold up."

She freezes, takes a deep breath, then spins. She forces a smile, but I know her well. She's about ready to cry, and it makes me feel horrible. She raises her eyebrows.

"Thanks for the cookies. I'll see you Saturday, okay?" I gently say.

"Mmhmm. Bye." She turns and quickly leaves.

The door shuts. I stare at it and sigh.

"Are you screwing her and my sister?" Hailee accuses.

I spin and growl, "What? Are you kidding me right now?"

"No. I think it's a fair question."

I shake my head in disgust. I'm beyond over Hailee interrogating me about Gemma every time she sees me. Now she's stepping into my personal business. "She's my best friend's little sister."

"So you're saying you aren't screwing her?"

My blood boils. I cross my arms. "Not that it's any of your concern, but I promised her brother when he left for a job in Europe I'd watch out for her. She's my friend. That's it."

Hailee purses her lips and tilts her head. "Does she know she's only your friend?"

I scrub my face and groan. If she hadn't come into the room, I could have set Molly straight. And I don't answer to Hailee, whether she's screwing Liam or not. "I'm not sure what it is about you O'Hare girls, but don't be spreading rumors around about Molly. She's a nice girl."

She points to the plate covered in foil. "I didn't say she wasn't. But women don't just bake cookies and bring them over to a man's house if they aren't into them."

"We're friends. She knows I like them and made extra. It's not a big deal," I claim, to shut her up. Molly has a crush on me. I see now. I'm not in denial anymore, but Hailee needs to mind her own business.

"Last week, it was a pot of fish stew," Gemma snarls, walking into the room, dressed for the day and her purse in her hand.

I scowl. After everything we went through yesterday, I expect her to cut me some slack. I promised her I would take care of it. Does she expect me to break Molly's heart with Hailee in the room? "This is getting old. Princess, why don't you and your opinionated sister butt out of my friendship?"

"Maybe you should stop leading the poor girl on if you aren't interested," Hailee retaliates.

"Right? Glad you see it, too," Gemma adds.

I groan. "What is with you two?"

"She likes you," Gemma points out, as if we haven't already discussed this.

"Yep," Hailee agrees.

"You two, stay out of my business. Where are you going?" I ask.

Gemma huffs. "Guess your statement goes two ways, doesn't it? Let's go, Hailee."

"Gemma—"

"Don't start, Nolan. The new bodyguards are here, so I don't have to tell you my every move. Or do you have concerns about them, too?" She glares at me.

I study her for a moment then shake my head. We came so far only to move ten steps back again. "Have a good day, princess."

"Yeah. You, too, prince charming," Gemma snaps back and slings her purse over her shoulder.

"How do you two live together?" Hailee questions, glancing between us.

Neither of us answer. Gemma gives me one final pissed-off look then they leave.

"Damn it!" I mutter and watch them get into the car with all the bodyguards. Several minutes pass before my insides calm down, but something nags me, and I'm not sure what.

I go into the kitchen and make my smoothie. I gulp it down then shower. The entire time, the uneasiness I felt when Gemma left only grows. Cold water starts to hit my back. I turn off the water, dry off, and my phone rings. I answer, "Liam."

He barks, "Did you let Hailee and Gemma go to their mother's on their own?"

My pulse increases. "I didn't know where they were going. But the bodyguards are with them."

"I'm pulling in. Get your ass in the car," he bellows and hangs up.

Shit. Shit. Shit!

Something is going on. I should have listened to my gut. I quickly get dressed and get in the car. I ask, "What's going on?"

The driver reverses, and Liam scowls. "Gemma lied. Orla didn't cut her because she turned off her tracker. She said Jane killed Riona. Hailee and Gemma researched it. They think it might be true, and Hailee also thinks Jane and Riona were sisters."

My stomach pitches. Not only did Gemma lie to me, but she did it several times. I swallow hard. "So Jane would be a Ryan?"

Liam's face turns darker. "Yeah. It looks like the O'Hare women have Bailey and Ryan blood running through them."

I grip the edge of the seat. The Ryans are just as bad as the Baileys. The two crime families have had an alliance forever. "How did we not know this?"

Liam clenches his jaw. "I'm not sure."

"Wouldn't Darragh have known this?"

Liam gazes out the window. He sniffs hard and lowers his voice. "I don't want you to repeat this."

"Okay. You have my word."

He turns to me. "My father's cancer is getting worse. I think it's affecting some of his memory and decision-making skills."

I inhale deeply. "Then you need to take charge."

"Go against my father?"

I tap my fingers on my thigh. "We all love and respect Darragh. But the clan can't afford long-term effects of him making bad decisions, and you know it."

The car parks on the curb of Jane's building. Liam doesn't say anything, and we go inside. Since he added protection on Jane and the O'Hare sisters, we have immediate access to all of their buildings. We go directly to Jane's unit and stand outside, neither of us talking.

Several minutes pass. The door cracks open and then slams shut. Liam spins in front of it, and I step next to him.

"Mom! Stop acting like a crazy lunatic!" Hailee yells.

"What do you think your father will be like? This isn't lunacy. You don't know what lunacy is," Jane's voice fires back.

Liam and I glance at each other.

"Mom!" Hailee yells again.

Jane says, "Go sit down. You aren't leaving until I'm ready to go."

"Get out of our way," Gemma cries out and then shrieks in pain.

The handle turns, and Hailee screams, "Move!"

Liam shoves his way through the door with me in tow. I tug Gemma into me. Her cheek is bright red with a hand mark on it. I seethe, "You hit her?"

Jane looks at Gemma as if she didn't even realize what she did.

I pull Gemma's head to my chest.

"Oh God. Gemma! I'm sorry! I..." Jane puts her hand over her mouth and breaks down crying.

I breathe through my nose, trying to stop myself from doing something I'll regret to Jane.

"We're leaving now. When you've calmed down, you can talk to your daughters. Until then, stay away. But know this, Jane Ryan. You and your daughters are under my watch, *my orders*. If you attempt to leave Chicago without my blessing, you won't get past your front door. Understand?" Liam threatens.

Jane's face completely crumbles. We whisk Gemma and Hailee to the car. I put my arm around Gemma, but the shame and pain on her face almost cripples me. And I wonder how much more she can take.

The one thing that sticks out from our conversation is what Hailee reveals.

"My mom thinks we should run. But they'll find us, won't they?"

I swiftly answer, "They had to have been watching you for years. It's not possible to escape them. For whatever reason, they left you alone all this time. Running again will only get you all killed."

Gemma shivers, and I tighten my arm around her. If Jane thinks she's taking my princess out of Chicago, she's going to deal with my wrath. I'm not letting Gemma anywhere out of my sight.

21

Gemma

THE COLD COMPRESS NOLAN HOLDS TO MY CHEEK MAKES ME wince. My mother has never hit me before. I've never seen that crazed look in her eye or imagined she could have any violent tendencies in her. Her hand left a mark on my cheek. A faint bruise has already appeared, and my face is swelling.

I thought I couldn't feel any more shame, but I was wrong. My mother hurting me creates an additional layer. It weaves around the lies I told Nolan and everything Orla's put me through.

Nolan's green eyes study me. Excruciating silence stands between us. He knows I lied to him. I see it in his expression. Every second that passes without him calling me out about it only makes my anxiety deepen.

My voice shakes. "Are you sending me to Liam's?"

His chest slowly fills with air. In a low voice, he asks, "Why did you lie to me, Gemma?"

Tears blur my vision. I turn toward the wall and attempt to contain them. My lips, hands, and insides quiver so hard, I fail at my attempt to stop my emotions. I wipe my cheek without the ice on it. "I didn't think it could be true. I-I know you already hate my mom. I thought if I could somehow prove it wasn't true, then maybe Orla would stop coming after us."

"Before today, I didn't hate your mom. After today, I'm not a fan. I don't know what to think, but I'm trying not to loathe her since she's your mom," he admits.

I close my eyes, wishing I could stop my tears, afraid Nolan's going to send me to Liam's.

He turns my chin and forces me to look at him. "You should have told me. I could have helped you."

I choke out, "It's my mom."

His arms circle me, and he pulls me into his chest. I lose it, not able to keep it together. He strokes my hair and mumbles against my head, "Shh."

"Please don't send me to Liam's," I cry out.

Nolan fists my hair and tugs it. "I'm not sending you to Liam's."

I sniffle. "No?"

"No. But don't lie to me again, Gemma."

Relief consumes me. I nod, unable to speak.

He kisses my forehead and slides me onto his lap so my unharmed cheek is against his warm flesh. He holds the ice pack on the hurt one, and I grimace.

"Sorry, princess. You'll thank me later."

I curl into him more, trying to ignore the sting of the cold on my sensitive skin. I mutter, "I like your slaps better."

He strokes my hair and kisses my head. "I wish we could have one normal day."

"Me, too," I agree, and the foil plate Molly dropped off catches my eye. I sit up and attempt to keep my voice even, but the stress I feel about her doesn't help. "What was Molly doing here?"

Nolan shifts and stares at the ceiling.

I quietly ask, "You aren't going to tell me?"

He pins his green gaze on me. In a firm voice, he answers, "She brought over thank-you cookies and to invite me to the surprise party her mom is throwing for her brother, Colin. I was going to talk to her, but your sister walked in and accused me of screwing her and you."

I blurt out, "I didn't tell Hailee about us. She asked, and I blew her off."

He clenches his jaw. "Did you miss the part where I said she stated I was sleeping with Molly?"

"I'm sorry."

He studies me then says, "I told her you're living here. Hopefully, she'll realize it's not ever going to happen between us. I still plan on talking to her though. And Colin is back Saturday. I'm going to discuss this with him, too."

I nod. "All right. I'm sorry about Hailee."

His face hardens. "Do you think you could tell her to back off? I'm getting tired of her coming at me every time we're together."

"Yeah. I'll talk to her," I promise.

He runs his hand through my hair and holds my face in front of his. "If I take you to the surprise party, can you be nice to Molly? Even if she does something to get under your skin?"

My stomach flips. "Do you prefer I stay home?"

"No. I want you to come with me and meet Colin. But I don't want any issues in his mom's house."

I understand why Nolan is concerned, but it still hurts. I assure him, "I know how to behave."

He sighs. "Gemma, I didn't mean it like that."

I force a smile. "I'm fine. Are you working all day?"

Nolan's phone vibrates. "Hold on." He glances at the screen. "Killian and Declan are on their way over. I have to discuss some things with them in private."

"About my mother?"

He furrows his eyebrows. "No. It's something to do with Sean's wife's family."

The hairs on my arms rise. "Are they okay?"

He smiles, but it looks as forced as mine. "Yeah. Hey, do you want to go to the gym and have a boxing lesson with my uncle Patrick today?"

I cringe. "Like a legitimate boxing session where someone is hitting me in the face?"

He laughs. "No. You're too pretty to risk your face getting destroyed. Plus, I think you got hit enough today. But he'll put us through a hard-core workout if you want."

"That sounds fun. I'm in. Can you take me to Ella and Ciara's apartment later tonight? I need to tell my sisters about my mom."

"Sure." He picks up his phone and sends a text message.

I put my hand behind his neck. "I have a question."

His thumb strokes my spine. "What's that?"

"Why did you tell me the first night we met you aren't a boxer?"

His face darkens. "I used to fight like Killian. All of us did. When I was thirty-two, I went down pretty hard. I got a concussion, and it screwed me up for a while. After that, I decided it was better to call it quits. So now I train, but I don't engage in combat."

"Unless you're kicking thugs' asses at the pub?" I tease.

He grins. "Yeah."

"Do you miss it?"

"Sometimes."

I lean in and kiss him then freeze.

"What's wrong?" he asks.

I swallow the lump in my throat. "I should tell you something else I just found out."

"What is it?"

My stomach quivers. "My father is being released from prison in two weeks."

Nolan's eyes turn to slits. "He's not coming near you. I mean it. He'll have to come through me first."

"He umm..." I stare at the ceiling and gather my thoughts. "When Orla made me visit him in prison, he said when he got out, my time was up. The man he said he's giving me to—"

"Giving you to? You aren't an object for him to hand over," Nolan growls.

I bite on my lip.

Nolan closes his eyes briefly. "Sorry. Please finish."

Fear fills me. The memory of the video Orla sent with the man telling me what he wants to do to me sends a chill down my spine. "My father said he's expecting me when he gets out."

Nolan confidently states, "Listen to me. As soon as your father is paroled, we'll hunt him down. My cousins are already tracking the man from the video."

I hold my breath. "You saw the video?"

He tilts his head. "I saw everything."

I look away. More shame fills me. I'm not sure what I thought Nolan saw the night he found me with the pills. Something about him seeing everything embarrasses me.

He turns my chin back. "Why does this upset you?"

"It doesn't. It I-I don't know. I just..." I stare at his chest as more tears fill my eyes. "I hate everything about that night and what I almost did. And everything Orla sent me..." My stomach flips.

He makes me look at him again then sternly says, "None of that is your fault."

There's a knock on the door then Killian and Declan walk in.

Nolan sighs. "I have to deal with this."

"It's okay. Want me to make lunch?" I rise.

"What are you making, Gemma?" Killian asks.

"She didn't ask you," Nolan reprimands.

I laugh. "Not sure. Are you picky?"

Declan steps in front of me. He sternly asks, "Gemma, what happened to your face?"

I glance at Nolan then say, "Nothing. I'm fine."

Killian peers closer. "Yep. You got a shiner."

I turn to him. "Does your mouth ever get you in trouble?"

He opens it to speak, and Nolan cuts him off. "Let's go into the office."

Declan and Killian scan my cheek again but finally leave. Nolan gives me a quick kiss on the forehead and a pat on the ass and follows.

I go into the kitchen and make a salad and sandwiches. Nolan and his brothers come into the kitchen as I'm finishing.

I put the platter of sandwiches on the table and chirp, "Just in time."

Declan and Killian sit across from Nolan and me. After we get salad and sandwiches on our plates, Declan says, "Gemma, Nolan said you're a kick-ass marketing guru."

I shrug. "I'm in marketing, yes."

"Stop being humble. She'll blow any graphic designer out of the water and can think of awesome slogans, too," Nolan brags.

"You should work on some things for the new company," Declan says.

"You should create a new hashtag for us to use when we launch. Something cool and easy to remember but trendy," Killian says.

"Maybe hashtag Killian jerks off to his selfies," Declan says with a straight face.

Killian grunts. "Hashtag Declan has to pay for it."

I laugh.

Nolan grins and puts his arm around my back. "What do you think? Want to design some stuff for our new tech company?"

I smirk. "Are you asking me because I'm unemployed, no one is responding to my job applications, and I'm bored most of the day?"

Amusement fills Nolan's face. His hand reaches under the table and he slides it onto my thigh. "Are you bored most of the day?"

My cheeks turn to fire, and I elbow him.

"Seriously. We should get started on all this stuff," Declan adds.

Nolan wiggles his eyebrows. "You should say yes."

"You haven't even told me what kind of tech company you're starting," I state.

"I didn't?"

"No, you didn't."

"Hmm. Okay. It's a cybersecurity firm."

Killian grabs another sandwich off the platter. "This is how it works, Gemma. Nolan's the algorithm guy. Declan is the hacker. Then you have me. Together we have three excellent brains."

"And what do you do?" I question.

Killian's arrogant expression fills his face. "Surprised you have to ask. I'm sales and marketing...just not what you do."

"Really?"

He sits back in his chair. "Why do you seem surprised? I'm the one with the personality."

I laugh.

Nolan tugs me closer to him. "What do you say? Want to give it a shot?"

Since I've got nothing else going on, I agree. "Sure. What are you naming it?"

Killian snorts. "O'Malley's. What else would we call it?"

22

Nolan

A Few Days Later

My brothers and I decide Declan will fly to New York and speak with Tully. Bridget may have cut off our access to my nieces and nephews and changed their last names, but they're still O'Malleys. If something is going on between the O'Connors and Marinos, then we have a right to know.

Twice this week, we had my uncle Patrick give us a boxing workout. Gemma quickly picked up the form and looks like a pro. Most days, we fall back into our routine we previously had. We get up, drink a smoothie, and run.

After we shower, we get to work. I make progress on the algorithm. She continues creating some super-cool marketing assets for O'Malley Cybersecurity.

Saturday comes, and Tiernan drops off the burner phone I asked him to pick up. I hand it to Gemma. "Thought you might miss having a phone."

Guilt fills her face.

I squint. "Why are you looking at me like you did something wrong?"

She sighs, goes into her bedroom, then comes out with her phone. "I had it in my dresser. I called Hailee before we went to see the baby at the hospital."

I focus on the ceiling, counting to ten. It was part of the lies she told me. We already talked about it, and it's in the past, but her dishonesty still makes my skin crawl.

She wraps her arms around my waist. "Nolan. I'm sorry. I forgot it was in there. I haven't used it except for that one call, I swear."

I glance down into her blue eyes and can't stay mad. "Okay. Don't do it again. This phone needs to stay off."

"I promise I won't touch it again." She reaches up and pulls my face toward hers. She kisses me, and I fall into it, forgetting about the phone I wish I could blow up but don't. From time to time, I check if Orla is trying to contact her to see her latest threats.

She ends our kiss and smiles. "Thanks for getting me a new one."

"It's a burner, nothing fancy."

She shrugs. "I don't use my phone like I used to. I don't need all the extra bells and whistles. This is perfect. Thank you."

I tuck a lock of her hair behind her ear. "You're welcome. How much time do you need to get ready for Colin's party?"

"Maybe an hour."

I glance at the time. "You should get moving, then."

She turns to leave, and I spin her back into me. My heart pounds faster. She arches her eyebrow in question. I say, "Why is all your stuff still in the other room?"

"Where's it supposed to be?"

"You're in my bed every night," I state.

She tilts her head. "And?"

"I think we should move it in my room, so you aren't going back and forth all the time."

Her lips twitch. "Back and forth as in down the hall?"

"Yeah." My stomach flips with nerves, as if I'm a kid again and asking a girl out for the first time.

She chirps, "Well, you do have that nice vanity no one is using."

"Exactly. And I have plenty of room in my closet."

She drags her finger over my Celtic knot tattoos on my biceps. "What about your drawers? Do I get a few?"

"I can make that happen."

"And who sleeps on the couch if we get in a fight? You or me?"

I chuckle. "Don't you mean sleep in the spare room?"

"That's just a detail. So you or me?" she repeats.

I palm her ass. "Do you plan on fighting with me a lot?"

"No. Are you avoiding committing to an answer?"

"Nope. I'll sleep in the spare room, princess."

She smiles. "Okay. I'll move my stuff in this weekend, then."

I happily kiss her. "I'll clean my drawers out. And maybe you should wear one of those sexy little outfits you've got stashed in them."

She gasps. "Nolan O'Malley! Have you been snooping through my stuff?"

I put my hands in the air. "No! I saw them when I grabbed your stuff the morning Hailee came over."

She pauses for a moment then questions, "What color did you like?"

There's no hesitation. I've been obsessing over what she'd look like in it since I saw it. "The blue one that matches your eyes."

She cocks an eyebrow. "Maybe I'll wear it under my dress tonight."

I groan. "Now I'm going to be distracted all evening."

She pats my cheek. "Good. Think about that when you're telling Molly to find someone else to post on her social media accounts. See you in an hour." She walks away.

Annoyance takes over. I'm not looking forward to having a conversation with Molly or Colin, but I also want to get it over with. I go shower and put on black slacks and a sage-green button-up shirt.

My phone rings. I glance at it and answer, "Boris. Everything okay?"

His Russian accent is thicker than normal. He angrily states, "Bogden picked up someone you and I need to deal with."

The hairs on the back of my neck rise. "It's him?"

Boris seethes, "Yeah. He had the balls to take photos of Nora and me taking Shannon out of the penthouse."

"He's at your place?"

"Ready and waiting for us."

I glance at my watch. Eamon Lynch, the man who Rory promised Gemma to and who sent her the vile video describing how he was going to defile her, is a man I'm itching to inflict pain on. But I'm not letting him ruin our night. "Colin's surprise party is in less than an hour. Let him sit until tomorrow."

Boris sniffs hard. "Done. Probably best if I have a night to calm down."

"Nora and Shannon are okay, right?" I double-check.

"Of course."

Relief soars through me. "Give Shannon a kiss for me."

"Will do. See you tomorrow." Boris hangs up.

Gemma comes into my room and puts her hand on my back. "Everything okay?"

I spin, and she steals my breath. Gemma can be full of sweat or just waking up, and she's the prettiest woman I've ever seen. But I don't see her dressed up very often. She's stunning in a simple light-pink sweater dress and knee-high black boots. Long curls frame her face. Her makeup is simple, but her eyes and lips pop more than usual.

I wrap my arm around her waist and rest my palms on her ass. "You look gorgeous."

She puts her hands on my chest. "Thanks. So do you."

"I have some great news."

"Oh?"

"Bogden picked up Eamon Lynch."

She inhales sharply then swallows hard. "Where is he?"

"The Ivanovs have him. Bogden caught him taking photos of Nora and Shannon when they left the penthouse."

"What?" she cries out.

"It's okay. Nora and Shannon are safe. He's in a secure location. Tomorrow, Boris and I will take care of him," I assure her.

She nods then her unsure smile appears. "So one less threat to worry about?"

"Yes. We have something else to celebrate tonight. Tomorrow, I'll drop you off at Boris's. You can stay with Nora and Shannon."

She slides her hands around my neck. Worry fills her expression. "And you'll be safe?"

I confidently state, "We're in control of this situation. Nothing can go wrong."

She releases a nervous breath. "Okay."

I push the collar of her dress aside and peek at the light-blue lace. "You're going to distract me all night."

She softly laughs. "I didn't know you were into lingerie."

I move my head back. "What made you think that?"

She shrugs. "I don't know."

I lean into her ear and take a quick lick of her lobe. She inhales sharply, and I murmur, "I'm very, very into it, especially on your sexy little body."

She grazes her nails on my neck. "Maybe I'll have to go shopping."

I tug her ass into my growing hard-on. "Don't tease me, princess." I give her a playful swat and a chaste kiss. "We should go so we aren't late for the surprise." I lead her out of the house. One of her bodyguards and a driver are in the front. The second bodyguard is in the back seat of the black SUV. We get in. It takes less than a minute to get to Colin's mother's house.

I step out and reach inside for Gemma. She gets out and takes a deep breath. I ask, "Are you okay?"

She admits, "Yes. I'm normally not nervous about meeting new people. I'm just a bit anxious being on Molly's turf."

I firmly state, "You don't need to worry about her. And my brothers will be there, too. When I get a chance to talk to Molly and Colin, you stay with them, okay?"

"Sure."

I hesitate, not wanting to piss Gemma off, but feel it's necessary to say, "Molly can be a loose cannon at times. If she is anything but friendly, try to ignore it."

"I'll be the bigger person," Gemma claims.

"Good, because you are." I kiss her quickly, satisfied with her answer, then lead her into the house. The room is full. Colin's mom is standing next to Molly. I hug Molly like I usually would then do the same to his mom but add a kiss to her cheek. "Rose, this is Gemma."

"It's nice to meet you." Rose smiles kindly and hugs Gemma.

Molly glares at Gemma. "I didn't know you were coming."

I tug Gemma protectively into me. "Sorry. Since she's living with me, I thought you would assume that."

Molly's face hardens, and she looks away.

"It's fine. Gemma, please make yourself at home," Rose assures us.

"Thank you. You have a lovely home," Gemma replies.

Rose smiles and glances around. "I've lived here for forty years. It needs an update." She steps back. "Please, grab some food and drinks."

Killian and Declan are in the back of the room. I steer Gemma to them, and the lights flick on and off.

"He's down the street, everyone quiet!" Molly yells then steps outside with Rose. The door shuts, and whispers fill the room.

"When did you get back?" I ask Declan.

Declan shifts. "An hour ago. It's an alliance. Tully said things are getting a bit rocky in New York."

"What does that mean?" I ask.

"You know Tully. He wouldn't go into details. But he trusts Angelo."

"And Bridget and the kids?"

Declan crosses his arms. "He claimed there's nothing to worry about."

"Did you see them?" I ask.

Declan's face turns dark. "Bridget wouldn't let me. She told Tully she doesn't want to confuse the kids."

Killian spouts, "Confuse them? By letting them see their uncle? Bridget's the only one confused."

"They're coming," someone half-whispers, half shouts.

The room goes quiet, the door opens, and Colin steps in. A chorus of "Surprise!" fills the air.

Colin's eyes widen, and a big grin appears. I let him make his way through the crowd. Molly is attached to his hip the entire time.

"Where's the restroom?" Gemma asks.

"Down the hall. I'll take you, lass. I've gotta go, too," Killian states. He leads her away.

Colin finally steps in front of us. "Nolan! Declan!" We all slap hands and embrace.

Declan says, "Never thought you were coming back."

I take a step closer to Declan to attempt to avoid Molly practically standing on top of me. I focus on Colin. "How was Europe?"

Colin's arrogant and mischievous expression appears. "Fun. Exhausting. Over it and ready to go back at the same time."

"That makes no sense," Molly chirps.

He glances at her. "Guess you had to be there." His face turns serious. He motions to Declan and me. "Let's step out back for a minute and talk."

"Good idea," I agree.

We get to the back door, and he says, "Molly, you stay inside."

"Why?"

"I have business to discuss, and it's not any of yours."

Molly pouts. "You just got home and are already leaving me out of things."

"Don't be dramatic." He nods for us to go outside.

Molly lets out an exasperated sigh.

We step onto the deck. The air is warm for spring and a hint of daylight is still out. Colin shuts the door.

Declan inquires, "What's going on?"

Colin steps closer. He gazes around then says, "I've got a message for you from Phelan."

Phelan runs the O'Malley clan in Ireland. He's our cousin and took over when his father died a few years ago. I scratch my jaw. "What is it?"

"The Baileys are sending more thugs over to the States. He said to make sure you're all prepared. The line Darragh and him speak on is compromised."

Anxiety flares in my chest. "How many are they sending?"

"Phelan thinks one hundred, maybe two."

"Shit," Declan mutters.

Colin nods. He steps closer to me. His eyes turn to slits. "Now, there's something else I want to know."

My stomach flips. "What's that?"

His face hardens. "Something going on with you and my sister?"

I groan.

His face turns red. "What does that mean?"

Declan puts his hand on his chest. "Cool it."

He jerks his head at Declan. "It's my sister."

I cross my arms. "I'm glad you brought this up. I was going to tell you that your sister has some wrong ideas in her head."

"Oh? Why is that?" he snarls.

"Stop getting defensive about assumptions. I'm here with Gemma. She lives with me. I can assure you I'm not interested in Molly, nor have I ever been. I never even saw her social media page until a few days ago when Killian showed it to me. If I had known she had a crush, I would have set her straight," I assure him.

He studies me. "You look pretty cozy in some of those pictures."

"He's drunk at the pub in almost all of them. Put two and two together," Declan claims.

"Why was she at your house? You were cooking her breakfast, and she was in your T-shirt," Colin interrogates.

The more he accuses me of being with Molly, the more pissed I become. "Your sister was drunk. Your mom was gone, and she was throwing up. I had her sleep in my guest room so she didn't choke on her puke. As I said, I didn't know she was taking pictures of me and posting. She's also been showing up at my house unannounced lately and needs to stop."

"So nothing is going on?" Colin asks.

"No."

Declan backs me up. "He's not with your sister. I can assure you."

Colin takes a deep breath then nods. "Okay."

All these years, I didn't mind watching over his mother and Molly. But now it seems like a big inconvenience. I remind him, "All I've done is watch out for her and your mom like you asked me to. And I'm going to take her aside tonight and tell her she needs to remove me from her social media and understand it's not happening between us."

Colin shakes his head. "No. I'll talk to her. Tomorrow, when no one else is around. I'll go through her social media with her and make her delete everything."

I can't lie and say I'm not happy to let him be the one delivering the message to Molly. "Okay."

He pats me on the back. "Thanks for taking care of them. I'm sorry if my sister is giving you issues. I hoped as she aged, she'd start reading situations better, but it doesn't sound like it."

Declan adds, "She's a good lass and hard worker. She just needs to put her focus on someone else."

"Let's go inside. I want you to meet Gemma," I say.

He nods and opens the back door.

"What!" Gemma's voice cries out.

"For real?" Killian barks.

"Oops. Sorry," Molly says.

"That was on purpose," Killian states.

"No, it wasn't," Molly claims.

I push past Colin and into the kitchen. A wet, red stain covers the back of Gemma's dress and her hair. I step in front of Molly. "What the fuck did you do?"

Her lips tremble. "I-It was an accident."

I scowl at her then turn to Gemma. I grab a towel off the counter and dab at her dress. She glances up at me, and tiny breaths come out of her mouth.

"That was low, Molly," Killian reprimands.

"It was an accident!"

"No, it wasn't!"

Colin steps between Molly and Killian. "Hey. If my sister says it was an accident, then back off."

Killian points at Molly. "I saw her with my own eyes. She didn't slip or fall. She tossed her drink on her. I was behind both of them."

"You're accusing—"

"It's all over Gemma's hair. Her drink wouldn't be in the air," I growl then squeeze the freezing liquid out of her locks. I shake my head at Molly. "This is low. I expected more out of you."

"It was an accident!" she claims again.

I toss the towel on the counter. "Good to see you, Colin. Text me tomorrow after it's done." I put my arm around Gemma's waist. Her body is trembling. "Let's go."

"Nolan. Wait!" Colin demands.

I spin with Gemma.

He steps forward and kisses Gemma's cheek. "It's nice to meet you. I'm Colin. I'm sorry about my sister." He throws daggers at Molly.

Gemma smiles. "It's nice to meet you, too."

"Let's get together another time?" Colin asks.

Gemma answers for me. "Sure. That would be nice."

"Okay. I'm sorry again about your dress and hair."

"Not your fault," Gemma replies.

"I'll see you later," I fume, so pissed at Molly, I need to get out of here or I'm going to say something I regret. I guide Gemma out the door and text my driver. He's only down the street and pulls up quickly.

We get in the car. I turn to Gemma. "I'm sorry. I can't believe she did that."

Gemma takes a deep breath. "Colin seems nice."

I slide my arm around her. "I'm impressed with how you handled that."

Gemma's face hardens. "It only took her destroying my dress for everyone to see her true colors."

I sigh and tug her into me. "I'm sorry."

"I take it you didn't get to break her heart yet?" She raises her eyebrows.

"Colin is talking to her tomorrow. He'll make sure she removes all the pictures of me off her social media," I inform.

She turns to the window and mutters, "She's lucky I didn't punch her."

"Especially since you've been working out with Uncle Patrick," I tease, trying to lighten the mood.

She pins her blue gaze on mine. In a cold voice, she replies, "The next time she wants to mess with me, I can't guarantee you I'll remain calm."

The car stops. I don't respond to her comment. I can't blame her and don't think I would have remained quiet. I move her dress over her shoulder and trace the blue lace on her lingerie. "Since you were such a rock star tonight, I think I'm going to have to show you how proud of you I am."

"Oh?" She tilts her head and bites on her smile.

"As I've told you before, good girls get rewarded. And you were exceptional tonight."

23

Gemma

THE FOLLOWING DAY, NOLAN DROPS ME OFF AT NORA'S, THEN leaves with Boris. Nora and I spend most of our time playing with Shannon. Whenever I get worried, Nora reminds me they're in a controlled environment.

A few times, she tries to get information about what's going on between Nolan and me, but I don't give her any insight into our relationship. I still don't know what we are. Nolan and I haven't put a label on us. I want to believe it meant something that he asked me to move my things into his bedroom, but I try not to read too much into it. I'm a hot mess with not much to offer anyone right now. At some point, it'll be time for me to move out. I'm not sure what will happen then, and I'm too scared to ask. I've already fallen hard. If he doesn't want me after this is over, it's going to hurt. But things are good between us right now. I don't want to risk rocking the boat and everything becoming awkward again.

The second night I'm at Nora's, my phone rings, waking me up. I answer it, assuming it's Nolan.

"Hey," I answer, with my eyes barely open.

"Hiding from me is impossible," Orla claims.

I open my eyes, sit up, and my heart races. *How did she get this number?* I turn the lamp on and glance around the room.

"Eamon has all sorts of new ideas about what he's going to do to you," she says.

My pulse shoots to the sky. How is this possible? Did something happen to Nolan and Boris? They were supposed to be killing Eamon.

She's lying, I try to convince myself, but her words have me shaken. What if something did happen to Nolan?

"Check your messages, dear sister." She hangs up, and my gut churns.

For several moments, I attempt to convince myself not to look. My curiosity wins, as it always does with Orla. I glance down at the screen and press play.

Eamon's devilish eyes send a chill down my spine. His thick Irish accent fills my ears. He stares into the camera and threatens, "Your father is getting out. I've prepared for you." He turns the camera. A king-size bed has ankle and hand cuffs ready to imprison its victim. Next to it, on the floor, is a dog cage.

Eamon's sinister grin turns my mouth dry. He taps the metal. "This is where you'll sleep. Unless, of course, I decide to restrain you." He opens the ankle cuff. Spikes are on the inside. He pushes his finger on one of them, and blood appears on it.

Instant nausea attacks me. I put my hand over my mouth, but I'm unable to tear my eyes off the video. I manage to swallow the bile rising in my throat.

Eamon points to the bar attached to the ankle cuffs. "This spreader bar I had made especially for you. Every time you move, it'll get wider."

My hand shakes so badly, I drop the phone. I pick it up.

Eamon's eyes gleam. "There's another thing I purchased." He picks up a flogger. It's black, with leather straps. He brings it closer to the camera, and nausea hits me again.

Dozens of pointy metal balls are on each leather strap. Eamon presses his finger on it just like he did with the cuffs. Blood quickly surfaces.

"Oh God!" I pull my knees to my chest and continue watching the video.

"You will be mine. You won't breathe without my permission. Every second of the rest of your life, I own. And I'm going to take extra pleasure in breaking you in, my future wife."

The video turns black. I stare at the screen. My lungs tighten, and it feels impossible to get oxygen into them. I rise and pace the room then torture myself by replaying the video again. Another message pops up.

Unknown number: *I just spoke with Eamon. You'll get an extra special punishment on your wedding night for sleeping with an O'Malley.*

I shudder and can no longer breathe. Heart pains streak through my chest so furiously, I think I'm having a heart attack. I bend over, hyperventilating, then kneel on the floor.

If Orla just spoke with Eamon, then something terrible happened. Are Nolan and Boris dead? Have I been sitting in this penthouse for two days on pins and needles while the Baileys have been the ones in control and not Nolan?

My body turns cold, but I break out in a sweat, gasping for air. I rock back and forth with tears dripping on the wood floor.

The door opens. Nolan's voice hits my ears. "Jesus. Gemma, what's wrong?" He picks me off the floor and sits on the bed with me on his lap.

I curl into him, sobbing, still trying to get oxygen into my lungs.

He fists my hair and tugs my head. His green eyes glow like a lightning bug. I focus on them as he commands, "Breathe. Deep breaths, princess." He inhales, trying to model for me what to do.

Forever seems to pass until the heart pain subsides, my breath returns to normal, and my shakes slow down. Nolan's face comes into focus.

He strokes my cheek. "Gemma, what happened?"

"I-I thought you were dead," I cry out, and more tears fall.

"Why did you think that?"

"Sh-she told me she just spoke with Eamon after I got the video."

Nolan's eyes turn cold. He snarls, "What video?"

I reach for my phone sitting on the pillow behind him. "I-I don't want to watch it again. Please don't make me."

He holds my head to his chest and kisses my forehead. "I'm sorry. I don't know how she got this number. Whatever she sent is a lie. Eamon is dead. He's nothing but ashes now."

I pull away and pin my gaze on his. "He won't get to me?"

He clenches his jaw. Hatred fills his expression. "No. I listened to him beg with his last breath. When there was no more life in him, I disintegrated his remains until any proof he was ever on this earth was destroyed. I shouldn't tell you this, but he's nothing but fish food right now."

Some relief trickles into my fear, but Orla found me. The images of the video and Eamon's voice don't instantly disappear. I shut my eyes, willing it to go away.

Nolan wraps his arms tighter around me. "What's on the video?"

I mumble into his chest, "Eamon showing me a cage next to his bed and things he was going to use to hurt me."

Nolan sniffs hard. "He's gone."

"I thought when she sent her message, they somehow found you, and you were dead," I admit.

"She's a liar. I'm here."

I glance up. "Can we go home?"

"Now?"

I nod. All I want to do is snuggle into Nolan and wake up in his bed. Nora and Boris's place is lovely, but it isn't the same thing.

"If you want to go, we'll leave. Do you have to pack?"

I shake my head. "I never unpacked. I just need my toiletries and to throw on some clothes."

"Okay. I'll get your stuff. You get dressed," Nolan orders.

I obey, and within a few minutes, we're in Boris's car. I sit on Nolan's lap, with his arms around me, neither of us speaking. His driver drops us off, and we go to bed. It's only then I notice the red in his eyes.

I kiss him and slide down until my head rests on his chest. He pretzels his limbs around me.

He strokes my back. "Go to sleep, princess. There's one less thing to worry about now."

Everything about his statement is true. But all I can think is how I'm not truly safe until my father and Orla are dead. It takes a while until I finally fall asleep, but when I do, I don't wake up again until music blasts from Nolan's phone.

He groans, and I sleepily open my eyes. His groggy voice quietly answers, "Colin."

I glance up.

Nolan kisses my forehead then says, "My phone wasn't on. I had something I had to deal with." He moves the phone away from his ear and pecks me on the lips.

I move on top of him and start to return his kiss when he retreats.

His eyes turn to slits. "Why would I hide something like that from Nora?" He slides toward the headboard and sits up, bringing me into a seated position. "My brothers agreed to it?"

I'm not sure how to take the conversation. Nolan isn't mad but doesn't seem happy.

He glances at me. "Fine. Come over. But that will be up to Gemma."

What's up to me?

"Give us thirty minutes." Nolan hangs up the phone and sighs.

"What's going on?" I ask.

He stares at the ceiling then meets my gaze. "Colin had Molly remove the photos of me off her social media pages."

"Okay. That's good, isn't it?"

Nolan slowly nods. "Yes. But he's bringing her over here to apologize. My brothers agreed not to tell Nora what happened at the party if I was okay with it. I told Colin that's up to you."

"Me?"

"Yeah. She threw her drink on you. It's your decision," he says.

I slide off him. "Why can't Nora know?"

"Molly is afraid Nora will fire her."

"It wasn't at work," I state.

"Yeah, but Nora isn't going to be happy when she finds out. Darcey didn't like the interaction between you and Molly on St. Patrick's Day. She put Molly on a warning and told her to be kind to you. Nora reiterated it," Nolan informs me.

Surprise fills me. "What did Darcey see?"

Nolan grunts. "Darcey can sniff out a problem better than a bloodhound. She has a sixth sense. And the woman always has her eyes on everything in the pub."

"Hasn't Molly worked at the pub for years?" I ask.

Nolan rises then pulls me off the bed. "Yeah. She still has to adhere to Nora's rules. And one of those rules is to treat all customers as if they are your family."

Molly isn't anyone I'll ever be friends with, but I know what it's like to lose your career. I blurt out, "I don't want her fired over me."

Nolan's face hardens. He looks over my head.

"You want her to get fired?" I question.

He shifts on his feet and scowls. "If she's going to assault you how she did, then she's made her own bed. But I'll leave it up to you. If Nora finds out, she will fire her."

I suddenly feel bad for Molly. Based on her social media profile, it looks like the pub is her entire life. Before Orla entered my life, I had very active social media pages, similar to Killian's. Part of it was for my job, but I had everything I did in my personal life on it, too. All my athletic events, pictures with guys I dated, and nights out with friends were nothing I thought twice about posting. I had thousands of followers I had never met. My life was an open book. Molly's is pretty bare besides her family and the people connected to the pub.

Nolan pats my ass. "Let's get dressed before they get here."

"How long do we have?"

Nolan glances at his phone. "Twenty-five minutes."

My gut flips. "I don't need a fake I'm sorry."

Nolan leads me into the bathroom. "Then tell her you don't accept it. It's your call. Let's get ready."

We take quick showers and put on clothes. I keep debating about whether Molly can be sincere or not. But there doesn't seem like there is any way to get out of this conversation.

Once we're in the kitchen, Nolan makes smoothies. I turn on the espresso machine, and the doorbell rings. I mutter, "Please tell me this won't be a long, drawn-out drama session."

Nolan grunts. "Not unless Colin has changed." He goes and opens the door.

Colin and Molly step inside. Nolan leads them to the family room. Molly avoids me and stares at the floor. Colin hugs me and kisses my cheek. "How are you, Gemma?"

I smile. Molly may be a pain in my ass, but so far, I don't have any issues with Colin. "I'm good. You?"

His brown eyes twinkle. "Still a bit jet-lagged, but I should get over it soon."

"Do you want an espresso or coffee?" I ask.

"Thanks, but I've reached my limit today."

Nolan motions to the chairs. "Have a seat."

Colin spins. In a no-nonsense voice, he questions, "Molly, aren't you going to say hi to Gemma?"

She meets my eye. Her stubborn Irish blood mixes with something I haven't seen in her before. Fear and defiance swirl in her expression. There's no doubt she's worried about her job. She straightens her back and, in a friendly voice, says, "Hi, Gemma."

"Hi," I respond, trying to be the bigger person but feeling uncomfortable. I wonder how to get this over with quickly.

Nolan takes my hand. "Let's sit down." He leads me to the couch and circles his arm around me.

An awkward silence fills the room. Colin stares at Molly, but she's back to focusing on the floor. Her cheeks turn pink, and she's twisting her hands in her lap.

Nolan finally speaks. It comes out gruff. "What you did to Gemma was bull shit, Molly."

She looks up and furrows her eyebrows. Pain emanates from her, and she whispers, "I'm sorry, Nolan."

Witnessing her squirm doesn't make me feel very good. Her social media feed pops into my mind. If Colin finally set her straight that she and Nolan aren't ever going to happen, she's dealing with a broken heart. Maybe it's all the times my heart got broken, but something about the agonizing expression on her face makes me sympathize with her.

Nolan fumes, "Don't tell me you're sorry. Tell Gemma."

I put my hand on his thigh, hoping he'll turn his delivery down a notch.

Molly stares at the floor again, takes a deep breath, then locks eyes with me. Her cheeks turn maroon. She offers, "I'm sorry."

I'm not sure if Molly is sincere or just embarrassed. Perhaps it's a combination of both. Regardless, I just want this over with so I don't have to see her anymore. I reply, "Thank you."

She swallows hard, and her eyes well with tears. She asks Nolan, "Are you going to tell Nora about this?"

My subliminal messaging must not have worked. In as cold of a tone as before, he informs her, "That's Gemma's decision."

Her lips tremble, her face scrunches, and she turns toward the wall.

Colin quietly requests, "Gemma, she needs her job. Do you think—"

"I'm not going to say anything to Nora," I state.

She jerks her head toward me, and her tears fall. "You aren't?"

I pin my gaze on hers. "No."

"Why not?" she chokes out.

I almost blurt out that I have Nolan and she doesn't. I'm the winner in this situation, not her. But I'm not that cruel. And I still don't know what will happen to us when it's time for me to move out.

The way I dismissed Molly the first night I met her flashes in my mind. So I take responsibility for my part in all this. "I wasn't my best self the night I met you. You were nice to me. I didn't treat you as I should have. For that, I'm sorry. Maybe if we hadn't started off on the wrong foot, this wouldn't have happened."

Nolan's body stiffens.

Shock registers on Molly's face.

Colin cuts back to the outcome. "So you won't tell Nora?"

"No. And if Nora does find out, I'll tell her I don't think it's fair for her to fire her."

"You would?" Colin asks as if he doesn't believe me.

"Yes."

"Thank you," Colin replies.

In a shaky breath, Molly adds, "Yes. Thank you."

"You're welcome."

A moment of silence passes, and Colin rises. "Thank you for allowing us to come over."

"You know you're always welcome here," Nolan says.

Colin smiles and addresses me. "Can the three of us go to dinner later this week?"

"Sure. That would be nice," I tell him.

"Great." He turns to Nolan. "I'll shoot you a text in a few days."

"Sounds good," Nolan responds.

Colin guides Molly out of the house.

Nolan shuts the door, and I exhale, happy the confrontation is over. He places his hands on my cheeks and tilts my head up. "You're a really kind person, Gemma O'Hare. Much nicer than me."

I tease, "Then I guess it's a good thing you're the killer in our relationship and not me."

But things can change when you get to your breaking point. And I'm not there yet.

24

Nolan

Several Months Later

"Stop! Please stop!" Gemma cries out.

I sit up and tug her onto my lap. "Gemma, wake up!"

Tears streak down her face. She sobs into my chest. It's the third time this week she's had nightmares. Over the last few months, they come and go, but Orla figured out the new burner phone number again. It's the fifth one I've bought for Gemma. I don't know how Orla can get access to them. Declan and I have done everything possible to secure the lines, but she always seems to find Gemma.

Every message she sends her is more graphic. Photos with Gemma's face look real. Videos with Gemma's voice edited on them are just as vivid. And since her father, Rory, got out of prison, some of the messages are threats from him.

Within days of his release, he sent a video of a new man he was giving Gemma to and the warning she was to turn herself over to him, or he was going to put her in one of his whorehouses.

My desire to kill Rory has never been greater. No matter how much we try to get to him, we haven't had the chance. Now that he's out of prison, Orla is constantly by his side. The problem is, security around Rory, his brother Mack, and Orla is so strong, we'd have to create a war in the streets. While I'm not naive to think it may not come to that, it's not a preferable option. Even the winner would have casualties unless a miracle occurred.

The messages always seem to come when I'm not home. It's as if Orla knows I'm not by her side to intercept them.

I push a sweaty lock of hair off Gemma's face. I murmur, "It's okay. You were having a nightmare again."

The shame-filled expression she always wears after she has a nightmare appears. It tears at my heart. No matter how much I tell Gemma nothing Orla does is her fault or how it affects her, she seems to carry an abundance of self-loathing over it.

Music blares from my alarm. I reach over and turn it off.

Gemma sniffles. "Is there something going on this morning I forgot about?"

Nerves suddenly swarm my belly. "I have a surprise for you."

"What is it?"

"Pack the smallest bikini you own."

She arches her eyebrows.

I chuckle, more from nervous tension, and I'm unsure why. Colin's on-again, off-again girlfriend from Europe surprised him with a visit. I finalized the new algorithm this week. Now, we have to wait for Jack Christian's company to go public. Gemma had several new clients hire her. We've both been working a lot. It's also the anniversary of my mother's death. I normally spend it with my family, but I don't feel like dealing with it this year.

The wars between all the crime families in Chicago are stressing me out. Boyra Petrov, Zamir's brother, came to town and kidnapped Sergey and Kora. The Polish mob gunned Adrian Ivanov down. My brothers, Liam, and I, took care of them and pissed Darragh off. Kora, Sergey, and Adrian are all okay, but since those two events happened, I can't stop thinking about how if it could happen to them, nothing is one hundred percent foolproof. Every day Orla and Rory live is another day they can get to Gemma. And all the messages they somehow figure out how to send to her have created a lot of extra anxiety.

Plus, my twin sisters, Erin and Nessa, won't leave my brothers and me alone about where their snake husbands are. Liam discovered they were cheating our clan out of money. One thing O'Malleys don't excuse are thieves among us. Once Liam brought it to the leaders of the clan's attention, they tore them to shreds and disposed of their bodies in a meat grinder. The longer they are missing, the more my sisters look at my brothers and me for information. Frankly, I'm sick of hearing their names and want to tell them their husbands were lying pieces of shit who never deserved the role my uncle Darragh gave them. Of course, I don't. So when Colin suggested we rent a yacht for the weekend on Lake Michigan, it seemed like a great idea. While Molly and Gemma are polite to each other, I don't think they'll ever be friends. However, Gemma and Colin get along well, and we see him often.

I drag my finger down her spine. "I hope you like yachts."

Her face brightens. She questions, "Yachts?" then bites on her lip.

"Colin and I rented one for the weekend. His girlfriend from Europe surprised him a few days ago."

Her lips curve up. "Are you serious?"

"Yeah."

"We have a yacht all to ourselves for the entire weekend?"

I chuckle. "Yep."

She gapes at me.

"Are you going to pack? Or do you want me to do it?" I tease.

She throws her arms around me. "This is awesome! Thank you!"

I squeeze her ass. "You can thank me later."

She softly laughs and kisses the spot below my ear. "I won't let you down."

My second alarm rings. "You have less than an hour before we leave."

She pecks me on the lips and jumps off the bed. "On it!"

We quickly shower, dress, and pack. When we get in the car, Gemma picks up my hand. "What's Colin's girlfriend's name?"

"Madison."

"She's from England?"

I nod. "London, to be exact."

"Have you met her?"

"Not yet."

Gemma bites her lip and stares at me.

My stomach flutters with nerves again. "What's the look for?"

She brings my hand to her lips and kisses it. "This is a nice surprise."

I lean my head closer to hers. "It's purely selfish. I get to stare at you in your bikini all weekend."

She softly laughs then presses her lips to mine, sliding her tongue in my mouth and creating a buzz in my veins. It's been months since I met her. At this point, I should be used to her kisses or how her body feels against mine. Nothing about her laugh, smile, or even tears should affect me the way they still do. Against all logic, everything seems to grow more powerful between us.

She straddles me. We make out until the car stops and the doors from the front slam shut. She pulls away, and we glance out the window at the dock full of yachts.

She starts to move off me, and I hold her to me. "Hey."

She gives me a tiny smile. Her blue eyes shine with excitement and curiosity.

The feeling I can't seem to get rid of around her intensifies in my chest. I'm not sure what I'm trying to say. Words merge together in my mind. I peck her on the lips and finally settle on, "You look really beautiful."

Pink creeps into her cheeks. Her smile grows. She places her hand on my face and runs her thumb along my jaw. "You aren't too bad to look at, either."

I grunt, grin like an idiot, and squeeze her ass. "Let's get on the yacht and pretend this is our life on a daily basis."

She continues caressing my jaw. Worry fills her eyes. "I don't know how you handle all this."

"What do you mean?"

"Everything. Your family issues. My family's threats. Me."

Blood rushes between my ears. I blurt out, "You make it worth it."

Silence fills the car. My heart pounds against my chest. Gemma and I are in a dance about who we are together. I'm not sure why I become a coward whenever the chance arises to tell her how I feel about her. Something keeps holding me back from expressing my feelings. Several times, I've told myself not to go there. We live together. I'm committed to protecting her. It's no longer because I want to know what Orla is threatening her about or because I promised her I would. It's an inherent need to make sure no one ever harms her. I would step in front of a bullet if it were flying toward her. But I'm not sure if Gemma's with me because we're living together and have chemistry, or if I'm more to her than that. So the voice in my head keeps telling me not to go there. Once it's out, I can't take it back.

The days Rory and Orla have on this earth are numbered. Once they're dead and Gemma no longer has threats against her, I don't know if she's going to want to move out. Maybe I'll have just been someone she's passed the time with and can easily move past. The thought pierces my soul and seizes my lungs.

There's a knock on the window. "O'Malley! Get your ass out of the car!" Colin shouts.

Gemma laughs. She rolls off me, and I open the door. I'm half relieved, half pissed off. Once again, I didn't have the balls to ask her what we're doing and if I mean anything past casual to her.

We get out, and Colin introduces us to Madison. She's a petite woman, with dark hair and eyes so blue, my guess is she's wearing contacts. Her nails are perfectly manicured, and everything about her is perky. She speaks, and her London accent is prominent. "Lovely meeting both of you."

"You, too. Are you here long?" Gemma asks.

She glances at Colin and wiggles her eyebrows. "A few weeks. We'll see how it goes."

I'm not sure what that means. Based on Colin's expression, my guess is he doesn't, either. I make a mental note to ask him later about it. I hadn't heard of Madison until a few days ago. According to Colin, they were on-again, off-again over the few years he was in Europe.

We make our way to the yacht. Three crew members stand at the entrance at the stern. They help us onto the deck and give us a tour.

It has four en suite bedrooms, a kitchen, and several sitting rooms inside the cabin. The bow has a small pool, hot tub, eating area, and plenty of sunbeds and shaded areas to lounge around in.

"Wow! This is amazing!" Gemma beams, and my heart swells. My only goal this weekend is to make sure she stays happy. A person can only take so much stress. I've watched her over the last few months try to juggle it and still keep going. She's the strongest woman I know. Yet, my biggest fear is something will happen. The night I found her with pills is always fresh in my mind. I cringe every time, thinking what might have happened if I hadn't arrived home at the moment I did.

"I can't believe this is a lake. It looks like an ocean," Madison gushes as her eyes dart from one side of the ship to the other, taking in the sparkling blue water.

A man in a captain's hat steps onto the deck. He holds out his hand. "I'm Captain Rick. Sorry I couldn't meet you when you arrived. I had a few issues I needed to take care of before we leave."

"No worries. I'm Nolan. This is Gemma." I shake his hand.

He leans over and kisses Gemma's cheek.

"Colin. This is Madison." Colin and Captain Rick shake hands. He kisses Madison on the cheek, too.

"Looks like we're going to have perfect weather. Any questions before we head out?" he asks.

None of us have any, so Captain Rick declares we're leaving. He excuses himself, and we decide to get our bathing suits on.

Gemma pulls a tiny white bikini out of her suitcase. She puts it on, and my pulse pounds in my neck. I step behind her, circle my arm around her waist, and drop my hand to her slit. I trace it and murmur in her ear, "When did you get this suit?"

She inhales sharply and sinks against my chest. She turns her face, and her lips twitch. "It was in the package that arrived last week."

"What else did you get?"

She smirks. "Maybe if you're a good boy, you'll find out."

My erection grows against her ass. "I plan on being a very good boy." I slide my hand under her suit and into her wet heat.

She shuts her eyes, and a tiny whimper flies out of her mouth. Her hands grip the sides of my thighs. She breathes, "That's good."

"What I'm doing to you, or that I plan on being a good boy?" I flick my tongue against the back of her lobe and circle her clit faster.

"Ummm... Jesus, Nolan," she whispers, and she digs her nails into my skin. Heat rushes to her face, and she blinks several times.

"God, I love everything about you," I mumble then freeze.

She jerks her head and holds her breath. Her blue eyes widen, and her mouth hangs open.

I'm not sure if I should feel relieved I finally admitted it or curse myself. Time stands still. The sound of the waves lapping against the boat competes with my heart. I'm sure she can hear it.

She finally breaks the silence. "Did you mean you love my body and the sex we have or me?"

My mouth goes dry. "Both."

She arches an eyebrow as if she doesn't believe me. I'm not sure if I just screwed up our entire weekend and home life or not. But I've crossed the line, so there's only one thing to do.

I spin her into me, cup her cheeks, and force her to look at me. "I love you. I have for a while."

She stays quiet, and my gut sinks.

My insides quiver like a bowl full of Jell-O. I quietly beg, "Say something. Please."

Her eyes fill with tears. She scrunches her face. "I love you, too. But how can you love me? I'm a mess."

Conflicting emotions plague me. I'm buzzing that she loves me. I'm horrified she thinks she's anything but spectacular. I firmly state, "No. You're nothing of the sort."

"I-I'm a ball full of anxiety all the time. I wake you up every other night screaming in terror. My career is barely existent. The money I make compared to what I used to is pennies on the dollar. My independence and the person I used to be, the one worthy of a man's love, they're both gone."

My heart breaks. There's no more analyzing or debating what to say or keep inside. I just start talking. "Then you don't see what I see. When I look at you, I see strength, beauty, and grace. You're a woman who should be bitter and maybe even cruel based on all you're enduring, but you're nothing of the sort. You're kind. And funny. Every punch that's thrown your way, you take and then get back up. And when I'm not with you, I feel off. Like something is missing. So if that's a mess, sign me up."

A river of tears stream down her cheeks. She shakily asks, "So when I can move out, you still want to see me?"

"No. I don't want you to move out." My entire torso is in chaos. I've never laid it on the line like this before with any woman.

She shakes her head, and my heart drops. I think she's going to tell me she wants to move out. She replies, "I don't want to move out."

A breath of relief flies out of my mouth. "Thank God you said that."

An emotion-filled laugh escapes her lips.

I dip down and kiss her. I put everything into it, as if my life depends on it. In some ways, maybe it does. Not moving forward with her might as well be death.

She clings to me, feeding my need for her.

There's a bang on the door. Colin shouts, "You staying in there all day or coming out to get some sun?"

Gemma bites her lip, and I turn my head toward the door. "Be out in a few. Now, fuck off." I wipe her cheeks with my thumbs then return to kissing her. When I pull back, I grin. "You did say you love me, too, right?"

She smiles. "Yeah, Nolan. I love you. Everything about you."

25

Gemma

NOLAN'S FINGERS SLIP UNDER THE FABRIC OF MY SUIT. TINGLES erupt under his touch, racing up my spine. Something warm slides over my belly button. He pulls the side ties of my bottom and yanks it away from my body. His hot breath hits my ear. "You awake?"

"Mmm." I open my eyes, inhaling his sandalwood and coffee bean scent. There's no more sunlight, and everything is dark. The sound of the water gently moving around the ship is the only thing I hear. All day, we spent sunbathing or in the pool, drinking with the others. It was full of laughs, kisses, and Nolan's warm flesh against mine. At some point, we crawled onto the oversized mattress inside the cabana. I must have fallen asleep. I yawn and sleepily question, "How long have I been comatose?"

"A few hours." He licks my lips then slides his tongue in my mouth the moment I part them. I reach to pull him close to me, but he grunts, pins my wrists over my head, then binds them together with something soft.

My flutters expand in my belly. "Where are Colin and Madison?"

Nolan locks his green flames on mine. "In their room napping before dinner." He wraps his fingers around my wrists. His lips trail my neck, down to my breast, and he rolls his tongue on my nipple.

I'm not sure when he removed my top, but I'm not going to question it. I arch my back and attempt to reach for him, but the cloth restraints stop me.

"I've waited to do this since the moment I met you," he mumbles then sucks on my breast while circling his tongue on my hardening pebble.

Zings fly to my core. I moan, "Oh..."

He drags his tongue over my cleavage, down my torso, and spends a few moments licking my belly button. His finger moves over my clit, but it feels warm like when I woke up.

"What is that?" I breathe.

He inhales deeply above my pussy, places his finger to my lips, and orders, "Suck it all off."

I open my mouth, and his finger glides inside. Sweetness erupts on my taste buds.

Honey.

I obey his command, and he dips his face over my sex. His other hand V's my wet folds. His tongue snakes over my clit, teasing and tasting me, as if I'm a gourmet meal to be savored and not rushed.

Whimpers fly out of me. He pulls his finger out of my mouth and plays with the nipple he sucked earlier.

Zings ignite and roll from my toes, up my body, until I'm sweating. "Nolan! Oh God!" I yank my arms, but they don't go past my head.

"I tied your wrists for a reason, princess," Nolan taunts then returns to torturing me with his mouth.

Adrenaline feeds my cells. The quivering in my belly expands everywhere. I squeeze my thighs against his cheeks.

Nolan groans then removes his hand from my pussy. He scrapes his beard on my inner thigh and nibbles on my clit.

"Holy...oh...oh God!" I cry out, trembling harder.

A long, wide object slides against my inside walls. Nolan's lips latch onto me and I explode, spasming against whatever he inserted inside me. I inhale sharply, and his wet, slippery finger bypasses the hard ridge of my forbidden zone.

"Nolan! I...oh..."

He doesn't release me, just flicks me faster and inches his digit in and out of me before adding a second.

There's no more room inside me, full of whatever he put in me and his fingers. I writhe, arching my back and gripping the cloth that binds me. My cries become louder, and a drop of sweat rolls down my cheek.

When I think I can't take anymore, he lunges over me, presses my knees under his torso, and sinks into my ass.

I gasp, closing my eyes, the sensation of him too much and perfection all at once. I thought he used all the available space in me before, but this feels like ten times the volume.

A deep rumble escapes from his chest. He places his elbows next to my head and palms it. "Jesus, Gemma," he mutters and fucks me with his sugary tongue.

I open my eyes. He pins his smoldering stare on me, thrusting his cock slowly, going deeper and deeper as I kiss him back with everything I have.

A click fills my ears, and whatever he inserted in my pussy vibrates then begins thrusting opposite Nolan's cock.

"Oh...my...God!" I manage to get out.

"Christ, you're perfect," he growls.

My fingers grip the cloth restraining my wrists. The earthquake inside me resurfaces. I arch my back into his warm flesh, whimpering in his mouth.

He pulls his face away, taking shallow breaths, and strokes my cheek. It's sweet and tender, and there's no more questioning what Nolan thinks of me. He loves me. I see it. Before today, I did, but I wouldn't allow myself to believe it. Now, I do.

As if he knows I need to hold him, he shimmies his hand up my arm and unties the fabric. My limbs fly around his shoulders, and my fingers slide through his hair. In a shaky voice, I whisper, "I love you."

"That's good because I'm not giving you up," he claims. His lips press into mine in a dizzy concoction of everything Nolan. It's possessive. It's passionate. It's all the things I've always wanted but never received from anyone but him.

There's another click near my ear, and the vibrations intensify. Nolan thrusts faster, and I come so hard, I soak both of us, screaming out his name. My nails dig into his shoulders, and my body convulses under him.

"That's it, princess." He pounds into me again and groans, "Fuuuuck."

My vision turns white. His cock stretches me to the point I'm sure he's going to break me, along with all the endorphins bursting in every inch of my body. He collapses over me and buries his face into my neck.

There's a click, and the vibrator stops pulsing. Nolan and I stay quiet, except for our lungs trying to find oxygen. I don't let go of him, and he doesn't move for several moments.

He finally lifts his head off me, shimmies down my body, and I stretch my legs. He removes the vibrator then scoops me up in his arms.

"Whoa! Where are we going?"

He grins. "Hot tub. You have honey all over you."

I softly laugh. "You were busy while I was asleep."

An arrogant expression floods him. He steps down into the hot tub then positions me on his lap. "Guilty."

I drag my nails over his shoulders. "Thanks for planning this trip."

His thumb strokes my hip. "It's nice to forget about everything for a bit, huh?"

"Yeah."

There's a loud boom, and an array of colors explode in the sky, lighting up an island in the distance. He tightens his arm around me, and I realize what day it is. I muse, "It's Fourth of July?"

Sadness mixes into his expression. "Yep."

I stroke his cheek. "What's wrong?"

He glances at the sky and takes a few deep breaths.

"Nolan?"

He studies me for a moment then quietly admits, "It's the anniversary of my mother's death."

I reposition myself over him so I'm straddling him. I cup his face. "I'm so sorry."

His expression hardens. "It was a long time ago."

I gingerly ask, "But it still hurts?"

He licks his lips, sighs, then slowly nods.

My chest tightens. I pull him as close to me as possible and kiss his head. He lets me hold him for a moment then glances up. "When this shit with your father and Orla is over, can I take you to Ireland?"

I sink on his thighs, so I'm face-to-face with him. "Sure. I'd love to go."

He stares out at the blackness of the lake. "My mom always wanted to go and didn't. She would talk about things she would do someday but never did. Then one day, she was just gone." He swallows hard. "I don't want to end up like her."

I quietly admit, "Sometimes I worry I'll die, never achieving the things I wanted, or doing anything memorable or of value. Then all my time on earth will be one big wasted event."

He slides his hand up my back and fists my hair, holding my head near his. "Nothing about you is forgettable."

"Says the man who has to protect me wherever I go."

He furrows his eyebrows. "What does that have to do with it?"

"I can't really go out and conquer the world right now, can I?"

"I happen to think you're tearing it up," he says.

I snort. "You don't have to patronize me."

He huffs. "I'm not. You should know me well enough by now to know I don't do that. And any other woman would crumble in the situation you're in. But you don't. So why don't you give yourself some credit."

"I don't crumble because I have you," I blurt out. My cheeks heat, and I shamefully turn away from him.

He grips my chin and makes me look at him. In a firm voice, he claims, "You don't crumble because you're strong. And the moment you own it, you'll understand Orla doesn't stand a chance against you."

"What do you mean?"

He strokes his thumb over my cheekbone. "Orla's a bully. She believes you're weak. You aren't. She doesn't have any more physical strength than you. The only difference between you and her is she owns her power. She's arrogant and underestimates you. If I put both of you in the ring and had to place a bet, I'm putting all my chips on you, princess."

I smile. "Patrick did say I have a mean right hook."

Nolan grins. "That's right. And I wouldn't want you to unleash a kick on me, either."

I circle my arms around him and lean an inch from his mouth. "Maybe you should show me how to use some weapons."

His body stiffens, jaw twitches, and he studies me.

I lightly drag my nails over the back of his neck. "Why are you looking at me like that?"

His chest rises then slowly falls. He cautiously states, "Maybe I should."

I initially said it without much thought, but it suddenly seems like a good idea. I blurt out, "Yes, you should."

Silence fills the air, making the sound of the lapping water seem louder. Blood pounds against my skull as Nolan's eyes harden. He finally probes, "Would that make you feel more in control?"

Will it? I'm not sure, but an obsession to understand how to use weapons and defend myself against Orla and my father roots itself in my gut. "I-I don't know. But it won't hurt, will it?"

More deafening silence surrounds us. He never stops assessing me. It's like he can see the wheels turning in my head. He opens his mouth, shuts it, then studies me further.

"Why are you hesitating?" I ask.

"If I teach you, it doesn't give you a pass to go anywhere without your bodyguards or me," he insists.

My mouth turns dry. I admit, "The thought of going anywhere without protection, whether I know how to use weapons or not, makes me feel so much anxiety, it might cripple me."

He sighs. "I don't want you feeling like that."

"But I do."

The truth hangs in the air. He slides his hand through my hair. "I'll teach you when we get back on shore. And once you know, maybe some of your anxiety will go away."

I smile and lean closer. "I don't feel it when I'm with you."

His lips twitch. "I think—"

"Sir, the captain told me to inform you dinner will be ready in thirty minutes," one of the deckhands shouts.

Nolan circles his arms around me, pulling my naked body closer to his. He turns his face. "Thank you."

The man nods and leaves.

Nolan grabs the towels on the table next to the hot tub. He pecks me on the lips, naughtily grins, and boasts, "I hope you don't need a long time to get ready. My appetizer is your pussy."

26

Nolan

A Few Months Later

"YES!" GEMMA EXCLAIMS AND PUMPS HER ARM IN THE AIR.

I toss my safety goggles and earphones off and carefully place my gun down. The bullseye on her target has a one-inch hole in it from the round she just fired. "You're getting good at this."

She beams then does a little happy dance. "You're buying dinner tonight!"

I chuckle then glance at my target. I only hit the bullseye half the time. The other bullets ripped through the ring next to it. Before we left, we made a bet. Whoever won had to buy the other one dinner. I wouldn't have let her pay since it's not in my blood, but she doesn't know that. I admit, "The new

French restaurant opened in Lincoln Park. I already made a reservation."

Her expression brightens more, and she checks the chamber of her gun, fastens the safety, and sets it down. She throws her arms around me and teases, "You were scared, weren't you?"

In the last few months, Gemma's confidence has grown. Not just when utilizing guns or knives, but in everything she does. I wish I would have known what empowering her with self-defense would do for her. I would have taught her these skills months ago. I reply, "Don't get cocky, now."

She smirks. "But you were scared, right?"

I open my mouth, but my phone rings. I pull it out of my pocket and answer, "Liam."

"We're leaving tonight. I'll pick you and Gemma up at five thirty. The women will stay at Boris and Nora's," he informs me.

My gut flips. Rory sent a message to Darragh he wanted to meet. Our guys have been in Indianapolis for weeks, getting ready for the meeting and making sure the Baileys weren't anywhere near the warehouse, but he didn't set the exact date yet. "It's tonight?"

Gemma's face falls, replacing her happy glow with worry. Disappointment fills me. I hate not keeping my word, but Rory also needs to be dealt with. I don't know what he has up his sleeve. For several weeks, it's kept me awake at night.

"Tomorrow. See you tonight." Liam hangs up.

"What's going on?" Gemma questions.

"I'm sorry, but we're going to have to go to dinner another night. I need to go out of town with my brothers and cousins."

Her eyes widen. "Why? Where are you going?"

"I can't go into it. You'll stay with Hailee at Boris and Nora's," I reply.

She reaches for my face. "Nolan, please tell me what's going on."

I tug her closer to me. "You know I won't go into O'Malley issues with you. Don't ask me. You'll be safe at Boris's."

She closes her eyes. "How long will you be gone?"

"A few days. As soon as we can come home, we will," I assure her.

She pins her blue gaze on me. "I hate it when you're gone."

"This isn't a choice. I'd much rather take you out to dinner and wake up with you in my bed," I remind her.

She sighs. "I know."

I tuck a lock of her hair behind her ear. "You know that account I set up for you at La Perla?"

Her lips twitch. "Yeah?"

Blood heats in my veins. I wiggle my eyebrows. "Use it. Pick out something to surprise me when I get home."

She bites her lip.

"You remember what I did to you the last time you surprised me, right?"

Her face turns bright red. "Mmhmm."

I lean into her ear. "I promise I'll top it."

She softly laughs.

I steal a quick kiss then declare, "Time to go."

We put our guns, glasses, and earphones away, then leave the O'Malley shooting range. When we step into the house, Declan is sitting on my couch.

"Liam call you?" he asks.

"Yeah." I turn to Gemma. "Why don't you go pack."

She obeys, and I sit across from Declan. "Something else going on?"

He leans closer. "We caught the Bailey thug who's Rory's right hand. Killian and I just spent the last two nights with him."

The hairs on my arms rise. "And?"

He glances behind him then refocuses on me. "He claims Rory sent Orla to New York until he returns from Indianapolis."

"Why?"

"Not sure. We couldn't get anything else out of him."

Several minutes pass as I analyze this new information. I finally say, "It could be a trap so we think she's not with him. I don't trust a word anyone with Bailey blood says. No matter how desperate they are, nothing could ever be one hundred percent truthful. You can't take scum and try to cleanse it."

Declan nods. "You're right. But you also know when a man's begging for his life, things come out."

I scratch my chin. "I guess we'll just have to wait and find out."

Declan rises. "I need to pack. I'll see you tonight."

"Me, too. Later." I walk him to the door then go into my office and pack my laptop and chargers. I take the bag to the kitchen and set it on the counter.

The doorbell rings.

I go to the door and open it. "Colin. Didn't expect to see you."

His face looks slightly green. "You have a minute?"

"A few. I'm leaving in about a half hour." I open the door wider and step back. "Come on in."

"You have a beer? I need something," he claims.

"Sure." I go to the fridge, unscrew the cap, then hand it to him. I grab one for myself.

He sits on the barstool and drinks half of it.

"Thirsty?" I quip.

He sets his beer down and stares at the ceiling.

I sit next to him. "Want to tell me what's rattling you?"

He spins and says, "Madison called."

"And?"

He gulps another large mouthful of alcohol. In a deadpan voice, he says, "She's two months pregnant."

I do the math in my head. I slowly imply, "And the baby is yours?"

He scrubs his face and turns, staring at me.

"Shit," I mumble, realizing he's not one bit happy about this situation.

"Yeah, shit's a good word. And you know what, I'm not sure how this happened. I'm super careful. She's supposed to be on birth control."

I focus on the word supposed to be. My gut drops. I probe, "You think Madison did this intentionally to trap you?"

"Yeah. The chances of the condom and her pill failing are practically a miracle," he asserts.

I whistle. "What are you going to do?"

He scrubs his face. "Hell if I know. She's in England. I'm here. And it's not like she's my forever."

"She's going to be now that you have a baby on the way," I point out.

He finishes the rest of his beer. "You aren't helping."

I hold my hands in the air. "What do you want me to say? You knocked her up. Whether she trapped you or not is a moot point. If it's your kid, then you're stuck with her."

Colin groans. "I'm going to have to marry her now, aren't I?"

I take a sip of beer. "That would be the honorable thing to do."

"And where do we live? I wasn't looking to move back across the pond," he states.

"Can you move her here?"

He lets out a frustrated breath. "I don't know. She's attached to her mother, who I can't stand."

I tap my fingers on the counter, trying to figure out what to say to help him, but nothing comes to mind.

He rises. "I've gotta go."

I follow him to the door. "I'm out of town for a few days. When I get back, let's get together."

He nods, shoots me another expression as if he wants to curl up in a hole and never come out, and leaves.

I shut the door then go into the bedroom. It's getting late, and I need to pack before Liam arrives. Gemma closes her suitcase and zips it.

I slide my arms around her waist and put my face against hers. Her body stiffens. I assume she's still worried about me leaving. I kiss her cheek and inhale her earthy, lavender scent. "I'm going to miss you."

"Mmhmm," she voices but doesn't sink into me like she usually does.

"Everything is going to be fine," I attempt to assure her.

She removes my hands from her waist and spins. "You should pack."

I reach for her cheeks, but she ducks under my arms.

"Gemma."

"Sorry. I have to go to the bathroom." She hurries out of the room, and the door shuts.

Unsure what's wrong, I focus on packing and toss a few outfits into my duffle bag. I go into the bathroom and pack my toiletries.

Gemma steps out of the toilet room.

I zip my bag and tug her into me. "You okay?"

"Yeah." She smiles, but it feels forced.

I tell myself it must be due to her worry. "When I get back, I'll make it up to you for our missed dinner."

"It's okay. I understand," she replies.

The doorbell rings, and I groan. "That'll be our ride."

She attempts to escape my grasp, but I don't release her. "Hey."

She takes a deep breath and looks at me.

"Why do I feel like you're upset with me?" I ask.

"I'm not," she claims.

I study her. "You sure?"

She nods. "Yes."

"Are you just worried, then?"

She closes her eyes and releases an anxious breath. Her lids flutter open, revealing her glistening blue eyes.

I cup her cheeks and dip my face to hers. "Everything will be okay. I promise."

She blinks hard. Her lips quiver. "Okay."

I kiss her, and at first, she resists. I hold her head firmly to mine then deepen our kiss. She finally relaxes and returns my affection.

The doorbell rings again. I don't retreat. I continue kissing her until her hands lace together around my head and we're no longer two people. I murmur, "That's better."

She opens her eyes. Something I can't decipher is in them. I tell myself it's her fear, but I'm not convinced. She swallows hard and says, "Please be careful."

"I will." I return to kissing her. The next few days will be torture without her. I already know this. She'll be safe at Boris's, yet I'll still worry about her. And until she's in my arms again, nothing will feel right.

"Nolan!" Liam shouts.

I reluctantly release her. "We need to go." I sling my bag over my shoulder, put my hand on her back, and guide her into the bedroom. I pick her suitcase off the bed and lead her to the main room.

"Ready?" Liam asks.

"Yep."

We all step outside and get in the car. Hailee is in it. Since the night Adrian got shot, her attitude toward me has improved. She smiles. "Hey."

"Hi. You doing okay?"

"Yeah."

Gemma stares out the window.

"Gemma, what's wrong?" Hailee asks.

"Nothing." Gemma continues looking out the window the entire way.

When we get inside Boris's, I carry Gemma's suitcase into her room and shut the door. She stands near the entrance, avoiding me. I comment, "You're awfully quiet."

She gazes at me then steps forward. She places her hand on my chest. "Be careful."

Part of me feels relieved. She's worried, and this is what her standoffish behavior is all about. I fist her hair and gently tug her head. I dip my face above hers. "I will. Don't do anything crazy while I'm gone."

Her lips twitch. "I'm pretty sure Boris would stop me before I got too far into anything."

I study her face. "I'll miss you."

She softly replies, "I'll miss you, too."

I kiss her until Liam knocks on the door. He hollers, "Nolan, we've gotta go."

She pulls her lips off mine.

I give her a final hug then leave. I'm not sure why, but something feels off. I convince myself it's because I hate leaving her. I'm also nervous about whatever Rory has up his sleeve.

Liam and I say nothing. We meet my brothers and Finn at Killian's. Declan gets in our SUV, and Finn and Killian follow us in another.

Declan assesses Liam and me. "You two need to wipe your lovesick expressions off your faces. From this point out, the only thing you think about is how to take out Rory and all those other Bailey fucks if it comes to it."

I don't deny or argue with him. He's right. No matter how much I don't like leaving Gemma and the feeling like something is bothering her, there's no other choice at this point. We all need to concentrate so we get out of this meeting alive.

27

Gemma

The entire time I'm at Nora's, I focus on Shannon. No matter how much I love her, nothing takes away my conflicting thoughts.

Before we left, I stayed near the bedroom door, thinking I could find out where Nolan was going. I eavesdropped on his and Declan's conversation and now wish I hadn't. And then I almost walked into the room when Colin was over.

Nolan's voice never leaves my head. It doesn't matter what time of day or night. All I hear are his words.

"I don't trust a word anyone with Bailey blood says. No matter how desperate they are, nothing could ever be one hundred percent truthful. You can't take scum and try to cleanse it."

I despise being a Bailey, but their blood is mine. Since Nolan told me he loved me, everything has been perfect between us.

It's been months since we had a fight, and all I've done is allow myself to fall deeper into our relationship. When I think of my future, he's in it.

His conversation makes me question everything. I've lied to him in the past. I cringe thinking about how that makes his declaration true. If I'm honest with myself, I've always been desperate for his protection and love. But if he doesn't trust me, how can he love me? And does he see me as scum?

I was upset and going to call Nolan out on it when I walked out of the bedroom and heard him talking to Colin. His statement, *"You knocked her up. Whether she trapped you or not is a moot point. If it's your kid, then you're stuck with her,"* keeps spinning in my mind, along with him telling Colin to marry Madison because it's the honorable thing to do. I'm not pregnant, and Nolan and I have been careful except for the one time we weren't, but it rubs me the wrong way. If I accidentally got pregnant, would he feel I trapped him? Would he think I did it intentionally? Would Nolan marry me so he could be honorable and not because he wanted to?

We've never talked about kids. I want them, but until Orla and my father are dead, there's no way I would risk bringing a baby into this world. Yet, everything involved in Nolan's conversation with Colin makes me think he wouldn't want kids. Spending my time with Shannon only makes me want it more while at the same time thinking I might never get it.

The days pass slowly. Merged into my disturbing thoughts is my worry about Nolan. He may not love me. Maybe he only told me that to continue to get in my pants. Regardless, I can't turn my feelings off for him. I'm worried, and I see the same anxiety on Hailee's face. Neither of us discusses it. I still haven't told her about Nolan and me. I'm not sure why I always avoid answering her when she asks me about our relationship status. Now I wonder if part of me knew Nolan could never really love me. That thought stings more than his comment about how you can't cleanse scum. So I spend days battling with my fear he doesn't love me and what that will do to me. Then I freak out he's going to get hurt and never come home doing whatever it is he's doing.

When I wake up after my second night at Nora's, it's the same as the first night. Sweat coats my skin. My heart's pounding. The visions and voices of my reoccurring nightmares with Orla annihilate me.

Everything is the same in my nightmare, except Nolan isn't here to calm me down. It's another slice in my heart.

I go into the bathroom, take a shower, and get dressed. I walk into the kitchen and freeze. Liam has his arm around Hailee. My insides quiver. I glance around then ask, "Where's Nolan?"

Liam reassures, "He'll be here later."

"He's okay?" I ask, wondering why he's not here.

Liam nods. "Yeah."

I take a deep breath and attempt to calm my worries. For several hours, I don't hear from him. Nora's phone rings and she answers, "Hey, Nolan."

My chest tightens.

Nora smiles and says, "Sure. She's right here." She hands me the phone.

"Hey." I walk toward the bedroom.

"You all right, princess?" His voice sends relief, pain, and all the desire I constantly feel for him straight through my heart.

My throat turns dry. I blink away tears. "Yeah. Are you?"

"I'm fine. Hey, I'm sorry, but I need you to stay at Nora's the rest of the day. Something popped up I need to take care of. I'll pick you up on the way to Skylar's grand opening."

I close my eyes. I forgot about her party. She just started a fashion line. I swallow the lump in my throat and reply, "Okay. Are you...are you safe?"

He confidently states, "Yes. There's nothing to worry about, and I'll see you tonight."

"All right. Thanks for letting me know."

He says, "I miss and love you."

I put my hand over my eyes, not sure whether he means it or if maybe he's keeping me close since he doesn't trust me. My voice shakes when I tell him the truth. "I love you, too."

"Gemma—"

"I'm fine. I'll see you tonight." I hang up before he can ask me anything else, or I lose it. I spend the day the same as before then get ready in the late afternoon.

Nolan arrives at Nora's in black dress pants, my favorite green button-down shirt of his that shows off his eyes, and smelling like his signature sandalwood and coffee beans. Everything about him, including the snake tattoo on his neck, creates a pulsing in my veins. Nora and Boris are in the bedroom getting ready. Shannon is with them, too. It's Nolan and me, and the minute he sees me, he sweeps me into his arms.

His mouth hungrily attacks mine, and I can't stop melting into him or the tears from falling. It's a cruel move on his part if he doesn't love me. He pulls back and swipes my tears with his thumbs. "Hey. What's going on?"

I sniffle. "Nothing." I'm not going to get into it; this isn't the time or place.

"Gemma—"

"I'm happy you're safe. Can we go?"

He studies me. Worry laces his expression. Is it because he knows I might be onto him, or does he really love me?

I hate myself for any of these thoughts. I want to return to a few days ago when I was in ignorant bliss.

Nolan nods and says, "Let me tell Nora we're leaving."

"I think Shannon is sleeping in their room."

Nolan picks up his phone, texts her, then grabs my suitcase near the entrance. He takes my hand and guides me into the car.

He slides his arm around me, and I sink into him. "Are you going to tell me what's going on?"

Nervous flutters fill my chest. I glance up, and his phone rings.

"Crap. Hold on." He answers, "Declan, we're almost—" The color drains from his cheeks. He sits up straighter then mutters, "Jesus."

The hairs on my arms rise. The car parks in front of Skylar's new office.

"We just got here." He hangs up.

"What's happening?" I ask.

Nolan turns. "Selena's ex-husband kidnapped her. I need you to go inside and stay with the others."

"Oh my God!" I put my hand over my mouth as chills fill me.

Nolan's eyes turn to slits. He steps out of the car, reaches in to help me out, then swiftly escorts me inside. The next few hours are scary. Both O'Malley and Ivanov bodyguards secure the building, but all of our men deal with the Selena situation. Sergey calls Kora to tell her they rescued Selena, but they're going to be a while. Toward the end of the night, Hailee and I sit on the couch in Skylar's office, not saying much, still worried about Selena.

Finn comes storming into the room. His face is red, and he barks, "Where is Liam?"

"I-I don't know. He's not back yet. No one is," Hailee answers.

"What's wrong?" I ask.

Finn's demeanor doesn't change. "When you see Liam, you tell him I'm looking for him."

"Finn," Liam says from the doorway. The two men pin an intense gaze on each other.

"I told you not to touch Mack," Finn growls.

Mack? My father's brother?

I grab Hailee's arm.

Liam claims, "I didn't. Obrecht did. It happened before I could stop him."

"Is he dead?" I ask, hoping he died a horrible death. Mack was one of the men I had to watch breaking women in at my father's whorehouse.

Liam closes his eyes then clenches his jaw. He stares at Finn. "Yes."

"And Jack?" Finn snarls.

"Ivanov garage. Obrecht gave me his word he'll wait."

Finn shakes his head in disgust at Liam then shoves past him.

"You can't go right now. I need you to finish this off," Liam calls after him, and a new chill runs down my spine.

Finn spins. "What are you talking about?"

He points for him to go back into the office.

Finn reluctantly returns.

"Rory threatened Hailee in her classroom today," Liam informs him.

"What?" I cry out as new horror fills me.

"He's texting her a location. There are no more options. We take him out. Tonight," Liam insists.

Finn glances at Hailee. "Are you okay?"

She nods. "Yeah. But he's going to blow up O'Malley houses and the school if I don't bring my sisters and mother to him at midnight."

"Hailee! What the hell? Why didn't you tell me this?" I accuse, upset she sat next to me all night and said nothing.

Finn looks at the ceiling then says, "I'll be outside. I need some air. I'll let you know when I can think again." He storms out.

I sternly fume, "Hailee!"

She ignores me. "Liam?"

He scowls. "Stay here." He turns to leave, and I grab his arm.

"Liam!"

He freezes and glances at me.

"Where's Nolan?"

His face slightly relaxes. "He's fine. You don't need to worry. Stay here with your sister." He shuts the door.

I spin on Hailee and scold, "Why didn't you tell me?"

She closes her eyes. "I'm sorry. I didn't think it was appropriate when Selena's situation was going on."

"You should have told me," I insist.

Her eyes fill with tears, and her lips tremble. She swallows hard and says, "He's so horrible."

I sigh, pull her into my arms, and we both cry.

Liam comes back into the room. "Go to Aspen's. When this is over, I'll come get you."

"What are you going to do?" Hailee asks.

His eyes turn cold. "Kill your father. Now, go with Aspen."

We don't argue and obey. More Ivanov bodyguards appear. All of us women get transported to Maksim and Aspen's penthouse.

We all wait on pins and needles. I don't know how they will kill my father, but I'm not naive enough to think this is a situation they have complete control over. They could die. I may never see Nolan again. And that thought almost paralyzes me.

I engage in the conversation as best as possible, but I'm on the edge of losing it. Too many days have passed since I was with Nolan. Too much time has been spent wondering what the truth is between us.

Nora asks, "What's up with you and my brother?"

Anna laughs. "Nora's keeping it real like always, I see."

Nora turns to her. "What? My brothers always interfered in my love life. Seems fair that I at least get to know what's going on in theirs."

"Nothing is going on," I claim, and heat rises in my cheeks. The last thing I'm going to do is proclaim my love for her brother when he might be lying to me.

Nora tilts her head. "You're a bad liar."

"Nothing is going on. What you should ask Nolan is what is up between him and Molly," I blurt out then cringe inside. Molly's been fine since Colin made her apologize, and I promised not to tell Nora she threw her drink on me.

Surprise fills Nora's face. "Molly?"

It's like I opened the floodgate. All the issues I had previously come rolling out. I reply, "Yeah. She's constantly bringing him food and sending him messages. And how many times can a person really have laptop issues?"

Nora winces. "She tends to make bad decisions and usually finds herself in some sort of pickle."

"Yeah, well, I'm sure some of it she creates so Nolan can save her," I assert.

Confusion fills Nora's face. "I thought Colin sorted her out?"

I roll my eyes and reveal, "She's still obsessed with Nolan." I immediately feel guilty. I still see her longing looks from time to time, and part of me feels bad for her. Nolan broke her heart, and it's written all over her face when we go into the pub.

"For someone who says nothing is going on with Nolan, you sure seem annoyed by it." Kora raises her eyebrows.

I stand up. "I'm not. I'm going to the restroom." I quickly leave the room and go into the safety of the bathroom. I stare at myself in the mirror. Why the hell did I bring up Molly again? If Nolan is lying about loving me, I'm going to be in worse shape than she is.

I put cold water on my face, tell myself to pull it together, and return to the main room. Hailee is pacing. I go up to her and say, "You're making me nervous."

She stops moving and stares at me. "Sorry. I...seeing him today..."

I swallow hard. "When Orla made me visit him in prison, I didn't understand how we shared his DNA."

Hailee nods. "I know."

I admit, "I hope Orla is there tonight and they take her out, too."

Hailee hugs me. "I'm so sorry she came after you. I wish she would have picked me."

I shake my head. I would never wish that upon any of my sisters. "No. I'm glad she didn't. But, Hailee, I swear to God, if they don't take her out, I will."

Hailee freezes. "Gemma—"

"I can't deal with it anymore. She's ruined my entire life. I lost my career, my home, and everything I thought I knew about myself. I-I don't sleep at night. She keeps breaking the firewalls Nolan puts on my phone and texting me. Every time he adds something, it only takes her a few weeks to bypass it. He's stopped giving me new phones. It doesn't matter. She still seems to find me. Sometimes, I think I'm going insane," I declare.

"All this will end soon. I promise," Hailee vows.

I sarcastically laugh then wipe my face. "I hope it's before I end up in a straitjacket."

"Gemma—"

"Everyone safe and sound?" Adrian's Russian accent fills the air.

Hailee spins and runs over to Liam. She asks. "Is he—"

"They're all dead," Liam affirms.

"Orla, too?" I hopefully ask as Nolan steps into the room. Relief fills me at the same time my stomach pitches. We stare at each other. I will my feet to move, but they don't seem to step toward him.

Liam's face falls. "We don't have any proof she was there. We'll have to wait and see if she was in any of the cars."

My heart sinks. I walk out of the room. Nolan follows me and shuts the door behind me. He slides his arms around me, and I lose it.

"Shh." He strokes my head and kisses it.

My entire body convulses. It's too much. My father is dead, but Orla might still be out there. Nolan is holding me, safe without a scar on him, yet I don't know if he really loves me.

I can't stop crying. Nolan moves me to the bed, and I curl onto his lap.

"Gemma, he's dead. She might be, too. If she isn't, I'll find her. I promise," he says.

It should make me happy. Right now, I can't even process that. I blurt into his chest, "I can't handle it if you don't love me."

He freezes then tilts my head up. "Why would you ever question my love for you?"

I sob harder.

"Gemma, I need you to calm down and tell me why you think this," he firmly demands.

It takes me several minutes. I finally say, "I heard you and Declan."

Confusion fills his face. "When?"

"At the house. Before you left."

He pulls me up, so I'm face-to-face with him. "What did we say?"

I close my eyes and try to compose myself. "You said you don't trust a word from anyone who has Bailey blood, and you can't take scum and try to cleanse it."

He furrows his eyebrows. "What does that have to do with us? You know how I feel about the Baileys."

My lips quiver harder. I look away.

"Gemma—"

"I have Bailey blood," I cry out, spinning toward him.

He gapes and swallows hard. He sternly says, "I don't consider you a Bailey. I haven't for a really long time."

"Then what am I?" I ask, not fully believing he doesn't still see me as one. "You even call me princess, and we know where that comes from."

He takes a deep breath then grabs some tissues off the nightstand. He hands them to me. "Dry your face. We're going home, and then I'm going to tell you exactly who you are to me."

28

Nolan

BESIDES THE NIGHT I CAUGHT GEMMA WITH THE PILLS, I'VE never seen her so distressed. The fact that my words caused her to question what she means to me for several days, pains me. Part of me curses myself for not coming straight to Nora's when I got back in town. I knew something was wrong when I left, yet I convinced myself she was only worried. The other half of me is glad I didn't. Maybe it's going to be the only way to show her I don't associate her with her dead father or anyone else who is part of the Bailey clan.

I wrap my arm around Gemma and keep her close to my chest, escorting her through Maksim's penthouse. I ignore everyone and all their questioning looks. Gemma's still a wreck. Her tears have stopped, but her eyes are puffy. She's on the verge of losing it again. As soon as we get in the car, I pull her onto my lap.

She buries her face in my neck. Her hot tears drip down my skin. I hold her head and murmur in her ear, "Did you sleep well when I was gone?"

She shakes her head but doesn't lift it off me.

"You had nightmares?" I ask.

She sniffles. "Yes."

I stroke her back and kiss the top of her head. "Maybe now that your father is dead, you can sleep again."

Her body stiffens. It's as if she's only now registering what that means. She moves her face in front of mine. "He's really dead?"

"Yes. I saw him take his last breath."

She shivers. "Did you kill him?"

I wish I could tell her it was me, but I can't take the credit for it. "No. Liam did."

She swallows hard then looks out the window. In a painful voice, she whispers, "But Orla is still alive?"

I turn her chin. I shouldn't tell her any details, but something in me thinks she needs to know. "Listen to me very carefully. A war in the streets occurred. Do you know what that means?"

She shakes her head and bites on her trembling lip.

I brush a strand of hair off her forehead. "We gunned them down. Every one of your father's men that he planted to kill us are now dead. I don't know how many men he lost, but there's a big dent in his clan. And Orla may have been in one of the vehicles."

Gemma squeezes her eyes shut. "Or she could be in New York."

I wince inside, knowing she heard my entire conversation and what she thinks because of it. I state, "If she is, we'll find her. Now that she doesn't have your father or his men to protect her, she won't be able to stay in hiding. And I promise you, when we locate her, I will kill her. But my gut says she's dead."

Gemma slowly opens her eyes.

I cup her cheek. "Take the win, princess. Your father is dead. He'll never again threaten you or attempt to give you to some thug." My stomach flips saying that last part out loud.

Her face crumples, and new tears fall.

I pull her into me. "Shh. Everything is going to be okay now."

She chokes out, "But I still have Bailey blood in me."

If I could take back my words from several days ago, I would. It never occurred to me she was listening or that she would take what I said and think it applied to her. I firmly declare, "I already told you, I don't see you as one of them."

The car pulls into my driveway and parks.

She says so quietly I almost don't hear it, "I need you to love me. I need us to be real."

"We are." I get out and carry her into the house. Her body trembles, and I take her right to the bedroom. I set her on the bed then remove all her clothes. She stares at me, conflicted about whether I love her or not. It's all over her face, and I curse myself some more. I hold up the corner of the blankets. "Get under the covers."

She hesitates, shivering, but then obeys.

I remove my clothes and slide in next to her, tugging her into my body. I pretzel my limbs around her cold ones then press my lips against her forehead. "You asked me who you are to me. I'm going to tell you. Once I do, there will be no more questions about how I feel about you."

Her voice shakes. "I can't handle it if you lie to me, Nolan. If I'm part of some twisted game of yours—"

I flip her onto her back and cage my body over hers. She gasps, and I hover over her face so she can't escape me. "I've never lied to you."

New tears fall. "But I lied to you. Just like you said all Baileys do."

My pulse increases. "You've lied to me about something I'm not aware of?"

She shakes her head. "No. Nothing new."

My blood calms. "Then it's in the past. We've already discussed it."

"But you don't trust me," she quietly says.

I wipe a tear off her cheek. "If I didn't trust you, I wouldn't have just told you we had a war in the streets and who your father's killer was. Do you not see this?"

She stays quiet, biting on her lip.

I sweep my arm under her and palm her head. "Ask me where I was today when you were at Nora's."

She pins her eyebrows together.

"Ask me," I demand.

In a scared voice, she questions, "Where were you?"

I reach into my drawer and pull out a box. I flip the top up and put it next to our faces. "I was buying this. For you."

She freezes, and her eyes widen.

The feeling in my chest I always get around her intensifies. "You wanted to know who you are to me. I'll tell you. You're my everything—the woman I want to marry and knock out a dozen Irish babies with. The only woman on earth who can push all my buttons and stand up to me, and I still can't handle having you out of my eyesight. You may have Bailey blood in you, but you're the exception to the rule, a miracle among a cesspool of vile human beings. And one other thing, you're not their princess. You're *my* princess. So get it through your head. You belong to me, an O'Malley. Not them."

Her eyes dart between the ring and me. She swallows hard. "Are-are you asking me to marry you?"

"Yes."

"And you want to have babies?"

"No. I want to have *your* babies."

She scrunches her forehead. "But you asked Colin if Madison trapped him."

"What does Colin's situation have to do with us?"

"You made it sound like you wouldn't want kids."

I groan. "Gemma, the next time you eavesdrop on me, make sure you don't take things out of context."

She winces. "Sorry. So you do want kids?"

"Yeah. Yours."

Her eyes brighten, and her lips curve up. "Okay. Ask me."

I kiss her quickly. "I love you—more than I ever thought possible. I also know you love me, too. If what we have between us isn't real, then nothing in life is. So will you marry me, princess?"

She reaches around my shoulders and slides her fingers through my hair. "Yes. And I do love you."

I shut the ring box and toss it on the table. I brush my lips against hers. "Good. I'll put your ring on you later."

She laughs and kisses me, widens her legs, and pushes my ass.

I sink into her in one thrust. She whimpers in my mouth, clutching me, giving me all of her the way she always does, the way no other woman ever has.

"God, I missed you," I mumble.

"So much," she replies then rolls her tongue back in my mouth.

I retreat and stare at her. "Don't ever question my love for you again. I don't give it out to just anyone."

"I'm sorry."

"Shh. No sorries. But no more doubt." I kiss her lips then jaw, moving toward her ear. She grasps me tighter and digs her nails into my shoulder, quivering underneath me.

I lick her lobe. "Don't come until I do."

"Oh God," she breathes.

I slow my thrusts down, wanting to savor her and this moment, and all that we are together, with her at my body's mercy. She's my gorgeous princess, soon-to-be bride, the future Mrs. Nolan O'Malley. Somehow, in the middle of the chaos, she became the person I trust the most. I'll protect, love, and kill for her. If I had to step in front of a bullet to save her, I would. And I'm going to make sure, every day going forward, she doesn't just know it, but she believes it.

"Nolan," she whispers, as her lashes flutter over her blue flames. Her skin glistens against her pink-flushed cheeks. Strands of her strawberry-blonde hair stick to her forehead.

Our hot breaths merge. The scents of sex, sweat, and her aroma of earth and lavender mix, flaring in the air. I inhale all of it, breathing it in with short breaths. My eyes dart across her face, studying her perfection. I flick my tongue in and out of her mouth, fucking her in unison with my erection. Unable to hold myself back any longer, I speed up my thrusts.

Her body convulses, eyes roll, and she cries out my name. She claws my back and arches her body into my chest. Her body spasms, gripping and releasing my cock with pleasant torture.

Everything within me turns to mayhem. Racing blood and

adrenaline pound into every atom of my being. The high she gives me magnifies. My seed pumps deep within her, and I growl in her ear, "My wife."

She trembles beneath me, breathing as hard as I am, clutching me. I don't move, breathing in the scent of her skin, wishing I could find a way to have it permeate all my cells and smell it all day long.

I keep my face buried in the curve of her neck and reach for the box. I lift my head and roll off her, pulling her on top of me.

She smiles. "Hi."

I chuckle. "Hi."

She slides her hands in my hair and kisses me. I'm not sure who's giving who life, but everything about us together makes the darkness go away.

I reach for her hand and sit up so she's straddling me. "If you don't like the ring, tell me, and I'll get you another one."

"I love it," she says.

"You barely saw it."

She bites on her smile.

My nerves flutter in my chest. I hope I chose what she likes. If she doesn't, I want her to tell me so she doesn't end up with something she hates. I slide the ring on her finger. Diamonds outline a Celtic crown. A two-carat heart-shaped diamond sits in the middle. Platinum Celtic knots are on both sides, with another diamond in the center. I had it engraved. It reads: *My heart, my soul, my princess.*

She studies it. My anxiety increases, waiting for her to tell me her thoughts.

She glances up, and tears shine in her eyes. She cups my cheek. "This is the most beautiful ring I've ever seen."

"You like it?" I question, still worried.

She shakes her head. "No. I love it. It's perfect." She kisses me.

I slide back down in bed with her. When she's snuggled against my chest, I trace her hand, staring at the ring. I suggest, "Now that your father is dead, and Orla probably is, too, I think we start focusing on us."

She tilts her head and pins her gaze on mine. "Do you really think she's dead?"

"I hope so. If she isn't, we'll find her. I promise you," I vow.

Her eyes light with hope. She asks, "What made you buy this ring today?"

I stroke her back. "I didn't like being away from you. I never do. But something about Colin not being excited about having a baby bugged me. Not because of his situation but ours. I realized I want that. With you. I've never wanted it with anyone before. If you told me you were pregnant, I'd be elated, not upset. I'd be happy you were stuck with me. And then I saw your father."

She rolls farther on top of me. "When you were out of town?"

The vision of Rory Bailey demanding we turn over his daughters to him makes my blood boil. "Yes. There wasn't any question when he left, the end was near. I wanted to make sure that when it did happen, you were clear that you're mine. And we aren't just passing the time for something to do, since you couldn't live on your own."

Her lips twitch. "You already told me you didn't want me to move out."

I confirm, "Yeah. I did. But it's not enough. I want you as mine, Gemma. Now. Forever. And I want the world to know you belong to me and I to you."

She tilts her head. "So we should start planning a wedding, then?"

"Yeah. Whatever you want, we'll do, but it has to be a Catholic ceremony," I tell her.

"I grew up Catholic. That's fine."

I wiggle my eyebrows. "Good. And don't forget something white for under your wedding dress."

29

Gemma

A Few Months Later

THE DRIVER PARKS THE CAR IN THE DRIVEWAY. I STARE AT THE picture of me in the wedding dress my mother just ordered. Things have been better between us since my father is now dead. Orla hasn't contacted me and hasn't surfaced. The police have kept the street war out of the press. Not one news outlet has reported my father's death, but Nolan promises me he saw Liam shoot him in the head before he took his last breath. Liam claims that the police often keep mafia business out of the press so it doesn't incite more violence. Both he and Nolan believe Orla would have been in one of the vehicles during the shoot-out.

The more time that passes, the more I start to believe she's gone. My nightmares have slowly faded. Nolan and I have focused our energy into planning our wedding. He paid the priest to allow us to take our wedding classes on an accelerated track so we can get married sooner. Boris asked him why he didn't pay more to skip the classes, but Nolan seemed offended over the thought. And it made me love him more that he takes our vows so seriously, even if we roll our eyes at almost everything Father Antonio says during class.

I still have bodyguards wherever I go. Nolan told me, no matter what, I'll always have them. I'm okay with it. It gives me comfort and helps me relax in public.

A lot has happened since we got engaged. Darragh passed away and Liam's now in charge of the clan. Nolan, Killian, Declan, and Finn seemed to have taken on more responsibilities to help Liam out. The five men are always together, which I don't mind since I like all of them. Even though Nolan is busier, we still spend most of the day together like before.

I toss my phone in my purse and hop out of the car. Another private vehicle sits in the driveway. The driver isn't one of the O'Malleys, so I assume it might be an Ivanov car. I go inside the house and walk in on Obrecht and Nolan having a heated conversation.

Nolan states, "We need a few more points. We're almost there. If you take him out now, we'll lose a lot of money."

Obrecht's voice is so cold, I shudder. "I don't care how much money is at stake."

"Obrecht, this isn't my call," Nolan replies.

"Selena said she won't give me the go-ahead to kill that bastard until Liam says he is of no more use to you. I need you to talk some sense into Liam. If it were any of your women, he wouldn't be alive," Obrecht seethes.

"We're almost there. Just give us a bit more time—"

"I've given it months. Selena's still having nightmares. Until that motherfucker is dead, she's not going to have any closure on this. Tell Liam to put my wife first instead of his bank account," Obrecht barks.

Nolan runs his hand through his hair. He lowers his voice. "I'll talk to Liam. But you know it's not about lining Liam's pocket. It's about securing the future for the clan."

Obrecht snarls, "I don't give a shit."

I clear my voice. "Sorry. I didn't mean to interrupt."

Nolan and Obrecht spin toward me.

Obrecht releases a frustrated breath. He kisses me on the cheek. "You doing okay, Gemma?"

I smile. "Yes. How's Selena? I haven't seen her since your wedding."

"She's good." He scowls at Nolan. "Most of the time."

Nolan shifts on his feet and clenches his jaw.

"I'll see you later." Obrecht storms out of the house.

I wince at Nolan. "Sorry to interrupt."

He pulls me into his arms. "You're fine. Did you find a dress?"

Excitement fills me. "Yes."

His green eyes turn to flames. "What about your lingerie?"

I softly laugh. "I'm not taking my mom with me for that."

"Fair enough. Hey, I have something for you."

"What's that?"

He takes my hand, leads me into the office, and motions for me to sit on the desk. I obey, and he sits in the chair in front of me, then slaps a box on the table.

"What is this?" I ask.

"Open it."

"Okay...should I be scared?"

He chuckles. "Nope."

I lift the lid and take out a card. It reads:

O'Malley Cybersecurity

Gemma O'Malley, CEO of Marketing

I can't hide my smile. "Gemma O'Malley? Jumping the gun, are we?"

He shrugs, wraps his arms around my hips, then teases, "I almost put Mrs. Nolan O'Malley."

I bend down and kiss him. "Thank you. When is this company going to be official?"

His face falls. "We're almost there."

I cautiously ask, "And then Obrecht will be happy and Selena will sleep better at night?"

Guilt fills his expression. "Yeah."

I lean forward and kiss the top of his head. He tilts his head up. "My brothers want us to meet them at the pub. You up for it?"

"Sure."

He rises and helps me off the table. We go to the pub, have dinner and drinks with Killian and Declan, and come home. Just like every night, I fall asleep in his arms, feeling safe and loved.

In the middle of the night, I wake up. My phone screen glows. I pick it up, and my gut drops.

Unknown Number: *You thought you could escape me, but it's not possible. Now I'm going to destroy every person you love, starting with him.*

A picture of Nolan, with blood all over him, pops onto the screen. I swing my legs over the bed and cover my mouth.

Unknown Number: *When you least expect it, I will slice him piece by piece. Then, I'm going to dump his body on your doorstep.*

Nolan gasps and sits up in bed.

I turn. "Are you okay?"

Sweat coats his skin. He takes shallow breaths.

I kneel and move closer to him. "Nolan. What is it?"

He swallows hard. His green eyes glow. "My brother, Sean. I- I haven't had the dream since the day I met you."

Chills run down my spine. "What is it about?"

Nolan looks away. "Nothing."

"Nolan! Tell me."

He closes his eyes briefly then opens them. "I'm sure it means nothing."

He's lying to me. It's the only time he ever has. Instead of calling him out, I say, "Tell me, then."

He stares at the ceiling.

"Nolan!"

He nods. "Okay. He said the Baileys are coming and to watch my back."

My stomach pitches, and bile rises in my throat. I run to the bathroom and throw up in the toilet.

Nolan follows me and holds my hair back. When I'm through, I sit on the floor with my back against the wall. He hands me a wet cloth and sits next to me. "Are you okay?"

I wipe my mouth and close my eyes. My insides quiver, and all the anxiety I used to feel races back. I barely can get out, "She's coming for you."

Nolan firmly asks, "Who?" But we both know who I'm talking about.

"She just sent me messages. I was reading them while you were asleep."

Angry red fury explodes on his face. He pulls me off the ground then leads me into the bedroom. He snatches the phone off the bed, and his cheeks deepen to maroon. He snarls, "I'll kill her. If she's alive and coming out of hiding, she'll pay for every threat she's ever made against you."

My voice cracks. "It's against you now."

"She's not taking me down," he claims, but all I can see is the photo of him with blood all over his body.

There's a ding, and another message pops up.

Unknown Number: *That dress you ordered today is going to go to waste. He'll be dead before February.*

I gape at the message. She's already following me again. She knows our wedding date. Why did I believe she was dead? I should have known if no one saw her, then she wasn't present in the street war.

Nolan tugs me closer, and another ding rings through the air.

Unknown Number: *Maybe it would be more fun to poison him.*

A photo of Nolan drinking a Guinness at the pub from earlier tonight pops up. Foam is coming out of his mouth.

I whisper, "Oh my God." My chest tightens, and pains shoot through it. My hand trembles against my face. "Was she there? How could she be there, and we never knew?"

Nolan takes the phone out of my hand and sets it on the table. "It wouldn't have been her. Someone else had to have taken it."

"Who?"

"I don't know. We'll increase security at the pub."

"You think that's going to stop her?" I belt out.

"No. But I'm going to hunt her down and end her," Nolan growls.

I rise and pace the bedroom. Tears fall. I declare, "She's going to kill you."

"Gemma—"

"She's lost everyone she cares about. This isn't an empty threat! She knows about my wedding dress and that we were at the pub."

He steps in front of me and holds my cheeks. "You're spinning out. Nothing is going to happen to me. Come back to bed, and we'll figure out new security tomorrow."

His face becomes blurry from my tears. "I shouldn't have believed she was dead."

He sighs and pulls me into him. Another ding fills the air.

I step toward the phone, and Nolan stops me. I push him. "Get out of my way."

"No." He grabs the phone and turns it off. "She's not getting any more of our night. Get back in bed."

I don't move.

He softens his voice and strokes my cheek. "You need to trust me."

"I can't lose you. Especially not by her hand," I admit.

"You aren't going to lose me."

"How do you know?"

"I told you. I'm going to find her and kill her."

I turn away from him. No matter what has happened, Orla's always been the one in control. She's untouchable. All I see are the photos with Nolan's blood all over him or foam coming out of his mouth. I ask, "Can you tell me you aren't going to question everything you put in your mouth from here on out?"

His face hardens.

"That's what she does. Even if she doesn't kill you, she'll threaten and plant so many seeds of doubt, she'll destroy us," I warn.

He confidently states, "No. She won't. Now come to bed."

He has his *I'm not backing down* look on his face. I go into the bathroom, brush my teeth, swish with mouthwash, then get into bed.

He pulls me into him, and it only makes my fears worse. The thought of not having him hold me every night or the future we're planning sends me into another panic attack.

I pretend to sleep, and at some point, Nolan's breathing tells me he is. I carefully take the phone and sneak into the bathroom. When I turn it on, my gut curls. More pictures of Nolan with threats on how Orla might kill him are on a dozen new messages.

Something in me snaps. I text Orla.

Me: *We need to meet.*

Unknown Number: *The whorehouse I took you to. Come alone.*

Me: *Leaving now.*

I put on a black hoodie, yoga pants, and dark running shoes. Then I open Nolan's safe.

My heart races, but I tell myself I know how to use it. I pick up his silencer, open the chamber, and fill it with bullets. I put the safety back on and toss it in my oversize bag, along with money for a cab, the phone, and a pair of black gloves.

Guilt fills me when I look at Nolan. He's still asleep, and I contemplate writing him a note, but he'll only try and stop me.

When I get to the kitchen, I rack my mind about how to slip by the O'Malley guards. I go into the garage and out the side door then sneak through the yard. Once I'm several blocks away, I get to the main road, then realize the possibility of a cab at this time of night in this neighborhood is low. I pull out my phone, log into my app, and schedule an Uber.

It arrives within a few minutes. I put on my gloves and spend the journey telling myself to shoot Orla the second I see her. When the driver pulls up to the house, my anxiety intensifies.

The house is dark, as if no one is inside. The yard is overgrown with weeds. The night Orla brought me, everything looked perfectly groomed and lights outlined the walkway up to the front door. I glance at the second story. There's a broken window.

It's deserted.

Maybe since so many Baileys died and Orla was hiding, there was no one in charge anymore?

I pull my phone out.

Me: *Where are you?*

Unknown Number: *Inside.*

Me: *Come outside.*

Unknown Number: *No. I'm in the playroom.*

I swallow hard. Memories of Bailey men breaking women flood me.

Unknown Number: *No one else is here. Just walk in.*

I'm not stupid enough to believe Orla would be all on her own, but I'm also not comfortable standing outside. It's a nice neighborhood. But her men could be anywhere. I'm trapped either way and need to do what I came to do.

A gust of wind blows against my back. I take a deep breath, fighting the urge to run. When I get to the door, I slide my hand in my purse and flip the safety of my gun.

The knob turns easily, but the door creaks as I open it. Goose bumps pop out on my skin. I glance in both directions. Nothing comes into view. The house is dark and smells like dust, unlike the last time I was here.

My eyes adjust to the darkness, and the grand staircase comes into view. I grip the gun tighter and move toward the playroom, creeping down the hallway. A faint light blinks on and off, as if a movie might be playing.

I get halfway there and freeze. Orla's bodyguard stands at the end entrance. His green eyes glow, and while I can't see his face, I'd know those eyes anywhere. He moves toward me, and without thinking, I fling Nolan's gun out of my purse and shoot him in the head.

He goes down with a thud. Blood pools everywhere, and I lean against the wall, shaking.

I just killed a man.

Jesus.

Pull it together.

I glance in both directions, worried another Bailey might be here, but no one appears.

Was Orla down to only one man? Did the O'Malleys cause so much damage there's no one left?

Nolan's voice pops into my head. *The only difference between you and her is she owns her power. She's arrogant and underestimates you.*

I spend several more minutes watching the blood pool around her bodyguard.

"Are you going to stand out there all day or come inside?" Orla calls out.

My skin crawls from the sound of her voice. It's haunted me for so long, creating anxiety, paranoia, and paralyzing fear. I don't know what the right thing to do is. Stay in the hall or step into the room are the only two options. I'm not leaving until she's dead.

"Let's play fair. No guns," she shouts. A gun comes flying out the entrance of the room and lands with a thud next to her dead bodyguard.

"I don't trust you," I yell back and take a few steps closer.

"Then come in, see no one else is here, then toss it," she directs.

No matter what she says, I'm not letting go of my gun. My gut tells me not to do it, but I inch around the corner. I almost drop my gun from shock.

An oversized projector screen is in the room. A younger version of my mother and Orla's is on it. Several scenes move quickly across it, as if Orla made a fast-forward version. They're little girls playing together. Then teenagers. Then my father is beating my mother while Riona smokes a cigarette. My mother has black eyes, and Riona is making out with my father. My mother is screaming as my father rapes her and Riona laughs. Then, they're fighting, and my mother shoots Riona. It's on repeat and starts all over again.

My insides shake. I'm too mesmerized to tear my eyes away from it. I manage to get out, "Where did you get this?"

Orla moves closer to me, and I finally look at her. "I told you she did it."

"Where did you get this?" I aggressively repeat.

She claps. "Bravo! You finally get assertive."

Another breaking point occurs. Shooting her would be too easy. I want to tear her apart with my hands. I lunge at her, my gun goes flying, and we fall to the ground.

What I didn't see was Orla's knife. She slices my hip, and pain sears through it.

I scream out, but more angry adrenaline surges through me. I pin her wrist, and we roll across the floor, both of us fighting to take control.

With all my power, I put my free hand on her arm and yank her forearm until it snaps.

She cries out and can no longer hold the knife. I secure it in my hand and begin stabbing her, over and over, until I'm out of energy and she's no longer making any sounds. I drop the knife, staring at her bloody corpse and watching the reel of my mother and hers. At some point, I hug my bloody knees to my chest and rock back and forth. Tears and tremors consume me. The room becomes lighter as the early morning darkness fades into a hint of daylight.

I don't hear Nolan, his brothers, or Liam come in. All I feel are Nolan's arms around me, and I start to sob harder.

He holds my face in front of his. "Gemma, we have to get out of here."

"I-I killed her."

He nods. "I know. We need to go now."

I glance up and see Declan removing the video. Killian has a bag and drops the knife and Nolan's gun in it.

"Time to go," Declan says. He and Killian leave, and Nolan picks me up.

Sirens fill the air.

"Fuck," Liam spouts.

"Hold on, princess," Nolan murmurs and speeds up.

We get to the staircase, and Nolan trips. I go flying, and a net sweeps him up, raising him to the ceiling.

"Nolan!" I scream.

Liam spins, and Declan yells from outside, "Liam! Nolan!"

I jump up under Nolan, trying to reach the net, but it's too high up.

"Get Gemma out of here!" Nolan growls.

"Use your knife!" Liam yells.

"Liam! Gemma goes now!" Nolan booms.

I jump one more time, and Liam scoops me over his shoulder.

"Liam! Let go of me! Nolan!" I pound on Liam's backside, but he runs outside and throws me in the back of the SUV.

Liam orders, "Go! He's trapped."

"What the fuck!" Killian shouts.

The sirens get louder, and Declan looks on his phone. "There's no time. Go!"

"Jesus Christ!" Killian barks and puts the car in gear.

"What are you doing? You can't leave him!" I scream.

"We have no choice right now," Declan replies.

"What? No!" I reach for the door, and Liam wraps his body around me so I can't move. I become hysterical, writhing and screaming in tears.

When Killian finally stops, we're in a warehouse of some sort. I can't stop shaking. Killian and Declan get out of the car and turn on a computer screen on the wall.

"I'm going to let you go now. I'm sorry we couldn't get him in time," Liam softly states.

I stay in the car, not sure what to do or say. I killed two people. The only reason Nolan was there was because of me.

The breaking news alert flashes across the screen, and cameras zoom in on Nolan coming out of the house in handcuffs.

More curse words fill the air from all the O'Malleys. Nolan gets put in a police car, and the screen says, "Double Homicide."

Nothing could ever prepare me for the pain or regret that sears through me.

30

Nolan

Two officers lead me through the police station and into a small room. It's hot. There isn't any airflow. One wall is a mirrored window. I wonder how many people are watching me.

Hours pass. I keep my handcuffed fists on the table and stare at them. I can't get the image of Gemma, covered in blood, rocking back and forth out of my head. The vile movie playing on repeat and Orla's bloody corpse were just as shocking.

How many times did she stab her? Fifty? A hundred?

Shit.

My guess is Gemma shot the thug outside the room and not Orla. The bullet went right between his eyes. It has Gemma's shooting skills all over it.

Did they get away?

They better have gotten to safety.

How the hell am I going to get out of this?

The door opens, and an officer I haven't seen yet walks in. Metal scraping on the floor echoes in the room when he pulls out the chair. He sits and taps his fingers on the table.

"I'm Detective Stillwater. Want to tell me what happened?"

I say nothing, not changing my expression.

"Cat got your tongue?"

"I'd like to speak to my attorney, please," I reply.

He leans closer. "You sure you have nothing you want to say to me?"

There's a knock on the window, and he lets out a long breath of air. He leaves, and more time passes. The air becomes thicker, and my thoughts spiral, wondering if Gemma is okay and if I'll ever get out of here.

The door opens, and Keiran Kelly walks in. Relief replaces my disturbing thoughts.

He sits down and scratches his beard. "Jesus, Nolan. What the fuck were you thinking?"

"Isn't my attorney supposed to ask me if I did it?"

He raises his eyebrows. "Do you think that matters right now? You were the only person alive in the house. That girl got stabbed over one hundred times."

I almost blurt out she deserved it, but instead, I inform him, "I was in a net. The police had to let me down."

"Okay. Tell me how you got in the net. And if you didn't do it, who did?" he interrogates.

I stare at him.

"Fuck," he grumbles.

"Call Liam. He'll talk to the captain. Darragh has some arrangement with him."

"Yeah, I know all about that arrangement. But here's the problem. The captain is on some other continent, probably paying to get his dick sucked by some hooker, and I'm going to have a hard time getting you out on bail with this being all over the news," he claims.

My gut drops. "How long is he gone?"

"Few weeks."

I close my eyes then scrub my hands over my face. "Fine. I'll just sit back and wait a few weeks."

"Did you say anything after they read you your rights?"

I huff. "Fuck no. I know how to keep my mouth shut."

Keiran leans closer and drops his voice. "I already told Liam to call Tully."

My pulse increases. "No. There has to be some other solution."

"There isn't."

"You're my attorney. Figure it out," I demand.

He shakes his head. "There aren't any other options. This isn't something we can sweep under the rug. Your picture is all over the news right now with double homicide attached to it."

My gut churns. "If you involve Tully in this, you know I'll owe him a favor."

Keiran's eyes turn to slits. "It's a favor to Tully, or you're looking at life in prison. Which one do you prefer?"

I focus on the drop ceiling, not liking either option.

Keiran lowers his voice. "I was best friends with your father. I understand the blood between the Baileys and O'Malleys has never been good. I'm not going to even ask why you did what you did. I'm sure the girl deserved it. But your father wouldn't want you here. A favor to Tully is a much better option than letting that woman you asked to marry you lie in an empty bed."

The possibility I'll never hold Gemma again sinks its teeth into my heart. I'm having a hard enough time dealing with the fact she's probably in shock, and I'm not there to help her.

Keiran rises. "It's already a done deal. Liam was calling him. Keep your mouth shut. We'll try to get you out of here as soon as possible."

I say nothing, my pride doesn't allow me to give my blessing to let Tully help me out of this mess. But I also want to spend my life with Gemma, so I don't argue anymore.

He's about to leave when I call out, "Wait."

He spins.

"Why were the cops even there?"

"Concerned neighbor called. Said the house was empty and thought there was a break-in. I'll see you soon."

He steps out of the room and a female officer comes in. She leads me to the booking area and orders, "State your name."

"Nolan Patrick O'Malley."

She points to the wall with a height chart. "Stand in front of the wall facing forward and look straight at the camera."

I clench my jaw and obey.

"Turn," she commands.

I spin and breathe more sour oxygen, wondering how anyone works in this place day in and day out.

She holds up a flat bowl. "Empty your pockets."

I toss my phone, wallet, and keys in it.

A male officer approaches us. "Follow me."

I get led back to a changing area. He hands me an orange jumpsuit then gives me a bag to put my clothes in. It disappears, and he takes my fingerprints, then does a full-body search. He checks I don't have any warrants out for my arrest then leads me into a cell with six other men. It's similar to the cell Killian, Leo, and I were in on St. Patrick's Day.

All night, I don't sleep. When morning comes, I skip the tray of food they shove inside the cell. A few hours later, a guard yells out, "O'Malley."

He escorts me to court. When I walk in, Gemma stands between Killian and Declan. Hailee is between Liam and

Finn. Nora grips Boris's arm. Gemma starts crying, and I have to look away from her.

A man in an expensive suit whom I've never met before stands next to me. I ask, "Where's Keiran?"

"I'm taking over. Quinn O'Connor." He holds out his hand.

I shake it. "You're related to Tully?"

"Fourth cousin. And plead not guilty."

The judge comes in and the session begins. Each attorney states their case. I block it all out, fighting the urge to turn around and look at Gemma. The judge asks me how I want to plead.

"Not guilty," I state.

When it comes time for bail, the defense attorney states, "Due to the violent nature of the crime, we ask that bail be denied."

My insides quiver at the thought. I have to get out of here.

Quinn rebukes, "My client has no felonies or even misdemeanors. We ask that you release him on his own recognizance."

"Bail is set at one million dollars." The judge hits the gavel, and Quinn turns to me. "You'll be out in a few hours. Continue to stay quiet."

Relieved I got one win, I nod. The guard leads me away and I don't look at anyone. Not my family, nor Gemma. I get taken back to my cell, and a few hours later, the guard calls my name again.

He leads me to an area to put my clothes on. They return my personal items to me, and I sign a form. When the door opens, Killian and Declan are waiting.

"Where's Gemma?" I ask, worried about her being on her own.

"Calm down. She's with Liam," Declan informs me.

I let out a breath. "Good. Take me to her."

"Yeah, it's going to be a bit longer," Killian states.

The hairs on my arms rise. "Why?"

Declan steers me toward the door. "Tully's waiting in his car."

I freeze. "What does he want from me?"

Declan shakes his head. "We don't know. Let's just get it over with so you can get home to Gemma."

I sigh, and we go out to the parking lot. We get in Tully's SUV. His chestnut hair has hints of silver in it. His forehead is wrinkle-free and shiny from too many injections. His dark-brown eyes hold no expression. He nods. "Boys. It seems like you got yourselves into a mess."

"My brothers don't have anything to do with it," I claim.

He raises his eyebrows. "Oh? I heard they left you behind."

"No. They didn't. I told them to go," I insist.

"Did Darragh not teach you to protect each other at all costs?" Tully asks.

"Don't talk about our uncle now that he's dead," Killian snaps.

Tully puts his hands in the air. "No disrespect. You know Darragh and I got along well."

"Why don't you cut to the chase? Tell us what you want," Declan bellows.

Tully pulls a metal cigarette case out of his expensive suit pocket. He takes out a joint and lights it. He inhales a long drag, holds it in his lungs, then cracks the window. He passes it to me.

I follow suit, as does Declan and Killian. Once it gets back in Tully's hands, he sets it in the ashtray. He presses the pads of his fingers together and studies us. "It's going to take a lot to make this go away."

My gut twists. I blow out the smoke. In a cold voice, I question, "What do you want from me?"

"I'm not sure yet." He points at us. "But if you want this to go away, all three of you are on the hook."

"My brothers don't have anything to do with this," I reiterate.

"They left you."

"I told them to."

"Doesn't matter."

"So you get all three of us for one thing? Seems a bit tilted in your direction," Killian fumes.

Tully looks at him. "You drove the car, didn't you?"

"I told them to go," I repeat, getting pissed that Tully seems to not be listening.

Tully doesn't take his eyes off Killian. "Answer my question."

"Yeah. I drove," Killian confirms.

Tully's lips curve. "Okay, then. Since you don't think I'm fair, your brothers are off the hook. You're the only one on it."

"No," I firmly state.

Tully turns to me. "You want to sit in jail for life, or have all this disappear?"

I angrily fire back, "Killian isn't—"

"I'll do it," Declan offers.

I jerk my head toward him. "No. You aren't, either."

In typical Killian fashion, he arrogantly interjects, "Fine, I'll owe you. One favor. That's it. But you're giving us one other thing."

Tully raises his eyebrow. "Oh? What's that?"

"We get to see the kids once a month. You give us access to fly into New York if Bridgett doesn't want them in Chicago," Killian insists.

Tully takes another drag of his joint and passes it back to Killian. "You know how Bridgett feels—"

"And you know it's bullshit." Killian rolls down the window, defiantly tosses the joint, then crosses his arms. He pins his challenging stare on Tully.

Tully grunts. "You've always had balls, kid."

I lean closer to Tully. "Killian isn't taking on my debt."

Tully keeps his gaze on Killian. "Fine. I get you, and the O'Malleys get to see the kids once a month in New York."

"Did you not hear what I just said?" I bark.

Killian holds his hand out. Tully reaches for it, and Declan and I exchange a pissed-off glance. Killian never backs down. He doesn't know when to shut his mouth. Who knows what Tully will make him do.

"I'll be in touch," Tully promises.

"Gee, can't wait," Killian snarks.

Tully turns toward me. "Consider yourself a free man. All evidence will disappear over the next few days."

"Just like that?"

He snaps his fingers. "Poof."

"I'd say thanks, but I'm not sure what you just conned my brother into," I seethe.

He grins. "Oh, come on now. We're family."

Declan snorts. "Someone should teach you how families behave."

I open the door, pissed off at Tully and Killian. When we get into our own vehicle, I slap Killian on the side of the head. "What the fuck were you thinking?"

He points in my face. "Do that again, and you'll wish you stayed in jail."

Declan shakes his head. "You never know when to shut your mouth, do you?"

Killian scowls. "I'm sorry. Did you want Nolan in prison the rest of his life?"

"It was my debt to take on, not yours."

Killian shrugs. "Whatever. I'm not scared of Tully. And at least I got us access to the kids now."

I sigh and grumble, "That was a good move."

He mutters, "Tully is right. I'm the one who drove the car. And there's no point in all of us being at his mercy."

"I told you to go," I reaffirm. "You did what you should have."

"Yeah, well, it sure as hell didn't feel like something I should have done. I hope Gemma is worth it," Killian adds.

"Don't ever say anything like that again," I warn.

Killian locks eyes with mine. "She's not blood."

Declan groans.

"Have something you want to say, old man?" Killian chides.

The car pulls onto my street, and news vehicles and reporters cover the entire block.

"Shit," I mutter.

Tiernan pulls into my driveway and goes straight into the garage. He shuts the door, but the sound of reporters shouting permeates into the car.

"Want me to go flex for them? Give them something else to report on? Actually, some of those lasses looked pretty hot," Killian quips.

Declan groans, gives me an exasperated look, then focuses on Killian. I don't let Declan speak, not forgetting Killian's prior statement. "Gemma's going to be my wife. She's as good as blood. If it's saving her or me, you better always save her. Don't ever forget it." I open the door then turn back to him. "Thanks for taking on my debt to save my ass, but you're a stupid motherfucker sometimes."

He grins and winks. "Love you, too, bro."

31

Gemma

"Gemma, come sit down," Hailee says.

I ignore her, continue pacing, and ask Liam, "How's he going to get out of this? I should turn myself in."

It's a conversation we've had so many times, I've lost track. I even attempted to call the police on one of the old burner phones, but Declan caught me mid-dial. He took away my access to all phones.

"We've been through this. You need to be patient," Liam advises.

I spin and lock eyes with him. "You've been in prison. If Nolan gets convicted, he won't get out. Is that what you want for him?"

His face darkens. "Of course not."

"You were convicted of much less than what I did."

Hailee steps next to Liam. "Gemma. You need to stop talking like this and listen to Liam. I know it's hard, but—"

"You don't know anything. You didn't shoot a man and stab a woman to death. Your man is next to you. Mine's possibly going to prison for life for something I did. I'm not going to destroy his life—"

"Gemma, stop talking like this," Nolan demands.

I spin then run over to him. I throw my arms around him. "I'm so sorry!"

"Shh. It's fine." He holds me close to him and kisses the top of my head.

I glance up. "I want to turn myself in. I can't let you—"

"Stop. I'm not going to prison. This will all be cleared up in a few days," he claims.

I gape at him then recover. "What? How?"

"I can't go into it. Just trust me." He gives me a chaste kiss on the lips. "I need to talk to Liam for a moment."

I nod, trying to figure out how everything can morph from him being arrested for a double homicide to getting out on bail to all charges disappearing. I put my confusion aside and ask, "Are you hungry?"

"Starving."

"I'll make you something."

He kisses me again. "Thanks." He and Liam leave the room, and I go into the kitchen.

Hailee follows me. She puts her arm around me. "Good news, right?"

"I don't understand how it can all go away," I admit, still worried.

She sighs. "There is always going to be a lot they don't tell us. If Nolan says it's going away, you need to trust him. Don't do something stupid, Gemma."

I spin away from her and open the fridge. I pull out the ingredients for Nolan's favorite avocado and goat cheese sandwich.

Hailee's voice softens. "Gemma, are you okay? We haven't even talked about it. All we've focused on is getting Nolan out of jail."

"I'm fine." My insides shake. I blink hard and take an extra few seconds pulling the skillet out of the cabinet.

"Gemma—"

"I don't want to talk about it. Orla's dead. Nolan isn't going to prison. There's nothing to dwell on." I set the pan on the stove and add butter to it.

My sister stays quiet.

I pull out the cutting board, wash the basil, parsley, and spinach, then concentrate on chopping it into fine pieces.

"Mom wants to see you. She's worried," Hailee reveals.

I glance at her. "I don't want to see her right now."

"Why?"

"Why do you always have to push me?"

Hailee smirks. "Because I'm your older, favorite sister?"

I work on pitting the avocado.

"If anyone knows what you're going through, it's her," Hailee quietly states.

It's only a half-truth. My mother killed her sister. Orla, no matter how much I want to deny it, was my sister, too. But everything ends there. I can't get the movie reel Orla made out of my head. Watching my father brutally rape my mother while her sister sat there and happily watched makes me feel guilty for ignoring her all the months I did. And no matter how much Orla or her bodyguard deserved to die, I'm confused about how I could so easily do it. The thought of my mother with four young children, fleeing several states and hiding out all on her own, makes me feel nauseated. The repercussions of my actions are nothing compared to the burden my mother had to deal with while alone. I'm not. I didn't have any of the gruesome things done to me that my father did to her. And I can only imagine what sick things Riona evoked upon her. So I don't have any right to cry to her over my guilty, confused feelings.

"I'm sorry, but she's on her way over," Hailee admits.

I drop the knife. "What!"

She holds her hands in the air. "I'm sorry. I didn't know, and she's been asking for days. She texted she's on her way."

I close my eyes, wanting everything to go away and wishing I would have talked to Nolan and killed Orla with some sort of better plan.

Nolan and Liam walk in, and my mom is with them. She strides over to me and hugs me. "Gemma! I've been so worried."

"I'm fine," I lie.

She embraces me tighter.

All the emotions I'm trying to hold back come to the surface. I swallow them down, determined not to become a sobbing mess and be the strong woman I used to be before Orla entered my life.

Hailee clears her throat. "Liam and I are going to go. I'll call you later, Gemma."

My mom releases me and hugs Hailee. "Call me, too."

Hailee smiles. "I will."

She and Liam leave.

I put the ingredients on the bread and cover the skillet. Nolan comes up behind me and slings his arm around my waist. "Let me finish this. Why don't you go talk with your mom in private?"

I freeze.

He kisses my cheek and murmurs, "Whatever you're trying to avoid, you can't."

I glance up at him.

He pecks me on the lips. "Go."

I sigh and lead my mother into the office. We sit on the couch, and I face her. "I'm fine, Mom. Really."

She stares at me, and her eyes glisten. "No, you aren't. You can't be. I know you. And everything you went through—"

"Isn't anything compared to what you did. I'm fine."

She wrinkles her forehead and turns toward me more. She puts her hand on my shoulder then admits, "Nolan and Liam told me about the movie."

My gut spins, and bile shoots up my throat. I manage to swallow it down. The last thing I wanted was my mother to know I saw what I did. My insides quiver harder, and the emotions I'm trying to hide spill down my face. "I'm sorry. I'm so sorry. I-I shouldn't have been so mean to you or been so selfish. What Orla did to me was nothing compared to what you went through."

My mother tilts her head and sighs. She strokes my hair. "Sweetie, what I went through doesn't negate what Orla did to you or what you're going through now."

"But my father...what he did...what Riona did... I..." I look away and hold my trembling hands together.

"Was horrible. They were evil people, just like Orla."

I spin back. "I'm sorry for what they did to you."

My mom's tears release. She pulls me to her. "I'm sorry you had to see it. I never wanted any of you girls to know anything about my past. Maybe I was wrong to try and hide it all these years."

I put my arms around her. "You saved us from a horrible life. I understand why you didn't tell us."

She pulls back. "Gemma, I'm worried about you. I thought when your father died, and we assumed Orla did, too, that everything would be okay. You sprang back to life. But this is a lot. I don't want you keeping all this inside. It's not healthy."

"I'll be fine. If you can handle everything you did on your own, then you don't have to worry about me," I try to convince her.

She shakes her head. "I didn't handle it on my own."

"What are you talking about?"

She shifts on the couch. "Several months after we moved, I almost committed suicide. Ciara pushed Ella. She fell and broke her arm. Social services came to talk to me. You were in preschool and came down with chickenpox then the school called. Hailee threw paint all over a little boy in school, and they were going to kick her out. My boss grabbed my ass at work. I flipped out and threw a mug of coffee at his back. He fired me. That night, I sat down with a bottle of pills. Amy came over and found me." Amy has been my mother's closest friend. They met at a park and were both single moms. We were always with her kids, growing up.

The shame of what I almost did the night Nolan walked in on me hits me like a dozen bricks. No matter how much time passes, it never gets easier to revisit.

My mom takes a deep breath. "I confessed everything to Amy. For several months, she came over after work and helped me with you girls. She made me see a counselor at the domestic abuse shelter. They also helped me get a new job."

"See. You had way more to deal with than I do. I'll be fine," I attempt to reassure her again.

She scrunches her face. "I kept having nightmares about killing Riona and the things they did to me. Nothing I did made them go away. I want you to talk to my old counselor. She's about to retire but said she would work with you."

"Mom! You told her?"

"No. I said my daughter had some things happen and needed her help. You can trust her. Whatever you tell her, she won't repeat."

"I-I killed two people. I can't tell her that!"

My mom nods. "You can. I promise. She's safe."

Talking to anyone about what I did seems wrong. "I'm not going to commit to that right now."

My mom squeezes my hand. "Okay. Will you think about it?"

I don't respond right away. I finally agree. "All right, but I'm not promising anything."

She hugs me. "I'm always here to talk, too."

"Do you want me to make you a sandwich?" I ask.

She smiles. "No, thanks. Simon is taking me for a late lunch."

"Did you tell him?" My mom and I talked a few weeks ago, and she said she was going to tell her boyfriend Simon everything.

She nods. "I did last night."

"And he's okay about everything, right?"

Her smile grows. "Yeah."

I hug her. "I'm really happy for you, Mom. You deserve a good guy."

"He is." She pulls back, and we go into the kitchen.

She hugs Nolan. "Glad to see you're back. Thank you."

He raises his eyebrows.

"For everything you did for my daughter."

He pins his gaze on her. "She's my life."

My mom smiles. "Let me know if you need anything." She pats him on the shoulder and leaves.

Nolan tugs me into him. "Are you all right?"

I reach for his face. "Are you? I'm so sorry. I—"

"You aren't doing this, Gemma."

"You shouldn't have taken the fall—"

"Gemma, sit down." He leads me to the couch and pulls me onto his lap. "I'm worried about you."

"I'm fine. My mom just had the same conversation with me. Now that you're home, everything is fine," I assert.

He studies me then says, "I know what it's like to kill someone. And the first time is the hardest to get over."

"Well, unless some crazy stalker wants to threaten me again, I won't be killing anyone else," I chirp.

He sniffs hard. "This isn't a joke."

My gut drops. "I know it isn't."

He slides his hand on my cheek. "I don't want you having nightmares the rest of your life. We need to talk about this."

I lean into it and close my eyes. "I'm not seeing that lady."

"What lady?"

I open my eyes. "My mom has a therapist she saw years ago. She wants me to see her. She claims it's safe to talk to and won't tell anyone what I tell her."

Nolan's expression turns neutral. I'm not sure what to make of it. He suggests, "Maybe it would be a good thing."

"Why can't I just talk to you and my mom if I need to?"

He tugs me closer to him. "You can always talk to me. I'm trying to do what's best for you though."

I put my arms around his shoulders. "Okay. Why don't you let me talk to you about it, and if it doesn't help, then I'll consider seeing her. When I thought Orla was dead, my nightmares went away. And now I know for sure she is."

He sighs. "Did you sleep last night?"

"No. I was too worried about you. Did you?"

"No."

I sniff him. "You need a shower."

He chuckles. "Yep."

I swallow hard. "Are you sure all these charges are going to go away?"

His eyes turn cold. "Yeah."

"Why do you look upset?" I ask.

"I'm not." He rises with me in his arms then pecks me on the lips. "I need a shower, you, then sleep."

I laugh. "In that order?"

He cockily licks his lips. "I'm pretty sure you might be a multistep task."

32

Nolan

Several Days Later

"You look hot." I squeeze Gemma's ass. "Are these leather pants new?"

She beams. "Yep. Forty percent off."

I tilt my head. "Are you a bargain shopper?"

"Of course!"

"Good job, then." I peck her on the lips. "I have to go to the pub and meet my brothers and attorney."

Worry fills her face. "Is everything okay?"

"Yeah. Routine stuff. It should only take ten minutes or so. I'll have Tiernan pick you up and bring you to the pub so we can go to our last wedding class."

She pumps her fist in the air. "Another awesome hour with Father Antonio!"

I grunt. "You're a good sport."

She smirks. "Well, it was super stimulating listening to Father Antonio discuss the importance of a healthy sex life. I especially enjoyed his lecture on making sure we give ourselves enough time to learn how our bodies respond to one another."

My lips twitch. "Conflict Management is tonight. Maybe we'll learn something."

She bats her eyes. "But we never fight."

"Nope. We avoid conflict at all costs," I tease.

She traces my Celtic knot tattoos on my biceps and innocently asks, "Do you think it involves hot makeup sex?"

I grin. "Why don't you ask Father Antonio?"

"Don't tempt me. You know I will."

"Dare you."

She pats my arm. "Done. What do I get when I fulfill this dare?"

"It wouldn't be fun if I told you everything. But I left a present on the bed. Make sure you wear it to class."

She arches an eyebrow. "Oh? What is it?"

"You'll see." I dip down and kiss her. "I've gotta go. See you in a few hours." I leave and get in the car.

Tiernan rolls the divider window down. "Nolan, are you ever going to put me back on bodyguard duty?"

"Not for my soon-to-be wife or anyone I care about," I reply.

"Seriously? Am I going to be a driver my entire life?" he whines.

"Talk to Liam." I roll the divider up. It might have been months ago, but I'm not giving him nor Fergal a pass. The day Orla sliced Gemma's thigh is still fresh in my mind.

The garage door opens. The news reporters begin screaming and flooding the street. I groan, ready for them to leave me alone and get on with my life.

My phone buzzes, and I glance at it.

Gemma: *Vibrating panties?*

Me: *Scared you can't handle it in front of Father Antonio?*

Gemma: *How does it turn on? I don't see a button.*

Me: *Trying to sample the goodies without me?*

Gemma: *I could video chat with you if you wanted.*

I laugh, and the car pulls up to the pub.

Me: *Sorry. Just got to the pub. See you soon.*

She sends me a kiss emoji. I put my phone in my pocket then get out and go inside. My brothers and Keiran Kelly are at a corner table. It's the middle of the day before the evening crowd comes in. No other patrons are anywhere nearby. I slide into the booth next to Declan. My chest tightens. "Keiran. What's going on?"

He takes a sip of whiskey. "The DA's office is dropping all charges."

I glance at my brothers. "So that's it? I'm off the hook?"

He downs the remainder of his glass then motions for Molly to bring him another one. "Yep. There will be a press conference tomorrow at noon. Dress up. Make sure Gemma is with you. The DA will make a formal apology and explain you were kidnapped, held hostage, and lucky the murderer didn't see you and kill you, too."

I huff. "I was kidnapped?"

"Yeah."

"Makes you look like a pussy, doesn't it?" Killian jeers.

"Shut up," I warn, but I can't deny it.

"Can he sue the DA's office?" Declan asks.

Keiran looks between us and points at me. "You three do realize he's a lucky motherfucker and not to push your luck, right?"

"I say we sue him for slander," Killian says with a straight face.

"Maybe some trauma, too," Declan adds.

"Watch it," I threaten.

Keiran shakes his head. "Tell me you're joking."

Killian leans forward. "What about sexual confusion?"

"What?" I bark.

Declan shoots me a concerned look. "Did anyone try to touch you, and now you aren't sure what side you bat on?"

I go to slap him, but he ducks. "Shut up, you two."

Molly comes over and sets his drink down. "You need anything else?" She avoids looking at me. It's something she does since Colin brought her to the house and made her apologize.

"No, we're good," Declan says.

She leaves. Keiran leans forward. "What did Tully want in exchange?"

Guilt fills me. I hate my brother volunteered to take on my debt.

Declan motions to Killian. "Him."

Keiran furrows his brows and stares at Killian. "What for?"

Killian shrugs and takes a sip of Guinness. "Who knows? He'll call, I'll have to drop whatever I'm doing, deal with some bullshit for a few days, then it'll be back to normal life."

"You underestimate him," I warn.

Killian sniffs hard. "What's he going to do? Chain me up in his basement and keep me there at his beck and call? It's one thing. Everyone needs to get over it."

Declan sits back and crosses his arms. "Have him chain you up naked. He could film it for your social media. You'll get a whole new set of crazies following you."

"Can't help it if the lasses like what they see," Killian states.

"Lasses? Don't you mean the guys who message you?" I add.

"Oh! Show Nolan what that one dude sent you when he was locked up," Declan says.

I take a sip of water. "Glad you two were having fun when I was behind bars."

"You three need to take this seriously. Tully is no one to mess around with or underestimate," Keiran reprimands.

I sigh. "I know."

Keiran downs his whiskey and rises. "Be careful. Nolan, I'll see you at noon tomorrow."

"Yeah. Thanks."

He leaves, and I ask Declan, "Is the stock price on Jack's company where we need it?"

"We've got another ten percent to go."

"Shit. Obrecht was over a few days ago. With everything going on, I haven't had a chance to talk with Liam."

Declan shifts in his seat. "Finn's not going to budge. He wants Jack alive until he finds Brenna."

"If Jack hasn't said anything yet, he's never going to. Besides, he's wasting away in that cage. Have you seen him lately?" Killian asks.

"No."

"He looks like he aged twenty years."

"Good. Serves the bastard right after what he did to Selena," Declan barks.

My phone vibrates.

Gemma: *I'm outside. Want me to come inside?*

Me: *No. I'll be out in a minute.*

I rise. "Agreed. I need to go."

We say our goodbyes, and then I join Gemma in the car. Normally we would walk since it's close to the pub, but since the media is following me, I decide it's safer to drive. Her woody lavender scent fills the air, and I inhale deeply. I lean over and kiss her. "Are you wearing the panties?"

She softly laughs. "Yep."

I reach into my pocket for the remote and click the button on the lowest setting.

"That all you got?" she taunts.

"Patience is a virtue, remember?"

She leans closer. "But do you have any?"

"Ha ha." I put my arm around her. "I have good news."

"About the charges?" Hope fills her eyes.

"Yeah. Keiran said tomorrow at noon, there will be a press conference. We both have to go. The DA will drop all charges," I inform her.

"Really?"

"Yep."

She throws her arms around me. "Thank God!"

Tiernan pulls the car up to the church. Gemma's bodyguard gets out and guides us inside. We go inside the room. There are four other couples in class with us. Since we're on a fast track, there are new couples each time. Father Antonio likes to wait a month between sessions so you can practice what you've learned. After I offered to make a donation of a few thousand dollars, he was more than happy to deem us capable of learning quickly.

When we sit down, I turn the notch up on Gemma's vibrator. She squirms in her chair and looks at me.

I arrogantly smirk.

Father Antonio begins his boring lecture on conflict resolution. We have to role-play and say to each other, *"What I'm hearing you say is..."*

I turn the vibrator up again. Gemma uncrosses and recrosses her legs. Her face turns red. She begins taking shallow breaths.

"Your turn, Gemma," Father Antonio directs.

I press the up button until it's at full power.

She pins her blue gaze on me. Her cheeks flush crimson, and she squeaks, "What I'm hearing you say is..."

I put my hand on her forehead. "Are you feeling okay, princess?"

She squirms in her seat again. "Umm..."

I say to Father Antonio, "I'm going to take Gemma to the restroom for a minute. She's pretty hot."

"Are you okay, Gemma?" Father Antonio inquires.

The other couples all stare at us with concerned expressions.

Gemma puts her hand on her stomach. "I think the bathroom is a good idea."

I rise and grab her hand. I quickly lead her out of the classroom and into the vestry, where the priest gets ready for mass.

"What are we—"

I press my lips to her, push her against the counter, quickly shove her leather pants to her ankles, then spin her, so she's facing the counter. I splay my hand on her back, place my other one on the vibrator, and maneuver it in a circle.

"Oh God!" she cries out in a shaky voice.

I slap her ass.

She gasps and arches her back.

I rub out the sting and bend over her ear. Now that the DA's dropping the charges, I need to set her straight. "That's for saying you're going to turn yourself in." I slap her again, and she shrieks. "This is for ditching my security and me in the middle of the night." I rub it out and repeat slapping her while getting her off with the vibrator. "This is for not letting me handle things." I slap her again, and her knees buckle.

Sweat drips down her cheek. I slide the vibrator out, move her panties to the side, and enter her in one thrust.

"Nolan!"

I hover over her and put my lips against her ear. "Who do you let handle dangerous things?"

She shivers. "You."

"Why?" I growl and thrust at a slow pace.

"I-I..."

"I handle things. I love you, and that's my job. Do you understand?" I assert.

"Yes."

"If something happened to you, I'd die. Don't you ever do something like that again!"

She nods.

"Give me your word. Say it in front of God," I bellow.

"I-I promise," she breathes.

I kiss under her ear. "Good girl. Now, do you want it hard or slow, princess?"

"Hard. Please!" she whispers.

I cover her mouth with my hand and pound into her while slapping her ass a few more times. She arches her back, whimpering. Her body spasms, and the room becomes filled with her muffled cries.

I fist her hair and tug her head back. My lips hit her cheek. "My wife will not put her life in danger, do you understand?" I pound into her one more time.

"Yes!" she cries out, and her eyes roll.

I pump my seed deep inside her, staring at the only woman I've ever loved. She's the one person in the world who can aggravate me and understand me at the same time.

In our aftermath, I spin her into me and kiss her, as hungry and greedy as ever. I need her, and she clutches me, returning every ounce of affection I give her. And maybe that's why we work. We're two trains headed right toward each other, but instead of colliding, we couple together, creating something more powerful than we were apart.

I end our kiss and hold her face in front of me. "I mean it, Gemma. You scared me. Don't ever do anything crazy like that again."

She nods. "I won't. I promise."

I tug her into me and kiss the top of her head. I murmur, "We better get back to class. You still have to complete your dare with Father Antonio."

She tilts her head up, and her lips twitch. "Was this my surprise?"

"No, princess. This was your punishment."

EPILOGUE

Nolan

A Few Months Later

The music ends for our first dance as Mr. and Mrs. Nolan O'Malley. My perfect, beautiful bride beams. Over the last few months, we've focused on the future and not the past. Her anxiety is almost gone. Sometimes she has a nightmare, but whenever that happens, we talk through it. I remind her everyone who ever threatened her is dead. She hasn't gone to the therapist her mom recommended. I can't say I'm not relieved. Discussing what she did makes me nervous. But she doesn't hesitate to talk to me and sometimes her mom.

I lean down and kiss her.

Colin comes up and holds out his hand. He declares, "I'm stealing you before anyone else does."

Gemma laughs.

Colin locks eyes with me, and my gut drops. "Your brothers need to talk to you for a minute. They're in the bar."

I wink at Gemma then say, "I'll be right back." I make my way into the side room and find my brothers, Liam and Finn, talking to Tully.

Shit. What does he want?

I nod. "Tully. When did you get here?"

"Sorry I'm late. I had some issues pop up."

I glance around. "Where are Bridget and the kids?"

"They didn't come."

Anger seeps through me. "Why? We agreed they could come since you were here, and we have security everywhere."

He nods. "Yes, we did. However, Bridget didn't want to come. So before I go to war with my daughter, I need my end of the deal fulfilled."

Killian tosses his whiskey back and sets it on the bar. "You think I'm going to screw you over? I'm an O'Malley. We're men who keep our word. You know this."

Tully nods. "I'm counting on it."

A chill moves down my spine. I bark, "Stop being evasive, Tully. And I'm not allowing Killian to do whatever it is you have up your sleeve. It's my debt. I'll do it. Now, what is it?"

Tully chuckles then pats my back. "No need to get all worked up. And you can't step in at this point."

"Why?"

He points to Gemma. "Because of her."

My blood boils. "What does Gemma have to do with this?"

"Nothing."

"Tully—"

Declan steps between us. "Spit it out."

Tully turns to Liam. "You know we've needed to form an alliance with the Marinos."

Liam's eyes turn to slits. "Your alliance is not ours, nor is it Killian's."

"Mmm, I beg to differ. The DA dropped the charges against Nolan. But as easy as it went away, something else can pop up."

I step closer. "Are you threatening me?"

Finn puts his arm across my chest, stopping me from going closer.

Liam seethes, "No matter what your daughter thinks, we're family. However, if you do anything to harm an O'Malley, we'll go to war."

Tully crosses his arms. "We had a deal. If you had an arrangement, as leader of your clan, you would hold whoever it was to it, or hell would come down over their head. I am no different."

Liam stays quiet, unable to deny the accusation.

Tully steps closer and lowers his voice. "I have made an alliance with Angelo. Neither he, nor I, can afford to break it. Things in New York are not like they were. Now I have promised him a favor, and Killian is going to keep his word to me and follow through."

Killian rises off the barstool. "Just get your lady fight over with and tell me what it is. Name the time and place. I'll show up and do whatever it is you want. Then we're done, Tully. You get one thing from me, and that's it."

Tully smiles and pats him on the back. "That's all you need to do. One thing, then you've fulfilled your promise to me."

Killian tosses back a mouthful of whiskey. "Fine. What is it?"

Tully taps his crystal tumbler full of scotch. "Angelo doesn't want his daughter, Arianna, in New York anymore. It's getting too dangerous."

"Surely, he has security," Declan states.

Tully nods. "He does. However, she got herself involved in some circles he's not happy about."

The hairs on my arms rise. I interject, "Then he should get her out of them."

Tully snaps his fingers and points at me. "That's exactly what he's going to do."

Killian rolls his eyes. "So I have to babysit this woman or something?"

Tully shakes his head. In a nonnegotiable voice, he states, "No. You're going to marry her."

READ BRUTAL DEFENDER - FREE ON KINDLE UNLIMITED

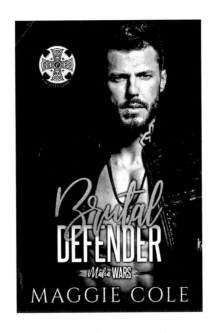

I choose Killian O'Malley out of desperation.

My papà gives me an ultimatum with one other option. I'll do anything not to marry the Italian mafia boss who lives in Italy and is twice my age.

So I become Killian's debt repayment. When I'm forced to pick, I don't know he's a boxer, a decade older than me, or has a body better than Zeus.

He's bossy.

Arrogant.

He calls me a mafia brat and creates rules like I'm his child, saying he'll tame me.

Our angsty relationship is so hot between the sheets my head is constantly spinning.

At times, he becomes a raging psychopath destroying anyone who even looks at me, including my ex who won't move on.

I thought Killian would be a playboy, but he takes our vows to the extreme.

Everything about him makes him my brutal defender.

READ BRUTAL DEFENDER - FREE ON KINDLE UNLIMITED

KILLIAN O'MALLEY
BRUTAL DEFENDER PROLOGUE

Killian O'Malley

REGRET IS SOMETHING I TRY NOT TO LET INTO MY LIFE. IT CAN swallow you whole and destroy you, inch by inch, until everything in your future looks dark. I learned that when my father died. It cursed me when Liam went to prison for avenging his killer. When my brother, Sean, got murdered, it almost destroyed me.

At some point, I had to remember I'm a fighter. I take knocks and then I hit back harder. There was nothing I could do about my father or Liam. Circumstances already set their fate in stone. But Sean's death was different. I could wallow in my grief and guilt over not finding out what Sean was involved in or use it to destroy the parties who ended his life. I chose the latter.

Moving forward, I told myself I'd never again regret anything I did. I would make my decisions and live with the consequences. My father always said, "Real men don't make excuses. They step up to the plate."

The problem with my thinking is I never considered my actions would harm one of my brothers. When my brothers, Liam, and I went to rescue Gemma, I'm the one who drove away from Nolan. I also left the house before he did, instead of waiting for him to carry Gemma outside. If I had made a different decision, maybe Nolan wouldn't have been arrested and booked for a double homicide.

So when Tully said all three of us—Declan, Nolan, and I—were on the hook for him solving Nolan's issue, it didn't make sense to me. I spoke my mind and didn't flinch or care when he said I would be the only one to owe him. Neither of my brothers were happy with my decision. They both tried to step in and shift the debt to themselves. But I wasn't going to let that happen. It's one favor then it's over. I'm not about to lose any sleep over it. A deal is a deal.

But Tully's power trip is getting old. It's Nolan's wedding, and I intentionally didn't bring a date. I learned a few years ago there are plenty of hot, horny, starry-eyed lasses who go to weddings looking for a good time to try and forget they aren't the bride. And right now, I'm bored with the women I casually date. I'm ready for some new excitement in my life, even if it's just for the night.

All was good until Tully walked in. And now this argument taking place between him and the O'Malleys is wasting my time. It's one little thing. I do it. It's over. I move on with my life. Nolan stays out of prison. Tully goes back to New York, and everyone is happy.

I toss back more whiskey. I'm ready to party at my brother's wedding, get laid, and move forward. Of course, none of that can happen with Tully around. He starts talking about his alliance with Angelo Marino. Then he brings up Angelo's daughter, Arianna. She got involved in some circles her father isn't happy about, and he wants me to get her out of them.

I roll my eyes. A mafia brat who wants to piss off daddy. Fine. I'll tame her rebel ass. I grumble, "So I have to babysit this woman or something?"

Tully shakes his head. In a stern voice, he states, "No. You're going to marry her."

My brothers, Finn, and Liam go quiet, exchanging shocked glances. I finish my whiskey. "That's funny. Now, what's the job, Tully?" I put my hand on his shoulder and point at a brunette who's been giving me fuck-me-eyes all night. "And stop with the games. You're interrupting my time with that woman."

He sniffs hard. His voice turns hard as nails. "This isn't a game. You will marry her. Next Saturday."

I still think he's screwing with me, but Declan scowls. "What kind of fucked-up arrangement is this? Have one of your sons marry her. Killian isn't—"

"He's joking. Calm down," I state.

Tully's face hardens. "Do you see me smiling?"

My gut suddenly sinks. He's serious. He wants me to marry this mafia princess who made friends with people to make some point to her daddy.

"Absolutely not," I tell him.

"I've promised Angelo, and I don't go back on my word," Tully states.

"You've got four unmarried sons," Nolan points out.

Tully puts his crystal tumbler on the bar. "They live in New York. Angelo wants Arianna as far away as possible."

I motion to the bartender that I need another drink. I fume, "Then send her to Italy. I'm not marrying her. Plus, did you forget I'm an O'Malley? We're Irish. We don't marry Italian brats."

"This is an alliance—"

"Your alliance, not ours," Finn seethes.

Tully tosses back the rest of his whiskey. He slams the glass on the wooden bar and steps closer to me, so we're face-to-face. His sweet, hot breath merges into mine, and his nostrils flare. "The wedding is next Saturday. You show up, and our deal stays intact. You skip out, and it won't only be Nolan who goes down."

"You better watch who you're threatening," Liam snarls.

"This isn't a job, it's a life sentence. Find someone else," Nolan hisses.

Tully spins. "The only one who will be serving a life sentence is you." He steps out of our circle. "Congratulations. Enjoy your bride while you still can." He slaps a wedding envelope with Mr. and Mrs. Nolan O'Malley on the bar then leaves.

The five of us watch him walk away. Upbeat music blares in the other room. I'd normally be dancing right now. Or shagging some girl in a dark corner. Or stepping outside to smoke a joint. Nothing about Tully's demands makes me feel like doing any of that, especially when Gemma walks up to us.

She puts her hand on Nolan's bicep and nervously asks, "Is everything okay?"

Nolan tugs her into him and attempts to cover up his fear, but everyone can see it. Tully doesn't make idle threats. The power he holds can destroy a person in a matter of seconds. He's a heavyweight in the ring with a featherweight. It's an unequal match where everyone knows the winner before the bell rings. If he's on your side, you're safe. If he's not, you're going to be knocked down and not able to get back up.

Nolan kisses the top of Gemma's head. I turn away. I can't look at my sister-in-law in her wedding dress and my brother in his tux and not allow them to have the future they deserve. There is no choice. It's a done deal. What Tully wants, he'll get.

I shout to the bartender, "Six shots of whiskey. Make mine a double."

The bartender sets down the glasses. I toss mine back and pull out my phone. I open my social media and type Arianna Marino in the search bar.

"Gemma, can you give us a few more minutes?" Nolan asks.

"Umm...okay."

"Thanks. I'll meet you for the next dance."

Gemma leaves, and my brothers, Liam, and Finn hover around me.

"Tell me you aren't considering this?" Declan says.

I scowl. "Would you prefer I destroy Nolan's life?"

"We'll figure something else out," Nolan states.

"What?" I ask.

He clenches his jaw.

I glance at the four of them. "Anyone have any ideas how to get Nolan or me out of this?"

Declan grabs the phone. "Let me see her. I'll do it."

I grunt. "Yeah, not having that over my head, either." I snag the cell back and hit the search button. The first account that pops up has over a million followers. I tap on it and am pleasantly surprised.

"At least she's hot," Declan offers.

"Not bad," I mumble, but she could be an Italian runway model. She has golden skin, big brown eyes under long lashes, and high cheekbones women would pay money to attempt to attain. Her pouty lips make me think dirty thoughts. She's not a stick. She's got curves in all the right places and long, shiny black hair.

If I saw her on the street, I'd follow her, strike up a conversation, and ask her out. I've always loved Mediterranean women, but I've never gotten serious about any of them. They're fun for a while, but I'm an O'Malley, meant to keep our Irish bloodline pure.

I hit her video footage, which disappears after twenty-four hours, and my blood starts to boil. She posted it within the last hour. In one slide, she's making out with some thug. In the next, she's dancing on a table while the bastard unbuttons her blouse. She's got a bottle of Cristal in her hand and she takes a long drink.

"Looks like you're going to have your hands full with that one," Declan mutters.

"Shut up," I bark. I grab another shot of whiskey, then walk off to the bathroom. I hit the follow button on the phone.

She immediately follows me back.

My pulse is still racing, and I debate about sending her a message, but one pops up.

Arianna: *Stalking me already?*

Me: *Where are you right now?*

Arianna: *None of your business.*

Me: *I think it is.*

Arianna: *In your dreams.*

Me: *I'd call this a nightmare, not a dream, lass. But if you're going to be my wife, you better get your body parts covered and go home to daddy while you still live with him.*

Arianna: *Body parts? Do you even know what to do with yours?*

Me: *I'm sure you'll have a hard time handling my body parts.*

Arianna: *Right. Sorry to inform you, but I'm used to more than a two-inch tadpole.*

I send her one of the many dick pics I've taken and sent to other women. Several minutes pass without her comments.

Me: *Yeah, I thought so. I better not see any more pictures of that thug's hands on you.*

Arianna: *Don't make empty threats.*

Me: *I'm an implementer. Don't ever forget that. Now, keep your clothes on and go home.*

More time passes. I keep staring at the phone, waiting for something. I don't get a message, but a notification pops up she posted another video.

I click on it, and every angry cell in my body lights on fire. She's on stage, dancing on a pole, and tears her shirt off. The thug who had his hands on her earlier gropes her.

The username for his account pops up. Donato Brambilla. I open up his page. Everything on it screams bad news.

He sends me a message.

Donato: *I had her first. And I'm going to have her tonight.*

My mouth turns dry. I stare at my reflection in the mirror, suddenly wanting to kill someone I've never heard of or met before this moment.

All night, I try to get her out of my mind and focus on my last few nights of freedom, but my blood never stops boiling.

READ BRUTAL DEFENDER - FREE ON KINDLE UNLIMITED

ALL IN BOXSET

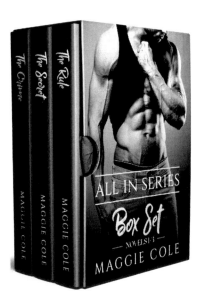

Three page-turning, interconnected stand-alone romance novels with HEA's!! Get ready to fall in love with the characters. Billionaires. Professional athletes. New York City. Twist, turns, and danger lurking everywhere. The only option for these couples is to go ALL IN...with a little help from their friends. EXTRA STEAM INCLUDED!

Grab it now! **READ FREE IN KINDLE UNLIMITED!**

CAN I ASK YOU A HUGE FAVOR?

Would you be willing to leave me a review?

I would be forever grateful as one positive review on Amazon is like buying the book a hundred times! Reader support is the lifeblood for Indie authors and provides us the feedback we need to give readers what they want in future stories!

Your positive review means the world to me! So thank you from the bottom of my heart!

PERFECT SINNER

MORE BY MAGGIE COLE

Mafia Wars - A Dark Mafia Series (Series Five)
Ruthless Stranger (Maksim's Story) - Book One
Broken Fighter (Boris's Story) - Book Two
Cruel Enforcer (Sergey's Story) - Book Three
Vicious Protector (Adrian's Story) - Book Four
Savage Tracker (Obrecht's Story) - Book Five
Unchosen Ruler (Liam's Story) - Book Six
Perfect Sinner (Nolan's Story) - Book Seven
Brutal Defender (Killian's Story) - Book Eight
Deviant Hacker (Declan's Story) - Book Nine
Relentless Hunter (Finn's Story) - Book Ten

Behind Closed Doors (Series Four - Former Military Now International Rescue Alpha Studs)

Depths of Destruction - Book One

Marks of Rebellion - Book Two

Haze of Obedience - Book Three

Cavern of Silence - Book Four

Stains of Desire - Book Five

Risks of Temptation - Book Six

Together We Stand Series (Series Three - Family Saga)

Kiss of Redemption - Book One

Sins of Justice - Book Two

Acts of Manipulation - Book Three

Web of Betrayal - Book Four

Masks of Devotion - Book Five

Roots of Vengeance - Book Six

It's Complicated Series (Series Two - Chicago Billionaires)

Crossing the Line - Book One

Don't Forget Me - Book Two

Committed to You - Book Three

More Than Paper - Book Four

Sins of the Father - Book Five

Wrapped In Perfection - Book Six

All In Series (Series One - New York Billionaires)

The Rule - Book One

The Secret - Book Two

The Crime - Book Three

The Lie - Book Four

The Trap - Book Five

The Gamble - Book Six

STAND ALONE NOVELLA

JUDGE ME NOT - A Billionaire Single Mom Christmas Novella

ABOUT THE AUTHOR

Amazon Bestselling Author

Maggie Cole is committed to bringing her readers alphalicious book boyfriends. She's been called the "literary master of steamy romance." Her books are full of raw emotion, suspense, and will always keep you wanting more. She is a masterful storyteller of contemporary romance and loves writing about broken people who rise above the ashes.

She lives in Florida near the Gulf of Mexico with her husband, son, and dog. She loves sunshine, wine, and hanging out with friends.

Her current series were written in the order below:

- All In (Stand alones with entwined characters)
- It's Complicated (Stand alones with entwined characters)
- Together We Stand (Brooks Family Saga - read in order)
- Behind Closed Doors (Read in order)
- Mafia Wars (Coming April 1st 2021)

Maggie Cole's Newsletter
Sign up here!

Hang Out with Maggie in Her Reader Group
Maggie Cole's Romance Addicts

Follow for Giveaways
Facebook Maggie Cole

Instagram
@maggiecoleauthor

Complete Works on Amazon
Follow Maggie's Amazon Author Page

Book Trailers
Follow Maggie on YouTube

Are you a Blogger and want to join my ARC team?
Signup now!

Feedback or suggestions?
Email: authormaggiecole@gmail.com

Made in United States
North Haven, CT
05 July 2025